BUBBA

The African Adventures of James Johnson

A Novel

WILLIAM G. SPAIN

Z

ZIWA BOOKS
Boulder, Colorado

Handwritten inscription:
To Marie & Robert
Thank you so
good friends over
re...
Hope you enjoyed!
Best wishes,
Bill Spain — 5-21-14

Published by Ziwa Books
Boulder, Colorado

ISBN # 978-1-3043-6180-6

Printed in the United States

This novel is dedicated to my wife, my two daughters and their lovely families who have been very supportive of my efforts to write and to complete this story. I thank them for the time they have spent in reviewing, editing and offering suggestions.

I would also like to acknowledge all of the wonderful Peace Corps Volunteers, past and present, who gave of themselves to help make this world a better place and to fulfill President John F. Kennedy's vision when he founded the Peace Corps. As a former Peace Corps volunteer, I understand and share the dedication required to go abroad and try to help others help themselves.

Table of Contents

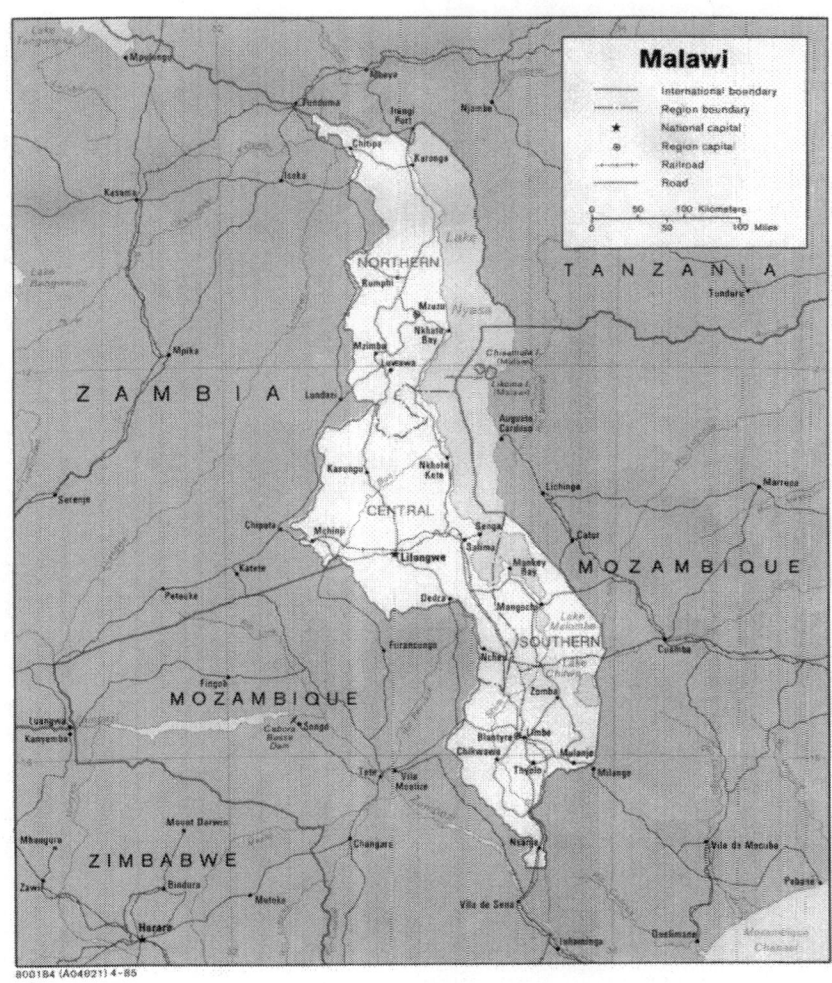

Prologue

It was a September morning in 1966. The stewardesses served drinks shortly after Trans World Airlines Flight 1140 to Los Angeles departed from Washington's Dulles International Airport. Most of the 178 passengers relished the pre-packed lunches served to them. The food, though, was small recompense for the long delay they had experienced on the ground. Tempers flared; now they simmered.

James Edward "Bubba" Johnson, however, seemed unaffected by the delays. As he sat sipping a cold beer, he withdrew into a comfortable, reflective mood. He had been too excited during the early part of the morning to care about the flight delay. In fact, he had enjoyed every minute of it—watching people finding their families, waiting for their luggage, locating their flight gates, scurrying for the exits, clutching their menus.

Yes, menus. A rather overweight middle-aged woman had lost her Air India menu, a 'souvenir' she had liberated from the seat pocket in front of her during her flight from London. She complained to the stewardess that she had paid a lot of money for her vacation abroad and she wanted everything she was due, including that Air India menu.

James thought to himself how stupid people can get over petty possessions, especially something as worthless as a flight menu. People should be more concerned with helping poor countries and feeding hungry people. He wasn't about to entertain the thought that this woman's flight menu meant as much to her as his 'greater issues of life' meant to him. How could they? Surely, the ideal is to place human values on a higher pedestal than such petty concerns. James had to believe these things, or why else was he on this mission?

Why, indeed, was he on this mission? Why was he leaving home for the first time in his life? Why was he replacing the comforts of old for the uncertainty of the new? He couldn't help thinking it had something to do with his name.

"To the folks back home," he thought, "I guess I'll always be 'Bubba,' the kid from around the corner. Leaving, though, is something Bubba wouldn't do. Striking out on my own—now, that's James."

Bubba was the fun-loving guy, the life of the party. But he was also sometimes wary of new things—not fearful, just cautious. James was something different, something more. James was a man with a mission, a man with a destiny. He resolved that he would be 'Bubba' no more.

"Excuse me, sir! Excuse me, sir! Sorry to wake you, but could you please fasten your seat belt? We are entering a patch of turbulence," she said in a soft but insistent voice.

"What?" James asked, realizing that he must have dozed off. "Oh! Sure. What's happening? Are we going to crash?"

The stewardess assured him that turbulence was normal over this part of Nevada. James was surprised and confused at having flown that far across America. He thought they had only been in the air for an hour at the most. How long had he been asleep? He turned to the lady sitting to his right and asked her to excuse him. He then made his way back toward the toilets and stood in a small queue. Having a chance to observe the other passengers on the flight, he was surprised to see so many different kinds of people. There were Chinese, blacks, whites, Hispanics and a few he could not identify. James wondered how many were Americans and how many were going to the same place as he. There could only be a few according to his calculations, since there were about thirty-nine volunteers selected for training and presumably they were selected from all over the United States. He waged a bet with himself that he was the only volunteer from Virginia, a notion he relished. The toilet queue had shortened. The door was opened and to his relief the cool moist deodorized towel was massaging his face.

James Edward Johnson was tall, dark and handsome. At 5 feet 11 inches, his 175-pound body was long and lanky with broad shoulders. He prided himself on his Yoruba features and took great pains to care for his dark brown smooth skin. The girls thought he was good looking and told him so often enough. The boys thought he was an okay guy. Although some of them envied his popularity with the girls, they respected his leadership and his gregariousness. He inspired confidence. Few would ever know his introverted side and fewer still would recognize that his "All American Boy" act was a cover for his own insecurities and hang-ups.

James would very rarely let it be known that he was insulted and he was an artist at keeping cool, calm and collected. One of his tactics was to disarm others by showing kindness and love, a combination few could refuse. He would also employ the old 'could you help, please?' approach. This not only caused others to feel needed, but also placed pressure on them to do a good turn. As he looked in the mirror he recalled one such situation.

One evening about 6:00 p.m. James was returning to the South Walk Community Center in Richmond, Virginia where he worked as a Youth Program Coordinator. The Center was noted for the violence and gang fights that continuously erupted over the slightest provocation. James had worked there for the past nine months, since he graduated from South Walk State College in 1965. He was proud of his Bachelors Degree in Social Work and like most new graduates, thought that he had all the answers to society's problems. His thoughts were often reflected in his actions, which some of the local boys resented. Pee Wee Patterson was a tough, mean seventeen year-old leader of the Corner Boys Gang. He disliked James and put the word out that he was going to 'get him.' Pee Wee never divulged what his first name was, although it was rumored to have been Shirley. This probably accounted for his violent temperament.

Pee Wee was waiting on the front door steps of the community center for James. Pee Wee's brother Larry and several other gang members were with him. As James approached the entrance he could feel the tension and he knew that the situation was bad. Most of these boys were known to carry knives, picks and other weapons.

Pee Wee had done a year in a Juvenile Detention Center for stabbing an old man in the arm. Since James was too close to walk away, or for that matter, outrun the boys, he had some quick thinking to do.

"What's happening, brothers?"

Someone replied, "You, man!"

James's mind was trying to think of the best thing to do because he knew by the sound of that greeting his turn was imminent. Already Mr. Hodge, the Center Director, had been beaten up twice and spent a month in the hospital with a fractured ribs and a concussion. The mere thought of Mr. Hodge's experience made James shiver. Then Pee Wee spoke.

"You gonna open up the pool table tonight, Mr. Johnson?"

They all called him Mr. Johnson, a rule imposed by Mr. Hodge to 'maintain a professional atmosphere.' James would have preferred to be called 'James' because he thought that formality inhibits communication. He was also not much older than the boys, being only twenty-one, and they resented having to call him Mister. James said that he wished he could open the table but Mr. Hodge had forbidden the use of the table for a week because some of the boys smashed up the cue sticks and cut the tabletop.

Pee Wee took a menacing step toward James.

"Ain't none of my boys messed up the table. Ain't our fault. Why do we have to wait cause somebody else messed up the table?"

"I agree with you Pee Wee," James said. "I've got an idea of how we might stop it from happening again, but I will need your help. Pee Wee, why don't you and the fellas come into the office with me and let's talk. You would really be doing me a favor if you could help me with this."

Perhaps he had taken Pee Wee off guard, but a few minutes later James found himself sitting at his desk across from Pee Wee and the other gang members. They were all drinking Coca Colas at his expense. James told Pee Wee that Mr. Hodge was getting a Job Corps grant soon from the Department of Labor. He would need some youth leaders to supervise the playground and recreation halls. He asked James to suggest names of good candidates for the jobs, people with leadership qualities who were not afraid of the tough guys and who liked kids. He asked Pee Wee if he knew anybody who would be interested.

There were several moments of hushed silence. The question really baffled Pee Wee. He was not only surprised at being asked the question as if his opinion would be highly regarded, but he was not sure he knew anyone with 'leadership qualities.' Someone broke the silence by shouting.

"Pee Wee ain't afraid of nobody!"

Then there was a chorus of "Pee Wee ain't afraid!"

There was a lot of laughing and joking. Someone shouted, "Yeah, there ain't nobody in the world Pee Wee is scared of, except his old lady."

Everybody roared laughing, including Pee Wee and James. Just as the tension seemed to break, Pee Wee turned around to the boy who cracked the joke, putting his hand to the boy's throat.

"Don't nobody talk about my Momma. Hear me? You jive-time dude!"

The boy's smiling face flattened as straight as a razor's edge. Everyone else stopped laughing. Finally, there was a collective sigh of relief as Pee Wee's huge hand slowly began to release grip on the boy's neck.

Pee Wee was big and burley. Standing at six feet, two inches and weighing two hundred and forty seven pounds, he was an imposing, even frightening, seventeen year old. He was sitting there in his dirty dungarees and his size thirteen Army Brogan boots that he stole from his English teacher's room. Of course, she was no small fry either. Miss Woods was all of six and a half feet and weighed fifty pounds more than Pee Wee. She was the only person at South Walk High School who could handle Pee Wee. Rumor had it that on no less than two occasions, Pee Wee was sent home in an ambulance after having a quiet word with Miss Woods.

"How about a butt, Mr. Johnson?" Pee Wee asked.

James knew this was going to be an expensive round because if Pee Wee got a cigarette then the others would want one, too. He also knew that Mr. Hodge did not allow the youth to smoke in the Center.

"What the hell," he thought. "While I am sitting here sweating for my life, old Hodge is probably sitting up watching the evening news with his feet propped up and a Budweiser in his hand."

Passing the cigarettes around, James told Pee Wee that he showed all the qualities needed for the job and if Pee Wee were interested, he would recommend him for one of the jobs. He also said that he would like to see Pee Wee get a job because he was such a 'nice' guy. Although it was true that the grant for the jobs was coming and that Mr. Hodge told him to look around for suitable candidates, James was less than enthusiastic about wanting Pee Wee in one of the jobs. The plain truth of the matter was that James was scared stiff of the prospect of having to tell Pee Wee what to do. Nonetheless he had tactfully got himself out of a nasty situation and made a promise that he could live with. It would then be up to Mr. Hodge to make the final decision. Either way, he felt that he now had Pee Wee in his corner and since he was leaving in a few months time, Pee Wee would no longer be his problem.

A voice over the intercom brought his mind quickly back to the present. Captain Walker was explaining that they were approaching the East Rim of the Grand Canyon. He said that Garcia Lopez de Cardenas, a Spanish explorer, was the first known European to see the Grand Canyon in 1540, although Native Americans had lived there for thousands of years. The canyon stretches 277 miles long, eighteen miles wide and 6,000 feet deep. The woman sitting next to James talked about how fascinating the view was. He agreed. They had exchanged smiles and pleasantries earlier in the flight and talked about how good the meals were, but they had not said any more. The woman looked very relaxed and appeared to have a smile imprinted on her face. James was puzzled by her, simply because he could not figure out how old she was. She looked to be about thirty-five with a very smooth olive complexion. What puzzled him, though, was her silver hair. It looked naturally grey. He wondered why a young looking woman, who was obviously used to smiling, would have grey hair. James dismissed the idea of malnutrition since she had a fine healthy looking body.

"Do you travel by plane often?"

James had not heard her question the first time, nor was he aware that she was reading his thoughts. It was obvious with his eyes fixed on her grey, shoulder length hair, cut with a fringe.

"No, I don't, ma'am. In fact, this is my first time on a plane. Do you travel much?"

"Oh, yes, I have done a lot of travelling. Sometimes I enjoy it, but it can be an awful bore at other times."

"Well, I don't want to bore you, lady. You started talking to me first!" James said defensively. He had totally misread the woman's statement.

"Oh, no! I don't mean that you bore me. I mean that traveling, changing planes and those types of things bore me."

She could not help but have a quiet chuckle at James's misinterpretation of her comment and she put it down to his immaturity. She introduced herself as Janice Blanche and asked James to call her Janice. He then introduced himself. By this time everyone sitting in the front section of the plane had turned to look at a man who became airsick. The poor fellow was already suffering the embarrassment of having to use the dreaded brown paper bag and then he had to put up with the further embarrassment of all those people looking at him. The stewardess quickly took the bag out of his hands and disposed of it. She asked him if he was okay and suggested that he go to the back of the plane where she could give him something to help make him feel more comfortable. He agreed to go with her, but as he was about to stand, he saw more people looking at him.

"Thank you," he said, "but I'll be all right now."

At that point a woman sitting on the other side of the aisle told the stewardess that she felt sick.

Janice leaned toward James and asked if he was on vacation. He explained that he was a Peace Corps Volunteer on his way to training in San Diego. There was an instant expression of excitement in Janice's face.

"Oh, that's interesting. I have heard a lot about the Peace Corps and I think it is one of the best programs created by President Kennedy. Which country are you going to?"

"I am going to Malawi in East Africa. I bet you never heard of it."

"I have heard of it. In fact, I have been there. This is quite a coincidence because I work in Zambia, a neighboring country to Malawi."

"Gee," James said, "I can't believe this. What a coincidence! What's it like there? I only have a little information about the country. We are supposed to learn more during training."

Janice talked continuously for almost half an hour, telling James about the climate, the rainy season and the dry season, the staple diet, the languages and a lot of statistics on the standard of living in both countries. She even knew what proportion of the gross national product was spent on defense in each country. James was fascinated by all of this information and thought Janice knew her stuff. Every so often he would peer up at her silver grey hair because he still could not figure that out. After listening to her for a while, she began to sound more like twenty-five than thirty-five. James was waiting for a chance to speak after listening to what turned out to be a long monologue.

"You really know a lot about Africa. How long have you worked out there and what do you do?"

"Oh, a few years," Janice said, "but I must tell you about the malaria pills. There are two kinds to take. There's the one-a-day brand that a lot of people forget to take and the one-a-month brand that the Peace Corps tend to—oh! I must be boring you silly. Perhaps I have talked enough. Would you excuse me while I get in this queue before it gets too long?"

Janice excused herself and James reclined into his seat exhausted. He thought that she was quite a talker and she had told him some interesting things.

"I still do not know what she does in Zambia," he mused. "She must be a teacher or something. She knew an awful lot about the Peace Corps. I guess when you've been around as much as she has you get to know a lot. She seems like a nice person."

Chapter 1: Training for a New Adventure

Once Upon A Friendship

There was a soft tap on the door at Sandra Whitaker's apartment. She rose slowly from the sofa where she had been sitting for quite some time. She answered in a snappy but soft voice.

"It's me, Linda. Are you okay, Sandra?"

"Yes. Just a minute."

Linda was Sandra's next-door neighbor. She had obviously heard Sandra cry because Sandra did everything dramatically, including crying. She grabbed a Kleenex tissue from the box to wipe the tears from her big, beautiful, hazel brown eyes. She had been crying for over two hours because James was gone. She told Linda that she cried more over James's leaving than she had cried for all her other boyfriends put together. Knowing Sandra as she did, Brenda thought that was quite a compliment to James. Sandra never did date a guy for more than two months until she met James. Linda sat down to have coffee with Sandra. She'd made sure she brought enough cigarettes to get her through the next hour and she had already made up her excuse for leaving. She knew from previous experiences that she was in for quite a talk-a-thon.

Linda took the first sip of her coffee as Sandra started parading up and down the living room carpet. She talked about the trip to the airport and how nice James's father was and how his mother did not like her and so on. Sandra had this irritating habit of trying to talk about five or six subjects at once. She then began to talk about her relationship with James. They met while he was in his senior year at college. He had just won the election for President of the Student Council and was also in several clubs including the popular

Debating Society. Sandra was in her junior year studying to be a teacher.

One day in the cafeteria Sandra went up to James and asked in a very demanding voice, "Hey, Mr. Student Council President, what are you going to do about this lousy food here?"

"What do you suggest?"

"Why are you asking me? That's why we elected you!"

"Hey, now, I can't do anything about it until I know what it is you are complaining about."

"Don't get uppity with me just because you've been elected Student Council President."

Thus began a turbulent, but exciting relationship. It is true that Sandra had few long-term relationships with men prior to meeting James. She was a country girl with a domineering father. He was a farmer in Suffolk, Virginia, an upright, religious, quiet, black man who did not believe in worldly goods. Sandra was not allowed to wear lipstick and never had until she went to college; even then, she would never let her father see her with it on. Her mother was a sweet and proud little woman of about forty-five years old. She stood five feet tall, but one got the feeling that she would actually have been two inches taller if she could straighten her back. She had worked so hard on that farm that she'd developed a hunch. She had the same pretty cherry brown skin as Sandra and very pronounced cheekbones. Sandra and her mother were really good friends and her mother understood her daughter's desire to get away from home. When Sandra left for South Walk State College, her mother was torn between happiness and sadness. Perhaps if she could have had more children, it would have been easier to let Sandra go.

James had told Sandra that his father, Earl Johnson, started work as a mail carrier with the South Walk Post Office in 1952. He was one of only a few black mailmen in the city and during that time it was a status job for blacks in the South. Top jobs for blacks included teaching (in black schools or colleges), Postal Service, Armed

Forces and owning a small business. In 1956, one of the first private housing estates was built in the area for blacks. Prior to that most blacks, regardless of income, lived in the same neighborhoods. Earl Johnson, a World War II Army veteran, was a proud man when he learned that his mortgage had been approved for one of the two hundred homes being sold at Fairfield Acres Estate in Richmond, Virginia. This was a great breakthrough, not only for Earl, but for his wife, Ida, and their daughter and three sons. It was also a breakthrough for the black community to know that maybe they would be able to own their own homes one day, too.

James was the eldest child, followed by Lillian, two years later. Lillian was three years older than David. After David came Randolph, who was a spoiled little brat, being the youngest. James was equally spoiled, being the eldest. James was a strict disciplinarian, just like his father. He did not want to be strict, but he was ordered to be strict with the little ones. He always thought he was kinder than his father and he would often play a mind game called 'Who can be the strictest and the kindest, me or Daddy?' James always won because his father did not even know he was playing a game. James was always kind to Lillian and David, and they helped to satisfy his notion that he was kinder than his father. But, poor little Randolph received the full wrath of James's pranks, including salt on his cornflakes and pepper in his lemonade. The pranks never got too heavy because they all basically loved each other. James even loved his father, although he wished his father would be more fun and less strict.

Sandra was a bit on the wild side. During her first year at South Walk State College, she went to most sports events and parties and she went on a lot of dates. She had been denied her freedom to smoke, dance, put on makeup and date for the first eighteen years of her life. She seemed determined to make up for lost time, all in her first year at college. Sandra's freshman year might have been a social success but it was an academic disaster, and she started her second year on probation. Sandra improved just enough that year to stay in school. Her relationships with some of her boyfriends were frenzied and volatile. She resented any long-lasting relationships because they meant commitment, which she was not ready to provide. The threat was dominance, and she had spent too many years being dominated by her father. She liked boys, and in some respects this was one reason why she wanted to be free: in order to like who she pleased on her terms. She had no trouble finding admirers. She was tall and not too slim, with beautiful eyes and even white teeth. Her lips were full, rounded and sensual. She also presented a downright challenge to James's male chauvinist proclivities.

James needed someone like Sandra. He had just recovered from a mild heartache after breaking up with Elaine Lavery. They had dated for three years in high school. He and Elaine were used to being apart since she had gone to a college out of state. They saw each other on holidays and during the summer months. Both had been dating other people and both knew it. It is difficult to know whether they were ever in love after their first year of dating. It is, however, very likely that Elaine's heartache was even milder than James's; she got married to someone else soon after she and James broke up. He became furious after hearing this. It was not so much the loss of Elaine, nor was it the fact that she got married, but what irked him was the *timing*. His pride was hurt because everyone knew that Elaine was getting married, except him. James felt he would not have to stick around Richmond once he graduated. He could go and see the world—no more ties and commitments for a while. That's where Sandra fit in. When he started dating Sandra he did not expect the relationship to blossom or, in their case, explode. In fact, he could not see it getting beyond the first couple of dates. They were poles apart and they both knew it. Perhaps the attraction they had was that they both wanted no commitments. On their first date, Sandra told James that she would see whom she wanted to see and he could see whom he wanted to see. James agreed. They fought like cats and dogs from that point until he got on the airplane at Richmond International Airport, but they mostly had a good time together. Neither one dated anyone else during the time they were together.

Just then, Sandra's conversation with Linda was abruptly cut short. There was a light tap at Sandra's door.

"That must be Betty," Linda said. "She asked me to go with her to the Laundromat. Gee! Have I been here over an hour, Sandra? I know you are going to miss him. Will you be okay now? I have got to go."

Linda left the room and Sandra began taking away the coffee cups and the dirty ashtrays. She opened the window to let some smoke out and fresh air in. She was glad that Linda dropped in because it gave her a chance to talk it out of her system. Sandra knew that she was very much like James. She would always be fond of him and could relish the good times they had together. She also knew that she could continue having good times just as he would. As she looked out of her living room window, she could see a silver-blue airplane high in the sky.

She spoke softly, "Goodbye James Johnson. I will always love you."

Hi, There! My Name Is. . . .

The plane landed at Los Angeles International Airport at 5:00 p.m. It was a September day in 1966 and the temperature in Los Angeles was in the upper 70s. The plane's engines were shut off and the air-conditioning was no longer working. It felt like an oven and passengers were taking off sweaters and jackets while waiting.

The voice on the intercom said, "Sorry for this delay, but it will only be a few minutes before you can leave the aircraft. Thank you for choosing to fly with us today."

That few minutes seemed much longer, as sweat began to pour off people's faces. Some were standing in the aisle of the plane while others sat in their seats. Those sitting down placed their hand luggage and other items in the spots where they would otherwise have been standing. This did not all happen at once. It seemed to occur along some chronological age pattern. First, an elderly lady placed her bag in the aisle. She was sitting in the front of the plane and most people could see her. That's fair enough because one doesn't expect little old ladies to stand under those conditions. Then a little old man looked around quickly and placed his box where he had been standing. This really did start off a new round of shuffling.

All of a sudden there were comments such as: "Excuse me, please." "Hey, buddy, watch your head!" "Sir, could you help me with this bag?" "Oh my God, I lost my passport!" and "Harry, get out of the lady's way!"

Finally, the gates to Dante's Inferno were opened and the crowd was allowed out to avail themselves of fresh air and water. James had just picked up his luggage when Janice Blanche appeared out of nowhere.

"James, it was really nice talking to you and I assure you this was not a boring trip. I have got to hurry now because someone is meeting me. Enjoy your training and I'll see you again."

Before he could reply, Janice had taken off and was quickly moving out of sight. He said to himself, "Goodbye, Janice."

He thought that she was a strange woman and he wondered what she meant by saying "I'll see you again." He quickly dismissed the matter, thinking that perhaps that was her way of saying goodbye.

A voice over the intercom intoned, "Would the following passengers arriving on TWA Flight 1140 from Washington, D.C. please report to the main reception desk: Mr. Joseph Veto, Mr. Stuart Steiner, and Mr. James Johnson."

"That's me! That's me! That's me!" shouted James, causing a few curious looks and lots of laughs.

It was not so much the hearing of his name over the intercom that excited him. He was used to that from his days in college. What excited him was hearing his name called out at Los Angeles International Airport, where stars like Sammy Davis, Jr., John Wayne and Dean Martin were known to travel. He thought for an instant that he was famous. When James got to the main reception desk, Alex Erskine, the Deputy Administrative Officer at the Peace Corp Training Center, San Diego, California and Susan Hart, Training Co-coordinator, were there to greet him. James was introduced to Stuart Steiner and Joseph Veto, both Peace Corps volunteers. They were among the few volunteers left to be picked up at the airport.

The drive to San Diego took about two and a half hours. However, it seemed longer to the group as they viewed the many new sights. This was California and it was just like the movies to them. The freeways were giant figure eight loops drawn into bows and drawn out again into eight lane straightaways with no end in sight. Although it was approaching dusk, they could still see the changing topography and sense the shift in the atmosphere as they drove out of the Los Angeles area heading south. Lush, green rolling hills began to change to gold dust desert country. As far as twenty miles away, they could see the Los Angeles smog set in the silhouette of the retiring autumn sun.

Stuart asked Alex Erskine what the training center was like.

"Oh, it's a nice place and in a good location, too. It's just about a mile from the old navy training barracks on the outskirts of San Diego. In fact, we're using the old command headquarters as the training center. Of course, there have been major repairs and changes to the place since Peace Corps started using it. You will like it a lot out there."

Before long, the new volunteers found themselves passing through the center of downtown San Diego. The night-lights had already come on and the streets were crowded with all types of people, including sailors. In fact, there seemed to be sailors everywhere. Alex explained that there was a large naval base located in San Diego and sometimes when two or three ships came in at one time, the whole city would fill up with sailors. Soon they were on the outskirts of the city and driving up hill. They climbed to a point where the entire city of San Diego could be seen in the distance behind them and a thick forest area lay ahead. Alex turned his head toward the rear.

"We will be there soon. I know you guys are tired and probably hungry by now. Dinner will be ready upon your arrival."

Alex drove left onto a loose gravel road about two hundred yards through thick woods and then all of a sudden there was a huge open space. Directly in front was a freshly painted, grey and white building with an American flag flying on it. Lights were on in the building and several people could be seen moving around the grounds.

"Here we are, guys. That's the administrative building straight ahead. Just leave your bags in the jeep until you know where you are sleeping. You can come into the office with me first."

They were all hustled into the building so quickly that they didn't get a chance to observe their surroundings. The training center complex was about the size of Yankee Stadium. Rows of wooden frame buildings were lined up at adjacent angles on each side of the Administrative building. There were eight in each row. About fifty yards behind the Administrative building were four other buildings, one of which was almost double the length and width of the others. It was the cafeteria/recreation hall. Next to it on the right was the supply building, which also housed the laundry facilities. The building on the left had been remodeled and equipped with showers, lockers and toilets. There were twenty showers all in a row. There were a total of twenty buildings on the complex, which was shaped like a rectangle with one short side missing. That was the entrance.

"Hi, there. My name is Rick Elliot. I am the training director. Did you fellows enjoy your trip?"

Rick Elliot was tall and weighed about two hundred pounds and was all muscle. He reminded one of a high school football coach. In fact Rick was once an all-American halfback for the University of Michigan. Since that time he had become a lawyer, worked in private practice, moved on to the State Department in some administrative post and was now with Peace Corps. He had been in his present position for three and a half years and spent eighteen months of that time as a PC Country Director in Tanzania. His credentials were good. Dick was fifty-one, married with two daughters, both in High School.

Greetings were exchanged and the three volunteers quickly found themselves getting instructions, timetables, and other logistical information from Claire Ferguson, Rick's secretary. They preferred to use the word cottage instead of barracks. James had been assigned to Cottage 3 along with Joe Veto. Stuart Steiner was assigned to Cottage 8, the last in that row. Cottages 9 through 16 were reserved for the girls. As they were walking the fifty yards or so towards the cottages, Stuart spoke hesitatingly.

"I'll meet you guys in the cafeteria in about thirty minutes—that's if it's okay with you."

Stuart was tall, slender and had yellowish white skin and black curly hair. He was twenty-three and sported a beard and mustache. He was from Stamford, Connecticut. He took a flight from Washington, D.C. after spending the last three days with his girlfriend in Maryland. Stuart was a loner, not by chance, but by choice. Each cottage had Navy issued single beds and small chest of drawers. There were also several large hooks screwed into the walls between each bed, which could be used for hanging suits, coats and other clothes. The floor was plywood, which had been painted deck red. It was clean and shiny, but noisy when walked upon. There were also two toilets and two washbowls in each cottage. Any serious personal hygiene would have to be dealt with in the showers next to the cafeteria. There was plenty of space. Males would share five cottages and females would share four cottages. Married staff would use the two cottages near the cafeteria and storage buildings. There were no married Peace Corps Volunteers in this group. James Johnson and Joe Veto found no one in Cottage 3 when they entered. The two other volunteers who would be assigned to the cottage had not yet arrived. Joe looked around curiously.

"Gee, I thought I was getting away from Vietnam but this place makes me feel like I am in the Army."

"It looks like those old Army movies," James said. "Every bed neatly made up and equal distances apart. Look at those thick greenish brown blankets. They remind me of my Daddy's old Army uniform."

"Oh your father was in the Army? Where was he stationed?"

"He was in Germany during World War II. He was a Mess Sergeant there. In those days, that was about the highest rank most black folk could get."

"Yes, I know." Joe Veto paused. "Blacks were not the only ones who had a hard time in those days."

James then changed the subject.

"I'm hungry, man. I am going to wash up quickly and get some grub. I wonder what kind of a spread they are laying on for us."

"Probably beans and franks!"

They both laughed and began to unpack.

More than three hours had passed since they had landed at Los Angeles International Airport. James and Joe met Stuart in the entrance to the cafeteria. It was a spacious long room with rows of tables and hard chairs. Some volunteers were standing in line waiting to be served and others were scattered all over the place in clusters. There must have been about twenty people in the room. Everyone appeared to be checking everyone else out. There was a sense of enthusiasm running through the place and everyone was being ever so nice, but cautious. Most of the girls wore shorts and t-shirts with a few miniskirts thrown in. The boys wore t-shirts, blue jeans and sandals or sneakers. There were fat people, skinny people, tall ones and short, extroverts and introverts, black, brown and white.

James noticed a rather round faced black guy with bubbly lips sitting alone at the far end of the room. He looked up and nodded his head to James, who returned the greeting. There was a rather attractive black girl talking with a Latino girl and two white girls. They were really having some laughs about something. In the far corner was a tall blue eyed, blonde boy standing next to a jukebox reading the list of songs.

"Two potatoes or three, amigo?"

The man serving the potatoes was Mexican American. The entire kitchen staff was Mexican American, including the Chef. James was not sure whether they were all part of the same family. He smiled.

"Dos, por favor. Gracias, amigo."

Joe Veto was the first through the queue and he found a table next to where four girls were sitting. They all checked each other out. They talked about where they were from, how they liked California, and the usual getting acquainted small talk. Stuart Steiner did not say much. Joe Veto and James Johnson did most of the talking, for the male side that is. All four of the girls appeared to be confident and equally gregarious. Time seemed to have passed quickly as they saw it was almost 11 o'clock at night. Exhausted, they quickly dispersed to their respective cottages. Before long, only the main flood light at the Administrative building shone brightly. The Peace Corp Training Center had gone to sleep on the first night of a training program that was to drastically alter the nature of all subsequent Peace Corps projects in developing countries.

The First Training Day

The remaining volunteers arrived on Sunday and were assigned cottages. Joe Veto and James Johnson met their two new roommates. Bob Newgate was from San Antonio, Texas and Phil Harrington was from Bismarck, North Dakota. It was 9:00 o'clock on Monday morning when the thirty-nine volunteers were assembled in the cafeteria building for their first orientation session.

"Good Morning and welcome to the Peace Corps training center here in San Diego. I have met most of you, but for the benefit of those of you I have not met, my name is Rick Elliot and I am the Director of Training. Over to my right is Alex Erskine, Deputy Administrative Officer. Susan Hart is over in the corner there. Susan is in charge of language training. In fact, Susan has a Ph.D. in Foreign Languages and speaks five languages fluently, including Chinyanja, one of Malawi's languages. Alex Erskine will discuss the agenda and timetable for the duration of your training. Oh, I must not forget Dr. Fred Mueller sitting over there. Fred is our Consultant Psychiatrist who will visit the center about three days a week. He has a private practice in San Diego, but kindly accepted an offer to work with this program. If you have any problems or anything you want to talk about, my door is always open. Please feel free to come in. I look forward to getting to know you all. Now I'll turn you over to Alex. Okay, Alex it's your show."

There was something about Rick Elliot that made you want to follow him. He was like a big brother or a coach. They trusted him but knew he could be tough if necessary. He also had a sense of humor and occasionally cracked the odd locker room joke, even in front of the girls. He would be as ruthless with them as with the boys and was often heard saying to both: "Get yourself together and fast! There are no mommy's apron strings to pull on around here and there will certainly not be any where you are going." Although Rick had never been in the military, there was something of a Platoon Sergeant in him. But the volunteers also got the feeling that he was genuinely concerned about them.

Alex Erskine began by reviewing the purpose of Peace Corps. He explained that the program was started in the early1960s by President John F. Kennedy to foster friendly relationships between America and developing countries and to provide assistance. One way of doing this was to send volunteers to work with and contribute to the development of these countries. These volunteers included doctors, nurses, teachers, health workers and people with certain agricultural and technical skills. The program had proved successful in many countries such as Asia, Africa and Latin America and they were requesting more PC volunteers. Alex further explained that their project consisted of a teaching program and a health program. It was the fourth PC group going to Malawi. There were twenty teachers and nineteen health workers in this group.

There would be two groups for language training since there were two main dialects to learn depending on which part of the country you were assigned. Language classes were scheduled for 9-12 a.m. on every weekday except Thursday. On those days, the afternoon would include cultural orientation and lectures in one's area of specialization. Thursday was set aside for field trips, which might include anything from learning how to construct a small dam to building a bridge. Teams of up to eight people could work on a project together with the idea of completing it within the three-month training period. Other projects included regular visits to nearby farms and health clinics in Baja, California. The purpose behind this type of trip was to get volunteers used to dealing with people whose language they did not understand and also to get them used to working in less than ideal situations.

Alex explained that the language teachers were all Malawians and all except one were students at various colleges or universities in the area. The one exception was a Malawian Head Master of a large secondary school. He had a dual role. He would teach the language as well as lead the cultural orientation sessions. Alex stressed self-sufficiency and co-operation. He asked everyone to tidy up their own beds, clear their own tables and generally help keep the place in tip-top shape. There were no cleaning people and the kitchen staff was only responsible for cleaning the kitchen and storage room. The weekends were free, but the volunteers were discouraged from going too far outside of the San Diego area. Alex talked about bus schedules, things to do in downtown San Diego and other logistical details. After entertaining a number of questions, he noticed that it was time for a break and directed the group toward the coffee and vending machines. For the rest of the day they could finish unpacking, take a look around the camp and play ball on the large field in the back of the building.

By mid-afternoon most people had finished their lunches and explored much of the training center. This included the insides of the storage rooms, shower rooms, each other's cottages and part of the surrounding woods. On the field in the back of the cafeteria, a group was playing a friendly game of touch football. Fat Ramsey Hall was touching everything but the football. Ramsey was round and portly with thin brown hair and a red nose. He was a jolly guy who weighed a lot. He was raised on a tobacco farm in Greenville, North Carolina. The girls actually enjoyed him and also teased him about his farm boy accent and his weight.

"Come on, Ramsey darling. Catch me if you can."

They knew Ramsey could not catch them. Actually, if Ramsey ran more than ten yards at a time, he would have to sit on the side lines for at least ten minutes to get his breath back. Ramsey was too fat and the doctors told him so. His specialty was farming, a skill that could be useful in a poor developing country. James and Joe were playing football along with Bob Newgate, their roommate, when Bob threw a long pass straight down center field. Joe missed the pass and the ball bounced off the field into a thicket. Joe went to get the ball and as he looked around he came upon a beautiful sight. Below was a cove with golden sandy beaches and blue-green waves forming clear white crests as they crashed on the shore. The beach was about three-hundred feet below the steeply declining escarpment.

"Hey, you guys, come over here," Joe yelled. "There's a beach down here and it's beautiful, too!"

Everyone ran over to the thicket—everyone except Ramsey, that is. He walked. They were all amazed at the magnificent beauty of the spot. Word soon got around that the beach was there and within walking distance and there was talk of having beach parties and barbecues. The day continued on into the evening with enthusiasm growing among all of the volunteers.

As James was to later put it, "This is a nice scene, man."—by which he meant the whole experience.

Jennifer Nolan

It was about 7:00 o'clock that evening when Jennifer Nolan finished her dinner and went to take a shower. She felt really grubby after all the walking she had done that day and wondered if the other girls were going to wear dresses or jeans that night. Jennifer turned the hot and cold-water taps simultaneously, and immediately jumped back letting out a shriek. The water was freezing! She then approached the cold tap from a side angle, trying to get the adjustments right. Eventually, the hot water began to merge with the cold, resulting in a comfortable, warm shower. She began to shampoo her short auburn hair that was cut in the style of the early Beatles. The suds began streaming down her slender body. Only her

28

face, arms and legs were slightly tanned from the sun. As she lathered the soap over her small, but bubbly breasts she was thinking of her four sisters and her parents.

Jennifer was from Wichita, Kansas. Her father was a wheat farmer who had come over from Ireland in 1935. Although he was born into a Catholic family, he never practiced Catholicism after he was married. Jennifer and her four sisters were brought up Protestant. She was the third born and did not receive the same attention as the first and last-born. Inevitably there were petty jealousies among the girls and Jennifer always felt last in line. She thought that her sisters were more attractive and had better personalities than she, not because it was true, but because they told her so. Her ambition was to get away from her sisters and that farm. None of them were strangers to hard work, thanks to their father, who had actually wanted boys. Jennifer was a quiet girl who wished that she wasn't. Throughout high school the boys did not talk to her, preferring her outgoing sisters. Her mother was a warm, but firm woman who would not allow the girls to date until they were eighteen years old. The two eldest sisters would often rebel by sneaking out anyway. Not Jennifer. She respected her mother and she also was afraid of her.

Jennifer went to Wichita State Teachers College to study Elementary Education. Almost all of the students taking this major were female. The odds for getting a boyfriend were slim. Jennifer did not even try, remembering the competition she had in high school from her sisters and others. She was, however, bright, attractive and studious and she graduated with honors, second in her class. She even got a scholarship to continue on at Wichita State for a Masters Degree, but she wanted to get away, and the Peace Corp offered the perfect opportunity.

Her thoughts were interrupted by this soft southern drawl.

"Hi, Jennifer. I thought I would find you here. What are you going to wear tonight? I am thinking about wearing this pretty Dashiki dress my boyfriend gave me. It sure is steamy in here, honey!"

It was Dianne Harper, the all-American black girl from Jackson, Mississippi. She had been telling everyone how she met President Lyndon Johnson when he was Governor of Texas and that she was a personal friend of Dr. Martin Luther King, Jr. She was also State Representative for the NAACP. Dianne was a bit of a show-off, but she had a winning personality. She was a very attractive tall, buxom young woman. She had a lovely brown complexion and pretty curly hair. She also exuded what one might call Southern sensuality. She was five inches taller than Jennifer and weighed about fifteen pounds more.

"I don't know what I'm wearing yet, Dianne. I was thinking of wearing jeans and a sweater. Do you think most of the girls will wear dresses?"

"Oh, yes. You always wear dresses to receptions. I mean, well, it gives you a chance to get dressed up, you know. It's not often the boys will see us dressed up. Yes, Jennifer, why don't you wear a dress?"

Jennifer thought, why should she get dressed up? No one would notice her anyway. Before long the showers were full of girls.

When James Johnson and Joe Veto arrived at the cafeteria that evening, music was roaring from the jukebox and some people were dancing. Most people had a drink, and the place was lively with conversation and laughter. James noticed Stuart Steiner talking to Catherine Horowitz, who shared the cottage with Jennifer and Dianne. The fourth girl, Maria De Angelo, from Santa Cruz had not yet arrived. Stuart looked serious and Cathy looked bored, sitting on the opposite side of the room alone was Jesse Jefferson. He was a short black guy from Newark who had not said much to anyone. He nodded to James, who returned the nod. Standing in the middle of the floor surrounded by a few people was Reggie Blackwell, a black guy from Atlanta, Georgia. Reggie was by far the tallest person in the complex, standing at 6' 8". He was a physical education teacher. Of the thirty-nine volunteers, there were three black males, one black female, one Puerto Rican female and two Mexican-American females from California and New Mexico. Everyone else was white, but from various ethnic backgrounds.

30

James was yet to understand the ethnic differences among white people. Where he came from you were either white or black. He had never differentiated Italian Americans from Polish, Irish, English, German nor other European ethnicities. He was aware of the religious divisions, especially of the Jews, but even so, most Jews were white, or at least the ones he knew.

Joe Veto spotted Dianne Harper.

"Hey, there's Dianne and her roommates. Let's go talk to them, James."

Joe liked Dianne Harper. James had noticed Joe looking at Dianne ever since she arrived. They both went over to Dianne and Jennifer. Ramsey Hall, the fat volunteer was already talking to them.

"Oh, boy! I got competition now," Ramsey joked.

"Nobody can compete with you, Ramsey honey," Dianne teased.

They all talked and laughed for a while. Dianne asked James where he was from and then said that she knew a lot of people who went to South Walk State College in Richmond, Virginia and began to ask James if he knew various people. James knew some of the names. Dianne then turned to Joe.

"Where are you from, honey?"

Joe did not know whether she was being condescending or whether the use of 'honey' was just a Southern expression.

In any event, he quickly replied, "Seattle, Washington."

Dianne said that she had once met an English professor from the University of Washington. According to Dianne, she knew someone from just about everywhere. As Joe and Ramsey became preoccupied with Dianne's adventures, James began talking to Jennifer. They must have talked for thirty minutes before James heard a husky voice.

"What's happening, brother?"

It was Jesse Jefferson, the black volunteer from Newark. They exchanged greetings and James introduced Jesse to Jennifer. Jesse gave a quick nod to Jennifer and continued to talk to James, who noticed that Jesse was ignoring Jennifer. James could sense that Jesse did not like Jennifer, not because she was skinny or perhaps not a beauty queen, nor because she was a girl. Jesse did not like Jennifer because she was WHITE. She must have sensed it too, because she quickly excused herself.

"Sure ain't many soul brothers around," Jesse whispered to James. "Notice how they split us all up. They always are trying to split us up just like what they did in slavery. You talked to the soul sister yet?"

"I talked to Dianne. She's all right. She likes to brag a bit, but she's all right."

James felt that he had to say something nice about Dianne because he knew that Jesse was the type who would think of a black person as an Uncle Tom if he were too friendly with white people. Jesse looked over toward Dianne.

"She's a good looking sister and I'm going to have to talk to her before she forgets who she is. She looks good in that Dashiki, but she would look even better if she wore an Afro instead of straightening her hair."

"Ah come on, man!" James said. "Lay off her. She's just trying to be friendly like everybody else. The sister knows who she is."

Jesse got the hint.

They talked about football and basketball for another ten minutes.

"How do you fellows like San Diego?" Rick Elliot came up and asked.

"I ain't been there yet," Jesse mumbled.

There was a long pause.

"It's really nice out here in California. This is a good location for training," said James, trying to defuse the tension.

Rick talked with them both for another five minutes and then moved on to mingle with others.

"You see, man?" Jesse said, as soon as Rick was beyond earshot. "See what I'm talking about? As soon as they see us in a group they begin to get worried."

"I thought I had hang-ups, but this guy is bitter," James thought.

He looked at Jesse and spoke.

"Look, brother. I know you don't like white people, but if you want to get to Africa you are going to have to work with them for the next three months. Now, why don't you just cool it?"

There was a pause before Jesse said, "You're right, man."

By this time just about everyone was out on the floor dancing. Joe Veto was dancing with Cathy Horowitz, Stuart with Jennifer Nolan and Fat Ramsey was trying to do the twist with Dianne Harper. James went over to Maria De Angelo.

"Come on. Let's dance, Maria."

"I can't dance."

"If you can walk, sweetheart, you can dance. Now, come on."

He pulled Maria out of the chair and led her onto the floor. Maria was right. She couldn't dance! James showed her how to do the twist. Eventually she caught on a little. The more she danced, the more she smiled. Maria was shy and lacked confidence. Twenty-nine and a teacher with seven years experience, she was still living with her parents. Some of her teaching colleagues had tried to get her to share an apartment with them, but her mother would not let her. The night was going well and most of the group enjoyed themselves. Someone near the jukebox shouted "last dance." James turned around to Jennifer Nolan and they both danced. It was a slow song. James put his arms around Jennifer's shoulders and she slipped her arms around his waist.

"Enjoy yourself tonight, Jennifer?"

"Yes, it was nice. What about you, James?"

"Oh, I had a great time."

A few moments passed.

"Your friend Jesse doesn't like me."

"Oh, no. That's not true. It's just his way with people."

Then James looked down at Jennifer and tapped her gently on the nose with his finger.

"Anyway, little sister, I like you."

Jennifer smiled, laid her head against his chest, and then held him tightly.

Joe Veto and Bob Newgate were walking back to the cottage together. Bob remarked that colored guys like to dance.

"Yes, I suppose so."

Bob asked Joe what he thought of colored people.

"I only know James, but he seems like a nice guy."

"That Nig—I mean, Negro has got too much confidence in himself. Now that other one, Jesse, don't talk too much. That's the way they ought to be."

Joe then whispered, "Maybe you and Jesse have a lot in common."

Bob was not sure what Joe meant by that since Bob had not met Jesse and did not know how racist he was. Joe knew that both were racist. Joe considered himself a liberal and believed in equal rights and equal opportunities for all. He also had experienced a form of discrimination as an Italian-American growing up in Seattle. Worse still was what his parents had gone through when they first moved to the Pacific Northwest. They could not live in certain neighborhoods, could not get certain types of jobs and were verbally assaulted. His father told him that Italian school children had to sit in the back of the class. Of course most of that had changed by 1966, but the memories lingered on.

"I am tired. Let's get some sleep," Joe said.

The Shrink

The next four weeks were busy ones at the training center. The volunteers had begun their language training, field trips and group awareness sessions. Some relationships blossomed and others fell apart. Jesse Jefferson made an enemy in Dianne Harper and James developed a platonic friendship with Jennifer Nolan, who was seeing a lot of Steve Manski. Steve was from Bloomington, Illinois and had a reputation for being a bit of a Romeo. He tended to go for the sweet, lonely and shy girls who lacked self-confidence. Steve was also somewhat ruthless in his tactics. He would build a girl's ego, wine and dine her, make love to her three or four times and drop her. A gorgeous, popular, outgoing Homecoming Queen had once dropped him when he was in college and he never got over the hurt. Now he avoided girls like Dianne Harper and Cathy Horowitz, both popular and outgoing. James and Steve got on well and did a lot of things together. Basically, what they had in common was that they liked girls. Their styles and approaches were, however, quite different. James was afraid that Steve would one day hurt Jennifer, but he noticed a great improvement in Jennifer's personality. She was more confident, thanks to Steve's sweet-talking. She began to think positively about herself. Steve was her first boyfriend and lover.

It was mid-afternoon one Wednesday in October when Dr. Fred Mueller arrived for the group awareness session. The thirty-nine volunteers were split into three groups. Mondays, Tuesdays and Wednesdays were set-aside for the group sessions. The Wednesday group included James Johnson, Bob Newgate, Jesse Jefferson, Fat Ramsey Hall, Jennifer Nolan and Maria De Angelo. Dr. Mueller as usual reviewed the purpose of the sessions and laid down the ground rules. The sessions were held to enable the volunteers to understand the dynamics of inter-personal and inter-cultural relationships. Participation was required. The volunteers were to become aware of their own sensitivities, how they perceived themselves and how others saw them. They were also to learn that their own cultural norms would, in many respects, be different from those of the Malawians. Although, they were not encouraged to change their own value systems, they would have to learn to respect those of the Malawians. There were three basic ground rules. First, they were expected to be honest. Second, they were to maintain strict confidentially within the group. This meant that volunteers could not talk with others outside of the group about what went on in the group. Third, they were to use the time to discuss their feelings, not their opinions.

The sessions normally lasted about two hours and each group had gone through three sessions already. Dr. Mueller played a rather passive role in the sessions. He would get the conversations started, keep the group on topic and take a lot of notes. No one had openly expressed feelings during the previous sessions. There was some joking, but the volunteers remained guarded. Dr. Mueller started the session by asking everyone how the group felt. They all said fine. He then asked how they felt about the training program. One of the girls said she thought it was great. There was a long pause. No one said a word. Dr. Mueller was quite prepared to wait because he knew the silence would be broken eventually. Someone began tapping on the leg of his chair. Another began shuffling her feet on the floor. Five minutes passed before a great roar of laughter interrupted the tension. It was Fat Ramsey. He laughed so hard that he fell out of the chair. Everybody laughed then—and did they belt it out! Tensions were released. After calm was restored, Dr. Mueller asked Ramsey why he was laughing.

"Well, I thought it was kind of corny, us all sitting here saying nothing. It was just funny, that's all."

36

Dr. Mueller asked the others if they felt the situation was funny. He knew from previous training programs that after about a month the volunteers would begin to release the pent-up tensions and anxieties, and he sensed that this session would break the ice.

Steve Manski, Jennifer's boyfriend, said he thought the training program was too long and people were getting bored. One of the girls challenged that assumption and indicated that the people she talked to were not getting bored. James said that he was not bored, but felt that as much could be accomplished in eight weeks as in twelve. He also believed that the number of group awareness sessions could be reduced.

Bob Newgate who did not like James, smiled and said in his Texas drawl, "What's wrong, boy? Is it getting too much for you?"

James gave him the "V" sign and continued to talk.

Others knew that Bob did not like black people and that he detested James. Bob was making enemies on both sides of the color line. The black folks did not like him because of his racist views and the whites, especially the liberals, were beginning to be embarrassed by his actions. The group continued to discuss a number of other issues that bothered them, including the food and the infrequency of transportation to San Diego. Someone reminded them that they were not on vacation. Dr. Mueller then told them that they were getting off the subject and that in his opinion they were still guarding their true feelings. His tactic worked because the comment elicited a volley of emotional responses including: "Bullshit!" "Crap!" and "Who is he trying to fool?"

Jennifer Nolan then began to speak. She told Dr. Mueller that the volunteers felt he was analyzing them and everything they said was being jotted down in his little black book. She pointed out that he never participated in the discussions, and therefore was thought of as an outsider. People were frightened of talking openly because they might damage their chances of completing training. When she finished, just about all the group agreed with her. James and Steve Manski were impressed by Jennifer's courage and newfound confidence. She said what all of them hoped someone would say.

Dr. Mueller waited for a minute or so before he responded. He knew that the group needed that outburst and he was inwardly pleased that Jennifer spoke up. He then assured the group that he was not there to spy on them and did not want them to think of him as a shrink. He explained that while his role was to facilitate the awareness sessions, he could participate as well, but did not want to until asked by the group. Dr. Mueller was able to alleviated most of their fears. The group was not altogether trusting of Dr. Mueller, but felt more confident and began to talk more freely. He took out a handkerchief and was cleaning his gold granny rim glasses when Maria De Angelo whispered something.

Dr. Mueller, then wiping the perspiration off the bald spot on the top of his head said, "Could you speak up, Maria? We can't hear you."

Maria sat back in her seat, folded her arms and muttered in a quiet voice.

"I don't know whether I will be able to cope with living alone in some isolated village in Malawi," she confessed.

Everyone seemed stunned by the statement. Bob Newgate became infuriated.

"For Christ sakes! What the hell are you doing here?" he screamed.

Emotions ran high and were mixed. It was not so much what Maria said as the pathetic way in which she said it. Some of the volunteers were appalled at the way Bob spoke to her. Dr. Mueller then stepped in.

"That's quite a legitimate concern," Dr. Mueller said. "None of you will know whether you can cope until you get out there."

Although his remarks offered some comfort to Maria, she was getting more and more upset over the way Bob Newgate spoke to her. Tears came to her eyes and she was breathing quickly. Sympathy was swinging Maria's way. Even Fat Ramsey Hall, who was usually smiling, turned around to Bob with a straight face.

"It wasn't necessary to come down that hard on her, Bob," Fat Ramsey said.

Maria got up from the chair and ran out of the room sobbing. Jennifer got up and ran after her. The session had run more that the usual two hours when Dr. Mueller made his summary remarks.

The group left the room quickly, leaving Dr. Mueller sitting alone. He was worried that things might have gotten of hand. He was also concerned about the effect the discussion had on Maria De Angelo. He thought she had some problems. He had seen her privately on a number of occasions and after a while she broke down and explained that she had once tried to commit suicide by taking an overdose of sleeping pills. She also talked about her upbringing and how strict her parents were. They were hostile and never showed her much love. Dr. Mueller's diagnosis was that, as a result of hostile and strict parental control, Maria was socially withdrawn and had low self-esteem. He agonized over whether to report Maria to Rick Elliot, the Peace Corps Training Director, or wait and have a few more private talks with her. He could not help feeling guilty over his dual role. On one hand, he was to be a friend and confidant to the volunteers, yet, on the other, it was also his responsibility to recognize any problematic behavior patterns and report them. He was genuinely concerned for the volunteers' well being. He had analyzed his role several times before. This was his fourth time working with Peace Corps training. Each time it seemed to get harder for him to come to grips with his role and he began to consider giving it up after this training program was completed.

Fred Mueller walked over to Rick Elliot's office to meet with him.

"It was a rough one today, Rick. We might have a slight problem on our hands."

"What do you mean, Fred?"

Dr. Mueller began explaining the approach he took in this session and how the volunteers became a little more talkative and relaxed. He then explained the details surrounding Maria De Angelo's emotional outburst. Rick was looking impatient.

"In plain language, Fred, is the girl a problem? Is she a risk?"

"It's too early to tell. I want to talk to her some more."

"Well, see if you can sort this one out quickly. I noticed a lot of extra talking going on among the volunteers. I don't want things to get out of hand. Where's the girl now?"

"I think she's in her cottage."

He then hinted that perhaps an eye should be kept on Bob Newgate, who was beginning to irritate the other volunteers. Rick said they would do that and Fred Mueller left for San Diego.

Dianne Harper, Jennifer Nolan and Cathy Horowitz went into the cafeteria for dinner about seven that evening. Some of the volunteers anxiously asked how Maria was doing. The word had got around. Jennifer said Maria was much better. The girls looked around to see where Maria was sitting, since she had left the cottage fifteen minutes earlier, saying she was going to dinner. Jennifer asked if she had been in yet. No one had seen her. The girls began to get worried and Dianne decided to look in the shower room. There was no Maria. They checked back at the cottage and could not find her. The panic was on and Jennifer became terribly frightened, as she had been with Maria all that evening and felt somehow responsible. James suggested that some of the guys look around the complex and that Rick Elliot should be informed. Dianne, Jennifer and Cathy dashed over to Rick's office.

"Maria's missing!"

"What? Christ Almighty! She's missing? What do you mean 'missing'? Is she not in her cottage?"

"No. We looked everywhere and some of the guys are out looking now."

Rick stormed off cursing, thinking to himself that this was all he needed, a missing emotionally disturbed female volunteer. He called his staff to his office right away and asked them to ring Dr. Mueller to inform him of the situation. A search party was organized and each of the four groups was to cover the four sides of the complex. More than two hours passed and still there was no sign of Maria. Rick's nerves were on edge as he contemplated calling in the police. The responsibility of being a Peace Corps Training Director was now weighing heavily upon him. If the police were called in, the incident might be reported in the press. Peace Corps headquarters in Washington, D.C. would not take too kindly to that. On the other hand, a girl's life could be at stake, an alternative even more serious.

James Johnson, Joe Veto, Bob Newgate and Phil Harrington were about halfway up the escarpment. They had gone down to the beach to look for Maria, but to no avail. It was a long, steep walk and it was treacherous in the dark. They all had flashlights, but could only see a few steps in front of them. Phil, who was in front, stopped walking.

"Wait," Phil said. "I hear something over in the bushes."

Phil being the outdoor camping type was quick to tune into noises of the forest. They all shined their flashlights in the direction of the noises.

"Oh my God!" shouted Joe.

They saw a figure crumpled on the ground in a fetal position, clad in wet clothes. It was Maria. Partially blinded by the flickering lights, she folded both her arms across her face. The boys ran over to her and held her up. She was shivering from the damp clothing and the cool night.

"Let's get her out of those wet clothes and put a coat on her."

They used Bob Newgate's coat since his was the biggest and would almost completely cover her. They sent Phil on ahead to tell Dick Elliot that Maria was found. It took twenty minutes to get Maria up to the complex. During that time, both Dr. Mueller and a medical doctor had arrived. Some of the girls ran over to see Maria, but Rick quickly got her to one of the cottages so that the doctor could examine her. She had suffered from slight exposure and exhaustion. The doctor put her to bed giving her a sedative. By this time, most people were relieved and weary. They gladly went to bed.

Dr. Fred Mueller was standing outside the cottage with Rick Elliot.

"She's obviously exhausted, so I'll wait until tomorrow to talk with her. In the meantime, it would be better if none of the others ask her about her ordeal. Just have one of your staff take her some breakfast."

Fred could almost read Rick's mind and knew Rick was annoyed about the entire incident. He also felt that he was to blame since he knew of Maria's problems.

"I don't think she will make it as a Peace Corps volunteer," Rick said. "It might be better if we were to release her soon. What do you think, Fred?"

Dr. Mueller felt that it was too soon to decide and that until they talked with her about what had happened, it would not be fair. He said it was possible that she went for a walk and got lost. Dick dismissed that theory in his own mind, but was quite prepared to wait a while longer. He asked Fred to prepare a full report on her disposition and her version of what happened. They both said goodnight.

As Fred drove back to San Diego, he wondered, "Am I getting too involved and losing my professional objectivity over this case? The young lady has problems and they are serious, but perhaps given a little more time she could overcome them. It is her first time away from her parents and the emotional adjustments must be difficult. Then, perhaps Rick is right. He can't really approve sending her out to Africa, not in her present frame of mind. This group is really beginning to affect me, much more than the previous ones. If we get through this one okay, I think I'll just stick to my private practice from then on. Sleep well, Maria."

The Hut

42

More than a month had passed since Maria's incident and the Thanksgiving Day Holiday was coming up soon. Maria was still with the training program and most of the volunteers were busy working on their field projects. There were miniature dams and small bridges being built on near-by streams. Phil Harrington was working on a project alone. No one knew what it was or where it was, and curiosity was running high. Phil, a quiet, unassuming person, would sneak out of bed at four or five o'clock in the morning and no one saw him again until breakfast. Even after his morning language classes, he would disappear until the next scheduled event. The guys teased him about having a secret lover somewhere. This would embarrass Phil whose mind was never really on girls.

One morning at breakfast, Phil sat with James and Jesse. Phil was one of the few white guys Jesse got along with, probably because Phil didn't give two hoots about a person's color, religion or background. Things like birds, trees, hikes and camping monopolized Phil's curiosity. In walked highflying, fast-talking, rich and randy Cathy Horowitz.

She put her arms around Phil's shoulder and slowly ran her fingers across his chest and said in a sensuous voice, "When are you going to take me to your hideout, darling, and show me what you got?"

Phil blushed and everybody roared laughing.

"Ah, get away, Cathy! You're always teasing."

It was true. Cathy was a great teaser and she picked on Phil most often. However, Cathy acted as if she was quite prepared to go beyond the teasing stage, and the rumor was that she was after James. He thought she was a joke and tried to avoid her. Cathy got her breakfast and rejoined the guys at the table. She sat next to James.

"I have got a great idea. Why don't we all go see a movie, have dinner and go to a disco on Saturday night?"

"Not me. I got a date with this good looking sister from San Diego State College and I ain't gonna miss that for nothing."

"You always stick to your own, don't you, Jesse?"

"Why change a good thing, baby?"

James proposed that Steve, Jennifer, Dianne and some others go to make it a big party. Cathy agreed to tell them and to organize the transportation. She told James that Steve and Jennifer's relationship was faltering slightly. Jennifer felt that Steve did not like her as much as he did at first and they argued a lot. James thought they would soon sort it out. It was time for language classes to start. Cathy got out of her chair, gave James a ticklish squeeze in his side, and ran off.

"I have been chased by girls before, but this one takes the cake," James thought. "She tells people that she's after me and tells them why, too. It's not for love and it's sure not for money. Her father is founder and Chairman of one of America's biggest paint manufacturers. She's just a rich and spoiled good time girl looking for new experiences. Well, I guess I would be a new experience for her, and vice versa. I can't say I'm overly excited about Cathy. She's got an attractive face and sensual looking lips and her long jet-black hair sets it off nicely. The problem is that she is too pushy sometimes and she wears too much makeup. Ruby colored lips and black mascara in the morning sometimes gets a bit much. The good thing about her, though, is that she's always full of excitement and she keeps the place lively."

James saw Steve Manski and Fat Ramsey Hall on his way to language class. They could see Phil talking to David Chilikwe, the Malawian language teacher who had been flown directly from Malawi. Phil was taking notes as usual. They wondered why Phil took notes so often when he talked to Chilikwe. It wasn't that Phil was so keen on learning the language, since he had not yet got beyond the basics. No, Phil was getting instructions of some kind and it probably had something to do with his secret project. They all entered the cottage used as a classroom.

"Muli Bwanji Bombo?" said this voice.

"Ndili bwino, Kayi inu?" was the answer. "Ndili bwino. Zikomo."

The language teachers used the direct method. This meant no translations, no books, just conversation in Chinyanja. Volunteers were allowed to study the translations after class hours, but in class, the technique consisted of repeating sounds and phrases aided by a form of pantomime used by the teachers. The classes lasted from 9:00 am to noon with a twenty minutes break in between.

During the break James saw Susan Hart, the training coordinator, standing next to a jeep outside. She was looking at her schedule when he walked up behind her and with an imitation James Cagney voice said, "Hello sweetheart. What's a nice looking girl like you doing in a place like this?"

Susan replied with an even better imitation of Cagney.

"I'm here, sweetheart, to see that little boys like you get your language training."

They both laughed. James had been trying to sweet-talk Susan for over two weeks. He asked her to go out to dinner with him on several occasions and she refused saying that staff were not allowed to date the volunteers. Susan had a great sense of humor and could keep her admirers at a distance without insulting them. She was twenty-seven and had plenty of experience at warding off admirers. She grew up in the California sun and her golden tan skin reflected this. She had light brown-blondish hair and a Miss World physique. James knew he would get nowhere with Susan, but he enjoyed the challenge. Susan did not think he was serious so she enjoyed the game. His blackness was no novelty to her, as she had dated several black guys during college. Nevertheless, he was too young to her way of thinking.

"Hey, sweetheart, why don't you and I take a cruise up the coast this weekend, or better still, why don't I come over to your place?"

"Ah, come on, James. You don't want me! I heard you and Cathy Horowitz got a big thing going."

Susan was laughing her heart out as James tried to wriggle out of that one, saying there was no way he and Cathy had a thing going on. James told Susan that all Cathy wanted was one thing. Susan then asked him, wasn't that all he wanted?

"Hey, that's not fair, Sue. I mean, I'd be crazy if I didn't want to go to bed with you. But that doesn't mean that's all I want. I'm not that crass."

Susan put her hand on James's shoulder and said in a soft and sincere voice, "I know you're not crass, James. That's why I like you."

It was time to go back to class, and as James turned, he reminded her that she owed him one dinner. He returned to language class and was soon engrossed in the conversations.

When the language class was over some of the guys talked about Phil Harrington's secret project. They decided to follow him after lunch. The group included Joe Veto, Fat Ramsey, Stuart Steiner and James. Stuart was not that bothered about the secret project, but he felt like a hike through the woods.

Phil finished with his lunch and went to the cottage to pick up a rucksack. He had a hammer, a trough and an assortment of other tools in his rucksack. He then walked across the open field in the direction of the path leading down the escarpment and was unaware of being followed. The group kept a good distance, but moved quickly because Phil was a fast walker. Fat Ramsey began to pant and puff and told the others that he did not think it was a good idea. They told him to keep quiet and keep up. Instead of going down the escarpment, Phil took a detour to the right just at the edge of the path. They all followed through thick bushes and briars. Fat Ramsey began to slow even more and with all the cajoling to get him to keep up, they somehow lost track of Phil.

Somebody cried out, "Hey, we've lost him and we're lost, too!"

Stuart then reassured them that they were not lost because they could still see the beach. They walked on for at least another twenty minutes before coming to a small stream about six feet wide. There was an old tree trunk straddling the stream that could be used as a bridge. It was wet and slippery. The water in the stream was not deep, only about four feet, but it was cold.

Fat Ramsey took one look at that stream and said, "See you fellows later. I'm going back."

They all said, "Don't be stupid. You can get across this little stream."

Joe went first across the tree trunk, followed by James. They told Ramsey to go next, but he was petrified. Stuart decided to go and stood halfway on the log. He was tall and with long arms. James held his hand on one side as he extended the other to Ramsey. They gripped each other's hands tightly and Ramsey began inching his way across the tree trunk. Except for a few birds and the sound of the rushing stream, there was dead silence. Fat Ramsey broke out into a cold sweat and his grip began slipping away from Stuart. There was a slow cracking sound. Stuart looked at Ramsey and Ramsey looked at Stuart, who then jumped on to the other embankment. Ramsey was dead center of the old wet, cracking tree trunk. Ramsey swayed back and forth as the log rolled. As it finally cracked under the strain of his weight, he threw up his arms and did a belly flop into the water. There was a loud yelp, splash and thud and then silence. Fat Ramsey was sitting there stuck in the water and mud. It took nearly ten minutes to pull him out. The fellows got bellyaches from laughing so hard.

Ramsey returned to the training center and the others decided to go on. After walking another ten minutes or so, they heard the sound of a hammer striking something. Following the noise they came upon a small clearing in the woods and saw a hut with grass on the top. James looked at Joe and Stuart.

"That's it. That must be Phil's secret project, an African thatch roof hut. Boy, is it funny."

They tiptoed over to the front of the hut after seeing that Phil was in the back.

"Muli Bwanji Bombo Phillip, you got company!"

They all started chuckling and made fun of how lopsided it was and asked Phil whose barn had he raided to get the hay. Phil was furious.

"How did you guys find me? This is a dirty trick. You were not supposed to know about this. Promise you will not tell the others, at least not until I finish."

They all laughingly agreed not to tell the others, knowing full well they wouldn't be able to keep this one to themselves. After Phil got over the initial shock or embarrassment, he gave them a grand tour.

The hut was six by four feet, muddy and wet. The walls were erected using tree limbs and branches as the frame, filled in with a mud and straw mixture that when smoothed out and dried, resembled a brick wall. There was a small window opening on the right side of the hut. Phil had stuck an empty quart-sized bean can through a hole in the roof to help channel out the smoke. The floor was the ground, but there was a large straw mat rolled up in the corner, along with a blanket. The place was crude by Malawian standards, but the fellows congratulated Phil for his unique idea and gave him an A for effort. Phil then rolled his mat out and invited them to join him for coffee. He put an old tin can full of water from the stream on top of a bunch of stones. He then lit the fire, put two teaspoons of ground coffee in the can and began talking about how he intended to sleep and eat there once he finished. The coffee had been taken from an old brown bag. The boys figured that Phil probably 'borrowed' the coffee from the training center store house and wondered what else he would borrow before this project was finished. It must have taken a half hour before that fire got hot enough to boil that coffee. In the meantime the inside of the hut was getting smoky.

"I know where you can get a good deal on a ventilation system, Phil," James said jokingly.

Everyone laughed. Phil told James where he could stick that ventilation system. As Phil was removing the tin can of hot coffee from the hot stones with a coat hanger, he apologized for not having enough cups. They all would have to drink from a tin can.

"I'm not drinking that stuff. You got any milk or sugar to go with it?"

"Ah, come on, James, you've had worse. Anyway, I sterilize all my pots and pans and tin cans."

There was another round of chuckles as they all sipped from that old tin can. By that time anything would have tasted good. It was almost dinnertime when they decided to leave. Phil said he knew a shorter route back to the complex and if they waited a couple of minutes while he collected his tools, he would show them. The route was much shorter. In fact it was only five minutes away from the training complex. When they asked Phil why he took the longer route coming, he said he was looking for some tall grass to thatch his roof. It did not take long before the details of Phil's thatch roof hut got around to the volunteers. In fact, even Rick Elliot wanted to get a guided tour of the place. Phil was going to have to get the place in tiptop shape because he was about to have a lot of visitors.

Saturday Night Out

The next morning James Johnson and Dianne Harper were walking across the complex on their way to breakfast when he asked Dianne how she felt about training so far. She told him that she still enjoyed it, but she was missing her family and boyfriend. He felt the same way. Almost two months had passed since training commenced and he was getting somewhat unsettled. They agreed that most of the volunteers were probably feeling the same way. They discussed Cathy's idea about Saturday night out and Dianne informed them that another girl named Sylvia wanted to come along, as she was feeling lonesome and needed to do something exciting. James then asked Dianne whether she and Jesse Jefferson were still on speaking terms. Dianne told him that she did not have much patience with Jesse because he came on too strong. Jesse believed that Dianne should stick to the black guys and specifically him. Dianne said that Jesse just wasn't her type and she saw no reason why she should date him just because he was one of three black guys around. She said that Jesse was the kind of guy that she would not have much time for if she was back home. She said that she was committed to her boyfriend and did not join Peace Corps to get involved with another guy. James said he understood and Jesse had no right to tell her how to live her life. Just as they were about halfway across the complex they met Jesse.

"What's happening, soul brother? What's happening, soul sister? This is the way it ought to be, all of us together. Look at them watching us. Bet they think we're conspiring or something."

Jesse had his usual sneaky looking smile as he made his remarks. He sounded as if he had scored a point. James turned to him.

"You're what's happening, brother! It's your world. I'm just passing through."

They all laughed and then Jesse replied, "It ain't my world, man! They got it all wrapped up."

The four of them talked about some of the great football matches held between the all black colleges they had attended and the football personalities, coaches, bands and good parties they had during Homecoming events. Then Jesse said he was starving and he missed his soul food.

"Sure miss them collard greens, black eye peas and pigs feet. This tasteless food here is getting me down, man. I'm gonna go talk to our Mexican brother and see if he can whip me up something greasy."

They laughed and agreed that some soul food would go down well. Reggie Blackwell, who was extremely quiet for his size, seemed to appear out of nowhere and greeted every one. Dianne liked Reggie because he was always gentle with her. He also called her by her name. Jesse had never called her Dianne, only sister. She did not mind being called sister occasionally, but the way Jesse addressed her, she felt he only saw a black girl, not Dianne the person.

"Ah! This sister's doing okay, man. She's very popular with them."

Jesse was not aware of how much he irritated James and Reggie by putting Dianne down. Dianne told him that he was suffering from delusions and hallucinations. Jesse tried to turn this into a joke.

"If you think someone is trying to screw you and they ain't, then you're paranoid. If you think someone is trying to screw you and they are, you must be black."

No one laughed.

They went into the cafeteria and before long were joined by others, including Cathy, who excitedly described the outfit she was planning to wear on Saturday night. Jennifer Nolan and Steve Manski were not sitting together as they usually did. They had had another argument. Cathy approached other volunteers about Saturday night, including Reggie Blackwell who said that he had some writing to do. The numbers dwindled down to a few who wanted a night out and included Joe Veto, Jennifer Nolan, Steve Manski, Cathy Horowitz, James Johnson, Dianne harper and Sylvia LeMaster. Thursday and Friday of that week were busy days for the volunteers. Their breaks in between language classes, group awareness sessions, and field projects seemed to get shorter. The Thanksgiving weekend was only a week away and their field projects had to be at least seventy-five percent completed. There would only be three weeks of training left after the holiday.

Maria De Angelo had improved, but it was quite evident that she would not make a good Peace Corps Volunteer. She had on two other occasions gone missing and many of the volunteers were fed up with her. They thought this was Maria's "attention getting" scheme and began to loose sympathy. Dr. Mueller had several more private sessions with her and came to the conclusion that her emotional problems would not be solved during that training period. He submitted his diagnosis and recommendations.

During the same period Rick Elliot talked to Bob Newgate about his negative attitude towards black people. He told Bob that whatever his racial views were, it would be better to keep them to himself. Rick did not want any racial incidents in his program. He asked Bob to try to modify his behavior because if he went out to Malawi expressing these views, he could jeopardize the entire Peace Corp program in that country. Although it was not said, Bob's skill as an Industrial Arts teacher was in great demand in Malawi. The Malawi government requested as many volunteers as possible that could teach electronics, carpentry, machine tooling and other crafts. Rick did not want to loose Bob and was not prepared to expel him unless some intolerable situation occurred. Bob told Rick that Jesse was as prejudiced as he was and asked Rick why he had not spoken to Jesse. Rick indicated that Jesse might be prejudiced but it was not directed toward Africans.

One other male recruit from South Bend, Indiana told Rick that he was dropping out of the program. His heart was no longer in it and he thought he would not do a good job in Malawi. He explained that he only joined the Peace Corps to dodge the draft because he thought the Vietnam War was wrong and wasteful. His conscience began to bother him, not so much about dodging the draft, but for using Peace Corps as a way out. He decided to move up to Canada to join the draft resistance movement. Rick tried to persuade him to stay on by assuring him that his service in Malawi was needed but to no avail. Flight arrangements were made for a departure before Thanksgiving Day.

Phil Harrington was in the kitchen trying to persuade Chef Rodriguez to loan him a large coffee pot and some cups. Phil was preparing for his 'hut' warming on Sunday. Some of the staff and volunteers planned to visit his hut and he was excited. This would be the big Sunday outing. The Chef could not understand all the excitement over going to see a wet, muddy hut with grass on the top.

"I won't let you take my good pot out to that dirty place. How you going to heat the coffee? You got a stove?"

Phil told the Chef that he would heat the coffee on an open fire and would use stones to set the pot on.

"What! Amigo, you think I am loco? You put my best pot on a stone fire. No! No!"

Phil pleaded with the Chef and talked about how important it would be to the volunteers. The Chef then went into a cupboard and pulled out a coffee pot. It wasn't one of his best. In fact, the thing was as old as he was. It looked like it was used as long ago as the Spanish-American War. Phil's eyes lit up when he saw the pot.

"Ah, come on, Chef Rodriguez. I can't use that battered old thing. They'll laugh me out of camp."

"Either laugh or no pot, amigo. That's the best I can do for you."

Phil asked for coffee cups, coffee, sugar and powdered milk. The Chef's face lit up in disbelief. He threw his hands in the air and began talking in Spanish. It did not sound so pleasant to Phil. Then the Chef briskly snatched a large brown paper bag from the counter and began throwing cups, spoons, some coffee and packets of sugar into the bag.

"Aquí! Vámanos!"

Phil grabbed the bag and smiled.

"Zikomo Kwambiri Bombo!" he said, which was Malawian for thank you very much. Then Phil ran out of the door in the direction of his hut.

James and Joe had just returned from the shower. They were to meet Steve and the girls at the entrance to the complex. They were both excited about this night on the town.

"Man, I am going to have a good time tonight. We ought to get some of that tequila everybody talks about. Are you going to wear a tie, Joe?"

"Yes, although it's been a while since I put on a tie and jacket. What about you, James?"

James explained that he had brought only one tie, which did not match his sports jacket, so he was thinking of wearing a polo neck sweater under the jacket. Bob Newgate who was sitting up on his bed reading a novel offered James one of his ties. Both James and Joe looked around at Bob with amused expressions. There was a long pause. Bob became slightly embarrassed.

"Well, do you want it or not?"

"Sure, Bob. You sure you don't mind? Hey, that's mighty kind of you, man."

There were smiles all around. James and Joe were wondering what got into the guy. They just couldn't figure out why Bob was all of a sudden nice to James. Both got dressed and slapped on their after shave cologne. The place began to smell like a perfume factory. Bob let a cat call out and they all chuckled.

"See you later, Bob. Don't wait up for us," shouted Joe.

"No chance. Anyhow, I don't expect you guys back until tomorrow morning sometime. Hey! Have a good time."

"Thanks, Bob."

On the way down the gravel road towards the entrance, Joe asked James what time the bus was due. It was due at about six o'clock, but sometimes they ran five minutes early or late. Steve, Jennifer, Dianne and Cathy were waiting at the entrance for them. Sylvia was not there. As they approached the girls, they began to whistle.

"My, my! Who are all these attractive girls you got with you, Steve?"

The girls were looking smashing. Dianne had on a light blue loosely fitting dress with matching shoes and a colorful blue and white scarf. Jennifer wore an ankle length peasant style dress. She also wore red shoes. Her eyes were slightly made up and her face was radiant. But Cathy stole the show. Not that she looked better than the other two, but she was so conspicuously expensive looking. She wore a black velvet knee length tightly fitting skirt with a six-inch split at the bottom left side. Merging into this background was a pair of black stockings and black alligator-skin high heel pumps. Her cream colored silk blouse had wide lapels and loose sleeves and fitted tightly around her waist with the effect of disguising her plumpness. Her wrap was a hand-woven wool shawl folded into an "M" shape. She wore ruby red lipstick and a real ruby ring on her right forefinger and three silver bracelets on her left arm. She looked smashing. Joe asked where Sylvia was. The answer was that Sylvia came down with a tummy ache and decided not to come. As they talked about where they were going that night, a big red bus could be seen about three hundred yards up hill.

"Here comes the bus, you guys. Gee, it's exactly on time."

After Steve said that Cathy said that they would not be catching that bus because she had arranged different transportation.

"Cathy, what are you talking about?" asked Joe.

"Oh, just wait and see, darling. It won't be long now."

Just as everyone was having a go at Cathy about what they would do if they missed that bus, a big shiny black Cadillac limousine pulled up next to them and stopped.

"Miss Horowitz? Miss Cathy Horowitz?"

"That's me, dearie!"

Then this small middle aged man got out of the car, put a cap on his head and ran around to the other aide of the car to open the doors. Joe looked stunned with his mouth gaping as the rest of them turned toward Cathy.

"For Christ's sakes, Cathy. What's going on here?"

Cathy was enjoying the expressions on their faces and thought that her expensive prank was great.

"Oh, don't be a spoil sport, Joe, just get in. This is our transportation, dearie. Don't worry, it's on me."

Joe begrudgingly got into the car with the rest of the group. The car carried nine passengers including the driver. The two rear seats were facing opposite each other. As they reclined into the soft leather seats of the Cadillac, no one said a word. They were either looking at each other or out the window at the trees swaying in the autumn wind. Many of the leaves had turned brown and yellow and the grass had begun to dry out for the winter. Most of the group was thinking the same thing. Why does Cathy get such a kick out of flaunting her money like this? She must be aware that as Peace Corps volunteers, they had a certain image to maintain and it was not conspicuous consumption.

Joe thought, "There is nothing wrong with Cathy being rich, but she has to learn that what she considers fun and jokes, others take seriously."

Then he said, "This is not what we're all about, Cathy."

"Now, Joe, don't you start again. By the way I hope you don't mind, but I booked a table for us at the South Bend Fisherman's Wharf. It's a neat little place and my cousin owns it. He left New York about five years ago and came out here. I haven't seen him since I was in high school. I'm sure you'll like it."

"Well, looks like you've got the whole evening planned for us. At least you could have asked us where we wanted to have dinner. I bet you have even organized the disco we're going to?"

"In fact, I have, Joe dearie. I hope you don't mind."

Joe threw his hands up in the air as if to indicate that he gave up. Everyone else began to look at each other and laughed. James turned to Joe.

"You got to admit, man. It is funny, isn't it? I mean, how often do you get picked up in a brand new Cadillac limousine and get taken out to dinner? I know it never happened to me before."

The streets of San Diego seemed extra crowded as the black shiny limousine cruised through the downtown main street. There were lights flickering on just about every building. Hoards of people were rushing in and out of movie houses, discos, massage parlors, peep show houses and bars. There were hundreds of bars and thousands of sailors all decked out in their white and blue uniforms. There were also a lot of girls walking about in miniskirts, long dresses, jeans and slacks. Some were prostitutes. The chauffeur explained that a more than usual number of ships were in port. As the group drove along, they made fun of some of the characters they saw on the way. Soon the limousine was driving out of the downtown section away from the lights. In the far distance they could see lights on a number of ships sitting out in the harbor. As they got closer, they saw restaurants and other places of entertainment.

"I am so excited about seeing my cousin David. It's been so long. I wonder what he is like now?"

Jennifer then asked Cathy if she knew her cousin well when they were growing up.

"Oh, yes. He was like a brother to me. Since I had no brothers or sisters, I used to visit David and his sister Sarah about twice a month when we were growing up. He's a great guy. You will like him."

The limousine turned right off the main coast road and soon entered a parking lot. In the background was a large old ship that looked like the Mayflower. The ship was not in the water, but sitting on land. Several smaller buildings had been constructed around it. There were lots of cars in the parking lot.

A sign on the top of the ship read "South Bend Fisherman's Wharf." Beneath that sign was a smaller one, which read "Quality Steak and Seafood Restaurant." Soon the limousine stopped in front of the main entrance and two men dressed in Pirates costumes immediately opened the door to the car.

"This place is ritzy looking," James thought. "I bet it's expensive as hell. That is typical of Cathy to choose one of the most expensive places in San Diego. I hope I have enough money. Boy, have I got the jitters!"

He was not the only one with the jitters. All the others except Cathy shared the vibrations, presumably because she was used to ritzy places and her cousin owned the place. As the group walked up a short flight of stairs, Cathy was talking with the chauffeur. She appeared to be giving him some instructions and he wrote them down. She quickly rejoined the others and the pirates escorted them to the reception desk. Cathy confirmed her reservation and also asked the receptionist to tell Mr. David Horowitz that she had arrived. The guys took their coats and girls' shawls to the cloakroom. The group was told to go into the bar/lounge if they wanted a drink before dinner and it would be about thirty minutes before their table was ready.

The bar/lounge was in the hull of the old ship. It was a large place with an oval shaped bar surrounded by various tables and chairs. Ship lanterns run by electricity gave light to the room and soft listening music could be heard in the background. The room was crowded. James thought he was completely out of his element and initially felt very uncomfortable. The group found a table and chairs for six and as soon as they sat down, a young dark haired handsome guy, wearing a white dinner jacket with a red rose in his lapel and black pants, came over to the table with arms extended.

"Cathy, darling! How are you? You really look wonderful! How are Momma and Papa? Gee, it's so good to see you."

Cathy was equally delighted as she gave him a big kiss and expressed her joy at seeing him. As they stood there with arms around each other's waist, Cathy introduced David to the group. He seemed like a nice guy and told them how happy he was to see them and then ordered drinks all round on the house. Somehow, he managed to reduce the nervousness in the group and particularly in

James. David talked with Cathy for another five minutes before he was summoned over the intercom. He told the group he would see them all before they left and to enjoy their meals.

The drinks did not take long to mellow the group and then they were called to their table. They were all feeling merry. There was a short walk up a flight of wooden stairs onto the main deck of the ship, which was completely enclosed by panel windows and a wooden roof. The ceiling had dark brown beams running at crisscross angles with long chandeliers hanging down. The group played a game in which each was a character out of Treasure Island. Cathy began to curl her long manicured fingers into the shape of a hook and then slowly pressed them into James's side.

"I'm Captain Cook and I'll catch you with my hook," he replied.

"If you don't remove them from my side, I'll give you twenty lashes across your hide."

They laughed.

The waiter arrived with the menus and the meal followed soon after. Time seemed to pass quickly during the meal. There were orders for steak, steamed lobsters, fried shrimp and scallops. The six of them had a feast and enjoyed every minute of it. It was nine thirty before they finished eating. David Horowitz came over to ask if they enjoyed themselves and he sat for about five minutes to talk to Cathy. He invited them all to have a drink in his office before they left but they all said they needed a breath of fresh air plus they wanted to get to a disco. David understood and escorted them to the door. Cathy kissed him goodbye and said she would write. There was no limousine waiting in the crisp cool southern California autumn night. Actually there was no need since Danks Disco was only about a quarter of a mile up the road. This gave the group an opportunity to walk off some of their dinner.

"Gee, that was fun. That's my kind of living, sweetheart," Steve said.

Jennifer looked at Steve Manski. A few hiccups and burps interrupted his speech. She knew he enjoyed himself, not because of the food or the company, but because he had dined with the jet setters. Steve was neither rich nor close to it, but he often told Jennifer that one day his name would be up among the stars. His ambition was to be editor of a girlie magazine that would outsell *Playboy*. Jennifer felt that with ambitions like that, Steve would have little time for a small town country girl like her.

"Yes, Steve. I know."

Danks Disco was located on the opposite side of the boulevard from the beach. Lights were flashing on and off. "Danks" "Disco", "Danks" "Disco." The building was three stories high and each floor had a separate disco. On the top floor a six piece jazz band was blowing out the sounds of the '40s and '50s. Most of the clients were middle aged. The first floor was used mostly by the just over eighteen year olds, all clad in jeans, shorts and sandals. The middle floor was used by the twenty to thirty year old group and a disc jockey played contemporary rock 'n' roll music. Flashing strobe lights blended with the frantic pace of twisting and sliding. It was on the dark side and smoky. The dance section was a large round floor sunk about three feet below the main floor. There were small tables and chairs, but most people tended to sit on the carpeted bleacher sections on the outer layer of the dance floor. There must have been one hundred people in the room and it was crowded. There were a number of Mexicans, Chinese, whites and blacks in the place, and it seemed like the place to be for James.

"Hey, this place is what's happening. Let's hurry and find a spot before all the seats get taken. We can then get out on the floor and do our thing."

"That's groovy, James. What about over there?"

Joe pointed toward some tables in the far corner of the room.

"That's all right. Let's hurry."

Before long, they ordered drinks and the group was on the dance floor twisting, shaking and perspiring. Dianne asked Joe to loan her his handkerchief.

"Sure, sweetheart. It is hot in here, isn't it?"

"You're telling me. We've only danced three so far and I am soaked!"

"Me too, Dianne. After this one, why don't we take a break?"

"That's a good idea, Joe."

Cathy and James by now were on the other side of the dance floor. Cathy was a good dancer, but she also liked to move around the floor. She would not dance in a small space, but all over the place. Her dancing was characteristic of her outgoing personality.

"This is fun, James! I love dancing, don't you?"

"Yes, that is when I can keep up with my partner."

They both laughed.

"Am I too much for you, James darling?" shouted Cathy teasingly.

"Oh baby, you're too much for anybody!"

"Ah, stop putting me on James. You can handle anything that comes your way."

James laughed and then paused.

"Well, I thought so until I met you."

They both chuckled as the perspiration began running down their faces. Soon everyone returned to the table and sat down in relief.

"Boy this place is wild, isn't it?" Steve said.

"Sure is hot," replied Dianne.

By this time they were all sitting on the carpeted bleacher section with their backs to the wall. Jennifer was curled up in Steve's arm and Joe and Dianne leaned shoulder to shoulder. James sat straddle legged on the floor and Cathy sat between his legs with her back leaning onto his chest. The music was very loud, so everyone had to shout to be heard. Cathy turned her head around and whispered in James's ear.

"Why don't you put your arms around my waist?"

"What? I can't hear you."

"Why don't you put your arms around my waist?"

The other four heard Cathy and began to joke with James saying that's an offer he can't refuse.

"Sure, sweetheart," James said in a playful tone, "anything for you."

The disc jockey had spun about three more records before they were all ready to resume dancing. As the other four got up, Cathy asked James to sit this one out with her. The corner was dark and filled with smoke. Several couples were necking in the background. No one seemed to pay any attention to what anyone else was doing. Cathy put her hands over James's arm and pulled them tighter around her waist. She then turned slightly towards him and gently placed her head under his chin. He looked down into her dark blue eyes as she looked up into his dark brown eyes. Her rosy lips were moist and slightly parted. As their lips gently touched each other, Cathy slipped her left arm around James's neck. Moments later, the gentle kiss had turned into sensuous and active passion with both firmly caressing each other. More than five minutes passed before they were interrupted.

"Hey, you two, can't you wait to have your sordid love affair somewhere else?"

It was Joe and the others returning from the dance floor.

"Yes, you're right, Joe. I guess we got a bit carried away," said James.

"Carried away is not the word for it," cried Jennifer in a disapproving tone.

Cathy sensed that Jennifer sounded a bit jealous, but could not figure out why, since she was supposed to be head over hills in love with Steve. Several more records played before the six got out on the dance floor again. James was now dancing with Dianne who was an excellent dancer. The record was about halfway over when Dianne noticed James gazing over into the far corner of the room. He was looking at a table in a dark corner and the three people sitting there. The heavy built dark black fellow had three dark scar marks on each side of his face. They were similar to African tribal marks. On his left was a robust and sinister looking character with a thick mustache and beard. He looked as if he were Latin American, maybe Cuban. The third person was an attractive longhaired brunette, who while obviously in serious conversation, managed to smile. It was the smile that captured his attention. He thought he had seen that smiling face somewhere but could not remember where.

"James, do you know those people over there?" asked Dianne.

"No."

"Why do you keep staring at them? Anyway, you're supposed to be dancing with me not staring at three people wearing safari suits."

"That's it! That's it! The safari suits. Now I remember where I saw that face. She is Janice Blanche, the woman I met on the plane coming from Washington, D.C. But her hair! She had silver grey hair. No, maybe it's not Janice, because she works in Africa and what would she be doing here again so quickly? I wonder if it is she. I never did find out what she did in Africa. Do you think I should go over and see if it's her?"

Dianne looked displeased as she replied, "No."

"Okay, let's dance."

They rejoined the group and talked about the three people in the safari suits and explained how James mistook the woman for someone he had met. As time passed they all noticed that these three people did not once get up to dance nor did they look around much. They seemed to be transacting some kind of business deal and all had pads, pens and some photographs. The group was joking about how the three could be international gangsters, conspirators or smugglers.

"My gosh! It's 12:30. We missed the last bus."

Cathy chuckled as she said, "Joe darling, I got you here and I'll get you back. There's a car waiting for us outside."

It was 1:00 o'clock in the morning when the limousine drove out of the parking lot of Danks Disco. The night air was cool and fresh and the wind was calm. The first few minutes of the ride were filled with laughter and jokes about the whole night and what a good time they all had. The ride back to the training center took only twenty-five minutes and three quarters of the ride would not be remembered by anyone except Jennifer.

The others had fallen asleep. As they approached the entrance to the center, Jennifer began shaking everyone.

"Wake up, you drunken sleepy heads. You're home."

Her soft, gentle voice was about the best way of waking them at that time of morning because they were grumpy and groggy. Then they got out. Cathy went to the other side of the car and gave the driver a bill. It must have been a good tip.

"That's mighty generous of you, Miss Horowitz. Thanks."

They stood and waved the driver off, then huddled around in a circle and began laughing. They were a loud bunch as could be proved by a husky voice shouting clear across the complex: "You guys shut the hell up! Don't you know it's almost 2:00 o'clock in the morning?"

There was a long pause. Then came a whisper.

"Hey, maybe we better break it up for the night. I'm tired and I can't guarantee you that I'm sober either."

Then James looked at Cathy and playfully said, "Hey baby, you were great fun tonight and thanks a lot for everything."

Cathy blushed and whispered something in his ear. He looked around at the others and then pulled Cathy a few yards away.

"You crazy? I can't go into your cottage. There are three other girls in there!"

"Well, we can go into the empty one over there. Nobody will know because they're all sleeping. Come on James, just for a few minutes."

"No way, Cathy. If we get caught we could be terminated from the program. You know how these people talk anyway. Word would be round camp before we were out of there."

"You're just scared James Johnson, that's all!"

She stormed off into her cottage without saying word.

Chapter 2: Festivities Before Goodbyes

Land of the Lake

The land lies baking in the sweltering heat of the November sun. It has been months since the torrential tropical rains penetrated the earth, yet the crops of maize, cassava, plantain and bananas are still growing. Malawi is a geographical paradise. Magnificent mountain plateaus of lush green foliage buttress the western border. The eastern border is filled with a beautiful glistening lake that looks from a distance like a ball of fire. Lake Malawi is 360 miles long and fifty-two miles wide. The country forms roughly the shape of a banana. The land between the lake and the mountains is flat bush country where the soil is fertile.

It is 1965 and most of Malawi's estimated six million people live in villages scattered along the main North-South highway and near to the lake. The main East-West road intersects the North-South highway at Lilongwe, the capital city with a population of around 75,000 people. It will become the largest of the three cities in the country. The mountain area is virtually uninhabited. Most of the roads in Malawi are dirt and gravel. During the rainy season many of them are impassable, which means that for three or four months of the year, people living in outlying areas are unable to travel by bus or car. Located south of the equator in Central Africa, the country enjoys a hot tropical climate except in the mountains where temperatures can drop to thirty-two degrees Fahrenheit at night. Large herds of kudus, water buffalo, zebra and other animal species roam the vast, dry flatland between the mountains and the lake. Waters from the mountains flow in three large streams southeastward into the lake, providing the lifeline for scattered villagers and wildlife throughout the country.

In the 1890s the Colonial powers carved out the new states of Africa on their maps with little or no account to tribal affiliations.

The inevitable result was tribal conflict and territorial disputes. Many Africans believed this decision was by choice and not by chance. Such clumsy manipulation of the various cultures would retard peace, harmony and economic progress for decades to come. Malawi is an example of the impact of these decisions. Here there are three main tribes each with their own language. Timbuka is spoken in the North. Chinyanja and Chichewa are spoken in the central and southern parts of the country. The latter two are Bantu languages. The President of Malawi, General Aleke Makube is from the Timbuka tribe, as are most of the country's top officials. The people from the other tribes are resentful of this elite group. The British government was the former ruling colonial power of Nyasaland. It had granted independence to the people in 1960 and appointed Makube President. The country was then renamed Malawi. The General's mandate was to establish a period of calm and stability, and within five years to hold democratic elections.

This has not happened. General Makube has chosen to remain in absolute power. He has an ambitious five to ten year development plan and hopes to turn this subsistence farming economy into a diversified economy with cash crops and the growth of light industry. More than ninety-five percent of the population is subsistence farmers. Their staple diet is millet, maize or cassava, a ground root potato-like plant that is dried and pounded into a fine powder and then boiled into porridge. Most of the population cannot read or write, and many do not use money but barter their produce. Over seventy-five percent of the secondary school teachers are expatriates either on contract or volunteers from different countries. Malawian teachers work in most of the primary schools. The country has no known oil and mineral deposits worthy of commercial development. It is a poor country. The average per capita income was $40 dollars per year in 1965. General Makube depends on the goodwill and generosity of other countries and he is not particular where assistance comes from. Being completely land locked, the Malawi government took great pains to establish friendly relations with its neighbors, which included Tanzania to the North, Zambia to the west and Mozambique to the West and South. The main airport in the country is located near Blantyre City the commercial capital.

"Could you please fasten your seatbelts and observe the No Smoking signs? We will be landing at Blantyre Airport in about five minutes. Please remain seated until the plane has come to a complete stop. We hope you have enjoyed your flight and thank you for travelling East African Airways."

Peering down at his watch, Bill Humphries thought the airline had achieved a mild breakthrough. They were actually on time. The time was 12:35 p.m. on November 23rd, 1966 and Bill had just returned from a long and tiring trip to the U.S. It was a week today since he was summoned to Washington to report to the Peace Corps Director on political unrest in Malawi and how events might affect the Peace Corps program in the country. One of Bill's responsibilities as Country Director was to monitor and assess political and other situations that may have a bearing on the program in the host country. This was not the first trip he had made during his twenty-one month tour in the country but this one was apparently more urgent. The President of the United States had requested information about certain 'non-political maneuvers' occurring in that part of Africa and whether there was any evidence of 'foreign intervention'.

As the plane approached the runway Bill considered whether he really knew all that was happening.

"I know that the northern tribes are not happy about General Makube's leadership because he will not allow democratic elections, but there has been no sign of a possible military confrontation between the government and the people up north. Anyway, their leader Chief Katumbi is hiding up north across the border in Zambia. He can't be much of a threat up there and he's only got a hand full of men with him. Maybe Washington knows more than I do about what's going on outside of the country. I have not been keeping up with 'non-political maneuvers' nor 'foreign intervention'. Surely that's the job of military intelligence or perhaps the CIA. My job is to see that the Peace Corps program is carried out successfully. I have told them all I know about the situation and I hope they are satisfied with that. I will have to brief the Ambassador about my talks in Washington since we have been instructed to meet with General Makube to discuss the situation."

A loud cracking and popping noise interrupted Bill's thoughts a few moments before the twin-engine propjet touched the ground. One of the engines had backfired with smoke and fumes fogging the outside of the window. The trip from Dar as Salaam was a bumpy one as usual. Since Blantyre Airport did not yet have facilities to handle international flights, passengers bound for Malawi had to transfer to smaller aircrafts usually in Dar es Salaam. To Bill Humphries this arrangement was all too cumbersome since inevitably there was a waiting period of anywhere from three to six hours. Only a few passengers were on this flight, so after the plane had stopped he was on the ground in no time.

Waiting in the main entrance lounge was Bill's wife, Sally, and his four-year-old son Norman. Accompanying them was Christine Dawson, Bill's secretary. Bill returned the many greetings and smiles as he walked through the passenger gate. He was well known throughout Malawi simply because he was Peace Corps Country Director and many Malawians viewed him as extension of America's foreign assistance program. He provided skilled manpower to the country.

Sally ran up to Bill and kissed him. Then Norman ran up and was hoisted high up in the air. After the family welcoming ceremony was over Jerry Weeks, Assistant Peace Corps Country Director anxiously approached Bill and as they walked out to the waiting Land Rover Jerry whispered,

"Have a good trip, Bill? There's been a couple of developments here you ought to know about. Two of the volunteers up in the Northeast region have been running off at the mouth. They are alleged to have said they support Chief Katumbi's fight for freedom and democracy in Malawi, among other things. President Makube is furious and called both the Ambassador and me in your absence. He wants a meeting as soon as you return and he wants the two volunteers deported."

"What the hell is going on, Jerry? Did the volunteers say those things? Have you talked to them yet? Hell we can do without this sort of agitation. Get me a full report on who said what, when, where and why."

Jerry was looking very nervous.

"The two volunteers are on their way down now. They should be here tomorrow. The Ambassador's office has scheduled a dinner meeting for this evening as the Ambassador wants to see you, too."

"Right. I want you to come back over to my place later so we can discuss this thing in detail. First of all, I want at least to get a shave and shower and have a couple of hours with Sally and Norman. You do that, Jerry, and tell Christine to be on hand as well."

Jerry and Christine left together in another car. Bill threw his luggage into the back of the Land Rover and got in. Sally was driving while Bill grumbled about the way things had been going recently. He was angry with the volunteers for getting involved in politics and not too happy with Washington's interest in outside interventions in Malawi, a situation he felt was not relative to his role. The Land Rover rolled along at about forty-five miles per hour on the dirt road to Blantyre. A stream of dust was left a hundred yards behind the vehicle. Sally knew not to get too close behind other vehicles unless she planned to overtake them quickly. Otherwise, they would be engulfed by red dust. If the windows were closed the inside of the vehicle would feel like an oven.

The Humphries arrived at their four-bedroom bungalow about thirty minutes later. The house was situated on the outskirts of the city nearer the airport. They lived in a comfortable suburban community, which before independence was reserved for whites only. Since then some of the houses were taken over by senior Malawian civil servants and military officers. Nevertheless, communities like this were still mostly reserved for expatriates who were on short-term contracts. They stepped out of the Land Rover into their spacious front garden, which was immaculately groomed and boasted some of Africa's most beautiful plants and flowers. Four domestic servants greeted them. There was the cook and his wife, who was the nanny. There were a gardener and a housecleaner. The cook had the highest status.

"Afternoon, Bwana Humphries, we happy you back."

"Thank you Geoffrey, it's good to be back."

Bill Humphries then went into the house with Sally and Norman. No further instructions were needed regarding the luggage. The servants knew exactly what to do.

At 6:15 p.m. that evening the U.S. Ambassador to Malawi, the Honorable Hewitt T. Smith, arrived in his chauffer driven Ford sedan. Jerry and Christine were already at Bill's house sitting in the back garden next to the swimming pool. Sally went to the door to greet the Ambassador and formality was observed.

"Good evening, Mr. Ambassador. I hope you enjoyed your ride over here. Bill's coming shortly. Would you like to come through to the patio while I fix you your usual?"

The Ambassador smiled.

"Oh, that's a delightful idea, Sally. You always did have a special way with fixing my drinks. I see you are looking radiant as ever. Did Bill manage to get some rest?"

"Oh yes, sir. He slept for two hours this afternoon."

When the Ambassador reached the patio, Jerry and Christine promptly stood up to greet him. There were polite exchanges all round, but they always found talking to him a bit of a strain. At sixty-seven years old the former Senator from Minnesota was an imposing figure who avoided small talk. He was at Bill's house on business and they knew it. To their relief Bill appeared through the door in a red short sleeve golf shirt and a pair of blue and white checked pants. Only the Ambassador was in a suit and tie. It was so hot that he insisted others dress informally, but felt he the Ambassador needed to be formal. Sally served drinks and left to supervise the meal being prepared.

"Now look here, Bill, I've got President Makube on one hand breathing down my neck over something a couple of volunteers allegedly said and I've got Washington asking a lot of questions about the political unrest in Malawi and neighboring countries. I know you just got back from Washington, but we have got to come up with some answers and fast! President Makube wants to meet with us tomorrow at 2:00 o'clock in his palace. What do you propose to do about these flippant volunteers up North?"

Bill Humphries knew the Ambassador was in one of his stroppy moods and that his tone would get worse before the evening was over.

"Well, Mr. Ambassador, the two volunteers are on their way to Blantyre now and should be here in the morning. As to what I plan to do about them. I don't know until I have had a chance to talk to them."

The Ambassador was trying to restrain his volatile temper, which most Americans had seen during various Senate debates on television.

"Don't know? Don't know? Dammit, Bill! These are the same two radical screw-ups that started that furor six months ago. They even admitted their views. How the hell they were ever allowed in the program I'll never know. Now I know you want to avoid sending any of them home, if at all possible, but this situation has got out of hand. We give them one chance and look what they do! I say let's send them home straight away; otherwise we might really have problems on our hands.

Listen, Bill, and listen carefully. Since you have been in Washington I've had reports from reliable sources that Chief Katumbi and his gang are planning something big and I'm not just talking about verbal political warfare. I'm talking about an invasion! Now President Makube has the same information as we do and Washington has been informed. The implications are far more serious than what might happen to the Peace Corps program in Malawi. Without going into any further details, we're talking about super power involvement in this entire region of Africa. Hopefully nothing will come about but what we don't want is a bunch of Americans, Peace Corps getting involved in further politicizing the situation here. Do you understand me, Bill? Do you understand?"

"Yes, sir."

Christine and Jerry were sitting on the opposite side of the pool while this conversation was going on. The Ambassador told Bill to call them over to share in the discussion. They talked about Bill's trip to Washington and discussed the best strategy to take in the meeting with President Makube the next day. After three whisky sours and forty-five minutes of talk, the Ambassador seemed to withdraw from his hardline stance about the two volunteers.

"Look, Bill, I am a fair man. Now, if these two kids promise not to make any more trouble, maybe we can let matters stand. I should be able to talk the President out of the idea of deporting them. You let me handle that but if there is as much as a murmur out of them after this. I want them sent home right away. Now, I'll stand by you if you stand by me on this but Bill I've got to be frank with you. If something else happens and you don't move firmly and quickly I will bring down the full weight of my influence as Ambassador and as former U.S. Senator to affect the necessary actions. You understand me, don't you, Bill?"

"I understand you, sir."

Before The Feast

No activities were scheduled for the volunteers on the day before Thanksgiving or on the actual holiday. Most of the arrangements for the Thanksgiving dinner were completed. Claire Ferguson, Rick Elliot's secretary, organized the menu, transport, music and drinks. This would not be an ordinary gathering of good Samaritans sitting around a table with a roof over their heads. It was to be held down on the beach in the cove beneath the escarpment. It was just after breakfast when James Johnson, Joe Veto, Bob Newgate and Phil Harrington picked up their mail from the Administration building. The four roommates ate breakfast together and decided to go back to the cottage to clean up the place a bit. On their way back they saw Dianne Harper, Jennifer Nolan and Cathy Horowitz. There were greetings and smiles all round, except Cathy did not speak to James. In fact, she had not spoken to him since that Saturday night out in San Diego, and most everyone knew it.

Returning to the cottage James thought, "Cathy is just silly, selfish and spoiled. If she doesn't get her own way all the time she acts like a child. I tried to talk to her the next day but she refused. I don't know. Maybe I did insult her by turning her down that night, but she could not have seriously expected me to go into that cottage with her. I like Cathy and I'm not afraid to go to bed with her, but somehow this is not the way it should be happening. Maybe if she were not so pushy, I would want her more. Anyway as Jesse said, that crazy chick might turn around and scream rape the minute you finish. I don't know. I just don't want any hard feelings between us."

Phil picked up a letter off the ground and handed it to James.

"You dropped this."

"Thanks, Phil. I must have been daydreaming."

The four returned to their cottage and got the place cleaned up in about thirty minutes. They then sat on their beds and began opening letters and small parcels. James received three letters that morning; one was from his parents, one was from an old schoolmate and the third was from Sandra Whitaker, James's former girlfriend. Sandra's letter was sprinkled with perfume and he thought that was typical of her. Then he opened the letter and sat back on his bed with his pillow between the bed rail and his back.

"My Darling James,

The past few months have been so boring for me. I don't seem to know what to do without you. I miss your love and tender care and as I write this letter my eyes fill with tears. I did not know the agony and heartache I would feel when you left. I hope you still care for me as much as I do for you, but I am beginning to think that you don't care at all. This is my fifth letter to you and you have not written to me once. Although I love you, I think that you are the most ARROGANT JERK I ever met in my life. Not even a postcard! Well! You let me tell you one thing, James Johnson. When you get back home, don't come looking for me, because I won't be around. I have had it with you, brother! All my friends are asking me how you are doing and what your training program is like and all I can say is that you're fine and you like it. Imagine how embarrassing it is for me. You don't care for me and you have proved it. Don't expect me to sit around here alone and waste away. I am finished with you, James Johnson, and that's it!

Sandra."

There was a great burst of laughter and the other fellows looked around.

"Well come on, James, what's so funny?"

"I just got a Dear John, but it's the funniest thing I ever read. It's just like her."

They did not know whether to laugh along with James or try to comfort him.

"Oh, it's all right, you guys. I won't lose any sleep over it."

After a few minutes they all settled down to finish reading their letters and do some writing. James was beginning to feel guilty about a few things. He felt he had not treated Sandra well and she had always been kind to him. He did not feel that Sandra loved him as much as she claimed, but there was a great fondness there and perhaps he should write back to her. He also felt guilty about his relationship with Cathy Horowitz. The way he had treated Cathy and Sandra bothered him because he was reared with Christian virtues and he thought he was getting a bit callous and not concerned about other people. James was no saint, but he was sensitive about other people's feelings. Another hour passed before they all finished their letter writing. Lying stretched out across the beds they began to indulge in small talk.

"You got a girlfriend back home, Joe?"

"Sure, man."

"What's she like?"

"What do you mean, what's she like? She's nice!"

Then James turned over on his side, "Are you going to marry her, Joe?"

There was an impatient response.

"How do I know?"

Maybe Joe did not like to talk much about his personal life, including his girlfriend, so James did not push him.

"What about you, Phil? I bet you left a string of heart breaks back there in Bismarck."

Phil's embarrassment began to show on his face. He knew that the guys knew he did not have a girlfriend nor had he ever had one.

"Everyone can't be as dandy with the girls as you, James."

They all chuckled, more so to relieve Phil's embarrassment than anything else.

"I almost got drafted, you know," James said.

James explained how he received his draft notice and his Peace Corps acceptance letter on the same day. His local selective service board decided to waive his draft until he completed his Peace Corps tour and he was very relieved.

"They seem to be drafting a lot of you people for this war."

Everyone braced when Bob Newgate made that remark.

"Who are 'you people', Bob?"

"I mean you colored people."

Phil was glancing at a book and appeared to be ignoring this conversation. After a few moments James responded.

"You're right, Bob, but there are still more of *you* people in the Army than there are of us."

Bob quickly responded, "You mean more white people?"

"No, I mean more non-colored people."

Joe Veto broke out laughing because he knew James had scored one on Bob. The tension was still on their faces as they wondered whether to take each other seriously or not. Then Phil smirked. As James and Bob eyed each other the tightness of their faces gradually loosened. Just then Stuart Steiner stuck his head through the cottage door.

"You guys heard the news? Trevor Orr has quit the program!"

"What? What?"

"Yes, and he's leaving right this minute on his way home."

They were flabbergasted. Not that they knew him that well, but the surprise of it all without even the benefit of a rumor beforehand was what got them. Stuart explained that from what he could gather Trevor was going up to Canada to join some anti-Vietnam War protestors, but that was all he'd heard. Everyone immediately went out into the front of the cottage and could see Trevor's luggage in the back of the jeep. He was still inside the Administration building.

"Why don't we go over and say goodbye to him?"

By this time the word had got around and volunteers began to filter out of cottages, the cafeteria, the shower rooms and the woods to watch Trevor Orr leave. No one knew if this was a quick decision on his part or whether Rick Elliot knew of it before hand. They would eventually find out.

Thanksgiving Day

The California autumn sun was benevolent on the day set aside to thank God for seeing Americans through a season of good harvest. The high of the day would be 74 degrees Fahrenheit and the wind would be calm. It was a busy morning for everyone, as groups were organized to take various items down to the beach. The heavier loads including barbecue stands, utensils, plates, four large turkeys, six fresh chickens and three Virginian smoked hams were taken in the jeep along with cases of beer and blocks of ice. To get to the beach below by vehicle was not an easy task. The drivers had to go to the main highway and drive in the direction of San Diego for about a mile. On the right side of the road was an inconspicuous gate covered in tall grass and weeds. Once found, the single-track road led to an escarpment on which the Navy had built a winding dirt road down to the beach. The road had not been used since the Navy was there and the conditions were treacherous. The drivers took at least three other people and a few shovels in case they got stuck. Six trips by road were made to get all the necessary equipment and paraphernalia down to the beach. The entire operation took two hours to complete.

It was exactly mid-day when Rick Elliot asked Claire Ferguson what time Captain Halsey was coming.

"The chaplain is expected to arrive by 1:30 this afternoon, Rick."

Captain Falsely was a Naval chaplain stationed in San Diego. Rick had invited him to give a Thanksgiving blessing before the meal. The Chaplain eagerly agreed, as it would be an opportunity for him to break from routine.

"Is Fred Mueller bringing his wife?"

"He didn't say, Dick. I asked him but he seemed to evade the question. What do you want to do about the straights and mixes? Should we keep them with the beer or set them up somewhere else?"

Rick looked along the beach toward where the vehicles were parked.

"Why don't we leave them in the back of the station wagon for now? That might be a good place to serve them from. Anyway, most of these kids will just want beer or wine."

Six large folding tables had been brought down to the beach. Some of the volunteers helped to put out the food while others gathered dry wood for fires. Some volunteers set up the sports equipment including volleyball and badminton nets. There were footballs, baseballs and bats; horseshoes and several hula-hoops. It was to be a day of fun, games and feasting. Most of the group brought swimming gear. The clean and sandy beach set against the background of the cliffs dotted with green and brown foliage was a picturesque paradise. The water in the cove was crystal clear. From a distance the interplay of the sun's reflection produced a vivid blue-green background highlighted by a huge rock formation about one hundred yards offshore. These rocks provided a haven for some of the sea life along the California coast. Farther out in the Pacific, multi-colored sails could be seen swaying with the waves. Beyond that point the huge ocean liners appeared as miniature toy ships in the midst of the vast waters. It was as if nature reminded man of its incomparable powers.

From behind the rocks appeared three beauties in bikinis. They were Dianne Harper, Jennifer Nolan and Lucinda Cruz, a Puerto Rican American.

"Hey, let's play some volleyball."

Fat Ramsey Hall ran towards the girls.

"I'll play volleyball with you girls anytime."

With Ramsey were Reggie Blackwell, Steve Manski and Phil Harrington.

"We need another player. Hey, there's Cathy. Come on, Cathy, get up off your fat fanny and play some volleyball with us."

Cathy looked at Ramsey as she reclined from her sitting position to stretch out and lay on her back.

"You got a nerve, Ramsey!"

While everyone else stood laughing Ramsey ran over to Cathy and began tugging at her right leg trying to persuade her to join in. She must have thought that anything was better than Fat Ramsey hovering over her and tugging at her legs, so she quickly jumped up and joined the others.

"Listen up, everybody. Captain Halsey, the chaplain has arrived. Gather round, everybody."

As the volunteers gathered around and sat on the sandy beach, Rick Elliot began to speak.

"I know that for many of you, this will be your first time away from your families at Thanksgiving. We will try to fill the gap somewhat and I would like you to think of your group as a family away from home. Obviously, we don't expect to meet the standards of Mom's home-baked apple pies, but I am sure you will have no complaints about this feast that Jose has so diligently prepared."

There was a round of applause for Chef Jose Rodriguez, followed by three cheers.

"Now, as is our tradition, it is the time of year when we give thanks to God for his generosity during the past year and I would like to turn the proceedings over to Captain John Halsey, chaplain in the United States Navy, San Diego. Captain Halsey?"

The chaplain was a medium built man with grey hair and a pleasant face. His blue deck shoes, blue plaid Bermuda shorts and white short-sleeve golf shirt made him look as though he were on vacation. He had a high-pitched light voice, but spoke eloquently.

"Thank you, Mr. Elliot, for asking me to come here today. I am absolutely delighted to be able to share this Thanksgiving Day with so fine a group of young people. When you have been in the Navy

80

as long as I have, you look upon opportunities like this as a bonus. I promise not to bore you with a long drawn out sermon. Indeed, I too have developed a gigantic appetite this morning."

With his fingers interlocked, the chaplain continued.

"Now let us give thanks and praise to the Lord God our Savior and keeper. God, the Father Almighty, we, thy humble children, are gathered here today to give thanks for Thy glorious bounty throughout the year. This day of Thanksgiving was set-aside over two hundred years ago by our forbearers to offer special thanks and praise for Thy help during the years of hardship. Heavenly Father, we again thank Thee for continuing to look over and protect us, for seeing us through another good harvest and for keeping our great nation unified. We pray for the hungry, poor and destitute and that one day such suffering will end.

We pray for this group of young people gathered here today, that their humanitarian efforts shall not be in vain, but prove to have a lasting and positive effect in the country where they will work. Remind us, oh Lord, of the sacrifices made by Thy son, Jesus Christ, who carried the burden of man's sins upon the cross, in order that we can repent for our sins. Remind us also, oh Lord, that we should try to be Christlike by expounding charitable virtues. Jesus Christ died for our sins; let us give special thanks, not just today, but every day. Let us share a few moments of silent prayer together."

The chaplain's sermon was short, as he had promised. Rick Elliot kindly thanked him for giving the service and invited him to stay for food and drinks. He then told everyone to dig in. The six tables lined with roast turkeys, hams, chickens, along with a range of vegetables, pies, cakes and puddings were a delightful sight. Queues began to form at both ends of the table as the volunteers picked up their paper plates and plastic eating utensils. The small chatter turned into a chorus of: "Wow! Oh boy! Gee, this looks good! Yummy, yummy, yummy, in my tummy!" It was not long before the first queue up was over and people began to queue for a second helping, led by none other than Fat Ramsey Hall.

"Don't overdo it, Ramsey! Leave some for us," someone shouted.

Ramsey turned around and grinned. He then promptly resumed stacking his paper plate with as much food as he could possibly consume. As the volunteers ate less food, they drank more wine and beer and by 4 o'clock that day a number of them were feeling no pain. A dozen volunteers were sprawled out on the sand just beneath the escarpment. Some were playing cards, some talked and others slept. Someone suggested that they play a game called "Truth." The object of this game was to say exactly what they felt about anything at that moment. Cathy Horowitz spoke first.

"I think old Mueller put the screws on us. Look what he did to that poor girl, Maria de Angelo. If it weren't for him she probably would have been all right. Look at him parading around in those silly looking Bermuda shorts with his paunch hanging out. I never did trust him!"

Many agreed with what she said and they gave Dr. Mueller a grilling for about fifteen minutes. This was abruptly interrupted when Bob Newgate said.

"Cathy, you don't know the first thing about psychiatry and what's involved in analyzing problem cases. Now, anybody with any common sense could see that Maria had problems even before she came here. Dr. Mueller probably did the best he could for her. I tell you one thing, I wouldn't want her stationed in the same village with me, would you?"

Cathy sat up and braced herself.

"What do you know about problem cases? You don't give a damn about Maria or anyone else in this program. Anyway, I heard you almost got thrown out of the program because you couldn't hold your racist tongue."

Bob was turning red with rage.

"Who are you calling racist? You think just because your father's got a little money you can have everything your own way. Well not down here in these parts you can't! I resent you calling me a racist. I'm no more racist than you. How many colored people did you know or mix with before you came here? You are running around here making a fool out of yourself by chasing them all over the place, but I bet my bottom dollar that you won't take one home with you. At least I am honest!"

The long silence was broken by the sound of sobbing and sniffing. Cathy Horowitz was crying. The group looked bewildered as they sat there with heads hanging down, some looking at Cathy and others looking at Bob. They had mixed feelings about what had just taken place, because most of them felt that a certain amount of truth flowed from the mouths of both Cathy and Bob. The embarrassment grew so strong that the group began to disintegrate and before long only Cathy and Bob were sitting together.

"Cathy, I'm sorry. I did not mean to say those things. It's just that you got me all worked up by calling me a racist. I lost my head and just wanted to hurt you. Can you understand that Cathy?"

Still emotionally shaken and drying her tears with the towel Cathy shouted.

"Don't speak to me, Bob. You're just mean. Did you have to say such nasty things about me, especially in front of the others? You're right. No, I did not know any colored people before I came here, but that doesn't mean I'm being condescending toward them. I like James. I like Dianne, so why shouldn't I mix with them?"

Bob put his hand on Cathy's shoulder in an attempt to comfort her.

"Look, Cathy, I'm not saying you shouldn't mix with them. Hell! I sleep in the same room with James, but you made me angry by passing judgment on me as if I was wrong. I never considered myself a racist because I never came in contact with them until I got here. I don't mind working with them, but there isn't any cause for all this social integration. I mean, they like to do certain things different from us. Back in Texas we don't go for all this integration stuff and the colored people don't either."

Cathy shrugged Bob's hand off her shoulder and appeared even more irritable as she stood up.

"I might not be perfect, Bob, but at least I can recognize my own faults. I feel sorry for you because you are blinded by yours."

She walked off briskly, leaving Bob irate. The rest of the day's fun was not marred by the incident between Cathy and Bob. By six o'clock that evening, the volunteers had finished most of the leftovers from the Thanksgiving dinner and began to drink wine and beer again. The portable record player was blasting out sounds of the Beatles, Beach Boys, the Supremes and the Four Tops. It was as if the party had just started, although it had been an all day affair.

The sun slowly set in the western skies and dusk brought with it a slight chill in the air. Dressed with sweaters, jackets, skirts and jeans, the volunteers no longer felt the chill. Three campfires were kept ablaze and the festive mood continued. Cathy had changed out of her bikini into a knee length cotton towel dress, which kept her warm, except for her arms. She had not noticed the chill because she drank, sang and danced so hard. She was trying to forget the incident with Bob Newgate and therefore was determined to get high on wine. It was only when she stopped dancing to take a rest that she noticed the coolness in the air. Others did not need an excuse for getting blasted. It just happened. James who miscalculated the potency of the beer stumbled over toward Cathy.

"Hello, good-looking! You talking to me tonight? I heard you had a rough day with that bastard Bob. Don't worry, sweetheart. I will deal with him for you."

There was a pause as James hiccupped. His voice was slightly slurred. Cathy began to laugh.

"James, you're drunk. You can't even talk properly."

"Who, me? Oh, no. I never get drunk—hiccup! Oh, excuse me."

"If you are not drunk then let me see you walk that chalk line over there?"

James's boyish face gave an expression of mild confusion.

"There's no chalk line on the beach. I'm not that drunk."

"Yes, you are if you can't see that chalk line. You must be drunk."

There was no chalk line on the beach, but James pretended there was and proceeded to attempt to walk in a straight line. As he strayed off course several times, Cathy laughed. It was a funny scene and both enjoyed the play. Then it was Cathy's turn to walk the chalk line. James nudged her off course several times to prevent her from walking straighter than he did. As the pushing went on both fell down into the sand with Cathy landing in his arms. They lay there for several minutes laughing before Cathy began to shiver from the coolness.

"Here, take this jacket and put it around you. I don't need it because I am hot now!"

While Cathy put the jacket over her shoulders she teased James.

"Oh, you're hot, are you?"

James mused over the statement before saying,

"You don't miss a trick, do you?"

"No. Neither do you. Thanks for your jacket."

James and Cathy made up without even trying. Also Cathy soon forgot about the previous incident of the day. They danced, smooched and drank. Some of the volunteers slowly made their way up the escarpment and back to the complex. Others along with staff took the heavy equipment back in the jeep. The festivities, however, were by no means over as more than half the group stayed down on the beach to continue partying.
James and Cathy walked along the beach arm in arm holding each other up.

Cathy whispered in his ear, "Let's go back to the cottage?"

"Hey, it's a bit early to go back, don't you think?"

Cathy smiled shyly.

"You know what I mean."

Returning the smile, he looked at her.

"Oh! Well, I don't think that's a good idea. There are a lot of people up there."

Cathy looked slightly disappointed as they continued to walk. Although the night was dark their shadows could be seen by the reflection of the moonlight upon the waters of the cove.

"What are you snickering about, Cathy?"

"Oh, nothing much. I was just thinking about how funny Phil Harrington's hut looks.

"It is a funny sight, isn't it?"

As they chuckled about Phil's hut, Cathy said, "Why don't we go up there tonight?"

"What, are you crazy? I don't want to go to that filthy, damp hut. Anyway, we can't see in the dark."

It took twenty-five minutes for them to reach the hut. James had to be persuaded almost every step of the way. With only two small flashlights, it was a tricky climb. The hut looked ghostly in the night-light and the forest was quiet and cold. Only the sounds of cracking twigs could be heard as they approached the entrance.

"Shhh! Did you hear something in there? It couldn't be Phil because we left him on the beach."

They cautiously shone their flashlights in the hut but only saw pots, tin cans, a straw mat and a blanket folded in the corner.

"I don't hear anything, James. You must be imagining things. Let's go in. It's so exciting, isn't it?"

Cathy led the way in quickly unfolded the blanket and laid it on the mat. James was nervous and wondered where Cathy got her courage.

"Come on, James! Sit down here. Isn't it cozy?"

He thought Cathy was out of her mind because the place was dark, damp and cold. After about five minutes of whispering to each other, they both began to feel the chills creep in under their clothes. Lying side-by-side facing each other, they wrapped the blanket around them and were snuggly tucked in from shoulders to ankles. Because the blanket was wrapped in an awkward and clumsy fashion their feet were dangling outside.

Within minutes they were warm, as a result of massaging each other's backs and arms. The warmth brought on a feeling of sensuality mutually experienced by both. While they lay kissing, they weren't paying attention to anything else. As far as they were concerned, they could have been in paradise.

Locked arm and arm Cathy whispered, "James, you make me feel good."

James, who was lying sideways, turned his head and shoulder to Cathy, kissed her and then rolled over onto her soft warm body. As he completed this move his foot hit a tin can and set off a strange sequence of events.

"Ting! Ping! Pang! Cluck! Cluck!"

Cathy and James sat up straight. They began to wave their hands furiously in the air as if to fan off some unseen intruder. All they could hear was fluttering noises from something flying around all over the place.

"What the hell is that?"

"I don't know! I don't know!"

"It sounds like something flying about like a bat or something?"

"A BAT!" Cathy screamed as she jumped up and ran to the door.

A split second later James followed clumsily. They ran several yards away from the hut before they calmed down enough to try and figure out what was going on.

"What do you think it is, Cathy? We've got to go back and get our flashlights or we won't be able to see our way out of here."

Cathy stood trembling, partially from the cold, but mostly from fear.

"I don't know, but I'm not going back in there. I want to leave right now!"

James became annoyed.

"It was your idea in the first place to come up here. This is the most ludicrous situation I have ever been in. Come on, it could only be a bird or something."

He then pulled a reluctant Cathy by her arm and they slowly approached the entrance to the hut.

"Do you hear anything? I don't; it must be gone. Come on let's get our things together and get out of here."

As they stepped into the hut, the fluttering and clucking noises began again. Cathy made an abrupt about face, followed by James, followed by three overgrown chickens.

"That's it. Phil Harrington's chickens made the noise. The sound of the tin can woke them up."

They both stood there in the moonlight and laughed hilariously.

Volunteer Postings

It was a sunny but chilly day in December 1966 just two days before the volunteers were to finish training. There was a new feeling of excitement among the group when they gathered in the cafeteria for their last orientation session. This was the day that they would find out exactly where they would be posted in Malawi. Although a few of them knew already, the majority did not. Part of the problem getting this information was attributed to bureaucratic delays in some of the Malawi government departments. Not only had they not decided on which schools or health clinics to place the new volunteers, but living accommodations were not yet confirmed either. There were other political constraints also. For instance, the Malawi government did not want too many volunteers posted in the northwest part of the country where political unrest was continuous. The underlying motive, however, was that President Aleke Makube did not want anymore of what he termed "American Rebel Rousers" up near the border "assisting" the exiled leader, Chief Katumbi. Aware of the President's sensitivity over this matter, Bill Humphries, the Peace Corps Country Director, worked to convince President Makube that any new volunteers sent to that region would be carefully selected and would avoid any involvement in Malawi's internal politics. At 9.30 a.m. the group sat waiting for Rick Elliot who was fifteen minutes late.

Dianne Harper and Jennifer Nolan talked together.

"It's too bad about Maria de Angelo, isn't it?"

Jennifer's face appeared full of compassion as she responded to Dianne's statement.

"Yes. It's tragic. I mean, it must have been enough of a setback for her not being selected for the program, but I think her parents are awful for putting her out like that. Poor Maria. God knows how long she might have to stay in that institution before she's okay again."

Dianne hung her head downward.

"She's lost her job, career and her freedom. Maybe if she had a boyfriend or someone else to go to, she might not have got herself into this situation. They say even if you go into some of those places sane, you end up going nuts. She looked so sad when she left the day after Thanksgiving. I guess she could no longer take her parents' bitching and just withdrew. What did they call her condition again?"

"Something like being in a catatonic state, which I think means she just stands in a certain position for hours sometimes. Oh, it's so sad."

Shortly afterwards, Rick Elliot entered the room followed by Claire Ferguson, Rick's secretary. They brought a lot of forms, documents and other written material with them. Rick opened the meeting by reviewing the training program. He then praised the group for being such good trainees and said they would all be model volunteers in Malawi. He said he was sorry that the program was unable to retain two of the original group. He explained the political situation in Malawi, but assured the group that there was no cause for concern because the Peace Corps volunteers in the country were not affected by recent developments. He did however urge upon them the need to avoid getting involved in Malawi politics. He made no reference to the fact that several volunteers who did get involved in politics were subsequently deported. After another fifteen minutes of answering questions, he turned the meeting over to Claire.

Claire passed out sets of forms and documents to the volunteers. They contained detailed information about each position, including location, job description, supervisors, background information on the schools, clinics or government departments where each was assigned plus maps of the local area. Air travel tickets and schedules were also included. Tickets were made out to Kennedy International Airport in New York from each person's nearest hometown airport. Everyone would go home for Christmas prior to leaving. Claire explained all the details and reminded everyone that they should meet at Kennedy Airport to board a charter flight from Kennedy to Malawi via London, Cairo, and Dar es Salaam. The entire group would travel together. The volunteers spent the next two hours filling in visa forms, medical records, income tax deduction slips and a host of other documents. Occasionally, the odd complaint was muttered: "This reminds me of college registration, all these forms!" and "Hey do they need all these silly forms?"

When the forms were completed, the group reassembled in the cafeteria to get the last of their injections. They had already received seven during the course of training and this one was for Small Pox. Rumor got around quickly that the small pox injection was a real "stinger" and a number of volunteers were apprehensive. The session broke up about half an hour before lunch was served. Some of the volunteers congregated outside the Administration building discussing their assignments. Phil Harrington and Bob Newgate sat under an old pine tree in the center of the complex. Bob took out a pack of Winston cigarettes and offered Phil one.

"No thanks, Bob, I don't smoke."

Bob knew Phil did not smoke, but for some reason felt compelled to offer one.

"Well, partner, I hear you've been assigned to Mzuzu too. Where exactly is the clinic you gonna work at?"

Phil took out the local zoning map of Mzuzu a town in the northwest region of the country. Mzuzu was also the Regional Headquarters for several Malawi government departments.

Pointing to the spot on the map, Phil said, "There it is. It's in a village about four miles outside the town center. It's a small village with only about three hundred people. People come to the clinic from other near by villages on market days, so I will be busy."

The tone of Phil's voice expressed how keen he was to get started.

"Here, let me see your map, Phil, and I'll show you the school where I'll be teaching."

Bob studied the map for several moments. He could not find the school or the name of the road where the school was located.

"That's strange. The school is not listed on your map, but is on mine. Anyway, it must be about right here. It's called the Mzuzu Agricultural and Technical Training Center. It's in the center of town and has an enrollment of two hundred students, most of whom are over fifteen years old."

"You sound excited too, Bob."

"Kinda. Do you know if anybody else is assigned to Mzuzu?"

Phil paused for a few moments before answering. Phil always paused before answering and hardly ever initiated a conversation.

"I know that Jennifer Nolan is going there because she told me. I heard that Stuart Steiner is assigned to a clinic about eighteen miles north of Mzuzu."

Bob seemed to be pleased about Jennifer and Stuart's assignment.

"They're okay. The four of us ought to make a good team up there. Two teachers and two health workers is all right."

Phil appeared to be pondering as if he forgot something.

"What's wrong, Phil?"

"Oh, nothing, I forgot that James is going to Mzuzu, too."

"James!"

Phil braced himself as he felt Bob's hostility. For a moment he thought Bob blamed him. He remained silent. There were several minutes of silence before either spoke again.

"Hey, partner, I'm real sorry about that. It ain't your fault about his assignment and I shouldn't have taken it out on you. It's just that I don't like the nigger, because he thinks he's so damn smart. I hate a smartass nigger! Anyway just because he's going to be up North with us, don't mean that I have to be friendly with him, and he'd better stay out of my way!"

Phil and Bob said no more. They just sat there under the pine tree. They could see Jennifer talking with Dianne Harper and Joe Veto, both of whom were to take up posts near Blantyre City, the commercial capital. Several others were assigned to Zomba City, including Fat Ramsey Hall and Reggie Blackwell. Joe was assigned to a health clinic and the others would teach in local secondary schools. Reggie Blackwell was to have a dual role as Physical Education teacher and Coordinator of Malawi's sports events. One of his jobs was to organize field and track events throughout the country and identify potential Olympic athletes.

A few yards in front of Cathy Horowitz's cottage stood Jesse Jefferson and Steve Manski. Cathy approached them.

"Looks like those of us who are posted together are forming little cliques."

They both nodded in agreement. The three of them would be working in the southeastern part of the country. Cathy was to teach at the only secondary school within fifty miles of this isolated outpost. Jesse and Steve would work in several small clinics within a twenty-mile radius of the town. Like all health volunteers they would be provided with motorcycles. The town called Chikwawa to which they were going had a population of about two thousand people. There was only one main street lined with about twelve shops and a few houses. There was electricity, but it came on and went off intermittently. There was also a small emergency generator for the town's clinic.

"You're going to be apart from Jennifer quite a lot, Steve. I know you will miss her."

Steve shook his head while responding in a very unconcerned manner.

"Oh well, I'll survive."

Cathy asked what Jennifer felt about being apart.

"I don't know and I'm not sure whether I care."

93

Steve's response only confirmed for Cathy what she perceived as a relationship gone sour. She even thought that she could fancy Steve and conjured up visions of Steve and her together in some isolated village. Steve then began to pry.

"What ever happened to you and James? I notice you two haven't had much to do with each other since Thanksgiving Day."

Cathy blushed slightly.

"Oh, we're still friends, but we're not each others type."

Jesse then injected a thought or two.

"Yeah, and that's the way it ought to be."

They both knew that Jesse Jefferson was implying that blacks and whites should not date each other, so the subject was changed quickly. After five minutes discussing whether Chikwawa was one of the best posts or not, the lunch bell rang. They all must have been ravenous that day, because everyone made a beeline to the cafeteria.

The remainder of the day was busy for everyone. The medical team completed injections for small pox and there were numerous complaints about the side effects such as the "sting." By 9:00 o'clock that night most of them were in bed. James lay awake thinking.

"I wonder what Mzuzu is like. I bet it's beautiful, especially with the mountains in the background. Rick Elliot must be worried about what's happening up there or he wouldn't have called the five of us into his office to tell us to keep our noses clean. I don't understand all this political stuff going on out there. Anyway, I can't see how it's going to affect me. As far as I'm concerned, I'm just going out to help my Malawian brothers. I'll leave the politics, rebels and all that kind of stuff for someone else to deal with. I wonder why he tried to discourage us from going across the border into Zambia. I mean, just because this Chief, what's his name, Katumbi is hiding out up there, is no cause for us not to travel to Zambia. Anyway,

I've got to get some sleep. I wish my mind would stop racing. Maybe I will try deep breathing. That's supposed to relax you."

James slowly inhaled and exhaled and soon he entered the initial stage of sleep. Ten minutes later he was awakened by the noise of bedsprings. Someone got up to go to the toilet, but half drowsy, James could not figure out who it was. Anyway, his mind was active again. For some reason his thoughts were about Susan St. John, the training coordinator whom he never got to date. She reminded him of Janice Blanche, the woman he met on the airplane while flying to California and the one he thought he saw at Danks Disco one night in San Diego.

"Funny how I feel as if I know Janice and I only met her once. Even funnier, this feeling that I will meet her again, but I suppose it's very likely if she works in Zambia. Hell, it is not far from where I'm posted. I didn't even find out what she does there or where she lives. She is similar to Susan in a lot of ways, but mostly they both seem like nice people.

I've got to give it to Susan. She's a shrewd one. She kept her word all right about inviting me to dinner at her place before training was over. I'll never forget the night I went to her place in San Diego thinking that it would be just us two. When I arrived there were nine other people including her boyfriend and an old Aunt of hers who happened to be in town. I know Susan was laughing at me, as I could not hide my surprise. I got stuck having to listen to her Aunt's boring stories all evening. I was so glad to get out of there that night."

By this time James's mind, body and soul were weary and sleep was imminent. His last passing thought before he was engulfed by sleep was this: "If that was Janice Blanche in Danks Disco that night, what was a nice girl like her doing with those two sinister looking characters?"

Goodbye, San Diego!

It was a dreary Friday morning when about half the volunteers left the Peace Corps training camp for the last time. The thunder and lightning during the night left a trail of broken tree branches and puddles of water all over the camp. The first group had left at 6:30 that morning to catch various flights, followed by a second group before mid-morning. Although they would see each other again after Christmas, the atmosphere the night before and during the day was one of sad farewells. Their training experience had ended and a new one would soon commence. Sharing each other's lives for three intense months, day in and day out, the volunteers had formed a close bond with one another. Even Rick Elliot and his staff felt a certain sadness as those young Americans left San Diego that day for far away places.

Rick Elliot reflected upon the overall changes in the American way of life and developments abroad and wondered what the world would be like in ten years time. He thought for a moment of what it must be like for School Principals, who each year sent their students out into a world of unknown challenges. He was nervous about what lay ahead for this group of volunteers. There would be no occasion for him to see them again but he thought he would like to hear how each of them coped with their assignment.

Although his staff provided the shuttle service to and from the airports that day, he personally said farewell to each volunteer as they left the camp. The last to leave were Bob Newgate, Dianne Harper and a girl from Florida.

As they loaded their luggage into the jeep, Rick went over, "Sally, you take care of yourself. They need good nurses. Dianne, you have done a super job during training and I'm sure you will be great volunteer."

"Bob, can I have a quick word with you before you leave?"

"Sure, Rick."

"Look, I've no doubt that you will make a positive contribution at Mzuzu Agricultural and Technical College and believe me they need you there. You will also find that the Malawians are very friendly people. Bob, I want you to make a good go of it for me. You know what I mean. Now I know you can do it, so don't let anything spoil it for you. Okay?"

Bob paused for a few seconds to contemplate the meaning of Rick's comments. He knew that Rick was referring to his attitude toward black people and was concerned that his behavior might cause a few problems, if left unchecked. Bob looked around at Rick, nodded his head and said,

"Okay, I'll try my best, coach."

Rick smiled as he escorted Bob to the vehicle. He then stepped back and waved to the three volunteers.

"Have a good trip!"

As the jeep drove down the wet gravel road leading out of the Peace Corps training Camp, Rick continued to wave with his right hand while wiping the moisture from under his eyes with his left. Again he whispered into the winter evening.

"Have a good trip."

Political Talk

Lukabi was situated in Zambia about twelve miles west of the border with Malawi. The village was normally quiet with the exception of occasional lorries transporting troops, food and guns. Lukabi had a population of 1,700 people. It was not even as large as the refugee camp located about five miles west. The climate was hot and dry except from January to May. Intermittent showers began in January. These were a prelude to the rainy season, which would start in earnest in about two weeks. The rain fell gently as Janice Blanche loaded her Land Rover with food supplies from the town's only grocery store. She was pleased about the rain and did not mind getting wet. It was so refreshing and cooling. By the time she got into the vehicle to drive to the refugee camp, she was soaking wet.

"At least the roads will not be dry and dusty. I wonder if Sam Hernandez has arrived?" she thought as she began the journey back to the camp.

Sam was from Cuba but had lived in various parts of Africa on and off for the past seven years. He had spent the last six months in Cuba and California and was now returning to Zambia for an unspecified period of time. It was difficult to categorize Sam. He had multiple roles. He was sometimes a mercenary, a schoolteacher, a Marxist revolutionary, and rumored to be a double agent working with Americans and Cubans. There was one thing for sure about Sam Hernandez. He lived well at home and abroad.

Sam was expected to arrive by car from Lusaka, the capital of Zambia. Lusaka was about 550 miles southwest of Lukabi and the trip could take as long as sixteen hours by car. Although the main highway was paved, the minor roads were gravel and could be treacherous. The last sixty miles over mountains were the worst. Janice remembered the last time she saw Sam. They had met in California back in November when she visited some relatives and colleagues. It was the first time Sam and Frank Myosa talked personally. Frank was Chairman of the Zimbabwe Nationalist African Party (ZINAP) that had been banned by the white-controlled Rhodesian government. Frank was also in charge of recruiting and training Africans from Rhodesia to fight for their freedom. As Janice drove along the muddy road toward the camp, she remembered how impressed the two had been with each other. Frank was impressed by Sam's understanding and willingness to help ZINAP and Sam liked the determination Frank showed in fighting for changes in Rhodesia. Sam told Frank it would not be easy and would take several years of patience, setbacks and hardships. Frank then said his whole life had been one of disappointments and hardships, so a few more wouldn't hurt.

Before long Janice Blanche was driving past the two-armed guards at the entrance to the refugee camp. The guards were not in Army uniform, but wore short Khaki trousers and green t-shirts. One of the guards wore a pair of blue plastic shoes and the other was bare-footed. They both looked to be about fourteen years old as they clumsily attempted a "right shoulder-arms" with their American made M-5 rifles. Janice nodded her head and smiled as she passed them. The center of the camp could be seen approximately five hundred yards ahead. There was a whitewashed building with corrugated metal panels serving as a roof. This was the school, partially funded and staffed by an international Christian organization. There were other buildings made of mud-bricks with grass thatch roofs, surrounding the school. Spread out as far as a mile and a half behind the school were rows of thatch roof huts. It was an enormous village with men, women and children moving busily. Some of the women carried babies strapped to their backs as they pounded maize and cassava, and cultivated their vegetable gardens. Others, mostly, young girls, were marching around in platoons, practicing military drill tactics. They used wooden guns and sticks in place of the real thing. Janice saw several classes in session out on the open ground as she neared the main building next to the school.

Refugees were taught English, Math and a host of other subjects, including political education. The latter was a combination of Socialism and Marxism. Capitalism was referred to in the most derisive of terms and used as an example of how they and their families back in Rhodesia were being exploited. Janice could see two men sitting in wicker chairs on the porch of the headquarters building. The one on the right was a heavily built bearded man with sun-tanned skin. He was wearing a light-blue safari suit and puffing furiously on a Havana cigar. He not only spoke with his mouth, but his gesturing hands appeared to accent his every comment. Janice knew it must be Sam Hernandez, the arms dealer from Cuba, because she had not met anyone else who gestured so eloquently. As she got closer, she could see Frank Myosa, ZINAP leader, listening intently. The tribal marks on Frank's face made him look even sterner than he was. He looked like a tribal chief, which he claimed to be. Sam's conversation with Frank was abruptly brought to a halt as he jumped up out of his chair. With great delight, he threw open his arms for an embrace.

"Janice Blanche, how are you? Come, give me a big hug."

Janice spoke as she embraced Sam.

"I am doing fine and what about you?"

"I'm okay. You know me. I take care of myself."

Stepping back a bit, while looking him over, Janice teasingly commented.

"Yes, I see you do. You have not lost one ounce, have you?"

Sam laughed jovially as he patted his big round tummy with both hands.

"Why lose weight? All my girls like me this way. Now you, you're getting too small. You should take lessons from me. Isn't that right, Frank?"

Frank nodded his head in agreement and smiled. He was amused by Sam's jolly disposition.

"Come, come Janice, and sit down. We must talk," urged Sam.

As the three sat down Frank Myosa signaled to one of the young boys standing near by. The boy ran over to Frank, who instructed the boy to bring a pot of tea. During the fifteen minutes or so before the tea arrived, Sam talked about his trip and told a few jokes. The laughter was interrupted by a young, boyish voice.

"Excuse me Bwana, tea Bwana."

"Thank you. Put it there on the table."

The boy nervously placed the tea on the table, bowed to Frank and said

"Thank you, Bwana."

The boy tiptoed quietly away. Janice understood the significance of that brief ceremony. When the Africans called each other Bwana, it was a sign of respect. The boy said, "Thank you, Bwana" because he was happy to serve Frank Myosa, his leader and Chief. Janice was also aware that for many years, the Africans called European colonialists Bwana, but the Europeans chose to interpret and use the word in the Master/Servant context.

An hour passed before Janice left the two men. She had an afternoon class to teach. With a Masters Degree in Economics, she taught Math, Statistics and Economics. She kept her lessons at basic levels because most of her students had not previously attended school. Janice learned to make these adjustments during the first three years teaching at the school. During the same period, she assumed other responsibilities, including fundraising for 'humanitarian causes' and coordinating training for refugee women. She also gathered information about developments in Rhodesia and elsewhere, which could affect ZINAP's plans for achieving freedom and majority rule in Rhodesia. In other words, Janice was responsible for intelligence and she was good at her job. She was also well versed on military history and war games and was an expert markswoman. She learned these things from her father, Three Star General Alfred T. Blanche, who led American Army forces during the Korean War and was a veteran of World War II.

Janice was twenty-five years old when she first went to Zambia. However, two years earlier she made what she considered to be the biggest mistake of her young life. She got married. Her parents talked her into marrying the son of a Senator from Ohio. The marriage lasted nine months. Fed up over the way her life was going, she decided to answer an advert asking for teachers to work in a mission school in Zambia. She had no idea at the time that she would subsequently become involved in a revolutionary movement. She had no regrets.

There were fourteen foreigners working at the refugee camp outside Lukabi, including Janice Blanche and Sam Hernandez. There was a black male U.S. Marine veteran who had served as a medic in Vietnam and a white male science teacher from a high school in Kentucky. There were also five French technicians, two German military trainers and three British firearms experts. Only three of the foreigners lived in the camp. The others lived in Lukabi.

Later that evening as the African sky turned black the group met again beneath a brilliant half moon. Janice, Sam, Frank and two of ZINAP's top lieutenants were in deep discussion. Wiping sweat from his brow as he fanned away the mosquitoes, Frank Myosa turned to Sam.

"Did you have any success in getting the price down, Sam?"

Sam, who was puffing on a Cuban cigar and blowing smoke rings into the African night, sat up.

"Frank, he would only come down six percent on the original price. I tried. Believe me, I tried. I explained that since this is such a large order, he should give us a concession. He said that if we did not buy the guns, there were dozens of other customers who were willing to pay the price. I didn't want to chance blowing the deal. It's not easy finding good arms dealers you can trust. The other bonus is that four hundred rifles and machine guns will be arriving next week and the remaining three hundred will get here the following week."

Frank looked at Sam rather suspiciously, but this was nothing new to Sam, because in his business his clients were always suspicious of him. He reckoned that Frank thought he got the price of the guns dropped by ten percent, which would give him four percent profit. In fact, he was only making one percent on the deal, plus his normal fee, which was substantial. Frank looked at Sam and began to smile cautiously.

"All right, Sam. I'll take your word for it. I've got no other choice. Nothing personal, but it's my job to be suspicious and you being a man of experience in these matters, well, I'm sure you understand my position."

Sam relaxed a bit more.

"Yes, I understand Frank, but believe me I got you the best deal I could. You've got to trust me, Frank. I too want to see your people controlling your own destiny. Remember, I was involved in the same thing in my country for many years before we achieved our revolution."

Sam Hernandez sat back and relaxed as Frank Myosa began to talk of other matters. Sam had made a small fortune over the years as he assisted various African freedom fighters, but he considered his fortune to be the price of his high-risk involvement and he was not ashamed of it. He prided himself on the fact that he genuinely wanted to see a change in the white-controlled governments in the southern part of Africa. He hoped for socialism in those parts. The years of poverty that he and his family experienced in Cuba prior to the revolution had caused him to hate the powerful elite. Sam's twin brother and a sister had died of malnutrition at a very young age and when he was fourteen years old, he saw his eighteen year old brother dragged and beaten to blindness by the Cuban police.

The discussions then centered on Chief Rodney Katumbi, exiled leader from a northern Malawi tribe. Frank Myosa brought the group up to date on his latest talks with the Chief, who was asking for more cash and arms to help his cause. His plan was to topple the present regime of General Aleke Makube, President of Malawi. The ZINAP leadership was sympathetic to Chief Katumbi and was not pleased with General Makube because he did not allow ZINAP's freedom fighters to use his country's borders to mount raids into Rhodesia. Chief Katumbi's troops had recently grown from 900 to 1500. About fifteen percent were women and children. The many months of campaigning by the chief's supporters in Malawi were paying off. About twenty to thirty people were crossing the border into Zambia each week trying to reach the chief's camp in Lukabi. This was causing problems both administratively and logistically for ZINAP, who allowed the Malawian refugees to share part of their refugee camp. There was the added burden of feeding the new arrivals since Chief Katumbi depended almost entirely on ZINAP's good will for food, clothing and arms. Frank Myosa was extremely worried about recent events because ZINAP was being hosted by the Zambian government. Although not pleased with General Makube, Zambia wanted to keep diplomatic relationships between the two countries on an even keel. Frank explained that they would have to do something about the Chief's people coming in. They were getting overcrowded and we're running short of food. He asked Janice to get an estimate of what it would cost to feed everyone if the present number of Malawian refugees continue to come during the next six months. Also, Frank wanted her to work out roughly the amount of money they could expect to receive from all sources during the next few months. Both Janice and Frank nodded in agreement. Frank then asked for ideas to cope with the growing population in the camp. Frank's accent was a mixture of African and American, due primarily to the six years he lived and studied at Hampton Institute, a predominately black college in Hampton, Virginia. His credentials were an odd combination. He had received a Bachelor's Degree in Electronics and later a Master's Degree in Political Science. Both had come in handy.

Janice began by explaining that if people continued to come at the present rate, there would not be enough food. The food stock from the previous year's crops was low and there would be months to go before the next harvest. ZINAP was taking in almost one hundred people a month from Rhodesia. Malawians were also arriving daily to support Chief Katumbi. Although the level of assistance received from all sources had been rising steadily, the rate of inflation had risen faster. With the increasing cost in food, guns, clothes and basic supplies, double the amount of money was needed to keep pace. Janice presented a couple of options. Chief Katumbi would need to start his own fund raising activities. He needed money that could only come from supportive international groups. She also suggested that the Chief's supporters should be separated administratively and geographically from ZINAP. With the present system it was difficult to figure out exactly what costs were involved for each group. For example, the Chief's forces had training with ZINAP's guns and used their ammunition. It was difficult to estimate what this was costing ZINAP.

When Janice finished talking, Frank and the others sat back in their chairs musing over her suggestions. They were logical and made good sense, but as usual, no quick decisions would be made on such an important issue. Frank responded to her suggestions.

"Yes Janice, you made some very good points. I don't think your second option poses a major problem because we can handle that one ourselves. About the first option, for them to begin their own fund raising, you realize that we would initially have to help them establish contacts. Also, we must take care not to over burden our own funding sources. The Chief has a different problem from us. As you know, the United Nations have already condemned that illegal regime in Rhodesia and a number of countries are sympathetic towards our movement. But Chief Katumbi is fighting to overthrow a legitimately recognized government in Malawi, which gets most of its aid from western capitalist countries. He will not get any support from them. He would have to approach the east European communists countries, Russia and perhaps Cuba. However, they are not convinced of his politics. They are concerned that he wants power for power's sake and they doubt whether he could be relied upon to further the cause of socialism, once he is in power."

Sam Hernandez finished his warm beer and crushed the aluminum can with his hand.

"Frank, don't you think the Chief's presence here is a liability we can't afford? I mean to say, what's in it for ZINAP?"

The question was pertinent and Sam knew it. Frank thought about it before speaking.

"Well, we are all interlinked in one way or the other. For too many years this part of Africa and our people have suffered the injustices of colonialism. Chief Katumbi as well as others and myself are struggling to gain self-determination for our people. We are all trying to get rid of governments that hinder African progress. You know what I am talking about. There are two benefits to be derived from helping the Chief. If he comes to power, we could rely on him for support and a certain amount of freedom to move our troops through Malawi. Secondly, when ZINAP is successful in purging foreign enemies from our land and restoring it to the African people, we can work together to make Africa great. I have no doubt that a ZINAP-led government in Rhodesia would have better relations with a Katumbi led government in Malawi. We consider Malawi's President Makube and his regime to be a puppet for the white-controlled countries in southern Africa. He lived in the west so long, he forgot how to speak his mother tongue."

Sam laughed, followed by Janice and then the two ZINAP officials who were present. After a few moments, Frank began to question Janice again.

"Were you able to find out anything about that new group of American Peace Corps volunteers arriving in Malawi? The Chief is anxious to know who the new replacements are for his region, and what they're like."

"Yes. A group of thirty-nine are arriving on January 9th. Five have been posted in or near Mzuzu and I gather Peace Corps officials screened them carefully. They are supposed to be either apolitical or right of center. According to my sources, General Mukabe was so enraged over the involvement of the previous group in that region that he decided not to send any more there. The Peace Corps officials must have persuaded him otherwise."

Then Sam Hernandez joined the conversation.

"I wonder how non-political they are. Did you get any detailed profiles of them?"

"No, only that there will be four males and one female working in and around Mzuzu, the regional capital. Oh! One of the guys is black."

Both Frank and Sam sat up in their chairs, looking surprised and interested.

"This black guy, you mean they classified him as a politically safe risk?" asked Sam.

"Oh, yes. In fact, they are under the impression that he is less likely to get involved than the others."

Janice paused to chuckle a bit and then continued, "Ironically, I think I may have met this boy on the plane back in September when he started his training. His name is James Johnson. Really, he was one of the nicest fellows you could meet, but he was also politically naive. He thought communism was a bad word. He was as American as apple pie and is probably the type who would do anything to prove his allegiance. Nevertheless, he is very impressionable and given a little time, I believe he could be educated."

Impatiently Frank asked about the others. She did not have many details but her sources were able to provide her with where they would be working and where they were from. She thought the biggest problem would be with the boy from Texas who openly expressed racist opinions.

The meeting was interrupted by the sound of running feet. Then there were shouts in a mixture of broken English and Bantu.

"Bwana! Bwana Myosa! Bad news! Comrade's dead, Please come!"

They all jumped up from the table and made their way in the dark towards a crowd surrounding two men. One was bandaged around the chest and left arm with dirty rags. The other was not wounded but complained of sore feet and hunger.

"What happened? What happened?" asked Frank.

The two men told how their patrol of twelve freedom fighters managed to penetrate the Rhodesian Security Force's defense line and blow up designated targets. They destroyed a bridge, electric cable wires and damaged a power station. After completing the mission, they walked for three days back to the Rhodesia-Zambia border. About a mile before they crossed into Zambia, they were engaged by the Rhodesian Security Forces and were outnumbered five to one by the all-white force. Four freedom fighters and some security force fighters were killed in the first five minutes of crossfire. After that, the fighting continued until only three freedom fighters were left. They managed to escape in the darkness but one of them died as soon as he crossed the border. They had been given food and water from sympathetic Zambian villagers, but could not find proper medical help. They were exhausted and wounded.

Frank ordered food and water for them. The wounded man was taken to the camp's makeshift clinic. The American ex-Marine medic was summoned to do what he could until a doctor came, which would be the next day. Frank Myosa then reconvened the meeting.

"We're suffering heavy losses in Rhodesia. This is the third raid in two months and our men are getting caught each time. They have captured or killed at least fifty men in that time and they seem to know our movements. You can see how important Malawi is as a location for launching our raids. If those men could have come back through Malawi, they may be alive today. We've got to have more support and better intelligence from that area."

Sam Hernandez was perspiring profusely and his blue safari suit clung to his portly body.

"What about those new Peace Corps volunteers assigned to that region? They could possibly be of some use. After all, they're very close to the border with Mozambique and will probably be able to pick up information from time to time. Maybe we should discreetly make contact. Let's face it Frank, they don't have to know who we are. There are ways of using people without them really knowing it. Janice, did you get any information about them?"

Janice politely covered her mouth as she yawned. She was tired and sleepy.

"Unfortunately, Sam, I could not get many details. I only know that two males and one female are located in a small place called Chikwawa. It's miles from the main towns and very close to the Mozambique border. Sounds like an ideal place for our troops to have support. I know nothing else about them."

Frank asked Janice when she planned to visit Mzuzu and Blantyre again. She explained that she thought it best to wait a few weeks until the new volunteers got settled. She would then make contact with her sources to assess the situation. Three weeks would provide enough time for them to gather information about each recruit and for some of Chief Katumbi's supporters to personally meet them.

Janice stressed caution because Malawi government officials including customs were getting more suspicious about anyone travelling back and forth across the border with Zambia.

Frank told the group that a meeting with the East German Foreign Minister scheduled for January 29th had been confirmed and the Russians had suggested that the ZINAP delegation visit them during the same trip. They would be away approximately a week. Frank was hopeful that they would get a substantial increase in aid from the East Germans and Russians.

Frank Myosa then said, "I know it's late and you all look tired, so why don't we discuss it tomorrow? Janice, what time are you coming tomorrow?"

"Well, I have a class to teach in the morning, so I could meet you for lunch."

"That's fine. Lunch it is. Sam, is that okay with you?"

"Sure I have no other plans for tomorrow."

The group retired for the night.

Chapter 3: Adjusting To Malawi

Into Beautiful Africa

The plane flew over one of the most strikingly beautiful spots in Africa. Mount Kilimanjaro is the highest point on the continent at 19,340 feet above sea level. Seen from above, the snow capped peak merged gradually into the brown rock of the mountain. Further down hill was lush greenery of bushes, trees and foliage. The skies were clear.

Once past the mountain, the plane hit turbulence. The passengers and crew felt the plane shake.

"Christ Almighty!" shouted someone. "Are we going to crash?"

Just at that moment the captain's voice was heard over the intercom assuring the passengers that everything was okay. He explained that it was normal to experience turbulence during that part of the journey. Jerry Weeks, the Assistant Peace Corps Country Director, had flown out from New York to assist in escorting the volunteers to Malawi. Jerry, who was normally quiet and subservient around his boss—the Peace Corps Country Director, Bill Humphries—showed quite a different personality when on his own. He talked with each of the new volunteers and developed a good rapport with them. He also shared the itinerary for their first few days in Malawi. They would stay at the Blantyre Valley Hotel for three days. There they would meet local officials and dignitaries. A reception was planned for the first evening of their arrival at Bill Humphries's home. They would also get a chance to explore the city.

It was noon on a January day in1967 when they landed at Blantyre Airport. Crowds of men, women and children lined the fields a few yards from the runway. The women wore colorful printed wrap-around dresses and many of them had babies tied to their backs. In the distance, clusters of round thatch roofs huts jutted up out of the green and brown like silver-grey spinning tops. The thatched roofs were sun baked. This caused the once yellowish green grass to change color. Watching airplanes land and take off was a major event for local villagers. They even knew the flight schedules. The weekends were best because the entire family could come out together.

The volunteers happily left the plane and walked over the hot tarmac towards the airport building. It was small and could barely accommodate more than fifty passengers at a time. Steps led up to the roof that was used as a lookout tower. Bill Humphries, his wife, Sally, his secretary and several Malawi officials from various government departments were waiting to greet the group. It took more than thirty minutes to complete the greetings. Then a journalist and photographer from the *Malawi Daily News* wanted to take pictures of the group standing before the airplane. This meant ushering everyone back across the fifty yards of hot tarmac. The new volunteers were tired and hot but cooperated. After group photographs were taken, the Minister of Education wanted a picture of him greeting one of the Americans. Bill Humphries quickly called Jerry Weeks over to the side and spoke to him privately. After about two minutes of talking, Jerry walked over to a tall blonde, blue-eyed male volunteer. Jerry spoke to him briefly and in a few moments the volunteer was smiling and shaking hands with the Minister of Education while photographs for the next day's headlines were being taken.

Jesse Jefferson, the black volunteer from Newark, New Jersey, saw what transpired and reacted immediately.

He walked over to James and whispered in an angry tone, "Did you see that shit that just went down? I mean, goddammit, those honkies don't give up, do they? Why didn't they ask one of us to be in the picture? They've always gotta have some lily-white, blue-eyed cracker standing there like he's so superior. Damn! Reggie Blackwell is taller than any of us. He could have been chosen, but these honkies don't want the African brothers to see a black guy representing America. I'll be glad when I get away from these people and get down to my post. I'm fed up with their crap!"

James nodded and said, "I see what you mean, man."

It dawned on James that he was not nearly as sensitive or as aware of what was going on around him as Jesse. It also worried him that he had not tuned in to Bill Humphries's motives.

"Damn," he thought to himself. "It was so obvious and yet I was blind to see it. Come to think of it, little incidents happened all during training and I never gave them a second thought, except the obvious ones like Bob Newgate's racist comments. Hell! I'd better start opening my eyes a bit more. I know Jesse's had more contact with whites than I have so he probably knows a lot of their devious ways. I grew up in an all-black community. I went to all-black schools, and just haven't had much to do with white people. Maybe that's why I've missed their subtle forms of discrimination. Where I come from there was discrimination and racism all right, but at least we knew where it was. With some of this Peace Corps crowd, you just can't tell. On one hand they smile in you and act so nice, but you get the feeling that they talk about you when your back is turned. Maybe a lot of what Jesse's been saying is true. Maybe to them, I do act like some kinda Uncle Tom they can laugh at."

Just at the moment that James realized how much he had to learn about life, a loud squeaking noise drew everyone's attention. It was a wheel on the luggage wagon being drawn and pushed by two young Malawians. As they passed the group, they smiled. This wagon was the last of three loads and signaled the time for the volunteers to pick up their luggage from the baggage room. Once inside the airport lounge, several volunteers began talking to some of the Malawians. They seemed typically American, as clusters of them would aggressively engage in conversation with one or two Malawians.

"Hi, there! My name is Ed and I'm with the United States Peace Corps."

As if the Malawians didn't know.

"Hello, I'm Sue. Is that your little boy? Oh, he's so cute."

"No, madam, this is my baby girl. Her name is Mela."

"Oh. Oh, I thought she was a boy. She doesn't have much hair, does she? Anyway, that's a pretty name. How do you say it again?"

"Mela, madam."

This type of scene continued for a half hour before Bill Humphries and Jerry Weeks could get the volunteers out to the waiting buses. The trip from the airport took them past an unfinished stadium a few miles out of town. Only half the seats were erected and the center field was dusty red clay. Dozens of African men worked on various aspects of construction, along with a few Europeans, who looked as if they were supervising the operations. Once past the stadium the road stretched straight ahead for about two miles. Scattered villages lay in the background while several bicyclists peddled back and forth on the single lane paved road. The cyclists were hazardous to drivers of vehicles because they would normally not give way. It was not uncommon, especially at night, for cyclists to be brought to local clinics and hospitals as a result of injuries received from vehicles.

Some of the volunteers began to feel slightly nauseated as the bus wove from one side of the road to the other, trying to dodge the cyclist. Added to this discomfort was the soaring heat inside the non-air-conditioned bus.

Soon they approached the outskirts of Blantyre City. In the far distance, perhaps seven miles across the other side of town, a pearl white palace glistened in the sun.

Perched atop a small plateau, the Presidential Palace resembled a pyramid without a peak. It was flat on the top. Surrounded by lush greenery, the palace had only one road in and out, and was heavily guarded. The bus came to a halt at the traffic light. Traffic police manned other intersections.

Hundreds of people were milling around the open market place on the right. It was a huge market, taking up about two square blocks. Although some wooden stalls and tables were erected, most of the vendors sold their produce and goods from straw mats on the ground. The market was well organized, with certain areas designated for certain wares. For example, fresh vegetables and other crops were at each corner of the market, while meat and fish were sold in the center. The bus passed just as a butcher slaughtered the next cow. The operation appeared to be quick and simple as the sharp blade swiftly severed the jugular vein. Blantyre comprised an interesting combination of buildings. Many of the government buildings were relatively modern complexes, but most of the shops were old whitewashed buildings. East Indians managed many shops with colorful displays of imported garments. Under colonial rule, the Indians were encouraged to set up shops and small businesses, while Africans were discouraged from participating in commercial activities. The Indians were allowed to continue their businesses under General Makube's government until such time as a Malawian merchant class could be developed.

The main shopping streets in Blantyre bore little resemblance to those in New York, London or Paris. Wares of all kind were displayed on porches and in the street just in front of each shop. Paraffin burners, lamps, pots and pans, rugs, mats and just about everything else added to an already congested street. Some shops employed Malawians to unload trucks and stock shelves. There were a number of churches including Roman Catholic and Scottish Presbyterian. The Seventh Day Adventists were once established in Malawi and maintained a large following, but the government banned their activities and deported their leaders, saying that the sect's activities interfered with Malawi politics.

The tallest building in Blantyre was a block of offices and banks. The major investor in this project, a large British Building Society, also had substantial investments in neighboring southern African countries. The building looked somewhat out of character as it towered above its nearest neighbor. The city was clean and well kept with lots of flowers and whitewashed curbstones. It had several small but beautiful botanical gardens that showed off some of Malawi's flora. Numerous bars came alive at night. The two movie houses, one showing Indian speaking films and the other English speaking, were always full when opened. Films came irregularly from Rhodesia and were censored. Although the city initially appeared small to the new arrivals, it would eventually appear to be a big city after a few months of living in a small isolated village.

The bus entered the spacious driveway of the Blantyre Valley Hotel. Gardens surrounding the hotel extended three to four hundred yards in each direction. It was a grand and elegant place reflecting the equally grand life-style of prior colonialist clients. Prior to independence, the only Africans allowed near the place were employees.

The name changed soon after independence from the Prince Albert Hotel. With eighty bedrooms, two huge dining rooms, three lounges and bars, and a swimming pool, the grandiosity of the place was accented by four gigantic Gothic pillars, which lined up across the front steps. The interior was adorned with imported chandeliers and local art. The new volunteers were both impressed and amused as they entered the reception area of the hotel. Hotel staff overheard various comments whispered by some of the group.

"Gosh, this place's got class!'

"Gee whiz! Look at those lights up there. Is that real crystal hanging from them?"

"Good golly! I never expected to see a place like this in Africa."

The British hotel manager and a few of his Malawian staff looked at each other and smiled as they cheerfully watched their guests browse around the room.

"Good afternoon to you all. My name is Robert Landers and I am the manager of the Blantyre Valley Hotel. We hope to make your stay with us as delightful as possible, and I am sure you will find our facilities most suitable indeed. Mr. Kylimbe is my assistant and he will assign your room numbers for you. If you have any problems do feel free to call upon us."

Within an hour most of the volunteers found their rooms, unpacked their bags and were back downstairs touring the hotel gardens. Some were sitting poolside while others took a refreshing swim. They seemed to be all over the place. What had been a slow but relaxing afternoon for other guests, turned out to be an exciting and amusing time, as the guests mingled with the volunteers.

"Did you say you were going to Mzuzu? We travel up that way often. I say, though, it's a dreadfully boring place!"

Speaking was the former Minister of Agriculture, who served under the colonial government before independence. He continued to tell several volunteers how much better things were run when the British controlled the government.

"Now, you take the labor situation in agriculture. In my day, those boys worked bloody hard from sun up to sun down. They were good boys, too. You never heard them complaining about work or wages, and they were obedient. Nowadays, they're sassy little bastards. You can't tell them a thing. I know we were no angels back in those days, but believe me, they would still be running naked if it weren't for us British coming in and civilizing the lot of them."

The volunteers were aware that this man, who spent forty of his sixty years living in Southern Africa, had his prejudices firmly entrenched, and no amount of progress by Africans would change his opinion of them.

"Don't you think they have a right to do things their way?" asked one volunteer.

Sweating profusely while smoking a pipe made of ivory, the man sat back in his chair and laughed.

"Have a right! Have a right! The worst thing that happened to these people is that they got their independence. Look what's happening all over the continent. They're having tribal wars and overthrowing governments every six months, and they are killing each other off like savages."

The volunteer looked straight into the man's eyes. He felt contempt for the arrogant bigot.

"They're doing no more than what 'civilized' white men have done to each other over the past thirty years. Excuse me."

The volunteer got up from the table and walked away briskly. The man sat back bewildered. He was contemplating whether he had insulted the volunteer.

Jennifer Nolan and Dianne Harper found themselves engaged in light conversation with two Malawian civil servants, who were having lunch and a drink at the hotel. Both the man and woman were administrators in the Health Ministry. They talked about the problems of not having enough trained nurses and doctors to meet the needs of the population, and lack of clinics and medical equipment in most places.

"How many doctors are there in Malawi?" asked Jennifer.

The Malawian woman said there were not enough doctors in the country. She explained that the Health Ministry proposed a substantial increase in grants for students to study medicine abroad, since Malawi had no medical school. With a population growth of approximately three percent per annum, the ratio of doctors per thousand people was expected get even worse. It was explained that teams of young men and women were sent to villages to teach health and hygiene methods. They concentrated mostly on the nutritional value of certain foods and they offered some first-aid treatment. For a while it appeared that each recruit was engaged in conversations with Malawians. They talked to hotel guests, waiters, cleaning staff, cooks, and floor sweepers. There was a certain degree of anxiety, mixed with a desire to show off in front of other volunteers. A subtle game was being played called "Look at me. I've made friends with a Malawian!"

It was a superficial game, but very American. Even Bob Newgate condescendingly invited the hotel janitor to have dinner with him one evening. Jesse Jefferson produced his widest smile for months as he laughed and joked with his African brothers. He told them how good he felt to be home. They, of course, thought Jesse was great. Cathy Horowitz cornered a cleaning woman in her room. The woman was bored stiff as Cathy rambled on about how much she liked African people and she once dated an African (James, of course). Unknown to Cathy, the woman did not understand a word she said, because the woman did not speak English. Finally after twenty minutes, the cleaning woman gestured towards the door, picked up her duster and pail and opened the door.

"Wait a minute, dearie!" Cathy shouted. "I have something for you and your little ones."

She then put a British pound note into the woman's hand.

"Zikomo Kwambiri."

Replied the woman and hurried down the hall. Even if the woman could have spoken English she wouldn't have had a chance to tell Cathy that she had no children, neither was she married. The rest of the day, Cathy boasted about her new Malawian friend. When asked what the friend's name was, Cathy was hard pressed to come up with anything. She had never asked.

James Johnson went from one Malawian to the other, shaking hands and chatting for five minutes. He acted as if he were a celebrity. At five minutes a chat, he could not have been serious about making any long-lasting relationships.

"How you doing? My name is James Johnson. I'm from America and I'm a Peace Corps Volunteer. What's your name?"

James consciously made a point of saying that he was from America, as if trying to eliminate any doubt in the Malawian's mind. It was four o'clock that evening before he got around to the bus driver who was waiting to take the group to Bill Humphries's house for a reception. The driver was a bearded, well-spoken man of about fifty. He was once a high-ranking member of General Makube's cabinet, but was sacked for publicly opposing the government's policy of open trade with Rhodesia and South Africa. The driver was leaning on the side of the bus smoking a cigarette when James approached. In an almost childish, but condescending manner, James started his introductory speech. When he got to the part about being from America, he was abruptly cut off by a terse husky voice.

"Yes, I know you are from America. You don't have to prove it!"

There was utter silence as the driver looked piercingly at James. The stare was so forceful that James turned his head and looked away. Feeling like an absolute idiot after considering how he must have come off, he was speechless. A few more moments passed.

"Have a cigarette, son."

"Thanks."

As the driver held out a match he said in a kind and almost fatherly voice, "We're are glad to have you here James. We only wish your government would send more of our American brothers and sisters. There are many problems facing us in Malawi. You will notice things both surprising and disturbing to you. Don't be impetuous, but act wisely. We know of your problems, too. I lived in your country for some time. I do not apologize for speaking sharply to you. You now understand it was in your interest. Where will you work?"

"The Ministry of Health in Mzuzu. "

The driver smiled.

"That is my birthplace. You will like it there. Before you leave I will give you the names of my family and village. They will welcome you. I must leave now. Remember what I have said today."

The driver disappeared into the back entrance of the hotel leaving James standing next to the bus.

"I'm tired. I don't want to think about anything else today. Too much has happened and I seem to be making mistakes whenever I open my mouth."

James then lay down on a shady patch of grass and closed his eyes.

Some time had passed before a soft female voice woke him.

"Sir. Sir. Your friends will be leaving soon. Are you going with them?"

His eyes opened slowly and he noticed a cute little round face peering down at him.

"Oh! Thank you, miss. What time is it, by the way?"

"The time is 4:35, sir."

"Thank you. What's your name?"

"My name is Nika, sir."

"That's a pretty name, Nika."

The girl smiled and her dark brown eyes glistened.

"Well, I guess I'd better hurry to get changed. Thanks again for waking me up."

He quickly jumped up and rushed into the hotel, leaving behind the full imprint of his body in the grass.

By 7:30 that evening all the guests had arrived at Bill Humphries's house, including the Honorable Hewitt T. Smith, U.S. Ambassador to Malawi. The spacious back garden comfortably accommodated the guests, who included officials from the Ministries of Education and Health, Malawian and American Peace Corps staff and several volunteers who had been working in the country for some time. Bill's wife, Sally, and his secretary, Christine Dawson, helped the servants serve drinks, while Bill supervised the barbecue pit. Although the Ambassador spoke briefly with all of the volunteers, he spent considerably more time talking to the five people assigned to Mzuzu. He considered this post to be critical since it was the region most supportive of Chief Rodney Katumbi. He had already warned Bill Humphries that he would not tolerate any more "sympathetic radical" volunteers in the area. The Ambassador spoke first with Bob Newgate and Phil Harrington. After five or ten minutes of talking he felt confident that these two would not cause any problems. Then he talked to James.

"You're James Johnson, aren't you?"

"Yes, sir."

"How was your trip, James?"

"It was a very good trip, sir, except when we flew over Mount Kilimanjaro. Gee, I thought the plane was going to crash!"

The Ambassador chuckled.

"Yes, James, I have often felt the same way when flying through that passage. Tell me, what is your first assignment in Mzuzu?"

"Well, sir, I will be working out of the regional headquarters of the Ministry of Health. My job is to visit all the regional clinics in order to assess medical requirements. I will collect information about the number of patients utilizing each clinic, the type of equipment required, medical supplies and other data. The ministry wants to build a comprehensive data base of its health resources in the region."

The Ambassador was impressed, not so much with James's job, but with the way he described it.

"I can see you are very enthusiastic about your new job."

"Yes, sir. I am. I can hardly wait to get started."

"What subject did you study in school?"

"It was Sociology with a minor in Statistics."

"Well, the Statistics will surely come in handy for this job. Tell me, were you active in any clubs or organizations while in college?"

James talked excitedly about his participation in the Student Senate, Debating Society and the NAACP.

"Oh, you were a member of the National Association for the Advancement of Colored People? Did you participate in any of their protest marches?"

James detected a note of anxiety in the Ambassador's voice and for a moment felt as though a lawyer in court was questioning him. He hesitated a moment before responding.

"I supported NAACP activities in all ways, sir. In fact I am still a member."

They chatted for another five minutes, before the Ambassador said, "You must excuse me. I want to talk to as many of the volunteers as I can, since most of you will be travelling on soon. It was nice talking with you, James."

The Ambassador moved quickly to the next group of volunteers standing by the pool. He talked for only a few minutes when James noticed him moving toward Jennifer Nolan. James wiped his sweating brow with a handkerchief.

"That's interesting," James thought. "He seems to be spending more time with Phil, Jennifer, Bob and me, than with the others. I wonder if he's trying to figure us out because we are going to Mzuzu. I bet that's what he's doing. He's a sly S.O.B. I'm going to time his conversation with Jennifer and also see how long he talks to Stuart Steiner."

The Ambassador talked with Jennifer and Stuart at considerable length.

He spent the better part of forty-five minutes with both of them. Afterwards, James joined Stuart.

"You must have had a very interesting conversation with the Ambassador, Stuart. You were with him for a long time."

Stuart produced an uncharacteristic smile.

"Yes, and it was interesting, all right. Did you ever get the feeling that someone was trying to find out things about you, without you knowing it? Well, that about sums up my feeling about talking with the Ambassador. But I didn't pull any punches. I was as straight with him as I would be with anyone. You do know that he has a special interest in Mzuzu? From what I can muster he's worried that we might get involved in politics there, just like those other volunteers, who were sent home."

James interrupted Stuart.

"I got that impression, too. In fact, I timed his conversation with you, Jennifer, and the rest of us. Do you know that he talked with us longer than he did with any of the others? Look at him now, Stuart. He has cornered Bill Humphries and they're going into the house. I bet you five dollars that he's going to discuss his conversations with us. I wonder what he thinks of us?"

Stuart kept his eye on the Ambassador and Bill as they moved into the house.

"He probably thinks that we should be watched, but I'm not going to lose any sleep over it. Let's go over and talk to Jennifer. See what she thinks. By the way, are you going shopping tomorrow or are you going sightseeing?"

"I haven't thought about it. I suppose shopping first, since there are quite a few things I need to pick up. Why?"

"Oh, no special reason. I just thought maybe we could go together. That's if it's all right with you."

James paused and then smiled.

"Sure, man! It's all right with me. Hey, you don't have to always apologize for asking. Just say what's on your mind. You're okay with me, Stuart."

They both smiled and walked over to Jennifer Nolan.

The Ambassador entered Bill Humphries's study and sat down on a comfortable leather couch, imported from America.

"Would you like another drink, sir?"

"Sure, Bill, why not? I would like a little less water this time."

Bill went over to the mahogany drinks cabinet standing in the center of the wall. Above the cabinet hung a large shield made of cowhide. On each side of the shield was a six-foot spear made of wood and iron.

"The Malawians produce some nice crafts out in the villages, don't you think so, sir?"

The Ambassador briefly noticed the shield as he scanned the room. He had seen it before, and hundreds like it and he was not in the mood for small talk. In an unenthusiastic tone of voice, he replied, "Nice stuff."

Bill handed him a stiff scotch with hardly any water. He took a big sip and reclined into the couch. As Bill sat in the armchair opposite him, the Ambassador spoke impatiently.

"Now look here, Bill. I had long talks with those youngsters assigned to Mzuzu, and I've got strange vibrations about all except two. Now this kid from Texas, what's his name?"

"Bob Newgate, sir."

"Yes, Newgate, he seems okay. The other one named Phil won't be any bother either. The one I'm most concerned about is that boy from Stamford, Connecticut, the Jewish kid. It was nothing he said

Bill, just his attitude. Something about the way he responds that makes me very uncomfortable with him. Now that colored boy, James, seems like a nice boy and he's not angry. He's not angry yet! Nevertheless, Bill, keep an eye on him because he could easily be influenced. Jennifer Nolan reminds me of my own daughter when she was coming of age. Do you know what she said to me, Bill? She said that organizations like Peace Corps could be doing more harm than good in developing countries. When I asked her to explain herself, she said that although she agreed that certain forms of assistance were needed, she felt that we were also changing these peoples' culture and lifestyle."

The Ambassador paused to take another sip of scotch. This gave Bill a chance to interject a comment or two.

"Sir, I'm sure that thought has cropped up in most of our minds, but I do not think that is a cause for real concern. Jennifer is a very nice girl and will make a good recruit."

The Ambassador slammed his drink onto the coffee table causing a little to spill out.

"I'm not doubting whether the girl is nice or not, Bill. Sure, we all have had thoughts about our role in these countries. But what I am concerned about is whether she or any of the others will express these views to the Malawians. That's what I don't want to happen."

There was a long silence before Bill offered to replenish the Ambassador's drink. Bill knew that the Ambassador did not like his opinions challenged, but felt it necessary to speak up for the volunteers at least occasionally. The Ambassador had spent ten to forty-five minutes talking with each one of the Mzuzu group and was already judging them. Bill thought that some of these judgments were premature.

"I think I have had enough to drink tonight. Perhaps I should be going now. All in all it looks like you got a good bunch of volunteers this time. Let's try to keep them that way. Sorry about my impatience, but you're used to me by now. I'll just slip out quietly, so could you say goodnight to Sally for me? It's been a good evening and an interesting one, too."

The Ambassador was soon whisked away into the night and Bill returned to the reception. By this time the party had livened up and everyone was dancing in the back garden to rock 'n' roll music. The occasional interruptions of someone jumping into the swimming pool fully-clothed only added to the joy and glee of the moment. It was eleven p.m. when the last record was played. Then the bus took the group back to the hotel. They were an excited but tired bunch by now, and surprisingly, there was hardly a murmur as they rode back to the hotel to slumber away their first night under the African stars.

Two Days in a Flash

Following a much needed rest and an early breakfast, which included boiled eggs, scones and toast, the volunteers scattered all over Blantyre City. It was a busy day for most of them, as they shopped and bartered for those necessary items that could only be bought in the city. After most of the shopping was done, some volunteers visited the Presidential Palace while the others walked to nearby villages on the outskirts of the city.

The village children were fascinated with people who had white skin. Some of the younger children became frightened when they saw two or three white people cautiously approaching their village. They would scatter and hide behind huts, trees or any large objects that they thought kept them out of sight. The village chief and a small delegation of men and women greeted visitors. The children stayed in the background until introductory ceremonies were over.

It was afternoon when Phil Harrington, Stuart Steiner and James Johnson approached a village about four miles from the city. The children playing near the entrance saw the three and immediately ran back towards the center of the village shouting "Nsungu! Nsungu!" The volunteers remembered that the word meant 'European' in Chinyanja, one of the Malawian languages. As they got closer to the village they saw a small delegation of people coming to greet them. They came closer and extended their hands while giving greetings in Chinyanja. Then they turned to James and spoke in the most familiar of tones. They thought he was Malawian. He could not understand the language because he had studied a different dialect. The Malawians looked on in curious silence as he tried to explain in English who they were. After a short discussion among themselves, they gestured for the three to go over to a large thatch roof hut and sit down on the porch. The hut had windows of glass. The village Chief lived there and the glass windows were an indication of his high status.

The Chief made a gesture to one of the teenage boys, which indicated that the boy should go and fetch something. They sat around in a circle for about fifteen minutes trying desperately to communicate with each other when a young man of about twenty-one appeared.

He first spoke to the Chief and then said, "My name is Joseph. I am Chief Seiko's grandson. I speak a little English. I will translate."

A sigh of relief fell over the three volunteers. They explained who they were and where they came from. This was then translated for the Chief. There was a long wait as the Chief discussed something with the other elders. They kept looking at James rather suspiciously and then they laughed. James, who was a little embarrassed, asked why they were laughing.

With a smile on his face, Joseph said. "They believe you are not from America. You are from Blantyre. You are African and there are no Africans in America, only Nsungus."

Then James, Stuart and Phil laughed, and they laughed harder.

"Can you believe this? They don't think I'm from America. Well I've heard it all!"

James explained to Joseph that many, many years ago, white men came to Africa and took many Africans back to America to work as slaves. He said that the African Americans have lived there ever since and there were over twenty-five million Africans living in America. Joseph looked at James in an understanding way.

"I have heard this talk. You are the first African Nsungu we see. What is your language?"

"I speak English. My people came from many parts of Africa and we were not allowed to keep our African languages. Do you understand me?"

Joseph smiled.

"Yes, I understand. I will explain to my fathers."

While Joseph explained to the elders what James said, they could still not conceive of James, who looked like them, being from anywhere but Blantyre. To them Africans were from Africa and since most of them had been no further than Blantyre City, Africa extended from their village to the city.

Three women brought three large pans of nsima, a thick mass of boiled grounded maize, which looked like cream of wheat. After this came five dishes, three of which contained stewed chicken parts and gravy, and the others with dried fish. So busy were they watching the food being displayed, the volunteers did not notice the mowa being handed around in a deep wooden bowl. The Chief gestured to them to drink. Stuart was first and said in a whispering voice.

"What's this stuff? It looks like muddy water to me," Stuart said.

Phil urged Stuart to taste it.

"It's called mowa, their homemade beer. Go ahead and drink it, Stuart. You might insult them if you don't."

Stuart braced himself, closed his eyes and tilted the bowl to his mouth.

"Ah! This stuff is awful!"

The Malawians grinned with delight as they saw Stuart's face grimace. They must have exchanged jokes about how the Nsungu looked when he drank their beer. The others drank and showed equally disconcerted expressions.

"My father say you like mowa."

"Sure, sure it's good," replied the three, as they wondered how many more lies they would have to tell before the visit was over.

After the bowls completed the circle, the chief picked up a pan of Nsima and placed it in front of his guests.

Then Joseph said, "You may share my father's food."

Luckily, they had Phil with them because James and Stuart had not the slightest idea of what to do next.

As they looked around for spoons or forks, Phil said, "You guys watch me. Use your fingers to pick up the nsima and then dip it in the chicken gravy like this. You should have paid attention to what our Malawian language instructors taught us back in training. Go on, James. Stick your fingers into the nsima. It's not going to bite you."

James ate it slowly. By this time the potent mowa had begun to have its effect on them. They drank only a small amount, but felt quite light in the head. The meal was followed by a series of belches and hiccups from the guests. The village elders roared laughing as they watched.

It was an intriguing and not to be forgotten visit for the villagers. They would talk about their visitors for many months to come and until some other event occurred that had more storytelling worth than this occasion. The trio left the village and began to walk back to their hotel. They gratefully acknowledged the splendid hospitality given to them and said that they would return one day.

Back in the center of town at the Peace Corps garage, several volunteers were trying out the motorcycles they would use during their tour. The garage was located on a hilltop overlooking part of the city. In the back of the garage lay an open field extending about one hundred yards towards a cliff. The field was fenced in, but the terrain was very uneven and rocky. Bob Newgate was checking the brakes on his motorcycle along with another recruit called Chuck Chandler. Other volunteers were there to check on their motorcycles. Chuck was also from Texas and considered himself a bit of a daredevil. He raced motorcycles, cars and even rode bulls in rodeos in Texas. When Bob completed the checks on his motorcycle, he helped Chuck with his. In his familiar Texas drawl, Bob turned to Chuck.

"Boy, these Honda 90ccs sure are different from the 175ccs I'm used to riding. They must feel like toys to you too, Chuck."

"Yeah, this doggone thing is just like a baby kitten compared to some of them broncos I'm used to riding. But I bet you I can make this run like a Harley. I'm going to take it out now. Just watch me, boy. See what I can do with it."

Bob showed slight signs of nervousness when he spoke.

"Hold on a minute, boy. Your dang blasted back brake clamp is loose. Let me tighten it up for you. It'll only take a second."

Chuck was obviously impatient and wanted to get going.

"No need for that, Bob. I rode these things with no brakes before. Thanks partner!"

Bob was desperately trying to restrain Chuck.

"Come on, buddy. Don't be foolish! Look how uneven that field is out there. You'll get out there and break your damn neck."

"Lay off me, Bobby boy. I know what I'm doing. Why, I've been riding these things since I was knee high to a wild cat. Man! It's only a little 90cc. I can stop these things with one drag of the foot. Now come on. Let's go!"

Chuck was off in a flash. The engine was revved up as high as it would go as he released the clutch. Chuck left behind a cloud of dust as he cycled almost twenty-five yards on the one wheel. When the front wheel finally touched the ground it landed at the bottom of a low spot in the field. Then up came Chuck and the motorcycle, leaping about five feet into the air.

"Yippee! Yippee!" shouted Chuck.

By this time, a small audience had gathered. The volunteers and several Malawian workers at the garage stood cheering Chuck on.

"Come on, Chuck. Show us some Evel Knievel stunts."

"Ride that bronco boy! You can handle it!"

Everyone, of course, was not so confident about Chuck's ability to carry out stunts on such rough ground.

"Does that crazy fool know what he's doing?"

"That's one sure way to break a leg!"

But Chuck was doing great. With only the front brake working on the machine, he was able to drive straight ahead at full speed and stop a yard from the barbed wire fence. He rode with one hand, no hands, feet on the handlebars and even sitting backwards. The performance lasted about five minutes before Bob Newgate shouted.

"Hey, partner, you did great. How about coming on in here now?"

Bob was worried that Chuck would push his luck too far and end up with something fractured. Chuck slowed up as he passed the crowd.

"Okay buddy, but just one more trip around. I'm gonna wind this baby up good!"

The engine roared and popped as Chuck raced down the one hundred yard straightaway. He was so bent on beating his own speed record that he forgot about the dip in the field only ten yards from the fence at the edge of the cliff.

It was not until he was a foot or so from the dip that he applied the only brake he had, but it was too late to halt the momentum of the motorcycle. When the front wheel touched the ground, it was locked, causing the rear of the bike to topple up and over. At nearly sixty miles per hour, the bike travelled more than seven yards in the air before crashing into the ground. Screams had already begun as the crowd saw Chuck somersaulting through the air. His neck seemed to bounce off the barbed wire at the same moment as the motorcycle blew up. The crowd became hysterical. They stood there with hands over their mouths and eyes in utter disbelief. They ran the hundred yards or so down the field shouting, "Chuck! Chuck! Oh my God! What's happened to him? Help!"

When they got to the fence, they noticed that the top wire was broken and stained with blood. Dianne Harper fainted. Joe Veto picked her up and moved her back a few yards.

"Hey, Jennifer, come over here with Dianne, quickly!"

He then sprinted back to the edge of the cliff. "You guys found him yet?"

The replies were hysterical.

"No! No! He must have gone over. Christ, it must be a thousand feet down that cliff. Oh no!"

At that instant a voice cried out. A Malawian by-stander stood petrified as he peered down a few feet below the cliff's edge. When the crowd ran over to see what was happening, the screams of horror were unbelievable. What they saw caused most of them to vomit. Jennifer ran up to see and was turned away.

"Get back, Jennifer. You don't want to see this. Oh God! Why this?"

Chuck's decapitated head was lying smashed between two rocks. His face was purple and his head stained with blood. There was no sign of the rest of his body, but the sight was too gruesome for anyone to care.

Later that evening in the hotel the mood was somber among the volunteers. No one talked much at all about their day's activities and many stood around in silent disbelief. Dianne Harper did not come down for dinner that evening as she continued to lie in a state of shock. Both Jennifer Nolan and Cathy Horowitz visited her room at intervals to watch her. Bob Newgate sat in a corner of the hotel bar drinking straight bourbons. Phil Harrington sat trying to console him.

"Bob, you shouldn't blame yourself for what happened. You tried to stop him several times. Why don't you go up and get some rest now. You'll feel better tomorrow. Come on, Bob, those bourbons aren't doing you any good."

Bob just shrugged Phil's comments aside and continued to stare into the corner of the room in an absolute stupor.

"Goddamn it, Chuck. Why didn't you listen to me? It would have taken only two minutes to fix that brake clamp. Why didn't you listen?"

Phil put his arms across Bob's shoulder.

"Look, Bob. You tried to stop him, but you know how Chuck was. Once he got an idea in his head, nobody could stop him. You can't sit here all night. Come on with me."

Phil slowly stood up hoping that Bob would follow. Bob continued to look ahead. Then Phil said, "Come on, Bob."

Bob hesitantly got up and followed Phil.

Sitting in the lounge having coffee were Stuart, Jennifer and James. Jennifer's eyes were red and puffy because she had cried so much that day.

"Are you feeling better, Jennifer?"

"A little. It was such a shock. I have never seen anything so terrible before. It's awful!"

She began to cry again and both James and Stuart tried to calm her.

"Thank you, guys. I'll be all right. It's Dianne I'm worried about. The doctor gave her something to help her sleep and to calm her nerves. She was in a terrible state today. Cathy is watching her now."

"When do you think we can see her? Did the doctor say how long those pills would work on her?"

Jennifer pulled a tissue out of her dress pocket and wiped her eyes dry.

"He didn't say but I think they will keep her sleeping through most of the night."

Then she broke down crying again.

"Oh God, it was so horrible. What about his parents and family? Why did this have to happen?"

Stuart looked at James and gave a non-verbal signal. They both stood up and helped Jennifer to her feet.

"Maybe you should go up and get some rest now Jennifer. It's been a tiring day for you. Come along and we will take you to your room."

After escorting her to the room, Stuart decided to go to his room for the night. James looked at his watch and saw that the time was 9:35. Too restless to sleep himself, he went back down to the hotel lounge and sat on a soft sofa. Very few people were about that night. He thought about a lot of things as he lay back.

134

"Too bad about what happened to Chuck Chandler. It's almost unbelievable that something like that could happen. They said it was a frightening experience seeing the accident. I'm glad I wasn't there or I probably would have fainted, too. I can't stand the sight of blood, nor can I stomach much talk about it. Everyone was in such a happy mood before it happened, but now it's a real sad scene."

A waiter interrupted his thoughts.

"Can I get you something, sir?"

"No, thanks. Wait. On second thought, I will have coffee, light with one sugar, please."

The waiter hurried off to fetch the coffee. He was not in a sad mood. In fact, he had done well on tips since the volunteers had arrived. James thought again.

"Well, we've got one more day in Blantyre City and then off to our assignments. I wonder if Mzuzu is anything like Blantyre. I like it here, but I wish I could find some razor blades to fit my razor. I can't seem to find the right kind anywhere. I'll probably have to buy a new razor. All they sell is British razor blades and razors. They sure look different from the American ones. They're much smaller. Anyway, I don't guess it matters much, since I only have to shave once a week. Twelve blades could last me a whole year. I better get a few extras though, since I have to cut my own hair. I don't like the way the Malawians cut hair. Looks as if they placed a bowl on top of some of those guys' heads and zip around with their hair clippers just below the bowl's edge. They're trying to imitate the British hairstyle. I think it looks stupid. Anyway, I'm glad I don't have the problem that Joe Veto has. He has to shave twice a day or otherwise he ends up looking like a bear. That's one hairy guy!"

The waiter smiled as he approached James.

"Your coffee, sir. I also brought some cheese and crackers for you."

"Oh thanks. How much do I owe you?"

"Two shillings, sir."

"Is that all? What about the cheese and crackers?"

"No charge, sir. It is on the house. Is that what you Americans say, sir?"

"Yes. On the house."

James placed two shillings on the tray and reached into a separate pocket. Out came a U.S. dollar bill. He put it into the waiter's hand and said, "This is real American money. Here it's for you."

The waiter was delighted and replied with thanks and a smile.

James looked around the room as he sipped his coffee. By now the room was almost empty of people. Only two volunteers and an elderly British couple remained. Then he saw the waiter showing the dollar bill to his colleagues. They were discussing the value of it in Malawian money. James continued his thoughts.

"Some of the Malawians appear to be so content. Sometimes they behave too subserviently. The brothers back home would say they acted like Uncle Toms. Maybe it's too early to judge them. After all, I've only met a few of them in the hotel. I suppose when you're trying to make tips, you behave extra nice. That bus driver doesn't act like them though. He seems tough and shrewd. It's almost a shame that his talents are being wasted driving a bus, especially considering he was a government Minister. He sure put me in my place. I guess I deserved that. He reminded me of my father. I wonder how mom and dad are doing. I have to write to them soon. I must tell them about my first impressions of Africa and what it feels like to be here. I must admit, though, I'm not sure what it feels like yet. A lot of the white volunteers have asked me what it feels like to be a black American in Africa. I've just told them it's great and then I asked them what it feels like for a white American to be in Africa. Some of their speechless faces were funny as hell! My feelings right now are confused. I did not expect so much European influence in the way government ministers appear to operate. I also didn't expect to see Asians running the shops and businesses and whites controlling hotels, bars, and banks. I suppose I expected to see Africans running everything, including flying East African Airways aircraft. I'm really not sure how independent these brothers are yet. I suppose it takes a long time to train and develop a skilled labor force. After all, the country is one of the poorest in Africa and the British didn't do much to prepare the Malawians for self-rule. Maybe these are examples of what the bus driver meant when he said that I would notice things both surprising and disturbing in Malawi."

James's thoughts were briefly interrupted.

"I say there, young man. It looks like you and I are the only ones left down here. I'm off to bed now, so, I'll say goodnight to you."

James was awakened from his reverie by the polite British voice. For a moment, he wondered if the man had overheard his thoughts especially those relating to the British.

"I must have dozed off. You're right. There's no one else around. What time is it?"

The man said it was 11:25.

"I didn't realize I was sitting here so long. I'm going up, too. I need the sleep tonight. Thanks for waking me, sir."

"No bother, young man. No bother at all. Well, goodnight then."

"Goodnight."

Most of the volunteers were up early the next morning. For those travelling on to assignments outside Blantyre it was their last day for shopping and dealing with any other matters, such as collecting first-aid kits, books and novels and a good supply of malaria pills. Last minute transportation arrangements had to be confirmed, so Bill Humphries and his staff had a busy morning at the Peace Corps Headquarters building. Volunteers assigned to the same locations tended to stick together that day, primarily because they would be travelling together. Jesse Jefferson, Steve Manski and Cathy

Horowitz arrived at the office early. Christine Dawson, Bill Humphries's secretary, greeted them. Christine explained that they would be taken to Chikwawa by Land Rover starting about six o'clock the following morning. One motorcycle was to be tied to the back of the Land Rover for Cathy. There were already two motorcycles in Chikwawa used by previous volunteers and supposedly they were in good condition. It was a long trip, taking up to twelve hours on dirt roads. Christine asked them to check lists of items required and make sure they got all their necessities that day, since Chikwawa was so isolated. During the rainy season the roads would be impassable and they could be stuck there for up to eight weeks.

As they walked out onto the front steps, they could see the bus driver who drove them to Bill Humphries's reception on the first day of their arrival. The driver gave a beckoning nod of his head. Cathy and Steve did not know whom he was beckoning. Then Jesse Jefferson went over to the driver. They talked in whispers for about three minutes, leaving Cathy and Steve with bemused expressions on their faces. They noticed the driver slipping a folded sheet of paper into Jesse's hand. They then shook hands and parted.

Jesse returned to the front steps and Steve asked, "What was that all about, Jesse? A friend of yours?"

Jesse paused and then replied, "Oh, he's just a friend. He gave me the address of some of his relatives. You talked to him, didn't you, Steve?"

"Well, just briefly. Anyway, where do you two think we should go first to that shop with the aluminum pots or to the linen store?"

Cathy suggested getting the linen first, so off they went. The rest of the day was busy, but the calmness among the volunteers was uncharacteristic. Each of them seemed to approach each activity cautiously. They were still very much aware of the tragedy of the previous day, and most were preoccupied with finishing their shopping as soon as possible in order to get back to pack their bags. That evening the thirty-nine volunteers were seated for dinner. Steak, chips and green peas were on the menu, followed by peaches and cream. They had agreed earlier to eat on time so that they could have a sort of farewell drink together. Although they knew they would see each other again at some stage, it was to be a send-off party. Soon after dinner was over, they gathered in the lounge. Chuck's death was still on their minds although they tried not to let it interfere with the excitement of their new adventures.

Dianne Harper looked well rested but sad. It wasn't just the tragedy that depressed her, but a combination of things. Jennifer was sitting next to Dianne in the large circle of people gathered around the center of the lounge.

"Are you okay, Dianne? You seem worried about something. Is it just Chuck's death or is there something else?"

"It's nothing, Jennifer, I don't want to talk about it."

Jennifer waited patiently for a few moments and turned again to Dianne.

"It might make you feel better if you talked about it. Sometimes people need to talk to someone else. That's what friends are for."

Dianne became annoyed with Jennifer.

"Look, honey. I told you it was nothing and if I've got anything to say to you, I'll do it in my own good time. Now just leave me alone."

"I'm sorry, Dianne. I was just trying to be helpful. If you feel like that about it, I won't say another word."

Both sat silently looking in opposite directions for five minutes.

Dianne got up and said, "Excuse me."

She abruptly left the group. Jennifer noticed that she walked outside into the front garden. Jennifer turned to Cathy.

"Dianne has been very upset since yesterday. Have you noticed it too, Cathy?"

"Yes. She seems to be bothered about a few things. I noticed it the first day she arrived. She wasn't her confident out-going self. I was surprised because I expected her to be even more confident once she got to Africa. I can't understand it. Maybe there are problems back home or perhaps she and her boyfriend broke up. Speaking of boyfriends, do you and Steve have much to say to each other these days?"

Jennifer's curious but caring mood turned to one of icy resentment.

"I don't see why that should concern you, Cathy. Why do you ask?"

Cathy noticed a change in the tone and intonation of Jennifer's voice.

"Oh, no reason, Jennifer, I just asked. Sorry, I didn't know you were still sensitive about Steve."

"Who's sensitive about Steve? It seems to me that you're the one sensitive about him. Let's just drop it, Cathy."

"Okay. Sorry."

As the party continued, some of the volunteers sang songs. They sang "Home, Home On The Range," "Yankee Doodle Dandy" and a combination of folk and religious songs. The noise got so loud that other hotel guests left the room. The assistant manager of the hotel asked them twice to keep the noise down. Eventually what seemed like a long night slowly came to an end.

Dianne's Big Decision

James lay on his bed and remembered Christmas in Virginia.

"It was good being around the folks again. It's funny thinking about it. They treated me as if I was a celebrity and a guest. I almost felt uncomfortable. Maybe it was all that publicity I got in the local weekly newspaper. They gave me a good write-up. I liked the title of the article, "A Native Son Goes to Africa." The photo wasn't bad either. Well, I'll try to sleep since we've got to start early tomorrow."

Just as James began to doze off, there was a soft tap at the door. He wondered who that could be at that time of night. Then he spoke.

"Who is it?"

A soft southern accent could faintly be heard.

"It's me, Dianne. Can I talk to you, James?"

"Dianne?" He said unbelievingly. "Oh Dianne, hold on a second, I'll be right there."

He leaped out of bed and scrambled around for his robe. He could not find it, so he quickly wrapped a towel around his waist and went to the door. While trying to unlock the door, he inadvertently locked it, since he'd never actually locked it when he first came back to his room.

"Damn this door! Hold on, Dianne. I won't be long."

When the door finally sprung open, Dianne stood there in a nightgown with eyes full of tears.

"What's wrong, Dianne? Are you okay? Come on in."

As he led her into the room she sobbed and cried.

"I have to talk to you, James. I have to talk to somebody."

James led Dianne gently to the side of the bed and sat her down.

"It's okay, Dianne. You can talk to me. Just try to relax now. I'm sure we can sort out what's bothering you. There now, dry your tears away."

Dianne took several deep breaths as she dried her tears.

"I feel awful, James. I feel guilty about what I'm going to say. I mean, I just don't think I can take it. It's not for me."

"What? What can't you take?"

"Africa, James. Malawi! It's not what I thought it would be. The flies, the mosquitoes and the smells in the market place bother me. Looking at those poor little children running around with swollen tummies is just too much. I'm frightened."

James patted her on the shoulders gently and said, "It will be okay, Dianne. Just give it a little time. You're not the only one suffering from what some call culture shock. Hell, I don't like a lot of what I've seen so far, but we've only been here three days. I bet after a week, you'll look back and laugh at tonight."

Dianne interrupted with another outburst of crying.

"No! It's not just that. I hate to admit it but I would rather be back home teaching in a nice clean school, having hot showers, going to the beauty parlor each week and driving my Ford Mustang. Oh! You must think I'm awful but I don't want to spend the next two years of my life being frightened by those little lizards called geckos and worrying about catching malaria. I can't blame anyone for not telling us about the conditions here, because they did. I guess it's easier romanticizing about what it would be like while you're enjoying the comforts of familiar surroundings. When I saw that cow being butchered in the marketplace I almost threw up on the bus. Then what happened to Chuck yesterday. . . Oh Lord! Oh no! It's just too much."

"Try not to think about it," James whispered. "Everything will turn out okay. Believe me."

He put his arms around Dianne and held her tightly for several minutes. The moon cast its light through the open window, drawing the silhouette of Dianne's lovely brown face lying against James's chest.

142

James helped Dianne to sit up straight. He then dried her tears from her cheeks.

In a soft low and sincere voice he said, "Listen to me, Dianne. You're tired and you've had a busy time during the past three days. I understand your feelings and I admire you for being so honest about them. My mom used to always say, 'Where there's truth, there's hope.' That probably means different things to different people, but to me it means facing up to your self and what you believe in and want. I believe that once a person can recognize his or her true self he or she is in a better position to cope with ups and downs in life. Dianne, you have a lot to offer, personally and professionally. They need you over here, but obviously it will have to be your own decision. I would only suggest that you wait and try it for a few weeks before making up your mind. Come on now, why don't you go and get some sleep?"

James held his arm around Dianne's waist as he escorted her to the door. When he placed his hand on the doorknob to turn it Dianne looked up at him and said, "Thanks, brother. Thanks for listening to me."

She kissed him on the cheek and left the room.

Chapter 4: A Party, a Clue, a Dose of Gossip

A Party and a Brawl

Three weeks later, most of the volunteers were reasonably settled into their new posts. There were still many things to do, such as arranging to get the odd chair or table and in some cases finding a comfortable bed from somewhere. It was a Saturday evening and James Edward Johnson was in the process of cleaning his house before his visitors arrived. None of the five volunteers had seen much of each other during the first three weeks in Mzuzu. They had decided to meet at James's house on Saturday. It was, of course, a BYOB get together; each would bring what he or she fancied in the way of drinks. As James swept the last pile of litter through the kitchen door, which also happened to be his front door, his mind wandered.

"I've got to get something to get rid of these ants or they'll get rid of me. I wonder if they sell Real Kill termite spray around here? Maybe I will fork out the ten shillings for a bottle of Malawi gin. That stuff's so strong, I bet it would kill a horse, let alone a little old measly ant! If the boys back home could see me now. They wouldn't believe this place here. It's hilarious. . . Bathtub in the kitchen, kitchen sink outside, backdoor is a bedroom door and that corrugated tin roof. Gee, it's got a six-inch gap between it and the top of the wall. I lie on my sleeping bag and look straight out at the stars. At least the geckos are friendly. There are so many of the little creatures around here. I heard they are supposed to help keep the place free of insects. I wish they would do as good a job on the ants as they have done on those cockroaches. Those roaches are some of the biggest I've ever seen. Bigger than a half-dollar coin. Anyway, the guy at the Ministry of Housing said he would send somebody over next week to fix the cracks in the wall and ceiling. He is a stingy rascal, though. He would only give me one gallon of whitewash to paint this place. Hell, that one-gallon will be soaked up in the bedroom alone. I wish he could have given it to me last week. I could have had this place looking a little better tonight. I'm almost ashamed of it. I hear Jennifer is living in a modern four bedroomed bungalow with some other teachers and Bob Newgate is staying at the training center. They have nice facilities there. Talk about roughing it!"

After James swept the kitchen floor, he went outside to fetch a pail of water. The water was used to splash over the cracked concrete floor in order to dampen down the dust. By the time his guests would arrive, the floor would be dry. His house resembled nothing of western architectural familiarity. It was built in three stages years ago. Each floor level was a different height, resembling some crude form of split-level housing. The house was located about a mile north of Mzuzu on the main road. It lay about fifty yards off the road surrounded by trees and pineapple plants that conspicuously lined the dirt driveway. About five hundred yards in back of the house was a large community of line-houses where junior African civil servants lived. About three miles north of the house was a small village of mud-huts and thatch roofs.

The lowest level in the house contained a kitchen about six feet by eight feet. In this space, an old Victorian bathtub was hooked up to the water mains. The previous occupant left a pair of horrible looking green and purple shower curtains that cordoned off the bathtub from the rest of the room. Entering from the kitchen, steps led up about three feet to the next level, which contained a sizeable living room and a tiny bedroom. The last section was an eight feet by ten feet bedroom, which had a door at the side. The building formed roughly the shape of an L. The only furniture in the place was an old wooden chair. James complained furiously to the housing people. He asked for a bed, a couch, a kitchen table and two chairs. The Ministry of Housing was obliged to provide these basic facilities to the volunteers, but there was no time limit on this obligation. Some previous volunteers had waited over a year before they got furniture.

James soon found out that getting furniture and other supplies depended upon whom you knew and how many favors you were prepared to do for them. In some instances, outright cash was quite acceptable. He thought it was ridiculous that volunteers had to go through such red tape just to get a bed to sleep on. James was in the bedroom splashing water on the floor when he heard a knock at the kitchen door.

"Hold on a second. I'll be right there."

He placed the bucket in the corner of the room and dried his hands with a towel. When he reached the door, a short elderly man who held out a small book greeted him.

"Good evening, Bwana. I have come to be your cook and houseboy."

"My what?"

"Your cook, sir."

"Who sent you and what makes you think I need a cook?"

The man showed James his small book with recommendations from his previous employer, who was an official with the U.S. Agency for International Development.

"I cooked for Mr. Martin. See here, Bwana. I know what Americans like and I am a good cook. You will be a busy man and I can keep the place for you."

James was embarrassed because the man was trying so hard to sell himself. James contemplated the matter seriously.

"If there's one thing I'm not going to do, it's employ servants," James thought. "I did not come all the way over here to have my brothers serving me as if I were some colonialist. I'd feel as though I was supporting that old master/servant colonialist system they operated for so many years in this country. No! It's not my style. I mean. What would my folks and friends back home think if I told them I had a cook or a houseboy. First of all, it just doesn't go along with our jobs as Peace Corps Volunteers. Hell, we're supposed to rough it a little at least. Come to think of it. I didn't like

146

what I saw the first day I arrived in the country. I mean, Bill Humphries, our Peace Corps Director, what does he need seven servants for? I might have overlooked one or two of them, but seven! I felt embarrassed seeing those brothers running around all night saying 'yes, Bwana; no, Bwana. I'll get it right away, Bwana'. Not only Bill Humphries, but also most of the expatriate community out here seem to have a host of servants. Anyway, what can I tell this brother without being rude?"

James looked around at the man who was waiting patiently with a smile on his face. James detected a note of pleading in the man's small dark eyes and wondered what to say to him. Before he spoke, the man said in an urgent voice.

"Yes! Yes! Bwana. I will be your cook?"

There was a long pause before James replied.

"Please don't call me 'Bwana.' My name is James. Hell, you are almost old enough to be my grandfather. I should be calling you Bwana. What's your name anyway?"

"My name is Geoffrey, sir. Geoffrey Malango."

"Look, Geoffrey, you realized that I'm with the Peace Corps and we're just volunteers who came over to do certain jobs. We're not like the expatriates who have government contracts to work here and we do not have families here. Since I live alone, I don't need a cook or someone to clean up the house. You get my meaning?"

Geoffrey was determined not to be outdone by that little speech.

"Many volunteers have cooks and houseboys, Bwana James. It is a good thing for many Americans to come to Malawi because we get work. I need the work, Bwana. I have five children and a wife. Please don't feel shame to give us work. If you have no cook or houseboy, the Malawians will think you are not a kind man with your money and you will not have much respect."

Geoffrey's statement left James at a loss for words. Although he had no intention of changing his mind about hiring a cook he could not bring himself around to saying no to Geoffrey.

"Just as a matter of interest, how much money are you looking for, Geoffrey?"

"Mr. Martin paid me six pounds a month, sir."

"Stop calling me, sir! Six pounds a month? I couldn't pay you anywhere near that salary."

"I would accept less, Mr. James."

Geoffrey was not used to addressing employers or potential employers, however young, by first names only. After so many years of saying 'sir', 'Mister' or 'Bwana', he could not bring himself to call James by his first name alone.

"Well, I will have to think about it, Geoffrey. I'll make you no promise, but come by sometime next week and I'll let you know then."

Geoffrey seemed delighted and felt optimistic.

"Thank you! Thank you, Bwana! Ah, Mister James."

The old man was off in a flash. As he reached the end of the driveway near the main road, James noticed a woman waiting for him. She looked much younger and carried a baby strapped to her back. On top of her head was a basket filled with fruit and vegetables. She beckoned to someone playing near the trees and two small children ran out and joined her.

As they moved off swiftly, James thought, "They must be Geoffrey's family."

Soon after Geoffrey left, Stuart Steiner drove up the driveway on his Honda 90cc motorcycle. It was 6:45 p.m. Stuart was posted up near the border with Zambia so it had taken him a few hours to travel to Mzuzu. James had already told him he could stay the night, but that he would have to bring his own sleeping bag. Then James heard the roar of the machine and quickly went out into the garden.

"Stuart! I see you made it. How's every thing? Good to see you. man!"

They shook hands and Stuart said, "It's good to be here, James. The last three weeks seem to me like three years. You wouldn't believe where I'm posted. It's literally in the middle of nowhere. Hey, I hope you got some running water. It doesn't even have to be hot, just running."

"Sure, man, not only is it running and hot but it runs into a bathtub, too."

"A bathtub?"

"Yes a bathtub. That is, if you don't mind taking a bath in the kitchen."

"Heck, no! I'll take a bath in the middle of the street if it's hot and in a bathtub. Man, this is the Waldorf Astoria Hotel compared to where I'm living!"

Stuart took his sleeping bag and rucksack into the house and James showed him were he could sleep. They talked about several things while Stuart got a hot bath. Afterwards they went into the living room and sat on some old cushions spread out over the floor.

"At least you've got plenty of room here. It will look like a normal house once you get your furniture. You should see my place. It's wild, man! It has four walls made of wood and plaster about eight feet by six feet, two windows with no glass and no floor except the ground. Do you remember Phil Harrington's thatch roof hut? Well my house is exactly the same except larger. It's located just next to the clinic and when it rains too heavily I move into the clinic. I was thinking of swapping the hut for the clinic."

They both sat back and chuckled.

"Seriously, Stuart. Is it that bad? I mean, where do you cook and wash up?"

"I kid you not, James. It's that bad, but, you know, somehow I don't mind. I like the place. I've got two paraffin burners I use for cooking. They're very similar to yours except they don't have the stand and shelf space. Do you know where I wash in the clinic? It's well water and we use a hand pump to get it out. The people are real friendly to me, though. They bring me fruit, vegetables and sometimes, cooked chicken or fish. They call me 'Doctor Stu'. Can you believe that? I told them that I was not a doctor, but they insist on calling me that. The second night I was there, the village headman held a party for me. It was very interesting. First, the women danced around in a circle. Then, the men danced in a separate circle and I was pulled up to dance with them. I really felt strange being the only white person there. I tell you one thing, James, I was sick as hell the next morning. I don't know what they put into their brew, but it gave me the worst headache—not to mention the runs."

James was enjoying Stuart's tales of his first experiences at his new post. There was a certain kind of romanticism about living in an isolated post far away from the towns or cities. On the other hand, he was very happy with his own situation. He felt that two or three weeks in a place like Stuart's would be enough for him. He did not mind living rough for short periods of time, but not for two years. He asked Stuart if he wanted a drink before the others got there.

"Great! Have you got any wine?"

"Sure thing. I bought a gallon of red wine when I was in Blantyre. I can't guarantee that it's good stuff, but after the first glass, you can't tell the difference anyway. Did you run into much rain on your way down?"

Stuart's attention was on two geckos in the far corner of the room.

"Sorry, what's that you said?"

"I asked if you had much rain while travelling down."

150

"Hell, yes! One spot in the road was so bad that I had to push the motorcycle for about a mile before I could ride it again. That's why it took me so long. Luckily I'm getting a ride back tomorrow."

James was interested since he knew that Stuart had to get his motorcycle back too.

"How are you going to get your cycle back?"

"This girl I met about a week ago was travelling down to Blantyre in a Land Rover. She said she was coming back through here on Sunday. I told her that I would be in Mzuzu this weekend. She offered to give me a ride back and I explained that it wasn't necessary since I had my own transportation. She insisted. I thought, what the hell. A pretty girl like that could be enjoyable company."

"I didn't know you were such a lover boy, Stuart. Hey, this could turn into a real big thing for you. Does she live nearby?"

"Well, yes and no. It's strange, but she showed up at the clinic one morning and said she had heard there was a new volunteer there. She said she passed through the village often and decided to drop in and introduce herself. She lives across the border in Zambia and said she is a teacher. Her name is Janice Blanche."

James was so startled that he spilt his drink.

"Janice Blanche? Did you say Janice Blanche?"

"Yes. Do you know her?"

"I don't know. I met a woman on the plane when I was on my way to training. She said her name was Janice Blanche and that she worked in Zambia. Does she have silver-grey hair and does she smile a lot?"

Stuart paused momentarily to visualize Janice in his mind.

"She smiles all right, but her hair is sort of brown. It's definitely not silver-grey. Maybe it's the wrong name. Are you sure you remember her name?"

"I'm sure all right, because I will never forget the silver-grey hair on such a young face and I definitely remember the name."

"Never mind, James. You will see her in the morning because she is picking me up here. That's okay with you, isn't it?"

"No problem there. I look forward to meeting your mystery lady."

Just as James poured the wine, there were several beeps of a horn. Coming up the driveway was a red Mini Cooper with four girls inside. As they got out of the car, they looked around as if amused by the house and garden.

"Do you see what I see, Stuart?"

"Yes!"

Both walked quickly to the car to greet the girls. It was Jennifer and her three roommates. They had each brought something to drink. James and Stuart helped them carry their bags to the house.

"James and Stuart, meet Marg Prudhoe, Fiona Crewe and Chrissie Chipenbere, my room-mates. They are teachers, so you boys behave yourselves."

"Come on in and sit down, girls. Sorry about the no furniture business, but if one of you has a friend in the Ministry of Housing, it sure would help."

"Where are the others, James?" Jennifer asked in a way to keep the conversation flowing.

She was not sure how James would react to her bringing along the other girls, but she didn't think he would really mind.

"They will to be here soon. Here, let me hang up your raincoat."

Jennifer gave him her coat along with a hug. When he took the coat into the other room Jennifer looked at Stuart.

"How long have you been here, Stuart? What's it like where you live?"

He talked for the next fifteen minutes while James fixed drinks for the girls. Stuart was boring in groups and he didn't change on this occasion. Just as the last drink was handed to one of the girls, the sound of motorcycles could be heard coming up the driveway. It was Phil Harrington and Bob Newgate. There was a fresh wave of excitement as they entered the room and were introduced to the girls. Marg Prudhoe, who was from Manchester, England, took a liking to Bob right away.

She whispered to Jennifer, "He's smashing, isn't he?"

Fiona Crewe was from Newcastle, England. Chrissie Chipenbere was from the Southern part of Malawi. Marg was by far the liveliest and most aggressive of the girls. She had been in Mzuzu for over six months, but gave the impression that she had been there all her life. She knew just about everyone in Mzuzu and Blantyre—that is everyone in the expatriate community. She did not have much time for the Malawians. She drove the girls to the party in the car that belonged to her boyfriend, a white settler from Rhodesia. Stuart disliked her right away and showed it while James remained cool. He felt that since he was hosting the party he would try to be pleasant to her. Fiona Crewe was very different in personality and in manner. She was pleasant to talk to and gave the impression of being an honest person who knew herself. She and Chrissie got on great together. Jennifer watched these relationships closely during her first three weeks and decided to be wary of Marg, who manipulated and used people if she could. Bob had brought along a portable tape recorder with the latest rock & roll sounds. After the group talked for an hour, Bob turned up the music. Everyone quickly got into the groove and danced on the empty concrete floor.

The time was close to nine p.m. when Stuart asked James, "Do you mind if I smoke?"

"Hell, no. Everyone has been smoking all night. Why should I mind?"

"I'm smoking pot."

"Pot?"

"Yes, pot."

James looked worried and not too pleased.

"Hey, man, I don't know about that," James said. "I guess it's okay, but not in here. Suppose someone comes and finds pot here, we would be thrown out of the country tomorrow."

"That's not true. They don't give a damn if we smoke pot. Have you seen all of the plants growing around here? They smoke the stuff, too."

James was firm.

"Look here Stuart. I don't mind you having a smoke. But if you want one, you got to go out in the garden. That stuff stinks."

"Okay, James. Okay."

Before Stuart left, he asked if anyone wanted to join him.

"Yes, please," Marg replied.

She tried to persuade the other girls to join her but they refused.

"Party poopers," she exclaimed as she followed Stuart outside.

James went into the kitchen to get some more potato chips and peanuts. He could see Stuart and Marg through the kitchen window. They were passing the cigarette back and forth while Marg was cheerfully talking about something. He then felt a hand on his shoulder as he poured the peanuts into a bowl.

"You got a big place here, James. Bigger than I thought it would be. You like it here?"

"Yes, it's okay, Bob."

There was a long pause as both contemplated their next statements. James found it difficult to talk to Bob since he was aware of Bob's racist views.

"Do you like where you're staying, Bob?"

With a curious expression on his face, Bob did not know if James was trying to be sarcastic.

"You know, it is the typical run-down building sitting out in the open. It looks like those Tarzan movies, you know."

James smirked.

"You like those Tarzan movies don't you, Bob?"

Without considering the question.

"Sure thing, buddy. I think they're damn good."

"Yeah, I thought you did."

This last statement caught Bob unaware. He was furious with James for trapping him.

"Up your ass, James!"

"Up yours too, Bob!"

Bob who was slightly heavier in build than James and about an inch taller, stood back in a huff.

"You think you're so damn smart, don't you? You better watch yourself, boy!"

"Got to be smart with redneck rattlers like you jumping out of every bush. I've been meaning to tell you a thing or two anyway."

James stood back from Bob and held his clenched fist in a defensive posture.

"If this wasn't your house, boy, I'd take you out there and whip your arse," Bob said.

"I'd like to see you try it! You redneck, gutless son of a bitch! Come on. Let's go out in the yard and see how tough you are, you racist punk."

"Yeah, I'd be delighted, you black bastard!"

Marg and Stuart were sitting under a tree enjoying their highs when Bob and James came tussling out of the kitchen door.

Marg screamed, "Ah! They're fighting! They're fighting! Stop them!"

By this time the others had come out of the house. Bob and James were hitting each other blow for blow. Marg screamed again.

"Somebody break them up. They'll kill each other! Oh, it's so savage."

"Just cool it, girl," Stuart said. "They'll be okay. As soon as they get tired it will all be over. Anyway, both of them have been asking for this ever since they met. It will do them good."

As soon as Stuart stopped talking, the fight was over. It was hard to say who won since it was too dark to see the punches land. But they both could feel the effects of each other's punches.

Marg ran over to Bob and tried to comfort him. He pushed her aside. Jennifer went over to James.

"You all right?"

"I'll be fine."

156

"Come on in and let me see your face."

"I'll be just fine, Jennifer. Thanks anyway."

Bob's shirt was torn and he had bruises on his face. He walked slowly toward his motorcycle.

"I'm getting out of here. Fuck this shit! I'm going home."

James was at the kitchen door and walked back toward Bob.

"Don't be a damn fool, Bob! You can't go home like that. Why don't you come on back in and get cleaned up? Hell, it's still early and I don't feel like fighting you any more tonight. Anyway, we're about even now."

After moaning another five or ten minutes, Bob was persuaded by the girls to come back into the party. Someone turned the music up and the girls asked the guys to dance primarily to help loosen the tension created by the fight. After about three dances they all sat down. James and Bob did not talk to each other and Stuart, as usual, didn't have much to say in a crowd. This left the onus on Phil, who hadn't said much all night. He sat next to Fiona Crewe trying to think of something to say. Finally, he came up with something appropriate.

"What subjects do you teach, Fiona?"

"I teach maths and geography."

"Are you a teacher, Phil?"

"No. I'm a health worker in a clinic."

Fiona could tell that Phil was shy with girls and appeared to be at a loss for words so she continued the conversation.

"Do you like your work, Phil?"

"So far, yes."

"Sometimes I wish I could have worked in a village setting. It must be interesting."

Several moments passed before Phil responded. He thought it was about time that he asked a few questions, but feared he might say the wrong thing.

"Have you been here long, Fiona?"

"No, Phil. I arrived about two weeks before you did."

"Then you must not have had the chance to see many villages and clinics."

"To be honest, I haven't. I've been so busy settling into the school and working on lesson plans that I've not really been anywhere."

Before Phil could stop the flow of words from his mouth, he had actually made his first date.

"Would you like to come out to see my clinic sometime?"

"Oh! How nice of you to ask, Phil."

He could not believe how easy it was to ask a girl for a date.

He thought for a moment, "That wasn't as difficult as I had imagined. Gee whiz, folks! The new Casanova from Bismarck, North Dakota."

After that very bold move on Phil's part, he found it was easy talking to Fiona for the rest of the party.

In the meantime, James was engrossed in conversation with Jennifer and Chrissie. He was trying to explain how he felt about having a cook. Chrissie assured him that most expatriates, most high-ranking Malawians and volunteers hired people to help out. She felt that there was nothing wrong with hiring Malawians as houseboys and cooks as long as they were paid the going rate and were treated with respect. She too detested these "latter-day neo-

158

colonialist mentalities" in which the master treated the servants as slaves. James asked her whether he should hire this man Geoffrey Malango or whether he should wait and meet a few other prospective employees. She suggested he wait and choose from several. She also knew that he would not have to wait long, because once word got around that new foreigners had arrived, people would come by in dozens looking for jobs.

More than half an hour went by before Jennifer, sounding like a schoolmarm chastising her pupils, said, "Come on, you two. Shake hands and come out smiling. You ought to be satisfied now that you almost beat each other senseless."

With a little encouragement from the rest of the gang and a few smiles thrown in for good measure, Bob and James begrudgingly shook hands. The two British girls and the Malawian girl were amused and rather flabbergasted over the entire scenario. They wondered how two guys who were entangled in such a fierce brawl were able to shake hands afterwards and act as if the incident never happened.

The party broke up when Marg Prudhoe said, "Come on, girls. I had better get Jerry's car back to him before he gets too worried."

Then she looked at James and said, "Literally a smashing event, James."

He didn't catch the joke until everyone else laughed. On their way out, Marg invited Bob Newgate over to her place for dinner one night. About the same time, Phil made definite arrangements to take Fiona out to his clinic. James and Stuart stood outside until they all left.

"Whew! That was a hell of a night, wasn't it Stuart?"

"Yes, I haven't seen a knock down drag out fight like that since 'Hop Along Cassidy'. I was worried about you two for a minute there. Actually, Bob deserved every bit of what you gave him. Maybe you knocked some sense into his head."

James felt his own head.

"The way I feel now, I think it's vice versa. I've got a splitting headache. What did you think of Jennifer's roommates?"

"They were okay, except Marg. She's a high flier, or tries to be. She's too stuck on herself and I don't care for her attitude toward the Malawians."

"Stuart, you're too good to be true. Do you really feel that way, or are you just saying those things around me?"

Stuart's face grimaced.

"Well, if you are asking me if I'm a liberal, James, I'm not. I just don't like to see people kicked around. We Jews have been kicked around for a long time now, and as far as my generation is concerned, never again!"

On that note, Stuart turned solemn and quiet.

About fifteen minutes went by before they went to bed in their sleeping bags. Stuart used the small bedroom next to the living room. The house was so empty of furniture and other paraphernalia that voices could be heard straight through the place. Lying in his room atop his sleeping bag, James called out.

"What's she like, Stuart?"

"What's who like?"

"Janice Blanche."

"Oh, she's nice, man. Smart looking girl and got smarts upstairs, too. Why do you ask?"

"Just curious, you know. Wondering what different people are doing out here. That's all."

"I know she teaches math, economics and a few other subjects in a mission school."

A long pause prevailed.

"Do you think she's religious, Stuart?"

"Hell, how do I know? I only met her briefly. I'm going to sleep if you don't mind."

It was ten o'clock the next morning before James managed to drag himself out of the sleeping bag. The torrential rains pounded the corrugated tin roof causing his head to throb even more. He pulled the bedroom window curtains back and the light caused his eyes to squint. He then went over to look into a small mirror hanging on the back of the door.

"Ah, I look horrible. Look at my eyebrow stained with blood. I feel awful. Too much wine and beer don't mix well."

When he finished thinking out loud, he went to the kitchen and turned the water on in the bathtub. By this time Stuart had awoken. The noise of the running water bothered him. He quickly put on his shirt and trousers and wanted to know the time. It was twenty past ten. Janice was supposed to pick him up about 10:30. Actually it was closer to eleven o'clock when Janice arrived at the house. The grey open-back Land Rover was covered in mud as she parked close to the house. James was not sure why he felt something ominous about meeting Janice Blanche. He chalked it up to the fact that she might just be the person he had met on the plane, and if so, why did she look different now?

"Stuart, why don't you go out and show her in? I'll put on some coffee."

"Okay, but why all the ceremony? Why are you so nervous?"

"I'm not nervous."

Stuart went out to greet Janice and they talked for several moments before coming into the house. At the same time, James peered out of the kitchen window studying Janice's face. She was young with brown hair and very attractive.

"Is that her or not?" James thought. "The nose and mouth look the same, but I can't really tell about the rest of her. Janice was slightly heavier than this girl. Oh well, here she comes. I'll know in a moment."

Janice walked into the kitchen, followed by Stuart. She smiled as they stood there looking at each other. He was not sure whether to greet her as if they knew each other or wait to be introduced. She continued to smile and gave no sign of familiarity.

"Janice, this is James."

"Hi, James. I am pleased to meet you."

As they shook hands he stared into her face.

"Is something wrong?" she asked.

"Oh no, no, sorry. You must think I'm rude. It's just that I thought we'd met before. Come in, Janice. I have to apologize for not having chairs to sit on, but the cushions are comfortable. Can I get you a cup of coffee?"

"Yes, thank you."

"How do you take it?"

"Black. Thank you."

James prepared coffee while the two sat in the living room talking. Stuart seemed more stimulated than ever while talking with Janice. James did not know what to think.

"She looks a little like the woman I met, but she must not be. If she were, I'm sure she would have remembered me. It's just too much

162

of a coincidence that two girls named Janice Blanche live in Zambia and that they resemble each other. If it was her I talked to, why then was she disguising herself? Gee! I have seen this woman before! It was at Danks Disco in San Diego. She was with two men that night. Hell, I'm not crazy! I wonder what's going on here."

James took the coffee into the living room and sat down on a cushion. They chatted about the weather and Janice's trip to Blantyre. He asked her about her school. He noticed that this woman was a lot less talkative and more restrained than the woman he talked to on the plane. He felt that she guarded and controlled what she said.

"I know this is a stupid question, but have we met before?"

"Not that I remember," she replied.

He waited for her to say something else, but she kept her cool.

"The reason I asked is that you look like someone I met once when flying to California."

Janice smiled.

"Sorry, it could not have been me, because I've never been to California."

James was absolutely stunned and at a loss for words. His mind ticked over quickly.

"Either I'm a poor judge of faces or this woman is lying. I might not be sure about the woman I met on the plane, but I'm sure I saw this one at Danks Disco."

After a long pause in which everyone was embarrassed, James persevered.

"How did you come to be a teacher in Zambia, Janice?

"I applied for the job. You're very curious!"

"Oh, sorry! I don't want to sound nosey. Perhaps we should change the subject. Will it take you long to drive back to Zambia?"

Janice answered the question and they talked for another twenty minutes before she indicated to Stuart that they should be off. Stuart put his motorcycle in the back of the Land Rover and, soon after, they were ready to leave.

"You should come up to visit me. I'll show you some real bush country living."

"Sure thing, Stuart. In fact, I start my tour of the regional clinics in about three weeks. I'll be up your way about then. I will drop you a line before I come, though. In the meantime, take care of yourself."

"Okay, you too, And, hey, stay clear of Bob! You guys could give us a bad reputation."

Although James was not amused, he decided to smile.

"It was nice meeting you, James," Janice said. "I am sure we will see you again."

"Me, too, Janice. Have a safe trip."

She started the Land Rover and drove off quickly. James stood there in his front yard. As he waved goodbye to them, he considered Janice's last statement.

"I heard that before. That's what the other Janice said when we parted at Los Angeles International Airport. There's something strange going on. I can't figure it out."

Still suffering from a hangover and a few bruises, he went back into the house and lay on his sleeping bag. As he dozed off to sleep, the heavy showers slowly abated, followed by brilliant sunshine. Grasshoppers cricked in the lush green garden while dogs could be heard barking in the nearby village. The rainy season was in full swing and showers were almost predictable. It would rain for about twenty minutes followed by about forty minutes of dryness. This pattern seemed to occur almost continuously. He slept solidly for four hours. When he woke up it was raining. Momentarily forgetting the timing of rainfall, he thought it had rained all day. He was starving. Having missed his lunch, he set about the kitchen to whip up some fried eggs and rice. A sparse eater, he had lost more than seven pounds since arriving in Mzuzu.

"I'd better start eating properly or I will wither away," he thought as he tucked his loose fitting shirt into his jeans. By five o'clock he had eaten dinner and washed the dishes. He then sat down to write a second letter to his parents. About halfway through his letter he heard a soft tap on the kitchen door. He went to the door and there stood Jennifer Nolan in a yellow waterproof raincoat with a hood attached. She wore jeans and a pair of hiking boots.

"Hi! Just thought I would call in to see how you're doing today."

"Jennifer, come in."

He helped her take off her raincoat.

"Want something to drink? Coffee? Tea? Something stronger?"

"I wouldn't mind a cup of tea. Thanks."

While he prepared the tea, they talked.

"What's happening, Jennifer? What brings you around this way today?"

"Oh, I felt like a walk, so I decided to drop in on my way back."

"It's a long way to walk, isn't it?"

"It's about three miles, but I've enjoyed it. What do you think of the girls? By the way, I want to apologize for bringing them without first asking you."

"Oh, you don't have to apologize for that. I'm glad you brought them. Anyway, looks like Phil finally found himself a girl. I like Fiona and Chrissie, but I've got reservations about that other one."

He handed the coffee to Jennifer and sat next to her on a cushion.

"What do you think about them, Jennifer?"

"I like Chrissie and Fiona. Marg is a bit different. She will take some getting used to. She's very gossipy, you know. Already she's told Jerry, her boyfriend, and a crowd of other people about what happened last night. She tends to exaggerate things."

Jennifer went on to explain that Marg had played tennis at the Gymkhana Club that morning and she told everyone she knew that the Americans got drunk and fought like cats and dogs. She even lied about who smoked pot, saying that everyone except her participated. Jennifer was furious after hearing Marg's version from the headmistress of the school. Jennifer told Marg how deceitful she was and that she would not invite her to any other affairs. James then expressed his contempt for Marg.

"That lying bitch! I knew the minute she stepped into the room last night that she couldn't be trusted. I didn't like the way she tooted up her nose at everybody, except Bob. Those two would make a great pair, wouldn't they? I mean they're two right-wing racists and they knew it the instant they met!"

"Well, I don't know about that, but I do know that I've had it with her and so have the other girls."

"Tell me, Jennifer, what's this Gymkhana Club all about?"

"It's a huge place up on the hill. They've got tennis courts, a swimming pool, a golf course, and a football field. However rugby is played more often than soccer. I hear it's a membership system and only a few Malawian ministers and Army officers are members. Otherwise it's mainly white expatriates."

"Sounds like a cliquish place where all the whites go."

"It is. From what I hear the few Malawians who are members very seldom go up there and the membership fees are so high that most Malawians can't afford to join. Also, a member has to sponsor new applicants so it's easy to select out the Malawians."

"You know, this is a damn shame! I mean, why does President Makube allow this sort of thing to continue in his country? After all, it's supposed to be an independent country now. It all makes me sick!"

Jennifer didn't answer the question. Instead, she told James about some other gossip she heard through the grapevine.

"Marg told me that there was some fighting about ten miles north of here last night. According to her boyfriend, the Malawi Army killed or captured twelve of Chief Katumbi's men. He said the battle lasted about two hours and one Malawi soldier was killed. Marg thinks the Chief and his men ought to be hunted down and hanged. I don't agree with her. Not that I know much about it, but it seems to me that Chief Katumbi has a point. He wants to share what little wealth there is more evenly among the people. He also wants democratic elections. Perhaps I'm talking too much. I could get into trouble talking like this."

James was quite intrigued with Jennifer's statements.

"There are a lot of things I'm beginning to notice. The top civil servants driving around in Mercedes-Benzes and getting all the perks while most of the people live in poverty. There is a residential community near Blantyre City that is reserved for whites from Rhodesia and South Africa. They are even allowed to import their own apartheid. I understand that this country is poor and has to rely on aid from elsewhere, but to me, there's no reason why President Makube should allow racism and discrimination in his own country. Do you know that he is the only African head of state that publicly courts the racist regimes of Rhodesia and South Africa? He has been called the Uncle Tom of Africa."

Jennifer had been sitting up and then she stretched out and lay on her side. In a rather agreeable tone of voice she said, "This is the first time I've heard you talk like this, James. You really do have deep convictions about what's happening here in Malawi. I admit, I have often wondered whether you were conservative in your opinions, but at the same time I know you're not a radical. Perhaps you're somewhere in the center like me."

He mused over her comments for quite a while.

"Tell me, Jennifer, what makes you unsure of whether I am conservative? If you thought that, others must too. I mean, how do I come off, as some nice guy who will not rock the boat?"

"No. I didn't mean it that way. It's just that up until now, you've not expressed any political opinions. I've seen you irritated about one or two things, but you seem to have changed since you've been here."

"Well, perhaps I'm beginning to open my eyes to what's going on around me. Talking about changing, you've done a fair amount of that since I first met you. All to the good I'm pleased to say. When I first met you, you were one of the shyest people I'd ever met. Now look at you. You are confident, opinionated and you even have a touch of aggression. Maybe this Peace Corps experience is affecting us all. By the way, since you're so good at classifying people in political terms, how would you place Stuart Steiner?"

Jennifer thought about it for a while before answering.

"To me, Stuart is an island unto himself. He closes people out and is very selective about who he confides in. It's interesting that out of all the people in the program, he's had more to do with you. It must be your trustful eyes, James. Ha! Seriously though, I think Stuart has very radical ideas and he's angry. I don't claim to be an expert judge of character, but to me, Stuart Steiner is dangerous."

James was surprised at that statement.

"Dangerous?"

"Yes. Dangerous and shrewd, too. He's the kind of guy who would fight to the death for a revolutionary cause. He once told me that he would not go to Vietnam even if he were drafted, but he would fight for Israel."

"Stuart, fight in a real war? I can't imagine it."

"Maybe you should listen to him more carefully and read between the lines."

James lay back on his elbow and gazed into the ceiling while thinking about what Jennifer had said.

"You know, Jennifer, you've got a lot more insight into things than I thought you had. That little brain of yours is ticking over pretty good. You probably got me beat by a neuron or two. Gee. We've had an interesting conversation today with eye-openers all around."

"Yes. I did not expect us to get this involved in political talk."

"Well, as long as we keep it among ourselves, we will be all right. You should watch that roommate of yours, though. Marg will twist any thing you say around."

Jennifer smiled.

"Yes, I thought of that already, James."

"Good."

Although it was light outside, the evening sun was setting slowly. Jennifer's hike back to her house would take about forty minutes. She decided to set off. James went into his room to get her raincoat. She stepped up two feet into his room and remarked.

"It is barren, isn't it?"

"You're telling me. It's a damn shame not to have a proper bed to sleep on. Here, I'll help you with this."

"Thanks."

"You sure you don't want a ride back on my motorcycle?"

She turned to face him after he helped her with the raincoat.

"Thanks, but no. I'll be okay and the walk will do me good. My, your face is all scratched up. You have a cut over your right eye. Come here and let me see to it."

He moved his head in the opposite direction.

"Oh, it's nothing but a scratch. It will be okay."

"Have you dressed it and cleaned it with an antibiotic, James?"

"I don't need that stuff. Anyway, stop trying to mother me and get along home before it gets dark."

Jennifer was insistent and urged James to get his first-aid kit so that she could dress the wound before she left. After a couple of minutes of haggling she finally got him to lay back on a cushion while she cleaned and dressed the cut over his eye.

"That should hold you until tomorrow when you're going to see a doctor. Okay?"

"Okay, Nurse Jennifer. Thanks."

She then patted his cheeks with two hands and, to his surprise, plopped a big kiss right on his lips. She jumped up.

"I'm off now. I'll see you next week."

He was so stunned by what had just occurred that he did not see her leave.

RT3—A Clue

Janice Blanche arrived at the refugee camp at 7:30 Monday morning. Frank Myosa was on a three-week visit to East Germany and Russia, so Joni Matabelli, ZINAP's second in command, summoned everyone to an emergency meeting with Chief Katumbi. Sam Hernandez joined them. Gathered around an old weather beaten table in the administration building they discussed the incidents that occurred the previous Saturday night when several of the Chief's men were killed or captured. The Chief spoke emotionally.

"My men are badly trained and ill equipped and we must have more money and support from ZINAP. We cannot hope to win a battle with the archaic weapons we used. Isn't there anyway ZINAP can increase its support for us? After all, if we are successful, then you will be successful."

Joni Matabelli who chaired the meeting, cautiously replied.

"Chief Katumbi, you must understand the position we are in. We also need more funds for our operations here. Frank Myosa is trying to establish some useful contacts that could help your cause by providing equipment and advice. You can see yourself how low our own food supplies are. When Frank returns he should be able to tell you something more concrete. In the meantime, I would suggest that you restrain your operations across the border. After all, if you want to topple that puppet regime in Malawi, you will have to deploy your forces much more efficiently."

The Chief resented the last suggestion.

"I think my operations are efficient. Under the circumstances, what else would you expect?"

"Please do not take offense, Chief Katumbi. I did not mean to insult you. What I intended to convey was the need to adopt a more precise strategy. Sending men across the border using guerrilla warfare tactics is not a good strategy given the present circumstances. The Malawi Army has about 2,700 troops and only three hundred of them are based in the Northwest to guard the border. Already your forces amount to a third of their troop strength and, given several more months, you could have a well-trained army of over half their present strength. You will waste lives, time and money with these hit and run tactics. I suggest you plan a swift take-over in one attempt. It may take almost a year to plan and execute the operation, but in some respects this would be more advantageous because it would allow time to increase recruitment, training and financial support."

The Chief then turned to his men and discussed what was said in their own language. Several minutes passed as they nodded sometimes in agreement and at other times disapprovingly. He then turned back to Joni Matabelli and spoke.

"What you say makes sense, but there are a number of constraints facing us. For instance, we do not know how to get outside support for our cause. Who would we turn to? Secondly, your proposed strategy for a swift coup d'état will require considerable intelligence. We do not have the means to gather this information."

"I can make no promises, Chief Katumbi, but I am confident that Frank Myosa will agree to provide you the help you need."

Both Janice Blanche and Sam Hernandez remained quiet during these discussions. It was ZINAP's policy that only the Chairman spoke unless others were asked to make a contribution. They knew the Chief well and on previous occasions had discussed a number of things with him at great length, but protocol was strictly adhered to in these meetings. The Chief asked Joni Matabelli if he could ask Janice a question.

"Yes, you may, sir."

"You have just returned from Malawi, Janice. What have you learned about President Makube's reaction to our latest incursions?"

Janice pulled her chair closer to the table and folded her hands in her lap. She spoke in a relaxed but authoritative tone.

"Sir, from what I have been told the President intends to deploy an additional two hundred men to the Northwest region. They will not be based at the barracks outside Mzuzu. They will set up camps along a twenty-mile stretch on each side of the border post. In addition, Army personnel and police will check all vehicles entering

172

from Zambia into Malawi. They are tightening the reigns, so to speak, in order to catch or restrict the movement of your men. This latest development could prove to be beneficial in the long run."

"Why do you say that, Janice?" the Chief asked curiously.

"Well, sir, assuming you were to take Joni Matabelli's suggestion of restraining your activities for several months until you have a larger force, I believe that General Makube would withdraw those troops after several months of inactivity. In nine months to a year's time, three hundred men will only guard the Northwest region. A well executed battle plan could make this one of the easiest targets."

Chief Katumbi, who was an obese elderly man with grey hair, sat back and considered Janice's comments for a few moments. Then he spoke to his men again and turned to Sam Hernandez.

"You are a man of the world and understand these things. Tell me, do you think there is much chance of us getting support such as weapons and supplies from other sources? You know our goals and objectives."

Sam seemed nervous and hesitated before he answered the Chief. He knew that questions like that should be asked through Frank or Joni, and since he worked for ZINAP not the Chief, he did not feel obliged to answer it fully.

"There is a chance, of course, but with all due respect, sir, you can appreciate that I am not in a position to elaborate further. Nevertheless, I will add that often those willing to provide support are looking for something in return and they would want to feel confident that such concessions would be forthcoming."

"What do you mean, Mr. Hernandez?"

"Well, speaking in general terms, for example, the Eastern European communist countries, while obviously concerned politically with enhancing communism, are more interested in long term business and financial opportunities. They would want contracts for infrastructure development, concessions on oil, minerals and mining rights if such resources are abundant, and research and defense facilities. Therefore, and this is hypothetical, if they offered you aid and you were successful in coming to power in Malawi, obviously they would want the first option in any development schemes. They would be highly disappointed if you turned to the Western countries instead. This is why it is important for a man in your position to develop a political agenda based on Communism or strong socialist principals. If the Russians, East Germans or Cubans for that matter, are not sure of your political and economic aims, they would be hesitant to give you assistance."

Sam Hernandez stopped talking at that point as he felt he had said enough. He watched the Chief as he considered Sam's comments and then discussed them with his men.

At the same time, Sam talked in a whisper to Joni Matabelli, "I hope I did not say too much but I felt there were some facts of life the Chief should face up to. Let's face it, you don't get something for nothing nowadays."

Joni agreed with Sam and hinted that Sam handled the Chief's question very well. Joni was slightly annoyed at the Chief for asking such a direct and loaded question. Normally, that's the type of policy question reserved for meetings between Frank Myosa and the Chief. In fact, Chief Katumbi had heard exactly the same answer from Frank Myosa before he left for Eastern Europe. It was as if the Chief was double-checking.

A few minutes passed before the Chief finished his conversation with his men. He turned to the three sitting opposite him at the table.

"We will not have the Russians, Cubans or anyone else dictating policy to us. We don't want to be communist puppets. That's not much different from President Makube, who is a capitalist puppet. When we come to power in Malawi we would prefer to stay non-aligned. That means doing business with everyone, except for those racist regimes in the South. We already have too much imported political ideology in Africa and I don't think it is good for us. I am a socialist, but not in the European sense of the words. I believe in

174

African Socialism, which takes into account African culture, and tradition. Now, Mr. Hernandez, do you think the Russians or for that matter your own government in Cuba, would accept that?"

Sam thought seriously before answering.

"Chief Katumbi, sir, you must accept that I am not in a position to answer for the Cuban government or any other, for that matter. I think this is a matter you should take up with Frank Myosa when he returns. However, I hope you did not misunderstand me earlier. I do not want to give you the impression that because a government receives aid from another country that it is a puppet regime."

Chief Katumbi and his delegation stayed for another hour discussing other issues. When he left the meeting, he was much calmer than when he first came. The Chief had been upset over the recent loss of his troops. He felt that things were going desperately wrong. Hence the urgency of this meeting and his almost reluctant acceptance of some of the alternatives placed before him that morning. He knew that if he was ever going to make any in-roads into Malawi, he needed help on a different scale altogether. The Chief was often heard remarking, "I'm not a military tactician, just an old politician."

It was true. Neither he nor his followers knew very much about modern conventional warfare. Most of what they learned was through ZINAP. Hence when Joni Matabelli spoke of 'new strategies and battle plans' the Chief felt uncomfortably inadequate. He was also astute enough to realize that he would have to pay a high price for communist support, but in his old but regal manner, he was stubborn enough to put up a good verbal argument against what he considered to be foreign intrusions into African politics.
At nine thirty that morning, Joni suggested that they break for coffee and meet again in one hour. Janice had not eaten breakfast and said that she was going to get breakfast.

"What time are you taking the girls for drill practice, Janice?"

"I normally take them out at eleven o'clock on Mondays."

"Well," Joni replied, "in that case, why don't we meet after lunch today because there are a number of things to discuss."

"Okay, that's better for me."

One of Janice's pupils came up to her.

"Good morning, Miss Blanche."

"Good morning, Chiwa. How are you today?"

"I am fine. Can I be a Squad Leader today, Miss Blanche?"

Janice smiled as she looked down on the thirteen-year-old girl.

"Why do you want to lead the squad so soon, Chiwa? You know the rules. As the older girls move up in rank, the younger ones can replace them. Be patient, my dear, you will have your turn. Now, how are you getting on with your fractions?"

"I am learning, Miss Blanche, but I am having problems with multiplications."

"Well, you continue to study those exercises I gave you and you will get better at it. If you have any problems just ask me about them."

"Thank you, Miss Blanche."

There was a long silence as Janice walked along with the girl. Then the girl looked up at Janice.

"Why do you stay and help us, Miss Blanche?"

The question was challenging to Janice because she had not considered her motives in a long time. She really did not know why she stayed on at the refugee camp but she did not want to tell Chiwa that.

"Oh, well, I enjoy working here, Chiwa."

176

"Don't you get lonesome for home?"

"Yes, I do. My, you're asking a lot of questions this morning, Chiwa."

"I am sorry, Miss Blanche."

"Oh, no need to be sorry."

Several moments passed.

"Miss Blanche, are you ever going to marry someday?"

"Chiwa!"

"I'm sorry again, but some of the girls and I noticed that you do not have a man friend and we thought you were lonesome."

"Well you tell the girls that I'm not lonesome and I am happy in my work. Now you shouldn't be so concerned about me. In fact, you girls should have enough other things to keep your wandering minds occupied, such as your fractions and decimals. Now run along and I'll see you at drill practice."

"Yes, Miss Blanche."

Janice stood for several moments watching the hills and mountains in the far distance. They reminded her of her own isolation both emotionally and physically. Her pupil had just asked a pertinent question which to Janice was a very private concern. Not only had she sublimated her reasons for working at the school and camp, but she had for some time chosen to ignore her own loneliness.

"I'm used to being lonely," Janice thought. "I've never been in love before so I really don't know what I'm missing. There's just an emptiness down there deep in my heart. Oh, Chiwa! Why did you ask me those questions, child? Loneliness hurts but empty loneliness is misery. I did not love my husband, Peter, nor did he love me. I guess both of us knew at the time we married that it would not last. I wish I could have been loved or if I could have loved someone. Dad was always away and Mom too busy with her social life to care about me. Perhaps that's why I stay here. At least I have a cause although it's not mine personally. I love those mountains and hills over there. I love this beautiful land. Oh! If I could find someone to love and if he loved me, too."

The midday rain showers pounded mercilessly upon the canvass canopies covering the caches of guns and ammunition, which had just arrived on two trucks. Seven men including a Brit accompanied the trucks. They each had either a pistol or a machine gun on their person and looked as though they were ready for action. The Brit got out of the cab of the truck and was accompanied by a machine-gun toting African. Parked just outside the guarded entrance to the refugee camp, the Brit went up to the guards.

"I'm looking for Mr. Hernandez. Tell him RT3 is here."

"RT3, sir?"

"Yes. RT3 and be quick about it!"

One of the guards dashed off in the rain to get Sam Hernandez. The other guard stood there watching curiously but nervously. None of the men on the lorry smiled nor did they say a word. They looked as though they would kill if the guard as much as flicked his eyelash. The guard was petrified but to his relief Sam Hernandez arrived accompanied by Joni Matabelli and several men.

As they approached the gate the Brit said, "Sam Hernandez?"

"Yes, that's me."

"How's your brother?"

"See no more."

"Okay. Sign here please."

Sam signed the receipt after giving the passwords. He always used codes when transacting business and chose them in such a way that

178

no one could break them. For instance, using his brother's blindness. The codes were used so that the guns would not he delivered to the wrong person. It wasn't the location that mattered but the person. Sam could have been anyone as far as the courier was concerned, so to protect Sam's interest as well as those of the gunrunners, this method proved useful. Sam never forgot the time when he was knocked over the head just prior to the arrival of a shipment of guns. Someone else posed in his place and got away with thousands of dollars worth of weapons.

The Brit gave a few hand signals to his drivers. They started the engines and waited. He then turned to Sam.

"Check them here or inside the gate?"

"Inside."

Then he motioned the drivers to drive through the gate.

"Over there is okay, RT3?"

"Right!" the Brit shouted. "Okay, boys! Pull the tops off! Let's hurry now. We got to move soon."

The canvas tops were off in a matter of minutes. Then Sam, Joni and the Brit climbed on top of the lorries and began to inventory the stocks. The unloading took about an hour. As soon as all was finalized, Joni offered the Brit and his men tea.

"No, thanks, old chap. We gotta be moving."

He got into the cab of the lorry and they left in a hurry with not as much as a good-bye or a wave.

Joni turned to Sam and asked, "Why are they in such a hurry?"

"I don't know really. Either they have another delivery to make today or they ran into a bit of trouble back on the road. Normally, the Zambian security forces don't check our supplies. I wonder if they ran into some of President Makube's forces that crossed over into Zambia. That would of course be a breach of territorial integrity. Maybe we should send some scouts out to investigate the border area. With what happened Saturday night, I would not be surprised if the Malawian Army was bold enough to cross over into Zambia, probably in disguise."

Joni knew that this was highly probable and he became worried at the prospect of Malawian forces raiding the refugee camp.

"Sam, it frightens me that you could be correct in your judgment. I must call a meeting of my platoon commanders and put this place on battle alert. I will send out scouts to find out what is happening out there and I will inform Chief Katumbi of the situation. On the other hand, I can't imagine the Malawians risking a break in diplomatic relations with Zambia over a small band of armed men."

Sam thought for a while and then replied, "Perhaps they perceive the threat to be greater than it is Joni. They don't know how many trained men the Chief has. Obviously, if President Makube thinks that the Chief's forces are powerful enough to overthrow him, then he would stop at nothing, including the risk of severing diplomatic relations with Zambia to save his own government."

"You're probably right, Sam. Come. I must hurry now. I will meet with you this afternoon."

They both walked through the gate together and then split up. Joni Matabelli went off toward the administration building while Sam checked over the new cache of weapons. During the rest of the day Joni sent out seven small squads of three to four soldiers each. They went north and south on the main road and east and west through the bush and hills. Each squad included a good distance runner since only two jeeps were available. About six o'clock that evening Sam Hernandez walked over to Janice, as she was about to get into her Land Rover.

"Oh, Janice, can I catch a lift back to Lukabi with you? I promised those two American guys a drink on me tonight."

"Sure, Sam, hop in."

180

"Oh, I forgot my cigars. I won't be a minute."

Sam took about five minutes to go to his room, fetch his cigars and change his shirt.

"That's the longest minute I've ever waited," Janice said.

"Sorry, Janice, you know how it is sometimes."

"No bother, Sam."

The puddles of mud and water seemed to have deepened during the day as Janice drove out of the camp. Darkness was falling as they drove out along the partially wet road. The rains had stopped and the evening air was damp and hot. They chatted for most of the five-mile trip. But suddenly about a mile outside of Lukabi Sam shouted.

"What's that over there?"

"What?"

"Over there! Look at the lights shining up in the sky."

Janice stopped the Land Rover and they both sat there for several minutes looking in the direction of the lights.

"They look like headlamps on a vehicle of some kind. But headlamps don't shine upwards. Not unless the vehicle has turned over or something. I'm going over there, Janice."

"No, wait. It could be dangerous."

"You stay here. If something happens you can go and get help."

"But you don't have a gun on you."

Janice put her hand under the seat and pulled out a .45 revolver.

"Here, take this. You might need it."

"Thanks."

Sam quietly got out of the vehicle and slowly climbed a small hill on the side of the road. The lights were no more than fifty yards away, but they seemed miles away to Sam who sweated profusely. When he got to the top of the hill, he suddenly heard a rock fall behind him. He jumped around quickly with the revolver pointing in the direction of the noise. It was nothing but rocks sliding under his weight. Nervously peering down the other side of the hill, he saw a lorry resting almost perpendicular to a small cliff. It was too dark to see anything but the lights and the shape of the truck from where he stood. There was still another twenty-five yards to go before he reached the truck.

"Oh my Jesus! What happened here? That's the truck that RT3 was in!"

After counting four dead bodies on the ground he noticed two more in the truck's cab. Since it was upright he could not readily see their faces. Then all of a sudden an arm drooped out of the window. It was a white arm.

"That's RT3! What the hell happened here? I'd better get back to Janice so that we can get back to camp. This is no accident. These guys were ambushed!"

Sam hurried back to the Land Rover and explained what he had seen.

"Let's get back to camp quickly. Whoever did this must still be around here somewhere!"

The drive back to camp only took twenty minutes. Janice drove right through the gate up to the administration building. They both jumped out and ran inside.

"Joni!" Sam shouted. "Something terrible happened out on the road near Lukabi. RT3 and some of his men have been killed. It looks like an ambush to me."

Joni and the two other men in the room were startled.

"What! RT3? I'll get some of the men to go out there. This ties in with one report we received today. One of the squads along the Zambia-Malawi road reported seeing suspicious troop movements. They spotted two lorries from a distance. They also saw what could have been a piece of heavy artillery being pulled by a truck. They could not be sure because it was covered with canvas. Later they found an empty bottle of Malawi gin. What do you make of that Sam?"

"I don't know, but if they've got heavy artillery, they're not here just to hunt down a few men. They've come to do serious damage and there objective might be this camp."

On that note, Joni Matabelli, second in command of ZINAP forces, ordered full alert and immediate evacuation of the camp. Most of the women and children were ordered to leave the camp taking only food and necessities. They left from the rear over a small hill in the back. They set up camp in a valley on the other side. This operation took three hours. At the same time the men took up defensive positions around the perimeters of the camp. Several platoons were sent to search out and engage the enemy. Amazingly the operations went like clockwork. At two thirty that morning all was quiet but everyone was alert. At two thirty-five gunshots were heard about a mile from camp from the direction of Lukabi. As the gunfire increased in ferocity, those inside the camp were getting jittery. Soon a jeep came racing into camp with its lights off. A sergeant jumped out and ran up to Joni.

He shouted, "Sir, we have found the enemy and fighting is heavy. It is too dark to assess their troop strength but there must be hundreds of them. They have what looks like a rocket launcher but they're having trouble mounting it. We've only got one platoon and we are concentrating on keeping them from mounting the rocket launcher. We need several more platoons immediately. Our losses are heavy but I think theirs are also. It's so dark we can't tell."

Joni ordered more troops to the fighting zone and the camp prepared to take in casualties. All available vehicles including cars and motorcycles were put into use to carry troops and ammunition. About twenty minutes later a four-door sedan carrying ten men packed in like sardines was travelling at high speed towards the gate. Suddenly a red flare lit up the sky. Everyone could see the flare and ran for cover. Just as the sedan reached the gate they heard loud booms. The noise from the explosion was horrendous and it was horrific. The sedan was blown ten feet into the air and its occupants died instantaneously. Bodies and parts of bodies were blown in all directions. There were screams and yells all around. The car's wreckage resembled twisted steel. It was still burning as crowds ran over to the remains. Just then three more flashes in the sky could be seen coming toward the camp.

"Heads down!" someone shouted.

Boom! Boom! Several seconds passed. Bang! Bang! Boom! The last explosion was mightier than the previous ones put together. It landed dead center on the ammunition warehouse. There was a succession of smaller explosions, which spread fire to nearby buildings. People ran around screaming. Some lost legs, arms and even their eyesight. Others lay strewn all over the ground either burnt to a crisp or with shrapnel sticking out of their flesh. Nothing as ghastly as this had ever happened in the camp and most refugees had not been prepared for such horror.

In the meantime a fierce battle was being waged just about a mile from camp. ZINAP troop reinforcements arrived quickly and outnumbered their enemy three to one. It was so dark that they could not tell whom they were fighting. Their immediate objective was to knock out the rocket launcher, which was having a devastating effect on the camp. The launcher had been strategically placed on top of a small hill, which meant that ZINAP forces had to penetrate the defenses surrounding it. As they closed in paying a heavy price in terms of lives lost, they managed to capture one of the enemies.

"Who are you with?" shouted a ZINAP Lieutenant.

The man did not reply.

"Who are you with or I will slit your throat. Now tell me!"

The man already suffering from bullet wounds in the stomach bled furiously.

"I am with the Malawi Army."

"You rat!" shouted the lieutenant as he slit the dying man's throat.

He then instructed five men to prepare for grenade throwing. His aim was to concentrate fire on one section of the enemy's defense line and send five men in with grenades, hoping that at least one would reach the target. His orders were swiftly put into effect resulting in a break in the enemy's defense. The five men ran up the hill and on signal from their leader, threw their grenades simultaneously. The launcher was blown clear off the hill leaving four of the enemy dead. They then started to scramble back down the hill and within seconds all five were mowed down by machine gun fire.

Fighting lasted another forty minutes before the remainder of the Malawi forces retreated into the mountains. More that fifteen prisoners were taken back to camp, some seriously injured. The sun seemed to rise without being noticed that morning. Everyone was busy treating the wounded and assessing their losses. Some people were still in a state of shock. The cost of revolution was high. More than one hundred men were dead. Losses were heaviest for ZINAP. Bitterness and contempt for President Makube grew rapidly among the refugees. ZINAP would make a formal protest through the Zambian government to the East African Community. Although the invaders were repelled, this gave no comfort to the many wives and children of some of the dead men. Chief Katumbi, who lost thirty men in the fighting, became infuriated and determined to get revenge at any cost. The day lingered on in heavy sadness. Neither the hot sun nor the torrential rain would be enough to clear the air of the stench and squalor of death.

Bush Country Gossip

Several days passed before full details were released of what was being called the 'Lukabi Massacre.' The Zambian government temporarily recalled its Ambassador from Malawi as a formal protest against what he termed "an aggressive act of war." Several other African countries joined in condemning Malawi for the "slaughter of innocent women and children." Frank Myosa returned from his trip to Eastern Europe and vowed to help "purge the puppet that dangles from capitalist strings." Even many Malawians began feeling more sympathetic towards Chief Katumbi's movement. It was whispered in official circles in Malawi that the President had been ill advised to allow such a military campaign to occur. In the long run, it was felt that the losses would be greater than the benefits, if in fact there were any benefits. President Makube was annoyed with his top Army officers because the plan had been fouled up. They were not supposed to bomb the ZINAP section of the camp and were to avoid fighting the ZINAP forces if possible. Their mission was to search and destroy Chief Katumbi's forces. Only after the incursion did they realize that their intelligence was wrong. They thought that Chief Katumbi's camp would be completely separated from ZINAP and they used an old site plan showing the layout of the camp and distances from their launching pad. Hence, their rockets landed in the wrong places. President Makube was prepared to sack two of his Army officers, but was advised to wait until the entire affair had quieted down.

Blantyre was a city of gossip and covert political talk that week. The incident caused considerable concern among Peace Corps staff and volunteers. News of the incident had reached the American press in a garbled version. Bill Humphries's office was busy on Friday morning as more telegrams and long-distance phone calls poured in from concerned and sometimes irate parents and relatives of the volunteers. Bill tried to assure them that the incident in no way affected the volunteers and that it was an isolated occurrence. To add to uncertainty, the volunteers living in and near Blantyre City came into the office in dozens. Some openly expressed their disapproval of what happened, while others were just curious as to Peace Corps' reaction. Among the visitors that morning was Dianne Harper. She wanted a meeting with Bill Humphries to discuss personal matters. Bill soon found out that Dianne wanted to leave the program and return home.

"Dianne! You want to leave? This is absolutely surprising. You're one of the last people I expected to hear that from. I mean that you were such a good recruit in training and you have so much confidence in yourself. I'm flabbergasted. Tell me, Dianne. What's the problem?"

Dianne sat there with a handkerchief in her hand ready to dry off the next tear.

"It's difficult to explain, Bill, and I'd probably explain it badly. It's just that this is not for me. I want to be home where the things and the people are familiar. I did not expect it to be like this."

Bill sat back in his chair and decided to approach the subject calmly. He could see that Dianne was nearly hysterical and he wanted to calm her down.

"Did you just decide this or has it been on your mind for some time?"

"Ever since the first day I arrived I knew then that I could not stay here for two years.
That seems like such a long time to be stuck here."

"Is there anything in particular that bothers you? We might be able to help."

Dianne lowered her head and began to sob.

"No. It's nothing in particular. It's just everything. I have a filthy old house with no hot water. Those lizards are all over the place. I'm frightened to death of those things. I don't have any transportation, since I'm terrified of that motorcycle and just everything seems wrong, including the politics. I don't want to work for a government that sends troops out to kill innocent women and children. Oh, it's so horrible!"

Bill waited a while to allow Dianne time to calm down.

In a soft voice he asked, "Dianne, have you made up your mind about this or will you consider it for a while?"

"My mind is made up, Bill. The sooner I go, the better. I don't want to stay in that horrible place another night if I can help it."

"Well, look, why don't you come back to the office about one o'clock and we will work something out? In the meantime, try to relax and take it easy. I know it must be a difficult decision for you, but I do understand. You take it easy and I'll see you at one o'clock. Okay?"

"Okay. Thanks, Bill."

When Dianne left, Bill called Jerry Weeks, his assistant, and Christine Dawson, his secretary, to his office.

"Christine, before you sit down could you get me Dianne Harper's file? I think we're going to lose her. It's a pity. I thought she was going to be a damn good volunteer but you never know in this business."

Jerry and Christine were equally surprised at hearing this news.

Jerry then remarked, "It's interesting. We assume the black volunteers will adjust better than the white ones, but I guess this has proved us wrong."

Bill Humphries looked at Jerry in a slightly disapproving way.

"Whose assumption is that, Jerry? I don't recall ever making that assumption."

"Oh, I mean no one in particular, just a general assumption. You know," Jerry said, smiling coyly.

"Yes, I know."

After Christine returned with the file, Bill explained the situation to them. Based on his assessment of what Dianne said, he was convinced that she was serious about leaving. Bill was the type who did not want volunteers hanging around if they wanted to leave, so he wanted to expedite matters as soon as possible.

"Christine, could you find out the next scheduled flights out of Blantyre to Dar es Salaam, please? Get the ones starting from Monday. When Dianne comes in at one o'clock, I can discuss with her which day she wishes to leave. Over the weekend we can arrange to get her things packed and shipped to the States."

"Okay, Bill. Actually I have the schedules sitting on my desk. Would you like to see them?"

"Yes. Thanks."

While Christine was out, Bill asked Jerry to arrange for someone to deliver a shipping crate to Dianne's place on Saturday morning. Jerry agreed.

"Here they are, Bill," Christine said. "There's a flight on Monday at 2 p.m. that has a connection in Dar es Salaam on an Air India flight to London. The next one is Wednesday morning at 8:35 a.m. The flight transfers to an East African Airways flight to London. Once she's in London she can transfer to any American airline."

"Thanks, Christine. Now which day should we suggest? The problem with Monday is that it's only three days away. Rather rushing things, I should think. Also, it gives us little time to notify the Ministry of Health about her leaving. However, Dianne seemed disturbed and frightened about the prospects of spending much more time in her house. I really don't want her sitting around for five days in an emotional state. Plus, it could have a ripple effect among other volunteers. No, I'd prefer to send her home as soon as possible. What do you two think?"

Jerry agreed with Bill as usual, although he may have had other opinions. Christine on the other hand was quite different. She was opinionated and not in the least afraid of her boss.

189

"Three days does seem like an awfully short time to pack up and leave. I know it would put me in a tizzy, but I think it depends on how Dianne feels about it. If she thinks she can make it to next Wednesday without being unduly upset, then I suggest we go for that date. But if she wants to leave immediately, Monday is almost perfect timing."

"That's sensible, Christine. I'll talk with her and sort it out. If there are no other questions about Dianne, I'll see my next appointment."

Jerry and Christine left the room and Bill continued his busy morning seeing visitors and answering phone calls.

It was six o'clock p.m. when Dianne arrived at her tattered old line-house near the outskirts of the Blantyre City. She opened the front door and was greeted by two huge cockroaches. She stamped her foot on the floor and they scrambled. The line-house had two bedrooms, a living room and a small kitchen. The cold shower was outside in an outhouse joining the back of the house. It was hot in the house as all the windows were closed. Dianne flopped down on her wood frame couch. The pillows were hard but felt good to her at the moment. She was exhausted from walking around aimlessly all evening. After she left Bill Humphries's office she was both happy and sad. The walk did her good because it kept her mind at ease. She was leaving Africa on Monday and she felt bad because she rejoiced at the thought of leaving. Somehow her romanticism and idealism had been shattered. She even thought how difficult it would be to tell people back home that she did not like Africa. She decided to tell a lie which she had not quite formulated yet. It would either be that she got malaria or some other illness, which required a long-term cure and prevented her from doing her job. After resting for ten minutes Dianne got up and looked in the mirror.

"My, you look scruffy, honey," she told herself. "Why don't you take a shower and fix yourself up. Oh! Don't you like cold showers? Is that why you're leaving? Well, aren't you a soft load of B.S. After all, if those other girls can take it, you ought to be able to take it. Why are you copping out on your brothers and sisters, honey?"

190

The thoughts brought tears to her eyes and she began to cry. She cried so hard that her eyelids got puffy. Afterwards, she took a cold shower and changed into a skirt and blouse. The shower felt good and refreshing after the heat of the day and it seemed to calm Dianne. She came back into the living room and sat down with a pen, pad and envelope. She was going to write one letter only.

Dear Jennifer,

I know this will come as a surprise to you but by the time you receive this letter I will be back home in the States. It is very difficult to explain in a short space my reasons for leaving Malawi, so I will not attempt to do so. However, I did want to write to you to say thanks for being a special friend. I enjoyed our times together during training and even the first few days here. I regret having to make this decision and personally it's been agonizing.

Nonetheless, I hope you enjoy your stay in the country and I'm sure you will do a great job. You are the only person that I'm writing to before I leave, but please do not keep it a secret. I really don't mind the others knowing. I did have a word with James the first week we were here. I explained to him then what my fears were. They did not go away but only escalated. You may ask him to explain and tell him I don't mind. Also give him a special thanks and a kiss for me.

I hope you don't mind my saying this since I'm leaving anyway, but I know you have a lot of feelings for him and I hope something works out for you. I'll say good-bye for now and thanks.

Love,

Dianne

A week passed before news of Dianne's departure reached the volunteers living in Chikwawa. Cathy Horowitz heard of it from one of the missionary teachers who had been in Blantyre that week. Cathy could hardly believe that Dianne left so soon, but somehow it gave her a feeling of achievement. She had doubts herself about her own tenure with the Peace Corps but now felt she had more stamina and courage than Dianne. She was determined to stick it out. It was 3:30 p.m. when she left the school building on her way to tell Steve Manski and Jesse Jefferson the news. They all lived relatively close to each other since the town was no more that two miles long. Cathy began the hike to Chikwawa wearing a pair of sandals and a light cotton dress. It was blistering hot that afternoon and the road was dry and dusty. Chikwawa was almost a barren outpost located in flat bush country. There were very few trees about to provide shade and although it was the rainy season, this part of the country received very little rain. Steve Manski and Jesse Jefferson lived within a stone's throw of each other. In fact, Steve's house was directly opposite Jesse's on the main road, an arrangement Jesse was not too keen on. Jesse liked his privacy and felt that having Steve living so close was an infringement. But there was little he could do about it since no other houses were available. Both lived in rather modest accommodations by Chikwawa standards. The houses, built basically the same, contained a living room, one bedroom and a kitchen. Privies and wash stalls were outside in the back.

Cathy walked up to Jesse's front door and knocked. Several moments later, Jesse's houseboy, or 'helper', as Jesse preferred to call him, appeared in a pair of American Levi jeans and a red plaid short sleeve shirt. He was obviously wearing Jesse's clothes.

"Hi. Is Jesse home?"

"No, ma'am."

"Do you know when he's coming back?"

"No, ma'am, but I think he will not return until Sunday night."

In a surprised tone Cathy exclaimed, "Sunday night! Where on earth has he gone?"

"I don't know, ma'am. He did not say, but my friend saw him get on a train to Rhodesia."

"Rhodesia? Why would Jesse Jefferson go to Rhodesia? Are you sure it was to Rhodesia? I can't imagine Jesse ever going there. Okay, thanks."

Cathy hurried across the road hoping that Steve would be there. She was anxious to tell someone about Dianne's departure, and she also wanted to have a bit of a gossip about it. This was big news for her in a place like Chikwawa. Since they had been there, nothing remotely newsworthy had occurred. The place was almost like a ghost town. Normally Cathy was in bed by 7 p.m. just to beat the boredom. She had also learned to rise with the chickens in the morning and found it to be the best time of day to get her chores done. Cathy enjoyed seeing students at the school performed traditional songs and dances. She found herself enjoying it thoroughly and could not believe how well she adjusted from her jet-setting past life to this.

Nervously, she tapped on Steve's door. Already they had argued and their relationship was cool. During the second week in Chikwawa, Steve told Cathy that she was a pest and to get lost. Cathy had been insistent during the first two weeks, dropping by his place almost daily.

Steve tried to be polite at first, but became downright annoyed and even remarked, "You and me? No chance, baby!"

So Cathy had seen neither Steve nor Jesse in about a week. The hinges on Steve's door needed oiling and made it squeaked badly when opened.

"Oh, it's you, Cathy."

Steve sounded irritated. Cathy became both defensive and apologetic.

"Well, if you are busy, Steve, I won't bother you. I thought I would drop by and tell you the latest news from Blantyre."

Steve was curious in spite of himself.

"Well, what is it?"

"You don't expect me to stand out here and tell you, do you?" Cathy asked.

"Sorry, come in."

Cathy walked slowly into the house and looked around the room as if she saw something new.

"Where did you get those?"

"What?"

"Those drums and spears. They're great!"

"I bought them from a man in the village. Now what is it you had to tell me?"

Cathy sat on one of two chairs Steve had in his living room. The decor was sparse. There were no pictures or ornaments on the grey walls and the floor was bare concrete. Cathy felt uncomfortable sitting there.

"Dianne Harper quit the program last week and she's gone home to the States."

Cathy spoke with a great deal of gusto and enthusiasm only for Steve to put a damper on it by saying that he had already heard about it.

"You heard? How could you have heard about it?"

"I saw the missionary from your school this morning."

Cathy tried to resume her composure.

"Well, what do you think about it? I mean, aren't you surprised about it?"

"Yes and no. Dianne impressed me as a girl who enjoys her goodies too much to work in these conditions for long. In fact, I'm surprised that one or two other people I know haven't left."

Cathy did not care to entertain his last comment because she felt he was referring to her. She browsed through a newspaper that she picked up off the floor.

"Oh, I forgot to mention that Jesse is away. His cook said that he got on a train for Rhodesia. I can hardly believe that, knowing how much Jesse detests what's going on there. Do you know where he is?"

Steve was slightly surprised.

"No, I don't, but I can't imagine why Jesse would go to Rhodesia. Are you sure you heard correctly?"

"That's what his cook said."

Steve excused himself to go into the kitchen. He had boiling water and wanted to turn the fire off. Cathy continued to browse through the newspaper to offset her discomfort.

Then she shouted through to the kitchen, "Steve, did you hear about the fighting up in Zambia this week? What do you think of it?"

"I think the Malawi Army should have wiped them all out," Steve shouted back. "This Chief Katumbi is nothing but a trouble maker in my book."

Cathy was amused at Steve's line of thought and decided to pry further.

"Well, you know that Chief Katumbi is espousing the cause of democracy. He wants democratic elections."

"That's bullshit. He's just another communist prop and once in power, would probably be a dictator. I would not support a communist regime and I'd be surprised if you would."

"Well, what makes you so sure he's being supported communists, Steve?"

"I heard that lots of Russian made weapons were used by the Chief's troops."

Cathy could hear Steve frantically moving pots and pans around.

"Steve? What are you doing in there? Do you need some help?"

"No, that's all right. You want some tea?"

"No, thanks. It's too hot. I suppose you support the white government in Rhodesia?"

There was no reply.

"Did you hear me?"

"Yes, I heard you. Who do you support, since you're so inquisitive?"

Cathy thought for a while before answering.

"Well, I don't really agree with the way they're treating the Africans there. They are using nearly the same system of apartheid as South Africa. After all, the Africans were there long before the whites arrived."

Steve offered a similar case to continue the argument.

"The Palestinians would put up the same argument against the Jews being in Israel."

Cathy, annoyed at Steve's dig, retorted, "That's not true at all! The Jews have just as much right to Israel as the Palestinians. What do you know about people's claims anyway?"

Steve paused for a while before answering.

"Remember, my people were pushed around by the Russians and even today, Russian troops still occupy Poland. The communists are nothing but aggressors with designs on any piece of territory they can get, including parts of Africa. Which is best, the present white-controlled Rhodesia or a communist-controlled Rhodesia?"

"I don't really know, but the way the Africans are treated now in Southern Africa, they might very well want an alternative."

Steve came back into the living room with a cup of milky tea. He sat opposite Cathy and just looked at her for a while. She became embarrassed.

"Why are you looking at me that way?"

"Oh, no reason. I'm just wondering why a rich girl like you decided to come and work in Africa."

Perturbed by the question, Cathy said, "Steve, I wish you would stop referring to me as a rich girl. I suppose my reasons for coming here are very similar to other people's, including yours. I came here to help in my small way and I came for the adventure of it all. Rich girl or not, my reasons are not very different from other people in the program. Why did you come? After all, for someone who has aspirations of being a girly-magazine tycoon, how do you justify being in a place like Chikwawa? There aren't many girls around here who would fit your bill."

"You do have a way of putting the screws in!"

"No more than you do. After all, I've tried to be nice to you since we've been here. You have not been nice to me. You have a rough way of treating a girl. I thought that since we're all isolated in this place, we could be friends. I don't mean lovers, but friends. I guess I was wrong. Anyway, Steve, I've got to go now."

Cathy got up from the chair and proceeded to the door. Steve grabbed her arm.

"Look, Cathy, if I seem to have been rude or unkind, I'm sorry. It's nothing personal with you. It's just that I haven't had time to adjust to this place yet. I hope you understand. Anyway, let's be friends and let's shake on it."

They both shook hands and Cathy said, "Goodbye, Steve. I'll see you around sometime. Oh, don't forget to tell Jesse about Dianne. I would love to see his reaction."

Steve waved good-bye as Cathy walked briskly down that dry dusty road toward Chikwawa.

Steve spent the rest of the day reading, writing letters and washing a few clothes. By evening he was exhausted. The heat bothered him more than the work. He felt as though his body worked overtime due to continuous perspiration. Temperatures remained a constant ninety degrees Fahrenheit during this time of year, and there was seldom much breeze. Actually, the cold showers provided the best relief of the day. Before long, Steve climbed into his bed, which was covered with a mosquito net. He fell asleep almost instantly. About one o'clock that morning Steve was awakened by noises coming from the kitchen. He heard pots and pans being moved, drawers opening and closing, bags rustling in the pantry. His first thought was the correct one.

"I'm being burgled!"

Steve's doors were never locked. Previously there was no need to lock doors in Chikwawa because people just trusted each other. Also, there were no locks or latches to be found within the town. In fact, those with doors considered themselves fortunate. Steve decided to warn the burglars by making noises before he investigated. He was too frightened to speak or call out, so he decided to take an old stick and pound the metal head board several times. The noise vibrated through the pipes right out into the night. The burglars hastily scrambled out of the kitchen kicking over bottles, utensils and other items. Steve waited several minutes before putting on lights and going to the kitchen. The place was in a mess. Steve was so relieved that they were gone that he didn't care what was missing. Checking around quickly he found that food and his first-aid kit were gone. After closer scrutiny of the place, he saw fresh drops of blood on the floor.

"Who in the hell were they? Somebody must be wounded. I can't imagine them getting cut in here."

His thoughts were interrupted by yet another fright. He turned around and saw a dark figure standing in the door.

"Ah!" He shouted.

Then to his relief he recognized the figure. It was Jesse's cook who had heard the commotion from across the road.

"Sorry to frighten you, sir."

"My gosh, you did! That's okay. What a mess."

"Yes, it is very bad. I saw two men leaving. One was limping."

"He must be the wounded one. Have you seen the blood on this floor? Look over there.
I wonder what sort of trouble they are in."

"I don't know, sir, but they could be terrorists who crossed over from Zambia."

Steve was startled by this last remark. The thought of armed wounded men in his house gave him the jitters.

"Terrorists! I could have been killed."

"I think they only wanted food and supplies, sir. This is the third incident in the past two months. They may come this way more often in the future."

Steve picked several items off the floor and said, "I hope not."

Steve and Jesse's cook spent the next hour cleaning up the mess and talking about the event. It was 3:30 in the morning before Steve finally got off to sleep again. He slept solidly until about nine o'clock. Still obviously shaken from the incident he got dressed quickly and went outside to start his motorcycle. He looked in the front and rear of the house but could not find the machine.

He thought: "They've got my motorcycle, too. That's funny. I didn't hear them start it and Jesse's houseboy said he saw them run off. Those S.O.B.s must have come back later to get it. I'm going to report this right away."

The police station was about a mile and a quarter down the road towards the Mission School. Steve walked briskly in the morning heat. As he passed people on the way, they nodded and greeted him. Although pleasant, he was in a hurry. He soon arrived at the police station. It was a one-room office building, which had been painted green on the outside. The paint must have been old because the finish was dull and dirty looking. Just above the front door was a sign that read. "Chikwawa Police Department." The sign was easily the most official looking thing about the whole operation. Steve tapped on the door and as he entered, bits of straw and dust fell from the roof. Two men were sitting at an old desk drinking tea. They both wore green uniforms with red shoulder patches. Behind them on the wall was a picture of President Aleke Makube. The picture looked sinister, as the President was not smiling. The room was about eight feet by eight feet, but seemed smaller because it was crowded with filing cabinets and old boxes stacked in a corner. The filing cabinets obviously had not been used for a long time since the dust appeared to be an inch thick and all sorts of papers and files were stuck on top of the cabinets.

Both men unfolded their legs and sat up straight at the desk. They tried to look official and efficient.

200

"Good morning, sir. How can we help you?"

Steve sounded impatient as he responded, "Good morning. Yes, I want to report a burglary."

"Would you like to have a seat, sir? Right there is okay. Would you care for some tea?"

The two policemen were quite excited, too. This was the first case they'd had in months and they were raring to get involved in what to them was a big event and mystery.

"Yes, thank you. I would like a cup of tea."

One of the men prepared the tea while the other listened to Steve's story. They seemed more amused than worried about what had happened but they were keen to give this case a thorough investigation.

"This sort of thing doesn't happen often around here. We will look into it and try to regain some of your stolen goods. Do you have many crimes like this in America?"

Steve detected that the policeman was more interested in talking about America than investigating the burglary.

"Yes, we do. Can we get on with my case now?"

"Oh, yes, sir. I will send one of my men to look around the place."

Unknown to Steve, there were only two policemen in Chikwawa. Both of them were right there in the office.

"When will he come, so that I can be there to show him around?"

"Oh, he can go with you now. First I must fill in a report. It will not take long."

Steve was there for forty-five minutes helping the policemen fill in the report. Although the policeman spoke good English, his writing was not so good. After the report was finished, Steve signed it and the policeman placed it on top of a pile of papers in the corner. Steve had a feeling that the report would never be referred to again and that the exercise had been one of formality only.

"How do you like our country, sir?"

"I like it."

"You are working with the Ministry of Health, aren't you, sir?"

"Yes."

"Are you a doctor?"

"No."

Steve politely excused himself.

"Do you think that I could show your man the house now?"

The policeman realized that he had kept Steve for longer than necessary.

"Yes, sir. I apologize for the delay, but these things take time. He's ready now."

Chikwawa Police Department had one government-issue motorcycle that they very seldom used. It took a few minutes to get the thing started after having initially flooded the carburetor. He then got two helmets from the bottom drawer of one of the filing cabinets and gave one to Steve. The helmets were old, dusty and smelly and Steve almost refused to put it on. Several minutes later they arrived at Steve's house. By this time, word had got around town that the American nsungu had been burgled. Crowds of curious Malawians gathered outside the house and gossiped about what had happened. Jesse's cook was the center of attraction as he relayed the tale of how he heard the commotion and then went over to rescue the American from the terrorists. They all believed him since they had not had the benefit of Steve's version.

The policeman proudly and officially dismounted from his motorcycle. This was his big day. Being seen by no less than thirty-five villagers to investigate and hopefully solve the case, gave him a certain amount of prestige. He stood up straight, placed his helmet under his left arm with a certain amount of finesse and proceeded to follow Steve into the house. Just as he reached the door, he took out a note pad and pen. This move was the final official touch. He then beamed with self-satisfaction and stepped into the house. Of course, some of the crowd realized he was putting on the big act and they exchanged comments jokingly about how funny he was. Steve showed the policeman into the kitchen.

"Look there. That's the bloodstain. We washed most of it away, but there."

The policeman walked over to the stain, kneeled down and closely inspected it.

"Are you sure this is a blood stain. It's very blue not red."

Steve impatiently responded, "It's been drying there all night. You can't expect it to be red now."

The policeman was annoyed at the forcefulness of Steve's voice.

"When are you going to track down and catch the culprits?"

"Now, sir, there's no need to get excited about that."

"Oh, I'm sorry officer. No offence intended. It's just that so much seemed to happen so quickly. Oh well, I know you are a busy man, and I wouldn't want to hold you up from other more important investigations."

The policeman felt complimented that Steve thought he had 'other important investigations' and he quickly completed this one.

After the initial fanfare was over that morning Steve felt like talking to someone who might understand his concern over what had happened that morning. Since he did not know anyone very well except Jesse and Cathy, and since Jesse was gone, he went to visit Cathy that afternoon. Cathy was surprised and delighted to see Steve. She and a Canadian missionary teacher named Brenda shared the house. They were having an early dinner. Their two-bedroom bungalow had been built as an extension to the school building only about three years earlier. It was fairly modern. From the dining room table they could see through the living room's large glass window.

"Steve, since you're here, sit down and join us."

"No, thanks. I'm not hungry."

"Oh, please. There's plenty here."

"Okay. I will."

Steve explained all that had happened in great detail. He also discussed his feeling that the policemen were not sympathetic although they were helpful. Brenda appeared to be a lot more sympathetic than Cathy and responded in such a way that Steve began talking more to her than to Cathy. After Steve finished his version of what happened Cathy tried to change the subject.

"Oh, Steve, did you find out any more about where Jesse went?"

"No, I have not. With all that's happened this morning, I haven't had a chance to inquire."

Steve was enjoying himself laughing and joking about the events of the day and getting the type of feedback from Brenda that he'd come for. Cathy felt slightly annoyed and envious. She was annoyed at Steve for being so selfish. He had come to the house to get some attention and be listened to, not to see Cathy. She was envious of Brenda's ability to cater to Steve and the fact that they both seemed to get on so well. Steve stayed there until late evening. He talked mostly to Brenda, since Cathy gave up trying to compete for his attention during the first hour.

When Steve left, Brenda said to Cathy, "He's a nice guy. We ought to have him back again soon."

"Maybe you would like to invite him back."

Brenda detected a note of jealousy, but chose to ignore it.

"I'll do the dishes tonight, Cathy."

Jesse Jefferson arrived back in Chikwawa on Sunday afternoon. Wherever he had been, he travelled lightly. He carried a small gym bag as he entered the house.

When he saw his helper, he said, "What's happening, bro? You made out okay while I was gone didn't you?"

"Yes, Jesse. Everything is all right here, but Mr. Manski's place was visited by thieves and terrorists last night."

"What? What are you talking about?"

"Thieves and terrorists broke into his kitchen and stole food and medicine. There was blood on the floor, so they must have been wounded."

Jesse decided to go over to Steve's house. He very seldom visited Steve. In fact, he had only been there twice while Steve had visited his place several times. Steve opened the door after hearing the loud knock.

"Jesse. Come on in. Where you been? I guess you heard about my little adventure."

"Yeah, man. That's some heavy stuff I heard about. Tell me all about it."

Steve told Jesse what happened.

"You mean they actually stole your transport, man? They sound like some bold dudes to me. Hey, did you hear them talking. I mean, could you tell whether they were Malawians or from Zambia?"

Steve thought about it for a moment.

"Hey, Jesse, it never dawned on me. Now that I think about it, the language sounded more like Rhodesian Bantu. They were probably terrorists."

Jesse did not want to engage in a political discussion at that moment. He just wanted to get as much information as possible about the incident.

"Hey, man. If those guys are running around here stealing and shooting people then I want to know about it."

Steve then asked, "Oh by the way, have you heard about Dianne Harper?"

"No. What about her?"

"She left the program and is now back in Mississippi."

Jesse almost leaped out of his chair.

"Man! Are you kidding? You mean the sister's gone home?"

"Yes, that's what I heard. Apparently she did not like it here and couldn't stand it any longer."

"Whew. I can't believe that she just up and quit like that!"

"Have you heard from any of the group in Blantyre or Mzuzu?"

"No, I haven't. It would be good to hear from them and to see them again. I'm thinking of taking some time off in June. Maybe I'll visit Blantyre and Mzuzu. Have you heard from James or Phil recently?"

"No. I guess they are all busy settling in, too. Your idea of going down that way in June sounds good."

Jesse did not want to appear to be imposing on Steve's plans but he wouldn't have minded Steve inviting him along. Steve decided not to take the hint. Steve asked Jesse where he had been during the weekend.

"I met this fine Malawian sister a few weeks back. She is a nurse at one of the village clinics south of here. So I visited her village this weekend."

"Did you enjoy yourself?"

"I had a great time. They gave a party with lots of village beer and dancing."

Steve cautiously approached his next statement.

"I am glad to know you had a good time, Jesse. We were worried about you for a while. We heard a rumor that you went to Rhodesia."

"Rhodesia? What gave you that idea? You know me better than that!"

" Cathy went by to see you on Friday and your cook said that his friend saw you getting on a train to Rhodesia."

Jesse became furious.

"That's a damn lie. Why would I even want to go to Rhodesia? In fact they probably wouldn't let me in if I wanted to go. They would hardly trust an American black man in that country. No, someone got their wires crossed."

It was very hot in the living room so Jesse stood up and walked over to an open window hoping to catch a breeze. Steve followed Jesse and as they both stood next to the window.

Steve asked, "How do you like it here, Jesse? I never got a chance to ask you before?"

"How do I like it? Well there are a few things I don't like about it, starting with this archaic civil service system which was instituted by the British during their colonial reign."

Steve seemed slightly confused.

"What do you mean?"

Jesse did not respond right away. He wanted to formulate his thoughts first.

"Well, if you think about it, colonial rule served British interest, not Malawians. The British were crafty enough to develop political institutions that would support their economic and political interest. Their aim was to 'civilize' the Malawians while at the same time exploit them. Just look around you. Most of the top ministers were educated in England. The educational institutions are based on the British system and even the highest ranking officers in the Malawi Army are British."

"Well, what's wrong with that?"

"What's wrong? I'll tell you what's wrong. The system is out of context here. For example the students studying for "A" and "O" levels spend a good deal of time learning British history and culture. What use is that going to be in a country that is highly dependent on agriculture? They should have more agriculture and technical training courses related specifically to African problems. Another thing, some of the African civil servants try to act more British that the British. They affect these phony accents and walk around in suits and ties, as hot as it is here. Even the British wear shorts and open-neck shirts. It's ridiculous."

Steve decided to sit down again and Jesse continued to stare out of the window.

"Is it what you expected to find here?"

"No, man. Some of the things I've seen in this country just blew my mind. These people aren't truly independent. If anything they're just the caretakers for foreign investments in the country. All the major banks, companies, and financial institutions are foreign owned and operated. Foreigners have used this part of Africa as a source of cheap labor. It's also been exploited for it's rich soil. What sickens me is that the Malawians don't seem to have got anything back in return. What do you think about it?"

Steve Manski was hard put to come up with a response. He did not agree with Jesse, but was initially reluctant to voice his opinion for fear that it would lead to another argument.

"What's up, Steve? Don't you have any views about this country?"

"Yes. I like it and I think President Makube is on the right track. Let's face it, this country is poor and these people can't be too choosy about where they receive their assistance. Granted, I know what you mean about the Malawians seeming subservient, but maybe they're happy about their way of life."

Jesse showed some irritation when he responded.

"Happy? Happy about kissing asses? Ah, come off it. You wouldn't act that way nor would you want to be treated as if you were beneath someone else."

"No, I would not. No more than you would. But what you got to realize is that these people did not have the same experiences as black Americans. They were once under colonial rule, but they were not slaves and maybe they don't have the same bitterness. Maybe you are imposing your own values on a situation which is totally different."

Jesse mused over Steve's last comment but for some reason chose not to challenge it.

Instead, he said, "That doesn't excuse the fact that the British imposed a system years ago, which still serves their best interests today."

"Well that's nothing new. Even America was a British colony once. Look at how much influence they had on our institutions. Our laws are still very much based on British jurisprudence, education, and industry. You name it. We still have a lot of British culture in our lifestyles. Maybe the people here don't have complete freedom of speech, press and so on, but I'm not sure whether our form of democracy would work in a country with ninety percent illiteracy."

"I disagree with you on that, Steve. You're probably judging their illiteracy by Western standards. They might not speak English nor write, but they aren't politically naïve. It's just that they are afraid to speak out for fear of reprisals. For many years the same argument was used against American blacks in the south. To reinforce this theory, the law allowed the Ku Klux Klan and other white groups to scare the blacks into silent submission and to prevent them from voting. No. I can't buy your theory."

Jesse had been at Steve's house for just over an hour. He looked at his watch and said that he should be going. Both had relaxed a lot and felt comfortable talking to each other about various issues. Actually they got to understand each other better within that hour than during all the time they had known each other.

"You don't have to leave now, Jesse. What about some coffee or tea?"

"Yes. I would like some coffee. Thanks, man."

Steve went into the kitchen to put on the kettle. It would take several minutes to boil. He returned to the living room and sat down with a smirk on his face.

"What's so funny, Steve?"

"People are funny."

"What do you mean 'people'?"

Steve paused for a moment.

"Well, it's like you and me. We've been acquainted ever since training in San Diego, but we hardly knew each other. I mean, we never really communicated with each other until now. I had put you down as being bitter with a chip on your shoulder, so I stayed away."

"Maybe you were right, Steve."

"I don't doubt that, but what I mean is that my prejudgment of you somehow inhibited me from communicating. You might be bitter and you might not like white people for all I know, but at least I feel as though I'm not afraid to talk about it with you."

"Sounds like you had more of a hang-up than I did. Sure I'm bitter about a lot of things. I would imagine though that most of us have hang-ups about something. Take you for instance. With a name like Manski, it's not hard to place you ethnically. Your people had a rough time, too."

"What do you know about the Polish?"

"I make it my business to know about the Polish. Not only that, black people in New Jersey had to fight like hell to survive around you guys. Then there were the Italians, Jews, Irish, Puerto Ricans, Slovaks and a whole bunch of other newcomers. What you guys don't realize sometimes is that we blacks got tired of you landing in New York from all parts of Europe and taking our jobs, housing and places in colleges. We've been in America since the English brought us over to the colony of Virginia back in 1619. So, hell yes, I'm bitter!"

Steve became defensive.

"Well, don't take it out on me. Anyway, my kinsfolk didn't take jobs from blacks. There were plenty of new jobs opening up during the turn of the century. They needed new workers from Europe."

"Like hell they did! They had a large number of able and willing black folk they could have used. By bringing in those newcomers, they only created high unemployment and poverty among black people. There is no use fighting about it now. I just thought I'd set the record straight for you, as if you didn't already know. I mean, an Illinois dude like you knows what's happening. Hey, your kettle's boiling."

"Yes, I'll fix that coffee."

While Steve was in the kitchen he shouted through to Jesse.

"Jesse, do you know much about this ZINAP business? You know, that exiled Rhodesian organization operating somewhere in Zambia."

"No, not too much. Why do you ask?"

"I just thought with all that's been happening recently, it might be good to know more about them."

"All I can tell you is that they're fighting for independence and majority rule in Rhodesia. But the way things are going, they've got a long ways to go."

"You don't sound very sympathetic. I'm surprised."

"Well, I've answered your question as best I can, Steve. What do you want, another speech?"

"No, just thought you might be a little more emotionally involved."

"Look, my plate's pretty full. Let's drop it."

Steve brought the cup in and handed it to Jesse. He was enjoying Jesse's visit and was amazed at the level of honesty in their conversation. He put it down to them being so isolated that they needed to really talk to each other.

"Did you work before you joined the Peace Corps?"

"Yes. Did you?"

"Yes. It's funny; I used to work in this bar in Chicago that catered to women. It was the only place in the City that women could feel free coming alone. Most of the bar tenders were young guys like myself. Man! You wouldn't believe the passes they made at us. They looked us over just like the guys would look girls over in a bar. It was a fun place to work. I learned a lot about what women think."

Steve then asked Jesse what work he had done.

"Nothing as exciting as that. My work was very boring. I used to file and stack old newspapers in the mailing room of a newspaper company. It was part-time work, twelve hours a week in the evenings. There were other people around the place, but the mail room was isolated from the main press and production room."

"How old are you, about twenty-one?"

"Twenty-one? No way man, I'm twenty-eight."

"Funny I thought that everyone was about twenty or twenty-one in the group. You surely haven't been working with that newspaper all of that time, have you?"

"No. I was in the U.S. Marines for three years and I did some other things afterwards. Anyway, it's boring, man. You don't want to hear about it."

It was four o'clock when Jesse left and the sun's glare was almost unbearable. Jesse looked down the main road of Chikwawa and didn't see a soul. Most of the people were either in their houses or some other place where it was cooler. The town was sleepy at that time on a Sunday afternoon. Jesse slowly entered his house and closed the door behind him. Then he called out to his cook.

"Ntalie, are you in there?"

"Yes, I'm preparing some tea for you."

"That's all right about the tea. Come in here. I want to talk to you."

213

Jesse could hear the kettle being taken off the burners. Then he heard cups being moved about. Impatiently he exclaimed.

"Come on, man. What's taking you so long?"

Hurriedly, Ntalie ran into the living room. Jesse asked him to have a seat.

"Is something wrong, Jesse?"

Ntalie called him by name because Jesse had instructed him to. However he felt uncomfortable owing to Jesse's serious tone of voice, and wished he could call Jesse 'bwana.'

"Listen. I know that sometimes we all may say something to someone without realizing that we're talking too much. I heard that you told Cathy Horowitz that I went to Rhodesia. Is that true?"

Ntalie's nervousness was showing.

"I only said that my friend saw you get on a train to Rhodesia. Have I said something wrong? I'm sorry if I did, Jesse."

"Well, I won't come down too hard on you, bro, but in future, don't tell anyone where I'm going unless I specifically instruct you to."

"Yes, sir, Jesse. I'm sorry. I will not talk again."

"Just do what I tell you and there will be no problem. Okay?"

"Yes, sir, Jesse."

There were several moments of silence.

"I'm sorry I had to talk to you that way, Ntalie, but there are certain things you might see or hear which I must trust you to keep to yourself. You still have a complete run of the place. It's like your home too, so when I'm away, I expect you to protect this place as if it was yours."

Ntalie nodded his head in agreement and then left the room.

Jesse reached behind his chair and grabbed his gym bag. The zip was padlocked. He pulled out a key and opened the lock. Then he unzipped the bag and withdrew some documents including his U.S. Passport. After browsing through the documents he opened his passport. There were several immigration stamps in the passport, including one for Rhodesia. He quickly put it back into the bag, locked the bag and took it in his bedroom. There he deposited the entire bag into a metal trunk that he locked.

Chapter 5: Between Love and a Rock

A Flower from Rhodesia

By early March most of the rivers and streams in Malawi were swollen. Flash floods caused considerable damage to crops, property and some of the already precarious roads and bridges around the country. The Northwest region was the worst affected. After almost three months of continuous rain, many villagers were cut off from the main towns. Not even the roads of Mzuzu could escape the huge mud puddles and sliding embankments caused by the frantic streams of water. Rain poured down continuously through the night and into Saturday morning. Muwalo Phiri was peering out of his line-house living room window hoping for a break in the weather. Already huge puddles of water flooded part of his walkway and he was concerned that if the rains continued, his guests might get wet feet that night. He did not want his party spoiled by wet feet. Not this party anyway. He had invited about twenty people and among his guests were three Americans and one Brit.

Muwalo Phiri was twenty-five years old. He worked at the Ministry of Health's Regional Headquarters in Mzuzu as a Planning Assistant. He was James's supervisor and they had become good friends. Muwalo received a Bachelor of Arts Degree in Health Administration from Cairo University. He was not married and was considered by the young single Malawian women as a good catch. Also, some of the top Malawi officials thought he would make a good marriage partner for their daughters. Muwalo wasn't ready to be tied down yet. He enjoyed his women and parties too much.

He was fortunate to have a line-house to himself. Nearly all line-houses were reserved for civil servants with families, but a top official in the Ministry of Housing was interested in catching Muwalo for his daughter. By providing a house, the only thing left to do was to get the two married. James had benefited from his friendship with Muwalo. About a week after having Muwalo over for dinner one evening, a shipment of good reconditioned living room furniture, beds and a dining room suite were delivered.

Muwalo wasn't short of a penny or two either. At least, by Malawian standards, he was well off. He received a good salary and his father owned a meatpacking and distribution warehouse in Blantyre. Muwalo soon left the window as he began to feel more depressed about the weather. He decided to arrange his record albums in the order that the music should be played. His brand new Philips record player and tape deck combination had taken six months to arrive. He was probably the only person in Mzuzu who had this most up-to-date equipment in home music. The albums were a mixture of rock 'n' roll, country western and African ballads, mainly from Rhodesia. Malawi did not have a recording company or many famous entertainers. After arranging his albums, he moved all the furniture out of the living room except his couch. This was done to provide more space, since twenty people would fill the room. This would not matter after the first hour or so because by then the discomfort wouldn't bother his guests. But he was apprehensive about their initial arrival because from his experience, people had a tendency to be nervous until after they've had a few drinks. Muwalo had bought plenty of drinks. Rain or no rain, he was excited about his party and was determined to make it a success.

Later that morning James and his cook, Geoffrey Malango, prepared to go to the market. James had reluctantly hired Geoffrey the week after he had first applied. Since then, James found he enjoyed having Geoffrey around and also his children who came by regularly. It was like having an adopted family away from home.

As they mounted his motorcycle to go to Mzuzu's main market place, Geoffrey said, "I think we will need the bigger shopping basket."

"Oh, we shouldn't need that, I'm not buying much this morning. I'm going to a party tonight. I'm going over to the teachers' house for tea tomorrow and I'll be leaving on Monday morning for my tour of the regional clinics."

Geoffrey seemed slightly offended and James noticed it.

"Okay, Geoffrey, but make it fast, I don't want to be in this rain any longer than necessary."

James knew that the bigger shopping basket carried a certain amount of status for domestic employees. Although Geoffrey might not fill the large basket with goods, at least he could be seen to have a large basket by his compatriots in similar jobs. He went quickly into the house and returned with a huge awkward basket. James looked at the basket and smiled.

"You don't think we're going to fill that this morning, do you?"

"The cabbages are bigger this time of the year," replied Geoffrey with a smile.

James knew that he would in fact have to buy enough food and vegetables to fill the basket, although he did not need that much. Since he was leaving on Monday for three weeks, Geoffrey and his family would put the extra food to good use. James didn't mind.

The trip took about twenty-five minutes. The roads were muddy and treacherous and caused several delays. They dismounted from the motorcycle at the entrance to the open market and stood there looking the place over. The dried fish let off an awful stench. They decided to get the fresh meat first since a cow had just been butchered. They could buy the best parts for the same price as any other part. Beef sold at one shilling and six pence per pound. It was up to customers to point out exactly which part of the cow they wanted to buy. The rumps and sirloin steaks were always the first to go. It was wise to get in the queue quickly.

"I will ask for four pounds of the best steak."

"Four pounds? Who's going to eat four pounds of steak, Geoffrey?"

218

"It will not be wasted."

James then scratched his head.

"Man, I got to give it to you. You could screw the spots off a leopard without it even knowing."

"What do you mean, James?"

"Ah, forget it. Go ahead and buy the steaks."

Geoffrey went over and bargained for the steaks, and managed to get a shilling shaved off the price. James stood looking at the mangos a few feet away. He decided to go over and buy a few. Just as he started to bargain over the price, Geoffrey came running over.

"Wait, Mister James. I will do that. I will get a better price for you."

"Well, I don't mind doing it."

"No. It is my job."

He stood back while Geoffrey bargained and thought.

"Damn, I can't even do my own bargaining with this guy around. Talking about division of labor! You would think that he belonged to a union or something. Anyway, I'm going to be doing my own shopping and bargaining over the next three weeks. I'll look forward to not having Geoffrey telling me what to buy and how much to spend. But, I guess he's only doing his job. He's all right."

They strolled around the vegetable stalls. There were ground nuts, cassava, maize, bananas, carrots, onions, rice, beans, smoked eel and even roasted 'flying ants', a rather large succulent extension of the ant family which tasted like fried bacon. Geoffrey seemed to know a lot of people including the vendors. He stopped at just about every stall and talked continuously. James joined in when he could understand what was being said.

Just when they entered the last row of stalls and were about to complete their shopping, James bumped into Phil Harrington.

"Hi, Phil. How's it going?"

"Okay, James. Have you finished your shopping?"

"Yes, touch wood. Geoffrey is so popular around here that unless I put my foot down, we will be here all day. Are you all set for the party tonight?"

"Yes, I'm looking forward to it. So is Fiona."

"I see you and Fiona have a big thing going."

Phil blushed with embarrassment. Although he and Fiona had got very tight since they met that night at James's house, Phil was still not used to having a girlfriend nor having other people comment about it.

"We get on okay. Are you going to their place for dinner tomorrow?"

"Yes, I guess so. By the way, do you see Bob Newgate much?"

"No, he was over at the girls' house one night when I was there. But we didn't have a chance to talk to each other much. Not with Marg Prudhoe hanging all over him."

"Are they going together? I wonder what her boyfriend Jerry thinks of all this?"

"Don't quote me, James, but I heard he called it quits after hearing about Marg and Bob."

"Well, I can't say I blame the guy."

"Have you heard from Stuart Steiner?"

"Yes. I did in fact. I received a letter from him yesterday. You see, I'm going to be up his way in a week's time so he agreed to put me up for a few nights. It saves me having to sleep in the back of that Land Rover. Anyway, Stuart's got a girlfriend who works just across the border in Zambia. I met her once. Nice girl about twenty-seven or twenty-eight. Her name is Janice."

Phil thought for a few moments.

"He must not see her much. I mean, we're discouraged from going across the border."

"Oh, I don't think that is much of a problem to them. She evidently drives down to see him on weekends. Anyway there's no law that says Stuart can't pop across the border every now and then. Hell, Peace Corps could care less about a couple of lovers trying to see each other on weekends."

"Yes, perhaps you are right. I've got some more shopping to do James. I'll see you tonight."

"See you later, alligator."

Phil laughed at James's song and walked off.

James and Geoffrey got soaked on their way back to the house. As soon as they drove into the driveway, the rain stopped, and all was calm. The heat of the sun was intense and within an hour, most of the paths and roads dried up. James was excited about all of his plans. Thoughts of the party that night, tea at the girl's house the next day, and his tour of the region prevented him from doing any serious concentration. He had picked up a *The Count of Monte Cristo* three times and found that he could not read more than a few pages at a time. So he decided to sleep.

James slept for two hours. It still seemed ages before the party that night. He decided to wear a blue shirt with a pair of smart trousers. Normally, he would have worn jeans, but since Muwalo and some of his Malawian guests were conscious of their appearance, he decided to fall in line.

He thought, "Do as the Malawians do when you're in Malawi."

Muwalo and his friends were considered middle class Malawians based primarily on the positions they had achieved in the civil service system. They included administrators, nurses, teachers and a couple of doctors. As it turned out, the weather was perfect. The last downpour at five o'clock lasted only twenty minutes. By the time most guests arrived, the sky was clear and the stars sparkled brightly. James could hear the Four Tops album blasting out as he walked up to the house. He knocked on the door and was greeted by Muwalo.

"Hello, James, my good friend. Come in."

"Okay. I' see you got this place swinging already, brother."

"Yes. It's a bit crowded, but who cares."

"I sure don't. I like it this way. Here I brought you a bottle of schoolboy scotch, better known as Vino di Headache."

They both roared laughing as Muwalo showed James into the room. Several people whom he'd already met greeted him and Muwalo introduced him to others. He saw Phil standing over in a corner looking very white and out of place. The three girls had not arrived yet. It took fifteen minutes for James and Muwalo to get through the living room to the kitchen where the drinks were. Initial greetings were quite a ceremony in Malawi. Muwalo fixed a drink for James as they talked casually.

"That must be the latest Four Tops album. I have not heard it before."

"Straight from Detroit. I know the people who run the big record shop in Blantyre. They always hold two or three of the latest albums for me. Do you like it?"

"Are you kidding? They're some of my favorite soul brothers. I like the Supremes, too. You got them?"

"I'm with it, man. I got them and the Drifters."

"Yeah, man. You're what's happening! Here's to you, Muwalo,"

"Cheers, James."

They both sipped their drinks.

"You know, you sound British when you say that."

"Say what?"

"Cheers."

"Oh. Ha, ha. We have picked up a few bad British habits."

"You can say that again."

They both smiled.

Just then an attractive Malawian girl came into the kitchen and in a pleasant and sweet voice said, "Muwalo, you have more guests arriving, the American girls."

"Thanks, I'm coming now."

The girl left the room and Muwalo said to James.

"Why don't you come and introduce your friends to me. I don't really know them."

"Okay, Muwalo. And by the way only one of the girls is American. Her name is Jennifer Nolan. Fiona Crewe is British and Crissie Chipenbere, I'm sure you can tell by her name is Malawian."

"I did not know that a Malawian girl lived in that house."

"You do now, brother."

Muwalo was relieved that James was with him to greet the girls and introduce them around. He was not used to having white people at his parties and wasn't too sure how to make them feel at ease. Nevertheless, it was he who had asked James to invite some of his American colleagues. James was very selective about whom he invited. He did not want Bob Newgate or Marg Prudhoe there for fear that they might embarrass him and his host. Stuart lived too far away, so this left Phil and the three girls whom he knew fairly well. Marg was annoyed when she heard that the other girls were invited and she was not. It wasn't that she wanted to go to a party given by Africans, but she felt slighted. James couldn't give a damn and was actually pleased that an opportunity had arisen for him to snub her. To Muwalo's delight, his new guests mixed quite well at the party. In fact, they were never left alone during the first hour of so. Most of the Malawians anxiously engaged the girls in conversations about America and Britain. Crissie, too, was getting a lot of attention. Many were curious as to how she felt about living with the nsungus. By 9:30 the party was in full swing. The men danced with each other and the women danced with each other. This followed traditional Malawian custom. There were, of course, some mixed dances. James noticed how unsociably some of the Malawian men drank. They did not just sip and chat. They drank one drink after the other until they were totally inebriated. Some people were going outside for breaths of fresh air or to cool off. Phil and Fiona went out and sat on his motorcycle. They cuddled and kissed. Crissie who had been entertained by Muwalo most of the night found herself being admired by another suitor. Muwalo wasn't too happy about that.

Muwalo was whispering to one of his girlfriends when James asked him about a certain girl at the party.

"Who is that girl over there with the one with the rose in her hair?"

"Oh, her name is Rose."

They both broke out laughing.

"Rose wears a rose?" asked James. By this time he noticed the girl looking in his direction.

224

"Oh, she knows we're talking about her now. Hey, brother. Can I break you away from your sweetheart long enough for you to introduce me to Rose?"

"Well, okay. But don't expect me to stay with you. My little lady here doesn't want me away too long."

"No, I don't want you to stick around. Just introduce me. I'll take care of the rest."

"Okay, James, but don't be too disappointed if you don't get anywhere with her."

"Just introduce us, Muwalo!"

There was an expression of nervous shyness on the girl's face as the two men approached her. She had stood looking radiant and glamorous for more than thirty minutes without talking to anyone. As James got closer, he thought that she resembled Diana Ross. She didn't smile until Muwalo greeted her.

"Rose, I would like to introduce a friend of mine from America. This is James Johnson and he works with me at the Ministry."

"Hello, Mr. Johnson, I am pleased to meet you."

"Hi, Rose. I am pleased to meet you. I hope we can be friends."

Rose stood there feeling rather uncomfortable knowing that James had watched her all night and that her boyfriend was in the next room. Muwalo sensed the tension and then spoke again.

"Oh, Rose, James has some interesting stories to tell about America. Maybe you can tell her a few, James. I'll leave you two now. My lady is waiting. See you later."

James approached Rose as she stood holding her hands and looking straight ahead.

"I didn't get your full name, Rose."

"It's Rose Nkoma."

"That's a pretty name. But pretty girls should have pretty names."

The comment provoked a smile from Rose, but she did not speak.

"Are you from Mzuzu, Rose?"

"No. I'm from Rhodesia."

"Rhodesia! Are you here on a visit?"

"No I work here. I've lived here for three years now."

"Why did you leave Rhodesia?"

There was no response. James felt that this girl was going to be difficult to talk to and he considered giving up. But decided to give it one more try.

"Look, Rose, I will not bore you any longer, but before I leave you, let me just say this. I've been watching you all night and you are the most beautiful girl I've seen in a long time. It's taken me all this time to work up the courage to come and talk to you because I was so afraid this might happen. I am sure you have reasons for rejecting me. Perhaps it is because your boyfriend is here or perhaps you just don't like talking to me. I'm both disappointed and glad. I am disappointed that you turned me away, but I'm glad that I was fortunate enough to have met such a lovely flower from Rhodesia."

Rose turned to James, looked him straight in the eye and laughed. She laughed so hard that tears came to her eyes.

James was both amused and flabbergasted. "Well, what's so funny?"

She laughed again and said, "I have met sweet-talking Americans before, but never one like you. Do you think for one minute that I am going to fall for those lines? Well, I'm sorry, Mr. Johnson, but I don't! Now if you will excuse me, I must go and get my friend."

James was left speechless as Rose pranced off into the other room. James rushed back over to Muwalo and said, "Whew. . . That chick is no push over! What's with her anyway?"

"Oh, forget it, man. There are plenty more girls around."

James wanted to know more about Rose, but Muwalo was pre-occupied with his girl and did not feel like discussing her any more. By this time Jennifer managed to make her way through the crowded living room to where James was standing.

"Hi."

"Hi, Jennifer."

"I haven't seen much of you tonight, James."

"I've been here. Are you enjoying yourself?"

Jennifer gave James a playful nudge.

"Well, are you going to ask me to dance tonight?"

They both got onto the crowded floor and danced.

"Who is that girl you were talking to?"

"Which girl?"

"You know. The pretty one with the rose in her hair."

"Oh her? She's just a girl named Rose. I don't know anything else about her, except that she's from Rhodesia and is here with her boyfriend. Why do you ask?"

"Oh, just curious."

While giving her a little light tug on the cheek he responded

"Oh, just curious, hey?" he said with a smile.

By midnight Jennifer, Fiona and Crissie were ready to leave. Fiona had managed to borrow the school's beat-up estate wagon to come to the party. As they left, they thanked Muwalo for inviting them and said what a wonderful evening they had. On the way out, Phil walked with Fiona to the car. They stood kissing while the other two girls shook hands with some of the other guests. James came out of the house and walked over to Crissie and Jennifer.

He put his hands around both girls' shoulders in a brotherly manner and said, "Now you girls don't drive too fast and take it easy. Hope you had a good time tonight. By the way Crissie, my friend Muwalo likes you a lot. He asked me to put in a good word for him but I said I was going to put in a word for myself. Ha! Ha!"

Crissie laughed too and replied, "If your friend is anything like you, I would have to be a very patient woman. He's very popular with the girls I see and I'm not up to the competition."

"Oh, he's not bad. Just likes to have fun. I'll see you guys tomorrow. What time did you say to come over?"

"About four," replied Jennifer.

"Okay, goodnight and sleep tight. You know the rest. Right?"

The girls said goodnight.

When they drove off James went back into the house. To his surprise he saw Rose Nkoma standing in the corner alone and he went over to her.

"Where's your boyfriend?

She snapped, "He's not my boyfriend. He's just an escort."

"Oh, I see. I imagine you expect him to escort you home tonight. In his condition I suggest you find someone else to take you home. Would you like a ride home?"

"You do think you are smooth, don't you, Mr. Johnson?"

James didn't know whether to smile or look on her statement as another dig at him.

"Look, Rose, I'm not trying to be a smoothie. I just want to get to know you better."

She stood there looking out into the room again. Her big beautiful brown eyes seemed as though they had seen a lot of different people and places. They would not be easily surprised. Muwalo walked over to them and in a jovial manner.

"How are you two doing? Getting to know each other?"

James murmured, "Hardly."

Then Muwalo turned to Rose.

"You have not danced much tonight, Rose. Don't you like my selection of records?"

"Yes, it's a very good selection, Muwalo. I am just a little tired tonight but I have enjoyed your party."

The girl whom Muwalo had been with for the past hour came up to him and pulled him by the arm.

"Come with me into the kitchen and fix me a drink."

"Some guys have all the luck," James joked.

"Oh? You don't seem to be doing so bad yourself," Rose replied.

"Well, I couldn't do much worse."

Muwalo and his girl went into the kitchen. James could hear their loud laughter and giggles. He surmised that they obviously were not fixing drinks since the kitchen light had been turned off. As he stood there thinking of how Muwalo brazenly went from one girl to the other without a care in the world.

"What did you mean when you said you could not do much worse?" Rose said.

He attempted to explain himself without insulting Rose further. She did not accept his explanation and showed her annoyance.

"If you don't like my company, Mr. Johnson, you can leave."

"I didn't ask you to talk to me anyway," James replied.

"Why are you so furious? I've stood here twice trying to be sociable and you've all but ignored me. Well, I'm sorry I bothered you Miss Nkoma and I assure you, it won't happen again, because I give up."

He stood pouting with frustration. He crossed his arms over his chest and turned away from Rose. She made a similar gesture and they both stood almost back-to-back without saying a word. The time was nearing one o clock and most of Muwalo's guests were leaving. He was busy saying goodnight to people and showing them to the door. Soon there were only five people left in the house, including Rose's escort who was not in any state to walk. Both Muwalo and James tried in vain to wake him. They even poured cold water over his face.

Eventually Muwalo said, "It's no use, this boy is out cold. Just leave him there for the night. It is too late for Rose to go home by herself. Do you mind giving her a lift?"

"No, I don't mind but she might."

"Yes, I see you two didn't get on too well tonight. Never mind I'll talk to her about you giving her a lift."

James went into the kitchen and talked to Muwalo's girl while he talked with Rose. She was obviously not too happy about her escort getting drunk neither was she pleased about James's rudeness as she put it to Muwalo. He explained that sometimes these Americans seemed brash but didn't mean to be. He also urged Rose to accept the ride since it was late for her to walk home alone. She reluctantly agreed. Muwalo then offered James advice on how to treat African women.

"You see, James, you move just a little fast for some of them. I know you don't mean it but they consider your smooth talk an insult. Rose for instance, felt as though you were propositioning her especially since you knew that she was with someone else tonight. So I suggest you be a little more polite and nice to her and don't rush things."

"Wow, man! You know I didn't mean to come off like that. I really feel bad about this. I guess I was too anxious and wanted to get to know her too quickly. She is a fine looking woman. Sorry about that, Muwalo."

"You don't have to apologize to me. I understand. See if you can make her feel better."

Entering the living room with a smile on his face, James offered Rose a ride.

"I'll drive you home whenever you are ready, Rose."

"Are you sure you don't mind?"

"I don't mind at all. I just hope you don't mind riding on the back of a motorcycle."

"I can manage."

They both said goodnight to Muwalo and his girl and mounted the motorcycle. James had only one helmet and suggested that Rose should wear it. She politely refused but he insisted. It was warm, pleasant and dry at that time of the morning and the breeze was refreshing to them.

"You will have to direct me, Rose."

"You drive back to the main road and turn right. I live about a mile up the road, but as we get nearer I will direct you."

James could feel Rose's long soft fingers clutching his stomach. The tension in her fingers indicated how nervous she was about riding on the motorcycle. She held him tightly and the touch of her soft body upon his back sent mild sensations through him. He glanced at her smooth slender thighs as the wind lifted her white dress and caused it to fly back like a cape. The thrill of the ride relaxed them both. He sang and clowned around a bit and Rose began to laugh.

"Do you want to drive?"

She laughed as she answered.

"No. I can't ride a motorcycle."

"Would you like to learn sometimes? I'll teach you."

Without realizing how she had committed herself, she responded with excitement.

"Oh, could you please? I've always wanted to learn how to ride a motorcycle."

"Sure, I tell you what, as soon as I return from my trip, I'll take you out and teach you."

"Where are you going?"

James explained about his tour of regional clinics and how long it would take.

"That's a long time to be away."

"Yes, but I'll be very busy so it should not seem too long."

Soon they came to a series of small shops about a mile up the main road. Rose told James to stop just ahead as he slowly came to a halt. He asked which place was hers. She hesitantly indicated that she stayed somewhere behind the shops.

"Shall I walk with you to your door?"

232

"Oh, no but thanks. I can manage from here."

He wondered why she was reluctant to be escorted to her door. He only saw the shops and was confused about where she lived. The road was completely deserted and quiet. The only noises to be heard were snores.

"Where do you work, Rose, if I'm not being too nosey?" he whispered.

"I don't mind your question. I am a typist at the American Information Service in Mzuzu."

"Oh, yes? Do you like working for Americans?"

"Yes, I do."

"I guess that's why you know so much about sweet-talking Americans."

They both laughed but she did not say anything. James seemed nervous again as he was about to pose another question.

"I'd like to see you again when I get back from my trip if that's all right with you?"

She smiled and said, "Remember you are supposed to teach me how to ride a motor cycle."

He was relieved.

"Oh, yes, that's right. Well, where do I find you when I get back?"

"You can come by the office either at lunch time or after work one day. Thanks for the ride, James. I must get home now."

Rose left quickly and James could see her long white dress slowly disappear into the dark like a ghost in the night. He was pleased that they made a date and he drew comfort in hearing her refer to him as James for the first time. He started his motorcycle and drove off toward home.

It was noon the next day when Jennifer Nolan emerged from her bed with a hangover. Jennifer did not drink that much at the party. She only had two glasses of wine. It was the mixture of red and white that made her delicate insides turn into convulsive eruptions of pain. Fiona and Crissie tried to comfort her throughout the morning. They brought aspirins, tea and breakfast, but she refused to eat. When she walked into the living room, Crissie asked how she felt.

"Oh, awful. This is the worst hangover I ever had. I'm not going to drink any more!"

"Here, sit down and don't move around too much."

"Okay, thanks, Crissie. You and Fiona have been so helpful. By the way, where is Fiona?"

"She went for a ride with Phil up the mountain."

Jennifer tried to read a book but her head was throbbing.

A red car drove up the driveway. As it got closer, the girls saw Marg Prudhdoe and one of her friends. They had been to the Gymkhana Club to play tennis. Marg got out of the car and tried to persuade the other woman to come in for a cup of tea. Unsuccessful, she waved goodbye and quickly skipped up the walkway. Marg was not a pretty girl, although she thought she was. Her thin lips and pug nose made her look crafty.

The well fitted tennis skirt and blouse complemented her well-formed 120-pound body. Although only 5' 3", she appeared to be taller due to her high waist line. She was long in the legs but short from waist to shoulder and given the wrong selection of clothes, she could look shapeless. She consciously and meticulously chose outfits that complimented her. At times Marg was funny. She would affect the most posh British accent when composed, but if ever ruffled about something, she lost her composure and broke out in a

234

broad Liverpool accent. "My Fair Lady" Marg was one of the biggest phonies in Mzuzu and her golden yellow dyed hair didn't help conceal the phoniness either.

Marg came swaggering through the living room door and loudly greeted the two girls. She then shouted unsympathetically.

"How's that head of yours? That should teach you not to stay out all night."

Annoyed at both the comment and the loudness of Marg's voice, Jennifer retorted.

"We did not stay out all night and do you mind, Marg? You don't have to speak so loud."

"Yes, I do mind. Why should I keep quiet while you sit and nurse your headache? You apparently expect everyone around here to sulk while you recuperate and I think it's awfully selfish of you, Jennifer."

Marg walked out of the living room in a huff.

Phil Harrington and Fiona Crewe were standing over looking the City of Mzuzu. They were 4,000 feet up the mountain and had a magnificent panoramic view. They were in love and talked of eventually getting married.

Fiona spoke with a mild Geordie accent.

"I just love this place. It will always be special to me. Looking across the hills and valleys around Mzuzu is awesome! It's so unspoiled and I hope it stays this way."

"I do, too. It would be a shame if this sort of natural beauty were spoiled by polluting factories, earth movers, and snarling traffic jams."

"I agree. It's beautiful up here on the plateau. The forestry commission does a good job of preserving it. Do they own those log-cabins up there, Phil?"

Phil looked at the crowded restaurant ahead.

"Did you hear me?"

"Oh. Sorry, Fiona. I didn't. I was looking at the restaurant and how it's built extending out over the cliff. A lot of work must have gone into the design and structure of that place. Shall we go over?"

As they approached the building, Fiona again asked Phil about the log cabins.

"I have heard that the Americans, British and French own some of the cabins. One of the American volunteers in Blantyre told me that the cabins are available for rent."

"Oh, that sounds like a smashing idea. Let's rent one for a weekend."

"Okay, but it depends on how booked up they are and I gather bookings have to be placed two months in advance, at least."

"We can wait. This will give us something to look forward to. Oh, Phil, book as soon as you can. I would love to spend a weekend in one of those cabins."

The Mountain View Restaurant was a popular place on weekends. Lunches and dinners would have to be booked two to three weeks in advance. Inside the building, approximately twenty tables filled the room. The place was owned and operated by a British couple that had come to Malawi in 1951. The inside decor was still very European in style, the only exception being a large photograph of President General Aleke Makube. In one corner of the room, an old riding saddle and boots hung on the wall. There were photographs of 18th century British Officers and troops, a picture of Queen Elizabeth and displays of Wedgewood china. The wooden floor looked well waxed and shiny and the chairs and tables had a

Victorian flair. The expatriate community patronized the place. There was an exclusive air about the Mountain View Restaurant, and the steep prices for meals and drinks helped to keep it that way. The outside patio that overlooked the east rim of the plateau provided a fascinating view of a waterfall in the distance. More conventional metal tables and chairs were placed around the open patio. Malawian waiters served inside and out. Their black pants, red coats and white shirts always looked immaculate, but somehow these uniforms were too formal for such a natural setting. T-shirts and shorts would have seemed more appropriate. In the rear of the restaurant were rows of little huts. This was where the staff and their families lived.

Phil and Fiona sat at one of the tables outside on the patio. Promptly, the waiter was there to take their orders.

"What would you like, Fiona?"

"I don't know really. Something cold and refreshing."

Phil, whose confidence and sense of humor had increased since dating Fiona, turned to the waiter and said.

"One tall lemonade and one something cold and refreshing."

The waiter laughed and so did Fiona.

Phil smirked as he said, "You do have something cold and refreshing, don't you?"

"Yes, sir."

The waiter hurried off. Fiona thought it was hilarious and anxiously awaited the waiter's return to see what he would bring. About five minutes later, he arrived with a lemon drink and a tall Coke float, with vanilla ice cream topped with crushed pineapple and a cherry, all floating on the Coke.

"Oh, Phil, look! Isn't that delightful?"

"Gee, you can say that again. The next time, I will order one, too."

The waiter stood there with a smile of success on his face.

"Do you like it, madam?"

"Yes, indeed. You made a very good choice. Thank you."

The waiter left after receiving a small tip and the two lovers sat and drank with arms locked across the table.

"Did you enjoy the party last night, Fiona?"

"Yes. I had a smashing time. I think Muwalo is such a nice person and he's very popular."

"Yes, I like him, too. Was Jennifer very sick this morning?"

"Oh, yes. I felt so sorry for her but there was not much we could do. I think she mixed her drinks and that leaves an awful after-effect. It should wear off soon, I hope. Did you feel all right this morning?"

"No problems at all. I had one beer all night. You know I'm not much of a drinker."

A young Malawian who worked with the Ministry of Health interrupted their conversation. He had met Phil during the week of Phil's arrival and remembered him only by face.

"Hello. Do you remember me? We met at Regional headquarters when you first came."

"Oh, yes. How are you?"

"I'm fine, thank you. Are you enjoying yourself in our country?"

"Yes. Very much."

"Good. I must go now. Bye."

238

"Bye."

When the young man was out of sight Fiona giggled.

"What are you giggling about?"

"You should have seen the expression on your face Phil. You obviously didn't know him from Adam. I think he picked it up, too."

"I do remember him vaguely."

Phil laughed, too.

"Oh, Phil, did you know that Jennifer fancies James?"

"No. Why do you think she fancies him?"

"She told me."

"She did?"

"Yes. We were talking one night and she told me how kind he's been to her ever since the first day they met in training. She says he's one of the few people she knows who is really like a friend and brother to her."

"It's true he's always been kind to her, but I don't think it's any thing other than that. You know how James is. He likes to be loose."

"Well, Jennifer feels it's more than just a platonic relationship. I think she loves him."

"Tell me, what did happen during your training program?"

"What do you mean? A lot of things happened. Do you have anything in particular in mind?"

"No, I've just heard rumors about some girl having a nervous breakdown, and people quitting. Are these things true? Come on, Phil, tell me what happened."

Phil, who wasn't much for gossip tried to relate as objectively as possible the incidents, which had happened during training at San Diego. They sat for almost two hours discussing various characters and incidents. Fiona was a good interrogator because she made Phil remember things that he would otherwise have forgotten. After they finished talking, Fiona felt that she had a greater insight into the Americans who had come to Malawi as volunteers.

It was afternoon when they started their journey back downhill. They were just in time to catch the downhill flow of traffic. The road was single track, so a timing system was set up to allow the one-way traffic to flow quickly in either direction.

A half hour later, they turned into the driveway leading to the house. James had just arrived and was strapping his helmet to the cycle.

"Hi, guys, where have you been?"

"Up to the mountain," Fiona exclaimed excitedly "It's beautiful up there. You must go up when you get back."

"Yes, I will. Good party last night, wasn't it?"

Fiona and Phil agreed. Once they finished affixing their helmets to the motorcycle, the three slowly walked up the walkway and entered the house. Jennifer, who was feeling much better, still looked washed out. James looked at her.

"My goodness. What happened to you?"

"I had too much to drink last night."

"You can say that again, the way you look."

They both smiled. Then he looked at Crissie.

"Now, you look in fine form today, Crissie. No hangover or anything, I see."

"I'm feeling fine, James. What about you?"

"Oh, me? You know me. I swim with the tides. One minute I'm down and the next minute up. Granted, I felt like I had rocks in my head this morning but it's all gone now."

Fiona and Marg had tea prepared. There were cucumber sandwiches, bread and butter slices, and an assortment of cakes and pastries. This was to be a "typical" British Tea. A tea cozy was place over a large pot of tea. Just as the girls finished setting the dining room table, a motorcycle could be heard roaring up the driveway.

Marg said gleefully, "That must be Bob."

Fiona seemed surprised.

"Oh, I didn't know that Bob was coming."

By this time, the group sitting in the living room saw Bob. James whispered in undertones to Jennifer.

"You didn't tell me he was coming."

"It's as much a surprise to me as it is to you. Perhaps Marg invited him although she didn't tell us."

Before they could sort out who invited Bob, he appeared at the door and knocked. It wasn't necessary to knock since the door was open, but Bob was slightly on edge. The type of edginess one gets when he's not sure whether he's welcome or not. Marg dashed quickly from the kitchen to the front door and held Bob's hand as he entered the house. He spoke to everyone and sat near the door. There was the type of silence that prevails when an outsider has intruded a group. James had no intention of trying to make him feel at ease and Jennifer was not in the mood. Phil decided to break the ice.

"How have you been, Bob?"

"Okay, Phil, and you?"

"I'm fine. I imagine you are very busy over at the training center."

Bob talked for several minutes about some of the projects the students were working on. When he finished, silence ensued. Fiona came out of the dinning room.

"Tea is ready."

They all got up and proceeded to the dinning room table. There were only 6 chairs.

"I'll get the stool from the kitchen." said Marg.

"Oh let me get it for you."

"No, you sit here, Bob."

Marg placed Bob at one end of the table. The other girls were annoyed, especially since they had not invited him. Jennifer said.

"James, you sit there."

This was the opposite end of the table. While Marg was in the kitchen getting the stool, Jennifer quickly arranged seats for the others. Marg ended up having to sit on the stool to her dismay. She also knew that Jennifer was pleased about her little maneuver.
The games people play continued. Marg refused to be beaten at the game of one-upwomanship, so she decided to take the initiative again.

"I will pour the tea. You take milk don't you, Bob? You, too, Phil. Oh, James, I recall no milk in your tea."

Marg poured milk followed by hot tea into cups. Jennifer thought to herself, "This silly woman will stop at nothing to get her own way. Well, not while I'm around."

After about five minutes everyone sat back in their chairs and silently thought.

"Whew!"

Bob and James talked for the first time that afternoon.

"I hear you're off for three weeks starting tomorrow."

"That's right, Bob."

"You must be excited about your trip."

"Yes, I am."

James discussed his trip and which route he would take. He told them that he would stay with Stuart Steiner the following weekend. Then Marg spoke.

"A friend of mine said he saw Stuart last week. Stuart's got a girlfriend who works in Zambia. I hear she teaches the terrorists."

"What are you talking about, Marg?" James asked with a certain vexation.

"Well, this friend of mine said this girl is involved with ZINAP. You know, that murdering gang from Rhodesia."

Even Bob knew how loose-tongued Marg could be and how she exaggerated things. He said in an unassuming tone of voice.

"Marg, you should not talk about things like that unless it's a fact. That's a pretty serious accusation to make against someone."

"It's true. It's true, I tell you. That's what Jerry told me."

After that outburst, a hush fell over the table. It was embarrassing even for James and Jennifer who didn't like Bob or Marg. She had inadvertently let on that she was still seeing her ex-boyfriend. Everyone assumed it was over since Bob Newgate was supposed to be her man now. The atmosphere around the table was awkward. Bob quickly finished his sandwich and said.

"Excuse me. Thanks for the tea."

He went into the living room and picked up his motorcycle helmet. As he walked out of the door Marg ran after him. He did not say a word as she followed him to the end of the walkway and down the steps. The others could no longer see them but noticed that several minutes elapsed before Bob Newgate got on his cycle and drove off. Marg ran back to the house in a fit of tears. She did not return to the table but ran into her room and locked the door. Fiona was about to go in after her when Phil said.

"Leave her be."

There was a feeling of relief as the others retired to the front lawn. They sat spread out in a circle about twenty feet away from the front door. They discussed what Marg had said about Stuart's new girlfriend.

"I realized she runs off at the mouth a lot but do you think there's anything in the rumor, Phil?"

"I don't know. Stuart's never said anything to me about a girl friend."

"Well, I did meet the girl the weekend of my party. But Stuart had just met her so it wasn't a big deal then. She teaches up that way somewhere and ZINAP operates up there. But that's no reason to associate the girl with them. Hell, there are hundreds of teachers from Europe and America working in Zambia."

Jennifer interjected a thought.

"It's possible that the girl teaches children whose families are members of ZINAP, but that doesn't mean she is involved in any of their activities."

"You might be right," said Phil. "But it's highly probably that she would be involved if she teaches their children."

Fiona joined the conversation and contributed a piece of information that might have explained the girl's involvement.

"You know, before I came out here, the agency that recruited me had a list of teaching vacancies in this part of Africa. The list also contained the names of organizations that sponsored mission schools. If my memory serves me right, there is a mission school just across the border in Zambia funded by an International Christian Organization. I remember, because I was interested in teaching in a mission school. This girl probably teaches at that school, which is apparently near the ZINAP refugee camps. But I doubt if a Christian sponsored mission would be involved in revolutionary work."

"Gee, Fiona, that makes a lot of sense. Maybe the girl is just a teacher."

James said that as if he hoped it were true.

"As a matter of interest, what do you make of all this ZINAP business?"

Fiona looked at Crissie as if she had to be cautious about what she said around her,

"Politics is not my forte, James."

"Right. I gotcha."

James implied that he understood her discretion.

Crissie was a middle-class Malawian teacher who obviously supported the government. She was shrewd, ambitious and one of the few Malawi women in the Malawi Congress Party, the ruling party. This was a good enough reason to speak discretely about Malawi politics around her. In fact, perhaps they had said too much already. No one suspected Crissie of being a government spy but it was known that Crissie dated one of the junior ministers in Blantyre. He had direct access to President Makube's personal secretary. An off the cuff statement could easily reach the President's office. He was a man so sensitive about political meddling by foreigners that any rumor, however farfetched, was enough to cause him to act impetuously.

It was six o'clock when James looked at his watch. It was almost dark as he walked to his motorcycle, accompanied by Jennifer. She considered him to be her guest, but he just thought of himself as one of the boys being invited by them all. When they got to the cycle she fiddled with the handbrakes while he put on his helmet.

"You'll probably need a good solid meal when you get back. Do you want to come over for dinner?"

"Oh, you don't have to bother Jennifer. I won't starve, you know."

Anxiously she said, "Oh, it's no bother, James. Three weeks is a long time. I'd like for you to come over."

It was then that he realized that their platonic relationship had ended. Jennifer was very fond of him and was sending out very strong signals to let him know. He had not thought of her in that context. He liked Jennifer, but did not want to get too seriously involved. He didn't want to let her down like Steve Manski had done. He also wanted to pursue his relationship with Rose Nkhoma, the girl from Rhodesia.

"I never could turn down an offer for a good meal Jennifer. Okay. I will either return on a Saturday or a Sunday. In the meantime, you should do more than just sit around this school all the time. Why don't you get out and meet a few more people. Otherwise a place like this could bore you silly."

She grabbed his arm, lifted herself by tiptoeing and kissed him on the cheek.

"Take care of yourself out there."

"Okay. Bye."

She stood watching as he drove away.

White Rock

James left early the following morning. He picked up the Ministry's Land Rover and drove out in a Southwesterly direction across barren dirt roads. His first clinic was in a village about thirty miles away. He hoped to cover at least one clinic a day and if lucky, two on some days. The interviews with clinic staff, along with inventories of their supplies could take up to eight hours to complete. This was assuming that the clinics were not too large. He was told that three of the clinics were almost double the size of the others. They had more staff, more supplies and more patients. It would be several days before he got to them. His plan was to spend the day at the first clinic and drive another fifty miles that evening. He would then spend the night there and start his work early the next day. He hoped to be able to stick to this schedule when clinics weren't too far apart, because long drives in the heat of the day were exhausting. Two hours later, he reached his first clinic. Mr. Chiwala was the resident nurse and he had one trainee assistant working with him. James got out of the Land Rover and introduced himself.

"Oh, yes. Mr. Johnson, we have been expecting you. Please come in, sir."

James went in and was offered a seat after being introduced to the assistant. Mr. Chiwala ordered tea and they sat talking for almost an hour. Then James was shown around the clinic. The building was relatively modern in comparison to its surroundings. Its cinder block walls supported a corrugated metal roof. The thirty by thirty foot structure was divided into four rooms. One was used as a supply room. Another room contained four single beds reserved for people recovering from serious illnesses. The largest room contained two tables. Mr. Chiwala used them to treat first aide cases. However, since he was not a doctor, he did not perform major operations. This was left for visiting doctors. James noticed that each room had a picture of President Mukabe hanging high on the wall.

Village houses surrounded the building. The people of the village felt fortunate to have such a facility although people from other villages also used it. It stood as a status symbol and a reward for the village's unstinting support for the Malawi Congress Party. James noticed that the children were not playing, but going about their chores. Everyone seemed to work, including toddlers who tugged away at the outer leaves of dried corncobs.

Soon they re-entered the supply room and Mr. Chiwala apologized for not having supplies in the right order. He said that they were so busy that they never got the chance to place things properly. They just look around until they found what they needed. James offered to help with ideas about keeping supplies stocked properly. Shortly after their tour, patients started to arrive. In three hours, James managed to inventory and catalogue only about half the clinics supplies. The job was proving to require a lot more time and effort than previously thought. It was the first time any kind of comprehensive inventory of clinics supplies and needs had been attempted in Malawi. No one knew how extensive the task would be. James emerged from the hot room and went outside the building to get some fresh air. Mr. Chiwala came over and suggested they go for lunch. The village chief had food prepared and wanted James and Mr. Chiwala to be his guests for lunch.

They walked to a larger than normal size village house. It too was made of cinder blocks and appeared conspicuously out of place among the thatch roof mud-brick houses. It was the Chief's house, built by the same people who had constructed the clinic. The cinder blocks were painted white and the windows had glass-panes, a sure sign of success and status in a village that small. There were three women of varying ages standing outside the door. They wore colorful wrap-around garments with beaded necklaces. They all smiled when their husband, Chief Ngumayo, made his regal exit through the door. He was an old balding man with a heavy beard. The Chief was dressed in his tribal gown and cap. James was nervous. He did not feel that his visit to the clinic warranted such a reception. The Chief did not speak English but Mr. Chiwala translated for him. James greeted the Chief.

"I am pleased to meet you, sir, and I am heartened by your kind hospitality. You have a wonderful village and my only regret is that I cannot spend more time here."

The Chief was pleased. They sat down at a table that was brought from the house. The Chief was interested in James's experiences living in America. They talked about several other subjects including the clinic. The Chief's next project was to get the government to build a modern primary school in his village. He also hinted that James could put in a good word for him. James did not want to disappoint the Chief by letting on that he was not that influential.

Lunch consisted of stewed chicken and gravy, dried fish and cassava. The Chief also passed around a bowl of village beer. After the meal, James shook the Chief's hands and bade him farewell. The rest of the afternoon proved to be tedious and exhausting. Interviews were conducted. Inventories and forms were completed. It was six o' clock that evening when James left the clinic for his fifty mile journey to the next village. It would take at least two hours to drive the distance. The winding narrow roads led uphill towards the mountains. Under the best conditions, only about twenty-five miles could be covered in an hour. James was concerned about finding the place in the dark. There were no road signs up that way and often the main road branched off into smaller tracks leading to nowhere. He did not want to sleep in the Land Rover parked in the middle of nowhere, although he had a sleeping bag.

After an hour of continuous driving, it was pitch dark outside. The only lights were those on the vehicle. Not even the stars were seen that evening. James noticed the temperature dropping. He was tired and weary and wished he had stayed at the clinic. He pulled over to the side of the road and stopped the vehicle. He felt as though he was pushing himself too hard. He put his sweater on and smoked a cigarette. He wondered if the tea in the thermos bottle was still warm. Tea might help me wake up. He had never seen nights as dark as these before. It gave him the jitters. He was getting closer to Kapango Village and could see the forest in the mountains ahead.

"Those people are really isolated. I would not want to live up there too long."

James Edward Johnson bounced along that lonely African road for another two hours. He could count on his fingers the number of times the speedometer registered fifteen miles per hour or more. It was a long, hard, boring drive not being able to see more than twenty feet ahead. The road became narrow and the bushes on the side seemed to grow into huge trees with sinister looking branches, which occasionally took a swipe at the windshield. It was nine o'clock. He had been on the road three hours and hadn't seen a sign of life anywhere. He was lost. Soon he came to another hill, which bore down to the right. A few hundred yards down, the road branched four ways. He couldn't figure out which was the main road since they all looked like dirt tracks.

"What now, James Johnson, all American Adventurer? What in the hell are you doing stuck in a place like this? Let's see you get out of this one. There's no one to ask, and you sure can't sweet-talk the trees, because they look mean as hell. Make up your mind boy because I'm scared."

James was alone, confused and afraid. He didn't know what he was afraid of which only served to exacerbate his anxieties. He drove down to the intersection and just sat there for about fifteen minutes trying to decide which road to take.

Suddenly, a small star appeared in the sky just above the road on the complete right.

"That must be my calling. I got nothing else to go on. Oh, thank you, Jesus! Thank you, Lord!"

He turned right on to the road and after several minutes found himself climbing higher and higher. Before long, he came to an old broken down gate. To the left of the gate was a signpost but all he could see were the letters R-E-A. The other letters were covered in mud.

"Well, somebody must live in there or why would there be a gate here?"

He drove through the gate and came to a clearing. There were trees on two sides and a rocky hill straight ahead. There was no sign of life.

"This place is deserted but I can't keep driving around all night. My arm is sore from changing gears so much and I can hardly see a thing. I'd better sleep here tonight. Sure is spooky around here, though."

The forest was damp and cold. James got out of the vehicle and shivered. The night noises were horrific. He had no idea that animals could be so loud. He went to the back of the Land Rover and untied the canvas cover. Once inside he shone his flashlight about to find his sleeping bag. It took ten minutes or so to move paraphernalia and equipment to one side of the vehicle so that he could roll out his sleeping bag. Before lying down he tightened the ropes on the canvas from the inside. He lay uncomfortably for several minutes listening and trying to identify various noises. Soon he was asleep.

Two hours passed before a pack of wild African dogs roamed across the clearing. They sniffed and barked and made scratching noises just outside the vehicle. The commotion woke James.

"My God! What's that?"

As he came to, he could see the canvas moving and heard clawing, scratching noises.

"Oh, no! A lion. No. Not, this way. Oh, God. Not eaten alive by a lion. . ."

James panicked while scrambling for the lift-jack handle. He could not see, but was afraid to use his flashlight for fear of attracting the intruders even more. Finally, he grabbed the jack and started hitting at any movement he saw in the canvas. There were so many that he thought there were several lions. His last swing must have caught the paw of one of the dogs because it yelped and screamed. Soon the scratching stopped, but he still heard sniffs and barks. Plucking up enough courage to peer through the bottom of the canvas, he saw about seven dogs outside. Two were attending the injured one by licking his paw while the others ran around.

The dogs slowly wandered off about fifty yards away. James couldn't see them, but he could surely hear them, they were growling and snarling at something. He didn't know what they had caught, but was glad they hadn't caught him.

"I'm getting out of here," he thought.

Then he felt that he was too tired. He quickly moved to the cab of the truck and found that he could not stretch out. He locked the doors and spread the sleeping bag over him as he sat crouched over with his head resting on the steering wheel. Soon he too added to the night noises.

About 4:30 in the morning the sun began to rise. James was oblivious to all that was happening around him. Birds began to tweet and water buffalo grunted. Kudu could be seen making fleeting passes across brooks and streams while herds of Zebra made their way down hill to bask in the heat of the flat bush country. By 5:30 that morning the forest was awake and aware. The survival game was in full swing as every living creature preyed upon another. James was too far away from the nearby stream to notice the frog gobbling up a green snake. Nor could he see the wild-hog being viciously torn apart while still living by a pack of wild Jackals. Buzzards flew high and parakeets merged in with the array of colors in the forest. Awakened by sounds of picks and shovels striking the earth's surface, he slowly opened his eyes. The initial glare of the sun in his face momentarily blinded him. As his eyes slowly re-focused, he faintly saw four metal rings pressed against the windscreen. He could not yet make out what they were. He rubbed his eyes and his vision cleared.

"Ah, no. I give up," he shouted.

He found himself looking down the barrels of four semiautomatic rifles. He looked up to see four gruesome looking burley black faces peering down at him. The men wore black berets and green Army uniforms.

"Open the door slowly and get out with your hands held high behind your head," shouted one of the men.

James was so stunned that he opened the door and fell out of the seat. The moment he landed face down on the ground, he felt a boot on his neck. He remained pinned down for several moments while some one handcuffed his hands behind his back. They grabbed him by the arms and forcefully lifted him off the ground. While being frisked by one man, another began to interrogate him.

"What is your name? What are you doing here? Didn't you read the sign that read *Restricted Area, No Trespassing?*"

The questions were coming so fast that James forgot them.

"My name is James Johnson. I got lost last night. I'm lost, I tell you. I didn't see a sign. Please, I'm with the Ministry of Health and I visit health clinics. That's all, mister."

"Where are your papers? Prove yourself."

"There in the Land Rover. I'm telling you the truth."

James was so shaken by events that he had not noticed he was in the middle of an excavation site. There were several Europeans and Africans digging samples of white rocks about twenty yards in front of him. There were also two Land Rovers and three Army jeeps parked near the cliff edge. One small tent stood brilliantly near a stream. The bright sun accented its orange color. While continuing the interrogation, two of the men searched his vehicle from top to bottom. Then he was ushered over to the tent as if he was a criminal and made to squat on the ground. One of the men went to the jeep and pulled out a short-wave radio. He called someone and then put the radio back. By this time a white man wearing the same type of Army clothes came up from behind a small cliff. He was a

Captain by rank and was accompanied by two African officers. When he got to the tent, he asked one of the men if he'd radioed.

"Yes, sir."

"Good. Now Mr. Johnson, who do you claim to be? Tell me why you are here and who you work for again."

"Look mister—I mean, sir—I'm just a planning assistant in the Ministry of Health. I came out here with the U.S. Peace Corps. I'm an American. I got lost last night trying to find Chipango Village. I got to the intersection a few miles back down the road and didn't know which way to go. When I saw the gate last night, I thought maybe someone lived up here and I could ask directions. That's all, mister. What's with this place, anyway? I mean, all the guns and soldiers, restricted area. . . Hell, I just want to get out of here."

"Mr. Johnson, I suggest that you don't concern yourself with what we're doing here. You're in enough trouble as it is. Now, you will have to wait a while until we check your statement. If you are who you claim to be, you will be released. But you must not mention this to anyone. Is that understood?"

"Yes, sir. Look, I'm innocent. These guys treated me as if I was some criminal."

"We will check your story. In the meantime, I will arrange for some coffee and breakfast for you. Those cuffs will be taken off, but you must be guarded. One thing is for sure, you obviously lived in America for a long time with an accent like that. Where are you from, the South?"

"Virginia."

"Yes, I thought as much."

The white officer with a British accent moved off briskly, followed by the two Malawian officers. Several minutes later a folding table was erected. A soldier brought a mug of black coffee and a tin of cold beans. That was breakfast. James sat there still dazed by the events of the night and morning.

"First dogs of prey, then dogs of war. I never bargained for this. Look at that guy holding that gun. He looks as if he'd take pleasure blowing my brains out this morning. He's a mean looking dude. At least the British guy was civil. I think he believes me, but obviously he has to check. What the hell is so secret around here anyway?"

James put his hand under his sweater to get his cigarettes. The soldier flinched and came closer with the gun. He didn't speak English but James figured he would understand cigarettes.

"Cigarettes," he said with a smile.

The soldier nodded. He took out the packet and offered one to the soldier, who looked happy and took one. The clearing was much larger than he had imagined. It was about half the size of a football field. Beyond the cliffs, a huge waterfall could be seen. Three small tributaries merged to form the waterfall. Below it was a large clear pool. Men were working near the cliff. They were putting samples of white rocks into a transparent plastic container. They wore gloves and used huge prongs to lift the rocks.

"I wonder what kind of rocks they are. Those are some funny looking instruments they're holding over the rocks."

A soldier who brought another folding chair to the table interrupted James's thoughts. Then he returned with a pot of tea. For a moment James thought it was for him. Then a young redhead freckle-faced white boy walked towards the table. He sat down and looked at James suspiciously. He thought James was a captured criminal. As he poured his tea, he spilt some on his Khaki shorts and shouted.

"Bloody hell," James said with a grin.

"What are you smiling about?" he asked.

"Nothing, just the expressions you British use sometimes."

"Who are you then?"

"Who? Me? I'm just a black American Peace Corps volunteer who happens to be sitting here being treated like a criminal."

"Oh. You're American?"

The suspicious look on the boy's face seemed to gradually disappear. He asked James what he did and how long he'd been in the country. They talked for about five minutes before James asked him a question.

"Are you an anthropologist excavating for old ruins or something?"

"No."

"What are you digging for then?"

The boy didn't answer. There was silence as the boy realized he'd talked too much. He got up quickly, finished his tea while standing and left. Two hours later the white Army officer re-appeared.

"You can go now. But remember, you've seen nothing here."

"Thanks. How do I get to Chipango Village?"

"Go back down to the intersection and take the first road to the right. It's about ten miles up that road. You can't miss the village because that's where the road ends. Now, I suggest you get moving and quickly."

"Yes, sir."

James drove out of the clearing like a bat out of hell. He left a trail of dust and tire tracks in the ground. It wasn't until he had driven about five miles up the road to Chipango that he realized how furious he was.

"I could shoot the bastards for treating me that way. I ought to report this to the U.S. Embassy. Hell, I've got rights, too. Who do they think they are, handcuffing me, pushing me around and making me sit out there for two hours? I'll fix them. I'll tell everyone. They must be trying to hide something important with all that security."

James eventually found Chipango Village and ended up staying there until the middle of the next day. He managed to complete his work at three more villages before Saturday morning. That evening he arrived at Stuart Steiner's house. Stuart lived in a thatch roof wood hut just off the main road next to a large village. It was no different from most of the other village houses. There was neither a door nor glass windows. Stuart roughed it. The only extension was a large tent standing next to the building. This was his "guest house" as he put it. Since his hut was already crowded and wasn't very large, he negotiated a tent from the Ministry of Forestry. James was to use the tent. Stuart had shaved off his beard and mustache and looked thinner. He asked what had been happening in the big city of Mzuzu and how his tour had gone so far. As they sat on the straw mats drinking Coke just outside the hut's door they talked about Muwalo's party, tea with the girls and his first clinic visit. Then Stuart was told about his ordeal with the Army up in the mountains. He was fascinated by the story and when James mentioned the white rocks Stuart became excited.

"Uranium, James. Uranium! That's big, man. Do you know that could put this place on the map? Didn't you say you saw white rocks in a container?"

"Yes, I did."

"Well, you saw uranium. That's how it looks. It's not a rock, though, it's more like metal.

"No wonder those guys gave you a rough time. That's probably top secret."

"Hey, you got me scared now, Stuart. I'm not supposed to say a word to anyone, okay?"

"Sure, but there's no reason for you to be afraid. I'm sure if you stumbled across the place, others have, too."

"Just promise me, Stuart."

"Okay, man. Okay."

They changed the subject and talked about some other things for a while. Then James asked how Stuart and Janice were getting on.

"We see each other every now and then," replied Stuart casually.

"What's 'every now and then'? Every weekend?"

"What makes you say that?"

"Oh, a little birdie told me."

"Hell, there are no secrets around this place are there?"

"I'm afraid not, Stuart. By the way, I've got something I want to ask you but I don't want you to think I'm being nosey for my own sake, rather for yours."

"What is it?"

"Well, do you remember I said I had tea with the girls last Sunday? Anyway, there's this British girl name Marg Prudhoe who lives with them and sometimes she suffers from diarrhea of the mouth. We were sitting around the table talking casually and Jennifer asked about you. Then this Marg chick said she heard that Janice teaches the terrorists. Well, of course, everyone got annoyed at her for spreading rumors. I thought I'd mention it so that you would know what people, are saying."

Stuart sat back and took another drink.

 "So do you think she's telling the truth?"

"Me? Well, I have no reason to believe her. She's always exaggerated things. Why? It's not true, is it?"

"Of course, it's not true. There are no terrorists up there anyway. They're freedom fighters."

James almost choked on his drink after that statement.

"Ah, wait a minute. Are you confirming or denying that the girl is involved with what's going on up there?"

"Neither. I've never been up there, so I don't know."

James remained quiet while he tried to analyze Stuart's remarks. He felt that Stuart was being evasive and he wondered if in fact Marg's rumor was true. He also wondered whether Stuart had begun to get involved politically. He still had suspicions about Janice Blanche, since she denied ever meeting him before.

"You must be getting hungry. I got a fresh chicken from the village this morning. It's out back stewing in a pot. Actually, I'm expecting Janice this evening. She's going to bring along a few dishes of food and some fresh bread."

"You mean Janice is coming tonight?"

"That' what I just said, man. Why are you so nervous about her?"

"I'm not nervous. I just didn't expect to see her. I hope I'm not intruding on your plans."

"Don't be silly."

"I am filthy with sweat and dust. Have you got any water around here?"

"Yes, there's a tub full out back. Also there's a washing pan. You can use that to put the water in."

James laughed.

"I always wanted to stay in a luxury hotel like this. Excellent facilities and the service ain't bad either."

Stuart chuckled.

"You've got to admit, James, it's not a bad deal when you're getting it free."

"Free? You ought to pay me for daring to stay here."

"You better get washed while the water is there. That's my supply until Monday, you know."

Janice Blanche arrived about seven o'clock and brought a box of food with her. There were canned peas and beans, fresh vegetables, two loaves of freshly baked bread and a chocolate cake she baked herself. James was in the tent when she greeted Stuart. He was surprised at how familiar they seemed with each other. Stuart held her in his arms and they kissed for several moments. She seemed happy as she showed Stuart what she brought. Janice wore a light brown skirt, white fitted t-shirt and tennis shoes. She looked more feminine to James than she had on previous occasions. He was surprised at how shapely her legs and body was. He slowly emerged from the tent clearing his throat to warn them of his presence.

"Oh, hello, James. It's nice to see you again."

"Hi Janice, same here."

"Did you enjoy your trip?"

"Some of it, yes," James said.

Then Stuart joined in.

"He had quite an ordeal a few days back, but I'm sure he will tell you about it later. Hey, we're starving, Janice. Shall we get the food ready?"

James offered his help, but was told to sit down and relax. It took fifteen minutes for them to return from the rear of the hut. James assumed that Stuart had told Janice all they talked about. The evening turned dark before they sat down to eat. Stuart brought two oil lanterns outside. It was hot and the mosquitoes were out in force. The three of them sat fanning away mosquitoes as they ate their dinner. James found it a strain to talk to Janice because he felt she was always on her guard. She seemed tense around him. She was more relaxed with Stuart. He sat wondering what she was hiding? He thought that she felt guilty because she denied meeting him and maybe she work for the terrorists and didn't want him to know. He didn't like her much and sensed that the feeling was mutual.

After the meal was over, Janice went to the Land Rover and got a bottle of expensive looking Portuguese wine. Stuart uncorked it and poured them each a drink. Stuart got up to gather the dishes. He took one lantern and said he would wash them.

Janice and James sat for a while without talking. Finally, he said that he remembered seeing her in California. She smiled.

"I'm not sure of that, yet."

"What do you mean?"

"Can we drop it, James? I'll let you know tomorrow before I leave."

He thought she was weird. His mind boggled.

"This chick is either crazy or playing games. How can she not be sure whether she met me or not? Why does she have to wait until tomorrow before she lets me know? Well, I'm not going out of my way to be nice to her. Hell, who cares anyway whether she admits to meeting me or not?"

He got up.

"Excuse me, I left something in the tent."

He left and didn't return until he heard Stuart's voice. The guys laughed about some of the incidents during training and they joked about the American Ambassador, The Honorable Hewitt T. Smith.

"Yes, that old fuddy-duddy thought he was shrewd, but I outsmarted him that night," Stuart said.

"Yes, and when I told him that I supported all the activities of the NAACP, he almost choked on his whiskey," replied James.

Janice changed the topic of conversation.

"What are your views about President Makube's leadership, James?"

"Wow. That's a heavy question out of nowhere. How do I know? I don't think I've been here long enough to assess his performance."

"Then you obviously think he's doing a good job or else you would have definite views."

"I wouldn't put it that way. Just because I didn't express any views doesn't mean that I support everything he's doing."

"I think the old man is conservative as hell," Stuart added. "From what I have learned about this country, he's put very little money into housing, education, health and other social needs. Just look around you, James. Sure, there are thriving businesses and a few Malawians drive around in expensive cars, but most of the profits go outside the country."

James realized that they both shared the same opinion of the President. He also felt they were trying to influence him for some reason.

"Well, I don't know. I've seen two new health clinics and three new primary schools during the past week. Plus there's a stadium and a University being built in Blantyre. Someone is putting up the cash."

Both Janice and Stuart laughed as if James's comments were stupid. She told him that the Presidential palace cost twice as much as all those other projects put together and that the President had three Rolls Royces and two Cadillacs that could pay for two modern secondary schools.

"No, Janice. I didn't know those things. Anyway, we can always find fault with any government, but what's the alternative?"

He played right into Janice's hand without knowing it. She sat back, smiled and began her political indoctrination.

"I see the President as an impediment to economic progress and true socialism. He allows wealth to leave the country through the greedy hands of his capitalist mentors. Even the little wealth that remains in the country is distributed unevenly. Look around you and see the poverty, disease and sickness. The alternative is to install a government, which would control the means of production and distribution of wealth, thereby assuring that the needs of the people are looked after. Karl Marx taught us that the people, the workers of society, are entitled to the full fruits of their labor. The worker provides the labor, which creates wealth. So why should this wealth be turned over to the fat capitalists? He also predicted the fall of capitalist systems as a result of the increasing misery of the masses of good, hard working, honest people. It's happening now, James. It's happening in Europe, Asia, and Latin America and to a lesser degree in America. Why shouldn't it? I'm all for nationalizing banks, key sectors of industry, education and welfare. At least the people have a better chance of receiving the rewards of their own efforts."

James didn't know what to make of that speech. He said his first thoughts out aloud.

"What are you, a communist?" Janice replied pertly.

"No, I'm a socialist concerned with seeing positive changes in this part of Africa and the only way that will happen is to get rid of those racist, capitalist regimes down south and their puppets. I'm surprised you don't see it that way."

"How do you know which way I see it? I have not said a word. No, I don't like what the whites are doing in Rhodesia and South Africa any more than I like what the whites are doing in Mississippi, Alabama or New York for that matter. It's easy for you middle-class whites to go around preaching revolution. You can go back home to white America and assimilate easily enough. You can also draw on daddy's big fat bank account. Capitalism has served you well so why isn't it good enough for Africans? Let me tell you one thing, Janice. Now, all those brothers sisters back home are running around getting their heads cracked open because they're trying to change the system to include them. Capitalism can provide good housing, education, health care and jobs. You want proof? Just look at yourself, a real capitalist product. I don't know who you are or where you come from, but I can tell by your conversation that you're not from the ghetto. So for myself and a lot of brothers and sisters back home, all we want is our share of the capitalist cake so that we too can have the nice things in life."

James blew her mind and Stuart's, too.

"I see you have changed a lot since I first met you, James."

"So you admit meeting me, Janice?"

"Yes, but I had good reasons for not acknowledging you before."

"I think I understand why now. Aren't you risking exposing yourself and your activities by talking with me?

"No, I don't think so. Am I?"

"No, but don't expect me to buy that communist crap. As far as I'm concerned, they'd do no better for the Africans than most of these fat ass capitalists do."

Stuart managed to get in a statement.

"James, don't under-estimate our commitment just because we're white. Some of us hold deep feelings about certain principals regardless of what color the victims are."

264

"I don't deny that, Stuart. Are you involved too with this ZINAP and Chief Katumbi thing?"

"It depends on what you mean by 'involvement'."

"Well, come on, Stuart. I'm no fool. You've sat me down here tonight and drilled me on your radical alternatives for some reason. You must be involved and want my involvement somehow."

"There's time for that," said Janice. "We just want your sympathy for the cause now."

"Well, look you guys. I sympathize with the cause but don't expect me to go around toting rifles or anything like that. Also this whole business scares me. I'll be honest. I don't want anyone knowing about this little get together. You're already suspected of being a terrorist by some gossiping female in Mzuzu, Janice."

She leaned back and picked up the bottle of wine.

"Don't worry about me. I'm well covered. We don't expect you or anyone else in this country to take up arms. In fact, no one should even know you're involved. What we need is information. That's all, information."

"What kind of information?"

"Different kinds. For instance, you've already provided us with some very important news. You, of course, didn't realize how significant it was, but a uranium find is big business and might help our cause significantly. Furthermore, a person in your position will see a lot of things, especially when you travel around the region. Activities such as troop movements, political meetings and so on. Also, you will eventually get a feel for which villages are loyal government supporters and which are not. You can help us without really trying. You will not have to steal documents or break into files and things like that. Most of what we need from you, you will already have. Another thing, you are preparing the reports on facilities at each clinic in the region. This information is valuable to us. At some stage I would hope you would share it with us."

James was exhausted just listening to the rundown.

"You know, I could get shot if I was found passing on that type of information. This thing's heavier than I thought. Look, let me sleep on it, because I don't want to get involved if it's going to be dangerous. Hell, I would be spying."

Janice backed down.

"Yes, you sleep on it. You should think about it for a while. We will in no way pressure you. Only when you think there's something that might be useful to us. Remember, these people over here have as much right to live in freedom as we have in the United States. All they need is a little help from a lot of people."

James was tired after having driven five hours that day. The conversations with Janice and Stuart were mentally exhausting. What they wanted placed a considerable burden on him. He was not however, surprised that Stuart was involved. He had always felt that Stuart had serious radical political beliefs. Stuart was not conservative, liberal or middle of the road. He was somewhere above and beyond conventional political stereotypes and James could not appropriately describe him. Taking one of the lanterns to his tent, he left the two sitting on the straw mats spread out over the ground. James quickly erected his mosquito net over his sleeping bag. Once in, he lay back trying not to think. The buzzing noise of a mosquito irritated him. He fanned it away several times and finally it stopped. He didn't know whether he killed it or whether it just decided to retire for the night. Considerable time elapsed before he began to fall off to sleep. Then he heard whispers, which grew into sounds of passionate sighs. He reckoned it was Janice and Stuart making love in the hut. He tried to cover his ears with the top of the sleeping bag, but even that did not block out the murmurs, whimpers and groans.

He thought to himself, "Ah come on you two; give a guy a break!"

Listening to the two was both frustrating and embarrassing. He began to think of Rose Nkhoma in that long sexy white dress. Later, there were sighs of joyful relief and then there was silence.

"Thank goodness that's over," James thought. "Anyway, it sounded as if they both needed that. Now I can sleep."

James woke up the next morning feeling refreshed. Unfortunately, though, he had a backache. The ground was hard. At this stage in his journey, the thing he wanted most was to sleep in a bed with a soft mattress. It was seven o' clock when he crawled out of the tent. Janice was sitting out next to her Land Rover. She looked radiant and appeared relaxed. They spoke to each other and James felt that she was more pleasant than she'd ever been since the first time they had met.

"Lovely morning, isn't it, James?"

"Yes, it is. I feel great myself, except for a backache. Where's Stuart?"

"He went to the village to get some fresh eggs. He should be back soon. When are you continuing your journey?"

"I'll set off early tomorrow morning. The next clinic is only an hour's drive from here. When do you go back to Zambia, Janice?"

"Just after breakfast. I've got a lot of things to do."

"Don't they suspect you at the border?"

"No, because they know exactly who I am. They're on our side, too."

James went over and sat next to Janice on the ground. They both casually looked around for a while. James noticed that her fingernails were short and jagged. He surmised that she bit them off and wondered why. Finally, he settled for the answer that she was a nervous person.

"Tell me, Janice, do you really think there's a chance that Chief Katumbi will push out the present leader?"

"I think there's a damn good chance. We wouldn't support him if we didn't think he would one day rule this country."

"Well, what about ZINAP? They have a formidable task trying to achieve majority rule in Rhodesia. Already, the Prime Minister has said no majority rule in his life-time, and anyway, they've got powerful military backing from the Republic of South Africa."

"Yes, you're right. It will be a tough job achieving freedom and independence for Africans in that country. But it can be done. Mao Tse Tung did it in China, Fidel Castro did it in Cuba and ZINAP will do it in Rhodesia. It might take ten or fifteen years of hard struggling to achieve it, but we're confident that the people's revolution will be successful."

Stuart returned with six eggs. Janice agreed to fry them and make the coffee. After they had eaten breakfast, James took the dishes out back to wash them. He wanted to give the two lovers a chance to be alone before Janice left. Soon she came around to the back of the hut.

"I'm off now, James. I'm really glad we had this opportunity to talk. Do think about what we discussed and by the way, if you do decide to help us, don't feel as though you're operating alone. We have a lot of support from some of your American colleagues. I'll be in your area in about six to eight weeks. I'll look you up then."

"Okay, Janice. I wouldn't want to make any promises I can't keep. One thing though, you have my word that my lips are sealed."

"Okay. Thanks."

Janice left soon after. James and Stuart spent the rest of the day looking around the village and meeting people. James found it a refreshing change and it helped take his mind off the decision he would eventually have to make. He and Stuart got on very well together and developed a bond of friendship. James even joked him about being "hen-pecked" and how Janice would drag him down the aisle of matrimony one day. He had been away from Mzuzu for almost a week and he found himself missing the place. He wondered what Geoffrey, his cook, was doing and thought of Jennifer Nolan's farewell comments. He knew that once he returned he would try hard to woo Rose Nkhoma, so he didn't want to make any commitments to Jennifer. There were two weeks to go before he would return to Mzuzu, so he decided to put it out of his mind.

Chapter 6: What Revolution?

The Illusive Compromise

The following Friday morning the three-man delegation that included Chief Rodney Katumbi, Joni Matabeli, ZINAP's second in command, and Sam Hernandez landed at the East Berlin airport in the German Democratic Republic. ZINAP's Leader, Frank Myosa could not attend due to illness. This was the Chief's first trip outside Africa and it was very important. The East Germans and Russians were willing to talk seriously to Chief Katumbi after hearing about the possibility of a uranium discovery in Malawi. Prior to this meeting they had turned down a request to assist the Chief. He was nervous and jittery as he stood up to disembark.

He turned to Sam Hernandez and asked, "How are these Germans to talk to? Are they difficult people?"

"Yes, they are, but they're after something, too. I suggest you listen to their proposals and think them over first. Then come back with your own ideas."

Joni Matabelli, ZINAP's second in command was nervous, too.

"I know that the Russians are shrewd, hard bargainers, but I've not had the opportunity to negotiate with the East Germans before," Sam said.

"Don't worry. Their interests are mutual. The Russians will also be represented at these talks."

As soon as they were off the airplane, a man wearing a dark blue suit and a dark overcoat came over and greeted them in English. He was obviously German because of his accent. English would be used for communicating throughout the visit. He led them to a waiting limousine. It was cold and damp that morning, although spring was near. The Chief shivered while waiting to get into the vehicle. Soon they were whisked away. The streets of East Berlin were busy as they drove along a major boulevard to the center of the city. The car stopped in front of a huge stone building. They entered the hotel carrying their brief cases. The rest of their luggage would be brought later. Their escort went to the desk and spoke in German. The receptionist gave him three keys and showed them to the third floor. Rooms 17, 18 and 19 had been reserved for them. Both the Chief and Joni Matabelli were impressed by what seemed to them, luxurious accommodation. Only Sam had seen better and knew that the hotel rated only about three stars according to British and American standards. However, he was in no mood to discuss standards of hotels, nor did he want to spoil it for the other two. The rooms were clean and functional. No extra frills, no lively colors and only basic furniture could be seen. They each contained a washbowl, but toilets and baths were at the end of the hall. Those facilities were shared. The German escort said he would meet them in the lobby in one hour to discuss the itinerary.

The three men washed and Joni shaved. The others sported beards and mustaches. Half an hour later they went down to the lobby since they had nothing else to do. Their bags hadn't arrived. As soon as they sat in the old, but comfortable leather chairs, a waiter came over and took their orders for coffee or tea.

"It is strange here, isn't it?" asked the Chief.

"Yes, it is, Chief Katumbi. It is different from our way of life," replied Sam Hernandez.

"Yes, too many people and too many cars in one place. It is also too cold here. I think you are familiar with these European ways, aren't you, Sam?"

"Somewhat, but I'm more familiar with American ways."

"Yes, you lived there for a long time. This man who brought us here, is he a negotiator?"

"No. I don't think so. He's probably assigned to look after us while we are here. A sort of secretary."

"I see."

At noon the escort appeared in the corridor of the hotel. He spoke to a man dressed in a waiter's uniform and then joined his guests for lunch. They got into an elevator and went up to the thirteenth floor. They then entered a small room situated in the corner of the building. It provided a panoramic view of part of the city. The meal was served along with German white wine. The escort told them that a meeting was scheduled for four o'clock that afternoon. This would allow them time to rest for a couple of hours. They would have dinner at eight o'clock that night and meet again in the morning at eight o'clock. After that meeting, he would give them a brief tour of the city. They were scheduled to depart at 8:15 on Saturday night and would arrive back in East Africa on Sunday. It was all so well organized that the delegation was impressed. As the escort handed them copies of the itinerary he asked if they had any questions about the German Democratic Republic.

Joni Matabelli asked about the size of the population and geographical area. He was told that the population was just over sixteen million in the German Democratic Republic with approximately one million of those living in East Berlin. Leipzig and Dresden are the second largest cities with each having almost a half million people. The country covers an area of 1,768 square miles and includes the five former German states of Brandenburg, Mecklenburg, Saxony, Saxony-Anhalt and Thuringla. The City of East Berlin covers 156 square miles.

Joni Matabelli, who was now peering out the window asked, "What is that large structure over there?"

"Do you mean down that way on the Umter den Linden?"

"I don't know what that means."

"Oh, sorry, that's the name of the street. You must be referring to the Brandenburg Gate. Just down on your left is Marx Engels Platz and straight ahead on Fredric Strasse is the border post, which the Americans refer to as Checkpoint Charlie. The border proposes a certain amount of contention between East and West Berlin, but you gentlemen will not be interested in that."

Chief Katumbi listened intently to every word the man spoke and was curious about the two Germanys.

"Once you were unified and now you are divided. What type of government have you chosen for your country?"

"Our second constitution, which will come into force next year, defines the German Democratic Republic as a socialist state. The ruling political party is the Socialist Unity Party and our laws and decrees are approved by what we call Volkskammer or People's Chamber. Political and economic policy is planned and formulated through our Politburo. We believe that we have an imminently more effective and efficient way of serving our people than some of the other forms of government practiced elsewhere. Gentleman, perhaps we should end our discussion in order to allow you time to rest before your meeting."

The men returned to the hotel. Before they each returned to their room, Chief Katumbi spoke.

"There is a certain amount of truth in the stereotype about efficient Germans. Not only is he efficient, but what he said was efficient, too."

"Yes, he sounded as if he could have been reading from a book," replied Joni.

The meeting started promptly at four o'clock p.m. There were two Germans and two Russians in the room. Only one German introduced himself by name. He was Herr Mielke and he presided over the meeting.

"Gentlemen, we know why we are here today, so shall we get on with our discussions. Chief Katumbi, you are seeking assistance to further your cause. We are interested in helping you, provided certain conditions are met. But first we wish to know more about your plans for your country's future. What sort of political ideology would you follow? What sort of economic strategies and development plans would you incorporate and how do you envisage your government's long-term relationship with countries such as East Germany and Russia if you came to power?"

The Chief was impressive when he dealt with issues concerning his economic development policy. He talked in terms of modernizing agriculture, introducing new technologies and industries and enhancing service sector growth and tourism. He felt there was a need to build up the infrastructure, including roads, sewage systems, dams for electricity and modern factories and warehouses. He explained that roads, rail and air travel systems were inadequate. Changing this would be a major priority.

"What policy would you adopt regarding government ownership of businesses?" asked a Russian.

"I am not sure whether there would be a need to nationalize all aspect of industry initially. I would prefer to experiment with a mixed economy first."

"How then will you control the production and distribution of goods and services, Chief Katumbi? Already the present government in your country has tried the free enterprise system and it doesn't work, at least for the masses of people it doesn't."

"That is because the present leader allows foreign investors a free hand. He is too liberal with them. I would impose certain measures to monitor both investment and profits. My policies would also ensure that money is put back into the country's development, economically, educationally and socially."

There was a long pause while the Russians and Germans, whispered among themselves, and then Herr Mielke continued to query the Chief.

"What guarantees do we have that a government led by yourself would give major concessions to our governments for investment in your country? After all, if you allow the Americans, British and other capitalist countries equal access, we could possibly lose a lot of money."

The Chief considered the question momentarily.

"Herr Mielke, we are a poor country with not much to offer. What type of assurances could I give you? Only my word that those governments who assist me now would be given first priority where investment is concerned."

"Chief Katumbi, your country is potentially rich. You have uranium there and we have an interest in developing that potential. We would expect to have sole mining rights to that venture. That is our price."

"Your price is very high, Herr Mielke."

"It's not very high when you consider that we could have you installed as President of that country before this year is out."

"You are even more optimistic than I am. That is a very short time to achieve such a thing. We need men, training, guns and advisers. How can this be done in a matter of months?"

"If we can agree, I could have advisers in your camp within the week. They would take care of the other logistics including the military strategy."

Joni Matabelli whispered something to the Chief. After a brief pause, the Chief spoke.

"Herr Mielke, I would be grateful if you could provide me with a list of conditions your government might require and allow me time to consider them."

"Yes, I will happily arrange this. You will have it shortly and we can discuss it tomorrow morning."

The meeting lasted for another hour, but the discussion centered mainly on political ideology. The Chief's line was that while he wanted a socialist form of government, he did not agree with the inflexibility of the communist bureaucratic systems. He also felt that a planned economy as the Russians practiced was too restrictive and would inhibit investment from other governments. He did not want to rely too heavily on one or two governments. His arguments did not bother the Germans too much as long as they got the contracts on the uranium. They were prepared to allow him political choice. Later that evening the delegation met in the hotel dinning room. The same gentleman who met them at the airport escorted them. They felt nervous about his continuing presence, but understood that they were there on business and were to conclude it as quickly as possible. Chief Katumbi did not like the German white wine or the beef stroganoff. He ate only the boiled potatoes and asparagus. The latter he forced down. There wasn't much conversation at the dinner table. The escort ate and smiled. He was not to entertain any discussions regarding their meetings. The delegation was relieved when the dinner was over. They sat out in the lounge after their escort said good night.

"I've heard tales about how the Russians place listening devices in the rooms of their guests," Joni whispered. "I wonder if the East Germans use the same tactics?"

"I don't know," Sam said, "but it pays to be careful. We should restrict our discussions to open places like this. Say nothing upstairs."

"I'm in full accord with you, Sam," replied the Chief.

The three men were all in bed by 9:30 that night. They slept solidly until early morning. They were used to rising with the sun and did not require a wake up call. After breakfast, they walked outside the buildings and stood talking. This was their last minute collaboration before their eight o'clock meeting. They had already agreed on which conditions the Chief should and should not compromise. They were going over the list.

"Good morning, gentleman," said the escort as he walked up to them.

They nervously greeted him as they stuffed the sheets of paper in their pockets.

"Do you not like the comfort of our hotel lounge?"

"Yes, we do, but we decided to get some fresh air. We're not used to spending so much time indoors in our country."

"Yes, I can understand. Would you like to come in now? I will show you to the meeting room."

They briskly followed the man to the lift.

The meeting started promptly at eight in the morning. Herr Mielke presided.

"Good morning, gentlemen. I trust you had a comfortable night. Shall we begin? Chief Katumbi, what is your response?"

"Herr Mielke. Gentlemen. I have considered your proposals and while there are areas in which I am in full accord with you, others pose a problem. The major issue concern is the uranium. You wish to have a joint venture in which you control fifty percent of the shares of ownership. This is hardly acceptable to me. I consider a fifteen percent share, along with sole rights to mine to be sufficient. Consider that we are only exploring now. We have no idea as to the amount of uranium is up in those mountains, nor do we know whether it would be a commercially viable venture."

Herr Mielke conferred with his colleagues.

"Chief Katumbi, we have reliable sources of information concerning the project. The Americans, British and Malawian government have estimated millions of pounds worth of uranium in that area. We are in no doubt that the venture is commercially profitable, but we do not think that fifteen percent would make our efforts worthwhile. Consider the investment involved in assisting

277

and equipping your forces in addition to the initial capital outlay, such as drilling equipment, earth movers, sophisticated processing factories and so on. We must be assured that our initial investment can be recouped. Now we are reasonable and fair. I'm sure you are too. At least a twenty-five percent share is what we want."

The men haggled over the percent of shares for an hour. They eventually agreed to a eighty percent/twenty percent ratio with the Malawian government having controlling interest. The next point of contention was the number of so-called advisers to remain in the country after President Makube's regime was overthrown. The Germans and Russians suggested a contingency of two thousand people. These would include technicians, administrators, teachers, nurses, doctors, agronomists and soldiers. They suggested a troop force of thirteen hundred men. Chief Katumbi thought the number of soldiers disproportionately high and felt that perhaps two to three hundred men would be sufficient to protect their interests. They settled on six hundred civilian advisers and four hundred military advisers or soldiers. It was agreed that the Chief would establish his own political and administrative institutions as long as they did not conflict with the German and Russian investment.

The meeting lasted four hours. Herr Mielke agreed to send out a group of twelve people the following week. Their initial task was to assess the situation at the refugee camp in Zambia and report on the assistance level required by Chief Katumbi's group. At the same time they would advise their government on ZINAP's long-term requirements. Their consultations would take one month. Both the Chief and Joni Matabelli were pleased at the way negotiations went, but deep down, the Chief felt that he had made too many concessions He knew, however, that he had no immediate alternative so resigned himself to believing that the compromises were necessary. He trusted neither the Germans nor the Russians.

They left East Berlin that cold windy night with not too many impressions of the city or its people. The entire visit was clothed in secrecy from start to finish. Even the brief tour they had of the city earlier that day did not leave any lasting impressions. They were shuttled around so quickly that they might as well not have gone. The Chief shuddered at the thought of how things had escalated in such a short period of time. He'd never imagined that he would receive assistance on such a scale, nor the speed with which it would be negotiated. The high level of East German involvement in his coming to power troubled him. Economic policy, political ideology, international protocol and hundreds of other mind-taxing issues would suddenly confront him.

It was no longer a parochial matter and even Joni and Sam detected the strain on the Chief as he said, "I hope I have made the right decision for my people."

Back in Blantyre City the U.S. Ambassador, the Honorable Hewitt T. Smith, was still in a furor over the news that a Peace Corps volunteer had trespassed into a restricted area. He asked Bill Humphries, the Peace Corps Country Director to conduct a full investigation of the incident. Bill suggested that it was obviously a mistake, which could happen to anyone and that he saw no need to take the issue any further. Bill arrived at the Ambassador's office on Tuesday morning at ten o'clock.

"Come in, Bill, and sit down. Would you like coffee?"

"Yes. Thank you, sir."

The Ambassador ordered coffee for two.

"Bill, Where's this boy now?"

"He's on a tour of the regional clinics and will not return to Mzuzu until the end of next week."

"Well, I hate to keep hammering home the point that these young people should stay clear of these kinds of situations, but I must. Do you know that President Makube's personal secretary has called me over five times already, expressing the President's deep concern over this matter? Well, he has and I'm told that that area is top secret."

"Are you privy to what is happening up in that area Sir, if I'm permitted to inquire?"

"Mining, Bill, mining. That's all I can tell you. Now this boy Johnson saw some things that he should not have seen. He was instructed by the officer in charge not to say another word about it. Perhaps you should have a word with him as soon as possible. I know the kid is innocent and that it could happen to anyone, but for his protection and ours too, lets make sure he doesn't speak too freely about this."

Bill Humphries finished his coffee and sat silently for a while. The Ambassador was getting impatient and irritable.

"Well, Bill? What do you say?"

"I think we would be creating more problems. If we cause undue suspicion in Johnson's mind, we can't be sure what his reactions will be. After all, he may not be aware of how sensitive this thing is and may soon forget about it."

"Dammit, Bill! You're too damn soft with these kids. Now just suppose he is astute enough to figure out what he walked into, just suppose that. If that information is passed to the wrong people, all sorts of problems might arise."

"Sorry, sir, but I don't understand."

"Well, listen, Bill, and don't pass on a word of what I'm about to tell you."

"The Ambassador stopped talking long enough to pull a bottle of whiskey out of his desk drawer and pour a measure into his empty coffee cup.

"My morning vitamins, would you?" he asked, pushing the bottle toward Bill.

"No, thank you, sir. Too early for me."

Bill knew that the Ambassador was a lush, but didn't know that he needed alcohol first thing in the morning. The Ambassador drank the whiskey in the cup and poured another measure. He put the bottle back in the desk drawer and said.

"Now! Where was I?"

"You were about to tell me something, sir."

"Oh, yes. Now Bill not a whisper of this to anyone. They have discovered uranium in those mountains."

"Uranium?"

"Yes, uranium. Just think about that for a moment. Think of the implications both internationally and for this country. One hint of this to the Reds is enough to trigger their commie appetites. They would stop short of nothing to get their hands on this stuff, even finance an overthrow of the government. This is big, and our boy Johnson is the only outsider who's ever bumped into that operation."

"Yes, as far as I know. This is why I'm concerned that he should be spoken to. You don't know this, but he evidently spoke to one of the young British workers while waiting to be released. They're not sure, but they think this fellow might have said something about what they were doing. Now this Johnson kid is no fool, Bill. I spoke with him at length over at your place and underneath that disguise of innocent naivety is a shrewd and quick mind. He could easily have guessed what they were doing."

The Ambassador paused to order more coffee. His secretary quickly entered and exited the room with the used cups. He then reclined into his big plush green leather chair.

"You think you could see him before the week is out, Bill?"

Bill was annoyed at the suggestion.

"I would not want to interfere with his work with the Ministry by recalling him, sir."

"Dammit, Bill! You obviously have not grasped the gravity of this situation. That boy's got to be spoken to and soon. Now, if you don't want to pull him off the job, then you can go to see him."

Bill Humphries did not like the Ambassador's tone of voice.

"Excuse me, sir, but it seems to me that the decision to recall or visit James is a Peace Corps prerogative."

"The hell it is, Bill! Not while I'm Ambassador to this country. Now lets get this straight. It is my responsibility to oversee American foreign policy in this country as well as looking after the interests of Americans living here. Now, I'm of the opinion that James Johnson could find himself in a very awkward if not dangerous situation. Not only that, we have American interests in this country to look after. If necessary, I can have a word with your people in Washington to clear this thing up for you. No I'm not trying to tell you how to run your ship, but when that ship threatens to sink with us on board, then it's my job to have a say. You don't want me to get on to Washington. Do you, Bill?"

Bill Humphries did not respond. He felt disgusted with the old bottle-toting Ambassador. The threats were clear. The Ambassador would contact Washington and try to have Bill replaced. Bill didn't like Hewitt T. Smith one iota. It didn't help either that the Ambassador was a right-wing racist. Oh he would deny it most profusely, but privately he called black people coons, niggers, and shifty eyed bastards. He had always opposed civil rights legislation when he was in the Senate and was once quoted as having said, "Now that we have machines to pick cotton, lets send them all back home to the jungle." The Ambassador had been recommended to serve in several other African Countries, but they'd refused to have him. Even France and West Germany refused him. He was lucky to be received by the Malawian government because otherwise he would end up at home with an old age pension.

Bill decided to change the topic by asking a few more questions. He asked who was involved in the explorations and how long had it been in progress. The Ambassador briefly told him. Then Bill asked who else knew besides the two embassies and the Malawian government.

"Well, of course, our C.I.A. boys are aware of it. They are involved to the extent that they're investigating any tip off about outsiders who might be curious about the project. They're also keeping an eye on Chief Katumbi's activities and have a pretty good network of reliable informers, I gather."

"I trust none of my group are being investigated?"

"I couldn't tell you, to be honest. However, I'm sure that if any of those volunteers become actively involved in anything, these C.I.A. boys will find out. They might keep an eye on Johnson, but not because they suspect him of covert activities understand."

"That's hardly fair on James, sir. He got lost and found himself in a tight spot. You already agreed it could happen to anyone. That's hardly sufficient reason to put the fellow under surveillance."

"It will not be Johnson they're interested in. It's who he talks to, Bill. You'll have to face reality, Johnson knows too much, although he may not be aware of it."

Bill Humphries sat back in his chair and sipped the second cup of coffee that was just placed before him. His mood was despondent. The meeting had exposed a number of pressing matters. He felt guilty about the fact that James Johnson had been put under the watchful eyes of the Central Intelligence Agency. He wondered what Johnson, who seemed like a nice earnest fellow, would do if he knew he was being watched. Bill wondered how many other volunteers were being watched and by whom. He had no idea who the C.I.A. people were, nor did the Ambassador, except for one contact. After the serious business was over, the Ambassador asked Bill how the new volunteers were getting on. Bill knew that the Ambassador very seldom engaged in small talk so he surmised that the Ambassador was interested in something more specific.

"They are settling into their jobs extremely well, sir."

"I hear the black girl left the program."

"Yes, that's correct."

"Well, too bad about that, but I suppose it's best that she made her decision early."

"Yes, you're probably right, sir."

The Ambassador finished his coffee and sat back in his chair again. Bill could sense that he was after something and sure enough the Ambassador said.

"Oh, by the way, how is this boy Steiner working out—you know, the Jewish kid?"

Bill tensed as he raised himself slightly out of his seat.

"Oh, Stuart Steiner you mean, sir. He's doing a great job up there from all the reports I hear."

"He's a long ways up there and very close to the border. I imagine he gets lonesome for familiar company. Do you know whether he's made any friends up that way? "

Bill gathered that the Ambassador must have heard something, which bothered him.

"No, sir. I know of no friends he's made except for people living in the village. Why do you ask?"

"No special reason, Bill. I just like to be kept informed on how your program is going. I will not hold you any longer. I'm sure you're busy over there. Don't forget, see this Johnson fellow as soon as possible."

Bill thanked the Ambassador for the coffee and said good-bye.

When Bill left the building, the Ambassador ushered his secretary into the office.

"Take down this letter for me and send it special delivery through the diplomatic pouch. It's to Mr. Allan Freeman, Director, US Peace Corps, Washington, D.C. Oh and send a copy to Mr. J. Miles, the Presidents Special Advisor. Our Mr. Humphries needs to be called into line a bit."

The P.C. Office was several blocks from the American Embassy. As Bill Humphries walked along the crowded streets of Blantyre City, he was glad that he hadn't driven to the Embassy. He needed the twenty minutes alone to think about what had transpired. He was concerned both with the situation that James Johnson found himself in and with Ambassador Hewitt T. Smith's hard line. He did not trust the Ambassador and he worried about what devious course of action he would take. After walking for five minutes he could see a very tall dark familiar face peering up over the crowds. It was Reggie Blackwell, the volunteer from Atlanta, Georgia. Somehow, Bill was glad to see Reggie at that particular moment. Perhaps a brief conversation with Reggie would relieve him of some of his anxieties.

"Hello, Reggie, how are you?"

Reggie Blackwell's high pitch Southern drawl always seemed incongruent with his huge physique. Looking down on Bill, he said.

"I'm doing all right, Bill. I'm out shopping for field chalk or lime to mark the lanes on the new track stadium."

"I hear you are doing a wonderful job over at the Recreation Department. You've organized the first nationwide track and field athletic games scheduled for sometime in June. Is that right? "

Reggie smiled as he looked away from Bill. He was embarrassed by his own success.

"Yes, sir. That's right. It will take place on the fifth and sixth of June, to coincide with the official opening of the new stadium."

"Well, Reggie, we're all proud of you. President Makube is coming, you know."

"He is? I didn't know that."

"Oh, yes, he along with a host of top officials. I'm sure he will be pleased with your efforts too. You might even get some sort of recognition, Reggie."

They both laughed, but Reggie wasn't that bothered about recognition. He was a quiet, hard-working fellow who shied away from publicity of any kind. Bill was aware of this, hence the laughs.

"I hope it goes well because it's been tough organizing these teams from all over the country," Reggie said. "You wouldn't believe the red tape and petty jealousies that go on Bill. For example, the Ministry of Education think that they should have more say in how the events will be scheduled than the Department of Recreation officials. They say that since eighty percent of the students participating are school children, then it's their responsibility. They argue about which colors the track suits should be and who's going to start the races, and a never ending list of un-related issues."

"Well, I guess this type of thing happens in all types of bureaucracies. Don't let it stop you from doing your job."

"No, I won't, Bill. By the time June gets here, we should have it all worked out."

"Do you like it here?"

"Oh, I like it here a lot. The job is rewarding and I like working with the Malawians."

"Yes, I've no doubt that you do Reggie. Are you in contact with the other volunteers?"

"Just Jesse Jefferson. We write each other often. I haven't heard from anyone else outside of Blantyre. I see Joe Veto and Ramsey Hall every now and then. In fact, I'm meeting them for lunch today at that little coffee shop around the corner from your office. Do you ever go there?"

"Oh, sure. It's a favorite place of mine."

"They make some good milk shakes and cheeseburgers in that place."

"Well, Reggie, I must get back to the office now. Hope you find what you're looking for and keep up the good work. Remember, if ever you have any problems, don't hesitate to come in and see me."

"Okay, Bill. Thanks."

It was close to one o'clock when Reggie met Joe Veto and Fat Ramsey Hall in the coffee shop. Reggie was about five minutes late so they had saved him a seat in the popular but crowded room. It was a favorite place for expats. The owner tried to imitate American and British menus. He prepared everything from hot dogs to fish and chips. Although it was called a coffee shop, it was more like a restaurant and the prices were steep according to Malawian standards. Fat Ramsey couldn't wait for Reggie to come. He'd ordered two hamburgers, a hot dog, a double portion of French Fries, a large milk shake and apple pie a la mode. This was enough to give a rhino indigestion. Of course, Ramsey had an appetite like a rhino and depending on the angle he positioned his body, he wasn't far off looking like one.

"How's it going, Joe?"

"All right, Reggie, and you?"

"Okay. I ran into Bill Humphries this morning. He seemed despondent about something."

"Well, I don't envy his position," Ramsey said. "He's got a lot to be despondent about. I wouldn't want to be responsible for over two hundred volunteers in this country."

"Yes, I know what you mean, Ramsey."

"Why are you so quiet this morning, Joe?"

"I'm not quiet, Reggie. I just haven't had a chance to get a word edgewise with you two running off at the mouth."

The three talked about their jobs and how they were getting along with their Malawian colleagues. Afterwards they exchanged tit-bits of news they'd received from other volunteers. Ramsey talked about a rumor he had heard which involved one of the volunteers in the North West Region. The way he heard it one of them was caught spying on secret government installations of some kind. He did not hear who it was or what type of installation it was. When asked how he learned about it, he said one of the Malawian girls who worked as a typist in the Ministry of Education was told by her boyfriend who was in the Malawi Army.

"I can't believe that."

Joe did not like rumors or wild gossip.

"Well, that's what I heard buddy. True or not that's the whisper around town."

Ramsey was determined to defend the rumor only because he had passed it on.

Reggie Blackwell shook his head in disbelief and then whispered, "Okay, assuming it's true. Who up there is likely to spy for anybody? Not anyone in our group."

"I don't know, Reggie. Personally I can't see Jennifer, James or Phil doing something like that. Bob Newgate would be more likely to spy for the Americans," Joe uttered defiantly.

"Hell, man! Don't you think you're talking too much? I mean, that's bullshit you're talking unless you get some facts to back it up."

Ramsey felt compelled to finish his statement and told Joe to cool down and not be so unimaginative.

"Now, as I was saying, the only one I would suspect, assuming it's true of course, is Stuart Steiner. You know how weird and way out Stuart can be. I could see him doing it just for a prank. Don't get me wrong. I don't think he'd be passing on any information to anyone, not unless they're Israeli."

Joe thought Ramsey was talking nonsense. Reggie Blackwell on the other hand was quite interested in what Ramsey said and even encouraged him.

"Come on, Joe, don't take it so serious. Let the man talk. About the Army guy, Ramsey, was he up there when it happened or did he just hear about it?"

"I can't say for sure, Reggie, but I think he was up there."

"You think!" shouted Joe, who simultaneously drew attention from the other customers. He then lowered his voice to a whisper. "You sound like you're making this story up as you go along Ramsey. It's no joke, you know, to accuse someone of being a spy. You could find yourself in a very embarrassing situation. I'm surprised at you Ramsey and you too Reggie for sitting here taking as if it were gospel."

They all finished their meals and Reggie said to Joe, "What are you so uptight about? You're too serious man! Don't you ever have any fun? Don't you ever relax? We know it's a rumor and I'm not going to run around shouting that Stuart is a spy. I couldn't care less if he is. You ought to relax more, Joe. You have so much moral certainty about you that it makes other people feel uncomfortable."

Joe Veto felt defensive but knew that much of what Reggie said about him was true.
He decided not to challenge him, but keep it all low keyed.

"Yes. Maybe you're right, Reggie. I guess I come off too straight-laced sometimes. I don't want to spoil our lunch. Go ahead, Ramsey. Say what the hell you want. Don't pay any attention to me."

Ramsey had already lost his appetite for more gossip, but not for more food. He ordered a third cheeseburger. The other two laughed.

The subject changed from spies to parties. The three had talked earlier of organizing a party together and one of the purposes of the lunch was to finalize the details.

"Yes, like I said before, we can have it at my place, but the only problem is that most of the people living around me have small children and I wouldn't want to disturb them."

"That's all right, Reggie. We can have it at my place. I've got loads of room and nobody around to bother."

"You live too far out, Ramsey. How will everyone get out there? There are no buses. Why don't we settle for my house? We can cram in a big crowd there."

So they all agreed to give a party at Joe Veto's house.

It was to be a weekend party with people invited from all over the country. They would have to bring their own food, sleeping bags and booze. This would be the first big bash for new volunteers, but a large number of Malawian colleagues would be invited as well. They planned it to coincide with the opening of the new stadium in June. Special grapevine word of mouth invitations would be sent out. Soon lunch was over and Reggie Blackwell made his exit first. Then Ramsey got up and stretched his huge arms about the place. A couple of teenage girls sitting in a corner giggled when they saw him stretching. In characteristic Bogart style, he winked at the girls. They burst out laughing and so did a few other patrons.

"Come on, Joe! Are you leaving now?"

"Oh, not just yet, Ramsey. There's someone I want to see first."

Ramsey leaned over the table, looked at Joe and smiled cunningly.

"It's that little girl you've been seeing, isn't it?"

290

Joe was embarrassed because he felt his sheepish expression was showing on his face, "What's it to you, who I'm meeting?"

Ramsey stood up again and replied, "Oh, it's nothing to me buddy. I don't care who you're meeting. Just joking, you know."

Ramsey left Joe sitting in the coffee shop. He had seen Joe on several occasions with this girl. She looked to be about twenty and was a very attractive African girl with large dark eyes. Joe liked black girls quite a lot. From the time he started training to after settling in Blantyre, most of his serious attention went to black girls. Ramsey knew that Joe liked Dianne Harper and was bitterly disappointed when he'd heard she'd gone back to Mississippi. He also believed that Joe had been jittery at lunch because he did not want Reggie Blackwell to know about it yet. Joe didn't know that Reggie could not care less. An hour after Ramsey left, Joe was still sitting in the coffee shop waiting for the girl to show up. He decided to leave and nonchalantly walked down the street trying desperately not to feel disappointed at being stood-up.

He thought to himself, "Why fuss over her when there are plenty more girls around?"

The waves of heat seemed to engulf him as he merged into the crowded street.

The following Friday evening in Chikwawa, Cathy Horowitz's roommate Brenda was busily preparing a dinner for two. She had invited Steve Manski over to celebrate his twenty-third birthday. Brenda and Steve had seen each other several times since the weekend he had been burgled. Cathy wanted nothing to do with the celebrations because she was envious of Steve's attentions toward Brenda. Cathy decided to go to the local bar that night with two local girls. Friday night was special at the bar because the three-piece penny whistle band played. Chikwawa was such a small place that this was the big event of the weekend. Also, it was not uncommon for girls to visit the bar on weekends. It was seven o'clock when the two girls came to Cathy's house. They wore skirts, blouses and scarfs wrapped around their heads. Both were once students at the school where Cathy taught. One of them was a clerk typist at the local railway depot. The other did not work.

"Hi, girls. Come on in. I won't be a second."

"We will wait out here on the steps for you, Cathy," replied one of the girls.

"Oh, don't be daft. Come on in for a minute."

The two girls nervously entered the living room and sat down. They seemed very shy while sitting in the house, mainly because they felt uncomfortable around Brenda.

This was their first time at Cathy's place, but they had met Brenda several times before. She was always very formal with them and her attitude was such that she constantly reminded them that she felt superior. Brenda was very patronizing to Africans. She found it difficult to relate to Africans who were either educated or had a higher job status than she did. A situation duly noted by the school's administration. Hence, this Canadian Missionary was not encouraged to take on any responsibilities that might involve tact and diplomacy.

Soon Cathy was ready to join the girls on the half-mile walk to the bar.

Brenda, who only nodded at the girls, said to Cathy, "Enjoy yourself, but be careful. Some of those men can get awfully familiar."

Cathy understood what Brenda was hinting at in her characteristic super-moralistic tone of voice and Cathy didn't like it.

"I think you will have more bother from your guest than I will from the Malawians," Brenda said. "Then perhaps that's what you want."

Cathy coolly turned to the door and spoke.

"Shall we go, girls?"

292

They left Brenda standing there with her hands over her mouth. She was aghast at how successfully she had been up-staged by Cathy. She was also embarrassed about the inference, which of course had a lot of truth in it.

A half hour later the three girls walked into the bar. The bartender greeted them. Cathy was the only white girl in the place, but there were two white men standing in the corner talking with some Malawians. They greeted her in a surprised, but pleasant manner. The place was crowded although it was early in the evening. Several couples danced to the tunes of the penny whistle band and the dry wood floors creaked with every movement. The room was about twenty-by-twenty square feet and mix-matched table and chairs were scattered around the place. The walls were bare except for a picture of the President of Malawi. The bar was made of two-by-four wood frames and untreated plywood, but to some residents of Chikwawa, this was the in-place. The bartender, who was also the owner, rushed over to the girls' table and took their order. Normally he left this task to his two waitresses, but because Cathy was there, he felt obliged to make sure the service was good.

"Three gin and tonics, it is, but sorry we have no ice."

"Oh, that will be quite all right," replied Cathy.

He smiled and walked briskly to the bar to fix the drinks. Cathy turned to the two girls.

"I didn't realize this place was so popular and there are a lot of girls here, too."

"Yes," replied one of the girls. "This is one of our favorite places. We know a lot of people here."

Soon the girls asked Cathy to join them in a dance. This was quite common practice. Not only did the girls dance together and hold hands as a sign of friendship but so did the men. They danced for more than twenty minutes before Cathy, who was sweaty said.

"Oh, it's too much for me, girls. I must take a rest."

When she sat down, one of the white men who had been standing in the corner appeared before her.

"Hi, my name is Hank."

"I'm Cathy. How do you do?"

"Fine, what do you do around these parts?"

"I'm a teacher at the mission school."

"Oh, you're from one of those religious organizations."

"No. I came with the Peace Corps but happened to be placed at a Mission School. Have you got something against missionaries?"

"Oh, no. They just try to do too much with too little. They expect instant converts and cultural changes. They want these people to give up their way of life and substitute it for ours. I think they go about it the wrong way."

Hank proceeded to give his opinions on the role of missionaries in Africa when Cathy interrupted him.

"Hey, mister—err, Hank! I'm not trying to be rude but that's a little heavy for me tonight. I came out here to enjoy myself and I'm sorry, but I don't feel like talking about religious politics."

"Well, excuse me!"

He then walked back over to his colleagues.

Cathy and her girlfriends went back to the dance floor after resting for a while. This time each had a male partner. The two girls were talking to their partners while Cathy's partner just eyed her up and down when she wasn't looking.

Then Cathy shouted, "Jesse! What are you doing here?"

Jesse Jefferson had just walked through the door with his house helper, Ntalie. Cathy shouting his name all over the place did not amuse him. She was delighted to see a familiar face. She excused herself from her dance partner and pushed her way through the crowds to the bar where Jesse stood.

"Hi, Cathy. What are you doing here?"

"I asked you first, Jesse."

"I'm having a drink, can't you see? How's it going?"

"I'm having a great time with the girls. It beats sitting around the house especially while Steve is over trying to make it with Brenda."

Jesse turned his head up towards the ceiling and said.

"Oh, so that's where Steve was going. I saw him just before he left and I asked why he was wearing his Old Spice Cologne tonight. He was funny as hell when he blushed and said to keep the mosquitoes away. Looks like he's attracting more than mosquitoes."

"Yes, and knowing him, he'll have it in Miss Stuck-up before she knows what's happening."

"Hey, Cathy, you don't sound as though you like what's happening."

"Me? I couldn't care less. You know Steve and I didn't hit it off to start with. Why should I care about him and her?"

Jesse decided to change the subject so he asked Cathy about a rumor he heard concerning some thieves at the mission school.

"Oh, yes," Cathy replied. "It happened about three nights ago and there were two of them. Actually I heard them at our back door first and I got up and turned on the kitchen light that probably frightened them off. It was 2:35 a.m. exactly, because I remember seeing the clock in the kitchen. When they left I turned the lights off and peered through the window. I saw them go toward the

295

school cafeteria but I was too frightened to go out. The next morning, the Headmistress said that the kitchen had been ransacked and a lot of food was taken. I thought to myself, well they couldn't have taken that much since I only saw two of them. Anyway Jesse, she reported it to the police. Actually, I feel sorry for anyone that hungry. I would have given them something to eat myself."

Jesse's keen ears and alert mind seized on Cathy's last comment.

"Suppose they were terrorists. Would you still help them, Cathy?"

"I don't know, Jesse, but I might. After all, who ever they are, they're entitled to eat."

"You could get in trouble, you know."

"Who cares? If I got in trouble for feeding a fellow human being, then something is wrong somewhere."

Jesse noticed that Cathy's glass was empty, but she also seemed quite high. He didn't want to encourage her to drink more because she was beginning to talk louder and about relatively sensitive issues. Ntalie's glass was empty too and since Jesse was treating him, he had to offer another drink.

"Same thing, bro?"

"Zkomo, Jesse."

"What about you, Cathy?"

"Gin and tonic."

"How many is that tonight?" he asked.

"Ah, come off it, Jesse, I'm not drunk. You're almost as bad as that classic bore I have to live with. Do you know that for all her pretenses of being an upright religious tea-toting Good Samaritan, she keeps a bottle of whiskey in her bedside drawer and she gets through it too? I know because I've checked the level on the bottle several times. She has very faint pencil lines drawn across the level she last left it. I have a good mind to go in and dilute it with water one day."

"Well, if she's that careful about the level of whiskey in her bottle, you can bet your bottom dollar that she would know if some one tampered with it."

The two talked for several more minutes before Jesse returned to the subject of the thieves. He wanted to know what they wore, what they had with them such as guns and other weapons and whether they appeared to be injured. After satisfying all his queries Cathy asked why he was so interested in the details. He explained that he was concerned about her welfare and then asked her to tell him of any more incidents that happened or anything she heard about. Cathy thought his answer was corny and was so uncharacteristic of him. She knew deep down that Jesse didn't give a damn about her or any other white people. She felt he only related to her in a very casual and indifferent way. Although she was high on gin and tonics, she could detect something different about Jesse that night. She thought she perceived a character that tried to present himself as someone other than who he was. On second thoughts she wondered if the drinks made her imagine things. Jesse Jefferson to her sober senses was in fact just an uptight black radical that could spew out street slang and send out racist vibrations with an ease that was natural. She questioned his motives no more that night.

Jesse was only there for an hour before he turned to Ntalie and said.

"Come on, bro, it's time to split this scene."

Surprised and disappointed Cathy exclaimed, "No! You're not leaving already are you? Gee! Jesse, the nights still young."

"Sorry, Cathy. I got things to do. Nice talking to you though and remember, we got to stick together so if you hear or see anything, let me know. You'll be okay, Cathy. Look, your friends are looking for you now."

"Okay, Jesse. You never were one for joining in anyway. Even during training you wouldn't come out with us. You're a real loner aren't you?"

"Right on, baby. See you."

Jesse and Ntalie left quietly.

It was an hour later when Cathy and the two girls reached the end of her walkway. They laughed and giggled as they stood there talking in the dark. Cathy told them what a fun evening she had and suggested that they go out again sometime. Cathy stood on the top step as she watched the girls walk back to the road. When they were out of sight, she slowly walked towards the house. The lights were out so she assumed that Brenda was in bed sleeping. Several steps away from the porch, she felt the force of a large strong hand pressing against her mouth. She tried to scream and twist loose, but the one-arm grip was too powerful. Frightful and shocking thoughts ran through her mind almost simultaneously. "I'll be raped, I'll be murdered. Help!"

Then she heard a soft but very young voice say in broken English, "Madam. I not hurt you. You must help. I not want to hurt you. Please make no sound."

Then he slowly released his grip from her mouth and she sighed with relief.

"Oh, please don't hurt me. I will do what you want. Please don't hurt me."

As he removed his hand and arm from her, he nudged her toward the back of the house. Cathy noticed that the boy's right arm was bandaged in a dark cloth stained with blood. He could not move the arm, but he held an automatic rifle in his hand.

"Please! What do you want from me?"

"I need medicine. You have medicine. Make arm well now and I leave."

298

"Oh, yes. I will help you if you do not harm me. Please do not harm me."

"I not hurt you. Medicine now."

"Okay, but I must go into the house to get it, you stay here."

"Madam, you trick me, I kill you."

"Oh, no. No!"

"Quiet! I go with you for medicine in house."

"Sure, mister, anything you say."

Cathy carefully opened the back door and tiptoed into the kitchen. She put the light on and gestured for the boy to sit down next to the sink. Nervously she untied the stained and filthy cloth and became almost sick at the sight of the boys arm. It was infected with bacteria resulting from a bullet wound he'd received. The bullet was still lodged in his muscle. He could see the horror on her face as she whispered.

"You need a doctor. You've got a bullet sticking out and the infection is bad."

The boy lifted the gun with his other hand and pointed it at Cathy.

"You doctor. Take it out now!"

"No I couldn't. Ah, I feel sick."

"Do it, madam, or die."

"Oh, no, please. . . Okay, I must get the first-aid kit out of the bathroom."

He followed her into the bathroom with the gun stuck in her back. She was careful to be as quiet as possible in order not to wake Brenda. She feared that if Brenda woke up and came into the kitchen, the boy would panic and shoot both of them. Several minutes later she was standing over the boy bathing his wound with disinfectant. He flinched in pain each time she touched it and this made her even more nervous. Cathy's dress was soaked from perspiration and her hands could not stop shaking. On several occasions she felt faint and almost vomited. Then suddenly she felt the nozzle of the gun poked into her side.

"Bullet out now, lady."

"No, I can't take it out. It's too far in."

"Get knife and cut out now or I shoot!"

Cathy went to the utensil drawer and pulled out a short sharp knife. She then soaked a cloth with rubbing alcohol and cleaned the knife. Her hands shook more as she held the infected arm across the back of the chair.

"Oh, this is horrible," she murmured.

"Now, I say. Now!"

The tone of the boy's voice carried more urgency about it and she didn't want to chance him pulling the trigger.

"Okay, Okay but this will hurt. I have some pain killers which might help."

"No pills!"

Before Cathy knew it the tip of the sharp knife was imbedded into the flesh of the boy's arm. Blood began to spew out as he writhed with pain. Cathy was sweating as she cut deep into his flesh.

Then she stopped and said, "I can't. I can't do it."

He shoved the gun into her ribcage. She continued to cut until the knife was imbedded as deep as the bullet. Somehow the pressure of her hand on the knife's handle forced the bullet out and it landed softly in the pool of fresh blood that already stained the floor.

The sight of the bloodstained copper toned bullet provided a moment of relief for Cathy and her patient. The only thing left to do was to stop the bleeding and patch up the wound. The boy looked weary and weak as he sat with beads of sweat pouring down his neck onto his bare chest.

"Water. Water."

She rushed to the sink and got a glass of water. This seemed to revive him for a few minutes. For some reason Cathy's fear abated. She confidently and courageously applied antiseptic and then a tourniquet. She then bandaged the arm. As she prepared a sling for his arm she whispered.

"I'm relieved that's over with. Who are you and what happened?"

His only reply was, "A soldier of my peoples liberation Army. We fight the evil invaders in our country."

"A terrorist!" whispered Cathy.

"A soldier. They terrorist."

"Who?"

"Rhodesia Security Forces"

"I see. What's your name?"

"No name for you!"

Then he waved his gun.

"Your name?"

"I'm Cathy Horowitz. I am a teacher here."

"You my people's friend?"

"Ah, I don't know. Yes, I suppose."

"Good. You are people's friend."

The boy gestured toward the food cupboard and Cathy opened it. He pointed at the loaf of bread and canned goods.

She got the message and asked, "Are you hungry?"

While Cathy prepared a sandwich for him, she asked a few more questions and found out that he was sixteen years old and from a village in Rhodesia. He had not lived there for almost two years, but he would not say where he lived or where he was going after he left her house. About half way through eating his sandwich and drinking a glass of milk, the boy dropped his gun and keeled over onto the floor. Cathy was horrified as she thought he was dead. She also felt responsible since she had performed an operation on his arm. She rushed over and kneeled down to hear if he was breathing. She thought the boy must be suffering from exhaustion and wondered what to do.

"If I wake up Brenda, she will have the police in right away. Surely they will kill him. Oh, I couldn't live with that. He's only a young boy. Maybe I should get him out of here. Yes, that's what I'll do."

She quickly bundled his shirt into a bag along with the rest of the bread, some meat and cheese. She then opened the back door and dragged him out of the house, through the back garden until she got to the thick hedges that surrounded the garden. She left him hidden in the bushes and quickly returned to get his gun and the bundle. The kitchen was a mess and she almost panicked again as she thought that Brenda might wake up and see the bloody mess. Cathy was concerned that if anyone found out that she helped the boy, she could be in a lot of trouble.

After taking the boy's belongings and laying them by his side, Cathy returned to the kitchen and quickly cleaned the place. The bloodstains were difficult to get up. She stuffed the old cloths and bandages in a paper bag and placed them at the bottom of the garbage can outside. As she stepped back in the house, she screamed.

"My God, Brenda! You gave me a fright."

"What are you doing, Cathy? What are those stains on the floor?"

"Oh, nothing. My nose was bleeding and I'm cleaning up the mess."

"You're making enough noise, aren't you? Are you drunk?"

Cathy had long since sobered up, but decided to lie.

"Oh well, I'm a little tipsy. We had such a good time tonight that I got carried away."

"I wish you could be a little less noisy, Cathy. I don't like my sleep disturbed you know. Good night."

Cathy was relieved when Brenda left the room. She also thought to herself.

"Goodnight, you silly cow."

Cathy woke up the next morning with a headache and a weak stomach. On top of this, she was still suffering from the shock of the previous nights events. It was market day and it was Brenda's turn to go shopping with the cook. Cathy could hear her shouting and telling the cook to clean up the mess in the kitchen before they left. Brenda was often rude and unpleasant to the cook and Cathy did not like her behavior. Nervous about whether the young boy was still lying in the hedges, Cathy did not want to leave her room until Brenda left for the market place. A half an hour later she heard the front door slam and foot steps walking down toward the schoolyard. Brenda and the cook were gone and Cathy was relieved. She jumped up and put on a t-shirt and pair of shorts, and rushed out to the back garden. Slowly approaching the spot where she left the boy she wondered whether several Malawian women who were walking along the road next to the house were noticing her. She felt stupid about creeping around in her own back garden.

The spot was empty and the boy gone. The only thing left was the brown paper bag that had contained the food and his shirt. She picked the bag up and placed it in the garbage can while simultaneously inspecting the bottom of the can to see if the dirty stained bandage was still wrapped up. It was. Cathy decided to spend the rest of her day in her room because she was exhausted and she did not want to talk too much with Brenda. Brenda asked too many questions. Cathy also made up her mind not to mention the incident to anyone, except Jesse. She knew she would be relieved if she could talk to someone, and Jesse was the only one she trusted regarding this incident. She believed that since he was black and radical, he would sympathize with the terrorists and would condone her actions. She did not trust Brenda and didn't want to see Steve. Cathy also hoped that she would never see another terrorist again.

The Party Pooper

It was a cool night and James slept restlessly. When he woke up the next morning, he felt the chill inside the house. He got up slowly that morning since there was no rush to get to work or go anywhere in particular. Once the bedroom curtain was drawn, he noticed that the pineapple plants lining his driveway were beginning to bear fruit. The sky was clear and the sun seemed to be set in a far-off distant place. It didn't seem to belong to Africa this time of year, but was sharing its favored warmth with some other part of God's magnificent earth. Even the birds appeared to be busily making their way to some other part of the continent. It was the middle of the dry season in Malawi, and literally everything was dry except the green foliage and crops, which had stored up enough water to see themselves through the harvest season. There had not been rain in four weeks and the once bubbling springs were now only a trickle. James had noticed that recently the popular but small lake twelve miles outside of Mzuzu was now a barren sunken cradle with only a few puddles of water. Even the last survivors of the fish family were fighting hard to maintain control over the few feet of water, although their fate would be a slow and smothering death as the sun would gradually dry up the puddles. It was a June Monday morning in 1967 and James Johnson was on his first holiday break since arriving in Malawi. He looked forward to the week off and planned to spend part of it in Blantyre with his girlfriend, Rose Nkhoma.

The two were reported to be in love with each other and saw each other often. They planned to attend the party given by Joe Veto, Ramsey Hall and Reggie Blackwell during the weekend and go to the track and field athletic events in the new stadium. James got up and fixed his breakfast. Geoffrey, his house helper was not there as he too was on holiday with pay. Somehow James was glad that Geoffrey and his family would not be around for a while. He figured they all needed a break from each other. After breakfast he turned on his transistor radio, which only got two stations. One was Malawi Radio and the other was an Egyptian station. He listened to African music while he made his bed and cleaned the house. Soon it was news time and he heard to his surprise a frantic voice proclaiming the victories of war. It was an Egyptian newscaster informing the world that President Abdul Nasser's forces were triumphantly engaged in a war with Israel and he went on to detail the successes so far. James thought at first this was some kind of a radio drama program, since he did not know much about the Israel and Arab conflicts. After the news in which the war took up ten minutes, the African music returned. He gave no more thought to the war that morning. It didn't affect him in the slightest so he wasn't that bothered. After cleaning the house he went outside to do some hoeing and digging in his small vegetable patch. The weeds in the ten-by-six patch were over powering the vegetables. He had planted cabbage, lettuce, peas and carrots and he enjoyed the exercise. Down on his knees digging with a small spade, his mind wandered. A lot had happened since he returned from his tour of the regional clinics. His memory of these events was very vivid.

"Bill Humphries had some nerve to come all the way up here to ask me about that incident in the mountains. He must have thought I would be foolish enough to admit knowing what they were up to. I told him I had no idea what those machines were doing up there. When he asked if I talked to that young British boy about Geiger counters, I said I didn't even know what a Geiger counter was. He irritated me that morning. Who does he think he is waking me up so early on a Saturday morning? Hell, I only got to bed around midnight. Someone must have put a lot of pressure on him because he was nervous as hell."

James's mind came back to the row he was weeding. He had come to the end of the row and had no idea how long his mind had drifted from what he was doing. He noticed that his carrots were not growing too well. The ground was hard and the reddish clay-soil didn't help either. The cabbages and lettuces were growing very well and he thought how hardy they were. As he knelt again to start another row of digging and weeding, his thoughts quickly drifted again to past events.

"I wonder if they suspect me of something devious? They wouldn't unless they know of Stuart's activities with Janice Blanche and I don't think Stuart would divulge information. I've helped them once during the past month by providing a list of health clinics and information about supplies and staffing. But I told Stuart that's it. I'm not getting involved anymore. This thing is bigger than I thought, especially if the East Germans and Russians are involved. Stuart let that one slip because he knows I don't want anything to do with the communists. He and Janice still don't fully trust me because they wouldn't let me in on what the East Germans were doing up there in Lukabi. Hell, I'm no fool. Anybody could guess that they must be training those boys to fight in a war. It makes me nervous thinking about it. Let me think of something else."

James was about halfway finished when he decided to take a break. He was in no hurry so he leisurely went inside and fixed a cup of coffee. He noticed how much more comfortable his house was since he got his furniture from the Ministry of Housing. He thought what a good friend Muwalo Phiri, his supervisor, had become. James and Muwalo double-dated almost every weekend since James started going out with Rose. They'd been up to the plateau twice and had taken several trips to the countryside in Muwalo's car. James tried to encourage Muwalo to go down to Blantyre during the weekend but his friend had other commitments. He did however offer his car to James for the weekend but James refused, thinking it was too much of an imposition. James and Rose planned to take the bus down. Sitting at the dining room table with his feet resting on a chair James thought about Jennifer Nolan.

"Too bad about Jennifer and me. We used to be such good friends. I mean, she was one of the few people I felt really comfortable talking to out here. Other than Stuart and Muwalo, she was the only other okay person. Now she acts as if she doesn't even know me. We speak, but I can feel an icy bitterness. It's strange. Since I've been dating Rose, Jennifer has never mentioned her by name, nor has she referred to our relationship at all. It's as if she's blocked me and Rose completely out of her mind. I don't know. I hope we don't continue this way because I'm still fond of Jennifer and would like for us all to be good friends. She makes me feel guilty as if I let her down or something. Hell, she's got no right to make me feel that way. I made no commitments to her. Haven't seen her in three and a half weeks now. Maybe I ought to pop by there this week. Then maybe not! I saw Crissie Chipenbere in the market last week and even she was cool toward me. I asked how they all were doing and she insinuated that they're doing fine as long as people like me stay away. Well, I had no fight with Crissie so I let that one pass. Stuff them all if they want to be that way!"

When he finished his coffee he decided to read Jesse Jefferson's letter again. He thought it was a strange letter because Jesse was hinting at things that James couldn't figure out. Jesse told James he would be in Blantyre for the party and that he wanted to talk to James about 'some happenings.' This was confusing enough and the letter went on to suggest that since they both were soul brothers they should stick together and share information with each other. The entire letter was so vague that James dismissed it as being Jesse's inability to express himself clearly on paper. The thing that struck James most about the letter was Jesse's reference to Cathy Horowitz. It read:

"Man! This Jewish sister is into some heavy activities down here. She's helping the brothers from Rhodesia. Only I know and now you know. When you see her next weekend don't mention it though. I'm the medium, you dig?"

James didn't dig it at all. In fact, he thought for a moment that Jesse had gone around the bend. James returned to the garden and worked for another two hours. He was stripped of clothing except for a pair of cut-off jeans he used as shorts. Even the jeans were

307

wet. He not only worked up a good sweat, but a terrific appetite as well. He went into the house to take a cold bath. Somehow the water didn't feel cold as he lathered his body with soap. He got out and dried himself with a beach towel. He skipped through the house and got another pair of shorts out of his chest of drawers. It didn't take long to fix a bologna sandwich and a glass of orange juice. It seemed to satisfy his hunger. While sitting at the dining room table he saw his love, Rose Nkoma, walking briskly up the driveway. He leaped up and ran outside to greet her.

"Rose, what are you doing here this time of day? Aren't you supposed to be at work?"

 Rose ran up to him and embraced him.

"I didn't feel like working the rest of the afternoon," she whispered. "I wanted to be with you. I told them that I wasn't feeling well so I'm supposed to be home sick."

"You silly girl," he joked. "You can't get enough of me, can you?"

"That's true, my love. Aren't you going to invite me in?"

"Sure, come on in, I was getting bored anyway. I'm glad you came."

They both went into the house and James poured an orange juice for Rose. They sat on the couch in the living room and laughed about their rendezvous.

"Boy, if your boss knew what you were up to he'd fire you tomorrow. You sure pulled the wool over his eyes."

"I'm too excited about the weekend, James. I've only typed about three pages all morning. You should see the mistakes I've been making. I think he knows I'm excited so he won't be too annoyed. I've got Friday off so we can leave that morning."

"Terrific! We should get the first bus in the morning to arrive in Blantyre at least by early evening."

Rose wore a tight fitting miniskirt with a frilly blouse. She looked delightful and sexy as usual. She was one of the few African girls who wore miniskirts. President Aleke Makube had spoken out against women wearing miniskirts and considered imposing a ban on them. Most of the Malawian girls never really bothered, but the expat women and a few African girls from other countries continued to wear them. Rose was not a country girl in the traditional sense of the word. In fact, she grew up in one of the large, urban African townships in Rhodesia and was used to western dress. She was 'together', as James put it. He enjoyed listening to her soft voice and her Rhodesia accent. She spoke good English since she had learned it from the time she was a child. Bantu was her mother tongue.

James sat with his bare legs stretched across the coffee table. Rose was curled up on the couch leaning on him. She began to make circling motions on his chest with her forefinger. They talked in between quick kisses.

"Hey, do you know what I'm going to do?"

"No, what are you going to do, James?"

"I'm going to take you back to America with me."

"Oh, you're always joking."

"I'm serious, Rose. You're my woman and where I go, you go. Don't you want to go to America with me?"

"Yes, I do. I will go anywhere with you, but it's a long ways off. You might not love me then."

"What makes you say that?"

"Oh, it just happens. Men are like that. When you get tired of me, you will go and find another woman."

"Oh, don't say that, sweetheart. I love you and I'll never get tired of you. Who knows, a pretty girl like you is more likely to get tired of me first."

"No. I love you, too, but maybe we shouldn't talk about things that will not happen. I would like to believe that you want to take me back with you, but things are not always as easy as they appear."

"What do you mean by that? Come on, Rose, what are you talking about?"

"I will explain sometime in the future. Please let's just be happy for now."

James became slightly despondent and got up to go to the kitchen. He poured another orange juice as he glanced out of the window while sulking. As he lifted the glass of juice to his mouth he could feel Rose's fingers massaging the back of his neck. She then leaned on his back and slowly slipped her arms around his bare chest.

"Don't be like that, James," she whispered. "Let's cheer up and have some fun. After all, I came all the way over here to be with you."

"Well, why do you say things like that and then leave them hanging? I hate being kept in the dark. What's up with you anyway, Rose? Several times now, you've hinted that our relationship won't last. Have you got someone else that I don't know about?"

"No. It's only you, James. I'm sorry. Sometimes I have trouble expressing myself. Let's forget it."

James went back into the living room and put on a record. He then stretched out on the couch. Rose followed him and as he lay there looking up, she came and stood right next to him. He looked at her long, thin brown legs and his eyes followed them up to the bottom of her miniskirt.

She smiled and said, "Aren't you going to leave room for me?"

He looked up and then smiled.

"Come here, you sexy woman."

Rose leaned over and kissed him on the forehead. He put his hands on the back of her legs and slowly felt them up and down until they rested on her soft but tight round bottom. He slowly pulled her on to the couch and they lay side by side kissing. They slept for almost two hours after they made love. The time was approaching three o'clock.

"Wow, we must have knocked each other out that time. You were great, sweetheart. Too bad we can't lay around and do it every day like this."

"You're very good to me, James. Maybe it is just as well that we can't do this every day. We would never get anything else done. Oh, it's getting late. I have to go now."

"What's the hurry? You can stay as long as you want."

"I've got to cook dinner."

"Cook dinner? Hell, it's only you. Stay here and I'll fix something for us."

"No James, too many things to do."

"Okay, then, I'll take you home."

James took Rose as far as the shops on the main street where she lived. He had never seen exactly where she stayed, but only knew that it was one of rooms behind the store. When she got off the motorcycle she kissed him hurriedly and said goodbye.

"Hey, wait a minute, Rose. Let me walk you to your door."

"No. That is not necessary. You should leave now."

"Should leave now! You say some strange things, woman. We're supposed to be in love and you won't even let me see where you live. I'll be damned, Rose! What are you hiding?"

Rose became annoyed.

"I'm hiding nothing! I have things to do. That's all. I wish you would trust me, James."

He felt guilty after that statement and decided not to push it.

"Hey, Rose. Okay, I'm sorry. I didn't mean to imply that I don't trust you. I do. Anyway, I'll see you Thursday evening. Have your bags ready and we can stay at my house that night. It's easier getting to the station from there in the morning."

"Okay, my love. Bye."

"Bye."

He threw her a kiss.

The next morning James lay in bed until mid-morning. He actually woke up at eight, but felt like being lazy. Moments after he got up, he heard a motorcycle roaring up the driveway. He wondered who it could be. Before he could finish dressing and making his bed he heard a loud knock on the back door. He ran to the door and unlocked the latch.

"Stuart. What a surprise. What are you doing around these parts?"

Stuart walked into the living room and sat sprawled in a chair. He looked nervous and worried.

"Hey, Stuart, what's up, man? You look like you received some bad news or something."

After catching his breathe and asking for a drink of water, Stuart calmed down a bit.

"James, I'm leaving!"

"Leaving?"

"Yes, leaving. I'm going to Israel to fight for my homeland."

"What the hell are you talking about, Stuart?"

"Israel is the Jewish Homeland. Haven't you ever heard of Israel?

"I just don't get it, Stuart. I know you're Jewish and all that, but what are you going to Israel for? I mean, you're American, man!"

"I'm Jewish and don't you forget it."

"Okay, Stuart. I'm sorry for being so naive, but just cool down a moment. Now has this got anything to do with that news I heard recently about Egypt being at war with Israel?"

"You're damn right, and we Jews are not going to go down without putting up a damn good fight. Maybe you can understand this. It's the only homeland we've had in almost two thousand years and we've had our share of being kicked around from one country to another and being slaughtered like animals."

James was absolutely flabbergasted. The morning just didn't seem real with Stuart breezing in talking about going to fight in a war that to James's way of thinking had nothing to do with Americans and particularly Peace Corps volunteers.

"What about your job here. What about the clinic?"

"The hell with the job, the hell with the clinic. Israel comes first!"

"Look, Stuart, I understand how you must feel, but don't you think you are rushing this decision. I mean you could go up there and get killed."

"James, I would gladly die for my homeland. Millions have died before me and a strong and united Israel is worth more to me than my life."

After that statement James realized how committed Stuart was to the cause and did not challenge him again about his decision to leave.

"Stuart, I'm sorry that I sounded ignorant about what's happening in Israel, but it's just that I don't know much about it. Anyway, will you come back?"

"No, James. I think once I get to Israel, I'll stay. It's not just an impromptu decision. I've thought about immigrating for the past three years. But hearing about the war was just what I needed to make up my mind. They're killing our people and invading from all fronts. Israel needs all her children's help now. Can you understand that, James?"

James's thoughts ran fast and furious as he recalled incidents in his own life and those before him in which black Americans died or were prepared to die to achieve freedom, equal opportunities and respect. He recalled the sit-in demonstrations throughout the American South and how the black People were beaten and abused by helmeted, truncheon-wielding white men wearing police uniforms and hooded white robes. James told Stuart that he understood what Stuart meant.

Stuart finished a cup of coffee and explained that he would drive straight to Blantyre and catch the first flight he could get. He indicated that he wouldn't be alone since there were quite a number of Jewish people in the country and a number of them would probably go, even though they would expect to return after the war was over. Then Stuart filled James in on the latest activities of ZINAP and Chief Katumbi's group. He hinted that James might be asked to get involved since he was leaving. They needed a good contact man in the region. He also said that he spent the last day with Janice and she was upset about him leaving. He asked James to be nice to her and said that she would be in contact with James within a few weeks.

"Well, I don't know about all this, Stuart. I mean, I've already got more involved that I intended but I don't feel as though I'm in a position to replace you as a contact man. Plus, there must be other people who could do as well as me. By the way, are any of the other volunteers involved and if so, who are they?"

"I can only tell you that there are others, but even as close as Janice and I are she would not divulge their names. The idea is to keep everyone totally ignorant of each other's activities therefore, if one person slips up, he can't implicate anyone else. It's just by chance that you and I have been working together on this. Anyway, James, Janice is a committed revolutionary but she's fighting for the Africans. I don't know whether that cuts much ice with you, but men like Chief Katumbi and Frank Myosa of ZINAP are only too grateful to have her assistance. Like me, buddy. You got a few causes yourself, and someday you will have to face up to them and make a decision."

Stuart's last comment achieved its desired effect. It was a stunning blow to James and left him seriously deliberating the matter. Stuart was about to leave and turned around to James and shook his hand.

"Thanks for being such a good pal, James. You've been one of the few people I've had a good laugh with and maybe one day we will run into each other again. If not, you will be written to by someone letting you know my fate."

"Ah, come on Stuart, don't be so morbid. We'll keep in touch and take care of yourself buddy."

"Okay, James. So long."

By the following Friday, Stuart Steiner and eleven other Jewish people who had worked in Malawi arrived in Israel. Also by Friday, a much different version of the war was emerging. There had been several years of uneasy peace between the Israelis and their Arab neighbors. Local clashes on the Syrian-Israeli border were followed by mass concentration of Egyptian Army units around parts of the Egyptian-Israeli border. President Nasser of Egypt expelled a United Nations emergency force and imposed a blockade on Israel.

315

This presumably precipitated retaliatory action by Israel who struck out at Egypt by land and air. The state of Jordan was also drawn into the conflict, which had spread to the Syrian border. The news received in Malawi on Friday was that the Israelis were actually winning the war. They occupied areas of the Gaza Strip and the Sinai Peninsula stretching from the Suez Canal in Egypt to the Jordan valley and the heights east of the Sea of Galilee. They even occupied the town of Quneitra in Syria. After hearing the latest broadcast on his way down to Blantyre, James felt he understood a little more about the conflict. He and Rose sat uncomfortably on the crowded bus after having travelled seven hours. He turned off his transistor radio.

"Do you remember Stuart Steiner, the guy I introduced to you from Stamford, Connecticut? The one who worked up near the Malawi-Zambia border? Well, he left for Israel to fight in the war?"

Rose who was wiping her forehead replied, "Why did he go there?"

"Well, it's a long story but basically, he's Jewish and he wanted to help his Jewish brothers and sisters."

"But the Jews shouldn't be there, should they? That land belongs to the Arabs and Palestinians."

"I don't know really. I know they've been there since the end of World War II and they came from all over Europe, the Middle East and from parts of Africa. The Arabs sure don't think they should be there. It's tragic, isn't it? I mean, they've been run out of one country after another and then the British decided to give them a homeland. The British didn't give them London or Birmingham, but they decided to take land from the Palestinians to give to them. I'm all for the Jews having a homeland but the British did the same thing there as they did in this part of Africa. They just threw darts at a map and said. "Right! You lot will live there and you lot push off over there," with no regard for cultural affiliations, languages or geographical boundaries. They've just created situations which will continue to reap conflict and war."

Rose laid her head on James's shoulder and closed her eyes.

"Okay, sweetheart, I get the message. I'm talking too much. I think I'll go to sleep, too."

They arrived at Blantyre Bus Station that evening. The station was crowded with people and their belongings, including chickens, goats and a few pigs. It had been a long and tiring trip and they were exhausted and felt dirty from the dusty sweaty ride. James decided to splurge a bit by taking a taxi to Reggie Blackwell's house. Reggie had agreed to put up a few people at his place. The trip across town took about twenty minutes and James was relieved to see that Reggie had a nice two-bedroom apartment near the Ministry of Recreation Headquarter building. It was a spacious apartment on the first floor of a three-story building. Rose was introduced to Reggie and told to make herself at home.

They took baths and changed into clean clothes. James had bought a few chicken sandwiches before leaving the bus station and they all sat around the kitchen table eating them.

"How's it been going, Reggie? You must be excited about tomorrow. I'd be scared stiff if I was to be congratulated by the President. I hear you're doing a great job. Congratulations, brother!"

Reggie responded in his usual shy and modest manner, "I hope the events run smoothly James, but you know I'm not one for a lot of publicity. I'll be glad when the whole thing is over."

"You're already famous. I heard your name mentioned on radio last week in conjunction with organizing the track and field events. Hey, can I have your autograph?"

"Ah, get out here. I'm not that famous," replied Reggie jokingly.

Rose excused herself for a few minutes leaving James and Reggie to talk.

"That's a fine looking woman you got, James. You two seem to be very tight."

"Yeah, she's great. We're kind of tight."

"What about you, Reggie? You got anything going for yourself down here?"

"No man, too busy. I've been out with one or two girls but you know how it is. I cannot see myself getting too involved, but if I could pick them like you do, I'd be all right."

"Oh, you're cool, bro. You probably got a string of girls digging on you. I mean a big time famous sports organizer like you will have no trouble pulling in the girls. They'll be swarming all over this place!"

Eventually they got around to filling each other in on what had been happening. Reggie told James that Joe Veto was dating a local Malawian girl and it looked serious.

"Aha! I always knew that Joe liked the sisters a lot. Did you know he had a real thing for Dianne Harper? I bet he was annoyed when she left."

"Yes, he likes the sisters all right, but then you can't say too much James because you like the white girls, don't you?"

"I'm not knocking Joe because he's dating a sister, neither am I denying that I like white girls. But you might as well get the story straight. I like them white, black, brown and yellow as long as they wear skirts and they don't have hairs growing on their chest. You're beginning to sound like, Jesse, man!"

"Now, now, don't get your back up James. I'm just joking man. I don't care what color girls you date. They can be candy-striped for all I care. Anyway, you got a fine sister there."

Rose returned to the room and cheerfully talked with the two for a while. Then Reggie heard a knock at the door. It was Jesse Jefferson and Steve Manski. Reggie was to put them up for the night, too.

"Reggie! James! How's it going, brothers? Hey, who's good looking sister is this? My name is Jesse Jefferson and I'm the brother from Chikwawa. Oh, meet Steve Manski. He works in Chikwawa, too."

318

Jesse didn't bother to wait for introductions and acted as if he were the host. They all went into the living room and exchanged their news. Rose enjoyed being fully admired by all the fellows and she received a lot of attention. While the conversation livened up, Jesse cornered James in a private conversation.

In a low voice he asked, "Did you get my letter? Did you understand what I was saying? I want to sound you out about something when we get a chance to talk alone, Okay?"

"Sure, Jesse. Okay."

It was getting late and Reggie's guests were ready to sack out for the night. James had brought two small sleeping bags for himself and Rose, but they did not need them that night, instead they used Reggie's single bed in his spare bedroom. Jesse and Steve slept on the floor in the living room. Reggie was up early the next morning because he had to be at the new stadium by seven o'clock. He left a note telling the others to make themselves at home and he would see them later. James decided to leave his bags at Reggie's place until after the ceremonies that afternoon. Although he planned to stay at Joe's place after the party, he thought it would be nice to have a place to get a hot bath and dress before going to the party. According to Reggie, they expected at least a hundred people at the party.

James, Rose, Jesse and Steve arrived at the new stadium before noon. The place was crowded and it was bedlam getting through the gates. Various track and field events had been in progress since ten o'clock that morning, but the finals for each event would not be held until after the President's arrival. Scores of buses drove in from various parts of the country and groups of African dancers completely surrounded the place. Once inside, the group pushed their way through the crowded bleachers, trying to get the best viewing spot. The array of colors and costumes along with the noisy bands gave the place a festive atmosphere. It was as lively as an American Independence Day celebration. Hundreds of white faces dotted up among the thousands of black faces peering down at the activities on center field. By the time the group found seats, a tall dark man wearing a golfers-cap fired a pistol. It was Reggie

319

Blackwell starting the four hundred meter relay. He seemed to tower above the runners as they lifted their heads and moved off in a fast sprint. Further to the east wing of the stadium a section of empty seats could be seen. Uniformed soldiers with guns surrounded it. It was reserved for the President Makube and his entourage. The Malawi flag flew high and the podium from which the President would speak was adorned with streamers of red, green and black paper, the national colors. The stadium was never void of entertainment and excitement. As each track event finished, a new group of dancers would emerge on to the field to perform their own tribal rituals until it was time for the next event. Groups of men with painted facemasks, spears and shields could be seen dancing franticly to the rhythms of the music. The women were not to be outdone as they proudly performed their dances. Their colorful beads and printed wrap-around dresses added to the festive atmosphere. Even the continuous beats of the drums seemed to carry a persuasive message of joyous certainty as the drummers compulsively reached higher and higher crescendos.

"Wow, this place is alive today," remarked Steve Manski.

"You can say that again," James said. "I wonder where those guys get all of their stamina. They must have been beating those drums for the last two hours."

"They're high!"

Everyone looked around at Jesse and said. "What?"

"High on laudanum. It's a tincture of opium, and don't tell me you never heard of opium before."

"How do you know, Jesse?" asked James.

Jesse looked at Rose and said, "You tell them, sister. Don't those guys take drugs to keep them going? You tell them."

Rose thought before she answered because she knew that Jesse was not exactly right.

"Well, yes and no. They use a root drug sometimes. They get it from the village doctor or witch doctor as you call them, but opium is not used much by villagers. It's very difficult to get in this country."

Steve looked at Jesse and laughed.

"You and your big words. You think you know so much, Jesse."

Jesse who was slightly embarrassed turned to Steve.

"You better watch your tongue, boy. Remember, you're in the minority over here!"

Everyone found his statement amusing except Steve.

The rest of the day at the stadium turned out to be very eventful. President Makube arrived in a motorcade and was driven around the stadium grounds twice. He shook hands and got out of his Mercedes-Benz limousine several times to dance with the women. He also waved a flywhisk that resembled a lion's tail. Once he was seated in the stands the ceremonies started in earnest. The Malawi Army Band played several tunes. This was followed by a mock-up version of the Malawi Army soldiers capturing terrorists. This exercise was performed to show the people how effective the Army was at capturing and killing terrorists and served as a warning to those contemplating aiding Chief Katumbi's forces. The message was that the Chief and his followers could not win. After the final track and field events were over, the President delivered a long and boring speech. He spent about five minutes on naming the stadium and 105 minutes on loyalty, dedication and anti-Katumbi slogans.

To some people's surprise, a well-dressed African about fifty years old was escorted to the podium. His hands were hand cuffed. Then President Makube spoke of how this man once ran with the terrorists and had now come back to ask for forgiveness. The President insinuated that he was prepared to forgive this man and others like him if they put down their arms and returned home. The man was asked to give his impression of Chief Katumbi. His speech was well prepared but no one knew for certain how much the

President had to do with the contents of the speech. It seemed very likely that this man was told exactly what to say. He denounced Chief Katumbi as a thieving renegade who was only interested in power for himself. He said that the chief used all the money for his own personal pleasures and that he was a communist. He stated that the Chief's supporters were leaving his hideout by the dozen and it was no use in anyone joining the Chief because he could not win and he was an evil man.

Most of the local people seemed to accept this dramatic episode in the day's events, presumably because they had witnessed this scenario time and time again. However, most ex-patriots who were new to the country could not believe their eyes or ears. James sat there shaking his head in disbelief.

He whispered to the others, "Is this for real? Man. I have never!"

"Quiet!" replied Rose. "You will be overheard. It is best not to discuss the President publicly. He has eyes and ears all over the stadium."

Jesse and Steve nodded their heads in agreement. James kept quiet after that. As the events came to a close, Steve spotted Phil Harrington and Fiona Crewe talking to Reggie Blackwell down on the track.

"Hey, there's Phil. I haven't seen him since we arrived. Who's that girl he's with?"

"That's his number one. Her name is Fiona. They're real tight, man," replied James.
"You mean Phil's got a girl?"

"You better believe it. Soon he'll have a wife the way those two feel about each other."

"I don't know. You guys in Mzuzu are doing okay for yourselves. Maybe I'm in the wrong place."

Then Jesse laughed at Steve.

"What are you grinning at, Jesse?"

"You, man. Why don't you tell James how tight you and that Church mum are?"

"Come off it, Jesse, she's just a friend. You know that."

"Oh?" said James. "So you're into some action too, eh?"

"Nothing to speak of James. Let's go over and see Phil and his girl."

"Okay," replied the others.

They all went over and greeted Phil, Fiona and Reggie. They talked for twenty minutes before Jesse asked James to step over on the side with him. The others didn't seem to notice them talking about ten yards away. Jesse told James about the series of house-break-ins and thefts which happened in Chikwawa. Then he explained how Cathy Horowitz came to him one morning to tell him how she was forced at gunpoint to aid a freedom fighter. Since that time, several more ZINAP men had showed up at Cathy's place looking for assistance. She began voluntarily helping them by providing food and medical assistance. Her entire involvement was secretive and only Jesse knew about that. The men usually came at an early hour in the morning and tapped on her window seven times. This was the signal for assistance. For some reason James could not believe that Cathy was so involved, but Jesse explained it in terms of her altruism. She did not particularly agree with their political motives, but she found it difficult to turn away a person in need. Jesse finally brought the conversation around to James's activities.

"I hear there's a lot of action up your way, especially regarding Chief Katumbi."

He waited for James's response, which was, "Oh, yeah? What have you heard?"

"Oh, nothing in particular. It's just that I thought some of you guys would be working for the cause."

"Come on, Jesse. You're being as vague now as when you wrote to me. What's on your mind, brother? You sound as if you're fishing for information."

"Who? Me? No, man. I'm not fishing. I'm just trying to relate."

"Well, relate then. Say, what's on your mind."

Finally Jesse told James that he heard some of the volunteers were passing information to ZINAP and Chief Katumbi. He did not know what information was passed on but he explained that he supported their activities and wanted to help in any way he could. He suggested that the two should liaison more closely with each other since they were fighting for the same cause. James began to feel suspicious about Jesse and asked him where he got his information.

"Oh, I get around and hear things."

"Who told you, Jesse?"

"I can't say, man."

"Well, hell. If you can't say, I can't confirm whether anybody up there is involved. What's up, Jesse, you don't trust me?"

"Sure, man, I trust you. You sound as if you don't trust me. You know me man. I'm all for helping to get rid of this Uncle Tom Regime and those honkies that are ruling Rhodesia. Listen, brother, if you're involved I'd like to know because I'm involved, too. We ought to work together, you know. What I'm prepared to do is tell you everything that happens down my way if you do the same for me. This way, the right hand knows what the left is doing. I've already given you a valuable piece of information by telling you about, Cathy. Now, if that ain't trust, I don't know what is. Hell! I've helped the brothers, too!"

There was a long pause while James studied Jesse's remarks. They made sense and seemed consistent with Jesse's expressed attitude toward President Makube's regime and those of Rhodesia and

South Africa. Jesse was a known radical with revolutionary ideas and James thought that if he couldn't trust Jesse, he couldn't trust anyone.

"What you say makes sense, Jesse, but let's face it man, living in this country makes you suspicious of everyone, including soul brothers. What have you got in mind specifically?"

Jesse then explained how he planned to visit Mzuzu about once every six weeks and they could talk then. In the meantime, they could write to each other using coded messages that Jesse would work out.

"What do you know about codes, Jesse?"

"Look, brother, remember I was in the U.S. Marines. Don't worry. We'll have a fool-proof system. Just trust me, baby! Another thing, it's important to know who else is working with you, so we don't get our wires crossed. You know how easy it is for different people to pass on conflicting information."

"I will think about it, Jesse."

By this time James noticed Rose beckoning him to join her. The others were still engrossed in conversation. Jesse and James returned to the group as inconspicuously as they left. No one but Rose missed them. Jesse asked Phil about Jennifer Nolan and Bob Newgate.

"Jennifer came down with us last night but Bob decided not to come."

"How did you get here, Phil?"

"We got a lift with Fiona's roommate's boyfriend. His name is Jerry. In fact, Jennifer is with him and Marg right now. They're probably lost in the crowd but you'll see them tonight Jesse. By the way, where's Cathy Horowitz? Did she come?"

"No. She said she felt ill," replied Jesse, but he knew the real reason she didn't come.

She was committed to her private cause of playing benefactor, doctor and godmother to the freedom fighters who came from Rhodesia. Reggie Blackwell was summoned by one of the officials and told the group he would see them later. They then dispersed and went in separate directions. Everyone seemed in a festive mood as the events of the day seemed to serve as a prelude to the party that night.

Joe Veto's house and lawn looked like a haven for hippies at a rock concert. Small tents were erected among the scores of sleeping bags scattered around the yard. There was hardly standing room as the blue-jean clad tee-shirted volunteers leaped across each other to get from one side of the lawn to the other. Close to a hundred people were attended including Malawians, Americans, British, French and Germans. In the back garden, a huge log fire was roaring and crowds of people gathered to roast their chickens, hot dogs, sausages and beef. There was plenty to drink and some marijuana was being passed around. Several people played guitars and on occasions their music blocked out the sounds of the record players, even though speakers were strategically placed in the windows of the house. Girls wearing miniskirts and shorts danced to the cool beat of the Motown sounds and the dust from the ground completely engulfed their bare feet. Everyone seemed to be having a great time.

James saw Joe Veto standing with his arms around his girlfriend. Initially, Joe seemed nervous but soon relaxed as the four chatted about various topics. The party was going well and Joe explained that he was apprehensive at first about having so many people. Soon Phil Harington, Fiona Crewe and Jennifer Nolan joined them. James spoke to Jennifer, but she hardly replied and she never once acknowledged Rose's presence. Her eyes were slightly red from a more than usual consumption of alcohol and her voice sounded slurred. Nonetheless, she appeared to be confident and almost aggressive that night. She dominated the conversation and moved about as if she were the queen of the party. Her new French style hair cut was set against the background of a low-cut black silk dress.

326

Parts of her bubbly breasts could be seen protruding out of the half-cup bra she wore. The dress seemed to cling to her and every time her body moved, the curves and crevices were accented. She had sex appeal and projected it in a very convincing manner. Jennifer talked with Steve Manski for a long while. During that period she had another drink.

Eventually she said, "Come on, Steve, dance with me."

They got out in the clearing and began dancing. Steve became slightly embarrassed because Jennifer was really letting her hair down. She began to perform the most sensual movements with her body. Then she slowly lifted the black dress above her knees and the crowds gathered around and cheered her on. Steve stepped back, leaving Jennifer at the center of attention. She seemed to be in her own world as she slowly stripped the black dressed from around her shoulders.

Someone shouted, "Take it all off!"

Then the dress dropped from her shoulders down to the ground leaving her standing in a pair of black lace panties and a black bra. She continued to twist and jump and shout with glee. It was as if she were having a pleasant catharsis. James began to get annoyed by her performance and for some reason embarrassed. Steve shared the same feeling.

James turned to Rose and said, "That crazy chick is drunk out of her mind tonight. Someone ought to stop her."

"Well, that's her problem, not yours. Why should you care since she hardly speaks to you and won't even look at me?"

"You're right, baby. It's just that we were friends once and I'd hate to see her make a fool of herself," Rose responded in an irritated voice.

"You should not care about her."

By this time Joe and Fat Ramsey went out to rescue Jennifer.

Ramsey said jovially, "Well that's it folks. This show is over. Time to put the little girl to bed."

"It's your turn now, Ramsey!" someone shouted.

He then gave a little shake of his fat ass and the crowd screamed for more. During the next hour Fiona Crewe and a few others tried to get Jennifer sober by giving her hot black coffee. It had little affect because she was still talking nonsense. She did not even remember dancing before the crowd, but accepted Fiona's word that she had. Rose was out among the crowd dancing with Jesse when Jennifer came out of the front door. James was leaning against the wall. He looked at her in disgust.

"Why are you looking at me like that, James Johnson?"

"Because you're drunk and you've made a complete ass of yourself."

"What, what, what's it to you what I've done?" she slurred.

"It's nothing to me if you want to strip in front of all these people."

She fell up against him.

"Would you rather I strip in front of you alone, James? What's wrong, James? Isn't this the way you like your women? Sleazy, sexy, randy?"

"What the hell are you talking about, Jennifer?"

"Well, look at what you chose, a long-legged whoring bitch who wears tight miniskirts. That's what you like!"

"You need to shut up, Jennifer, before you make an even bigger fool of yourself," James said. "Don't you ever call Rose a whore!"

Jennifer had never seen James so angry before and she was temporarily frightened, but somehow the booze stopped her from being rational.

"Don't take my word for it. No, I may be drunk. But ask your friends. Ask Muwalo Phiri. He knows all about Rose and so does everyone else except for you. You're a blind fool, James!"

Jennifer ran off into the crowd.

James stood there in anguish. Had she only said those things in a fit of jealousy? He felt like wringing Jennifer's neck for the insults she hurled and the doubt she planted in his mind. It made him wonder why Rose never invited him to her place and how she often hinted that their relationship would not last. Then he tried to rationalize Jennifer's remarks by putting them down to her own selfish motives. Her behavior was so uncharacteristic of her, at least when she was sober. Rose returned and noticed that he seemed upset.

"Are you all right, my love?"

He looked down at her and smiled.

"Yes. I'm just a little tired, Rose. Come here. I want to hold you for a while."

Sitting around the fire in the back garden, Jesse Jefferson was engaged in a lengthy conversation with Fiona Crewe about African politics. Phil was there, too, but as usual did not have much to say. Jesse argued that the traditional extended family system in East Africa was essentially a socialist system and was totally alien from the European concept of class and class struggle. He went on to suggest that given this close bond between the individual and the community, especially in rural areas, a system of cooperative sharing should form the basis of economic policy in Africa. Fiona's argument was that until a more progressive form of capitalism involving a full injection of investment funds from other countries became a reality, African Socialism would have little impact on the growing income disparities between the rich and poor nations. She cited an example of how Zambia had nationalized most of its industries and businesses, thereby frightening off potential western investment. Jesse challenged this assumption.

"There's no evidence to suggest that Zambia's development since independence has been hindered by its economic and political policies. I would say that the reverse has occurred. They've set up profitable cooperative villages, introduced agricultural and technical improvements and resources are more equally distributed among projects that directly help the people. Look at their new roads, rail systems, education systems and health facilities. They're a damn sight better off than they were before independence and miles ahead of Malawi."

"I would agree with you on the last point, Jesse. I'm not convinced that this government is doing all it can for these people."

"Now we are finally seeing eye to eye about something. Tell me, Fiona. What do you make of all the fuss over Chief Katumbi?"

Fiona talked at length about her impressions of politics, and to Jesse's surprise she was quite adamantly opposed to President Makube's way of doing things. He pried gently to find out whether she would put her views into action, that is, would she assist Chief Katumbi in any way? She refused to comment on that. When they finished talking Jesse went to look for James. He found him sitting on a sleeping bag next to the house. Rose was out dancing with someone.

"Hey, man, I've just been talking to Phil's girl, Fiona. She's a shrewd chick and she's got the right attitude, too. Have you talked to her much about her political beliefs and her attitude towards President Makube?"

"No, I haven't."

"Well, when you get a chance, you ought to sound her out. She could be very useful."

"But what about, Phil? You know how non-committal he is about politics."

"The way it looks to me, Phil is hen-pecked. He'd do just about anything she tells him. Sound her out, man. You'll see what I'm talking about."

"Yeah, okay, Jesse, but I'm tired now, brother. Why don't we give it up for tonight? I want to enjoy as much of the party as I can."

"Right, man. I'll see you later."

It was 6.30 a.m. when James woke up. He had dozed off to sleep despondent and woke up depressed. Sleeping under the stars was not a beautiful experience that night. His nighttime fantasies had been twisted into a series of nightmares about Rose owing to Jennifer's remarks. As he lifted his head, he was amazed at the sight of scores of people sprawled out around the lawn. The place looked like a refugee camp at best and a disaster area at worst. The garden was cluttered with beer cans, bottles, debris and garments of all types. A few other people sat up looking dazed.

He shook Rose who was sleeping next to him and said, "Come on. Let's get out of here. We got a bus to catch."

Within an hour they had packed and gone down to the bus station. The cafe was open and business was brisk for a Sunday morning. Hundreds of other people who came to Blantyre to watch the festivities were lined up waiting for their respective buses. Rose and James ate bacon, eggs and toast that morning and bought enough sandwiches to see them through their long journey back to Mzuzu.

After getting their seats on the bus and settling down Rose asked, "What's wrong, James? You've not said much to me this morning."

"Oh, nothing. Just a hangover."

James would not dare ask about what he considered vicious rumors bordering on slander. He also found it difficult to squelch his utter disdain for Jennifer Nolan that morning. His last thought before he drifted off to sleep again was: "I am really ticked off with Jennifer. Why did she have to say those things about Rose? She spoiled the party for me and the weekend, too."

Chapter 7: The Price of War

Momma's Operation

Frank Myosa and Sam Hernandez stood at the end of the runway, which was being constructed. The wind was very strong that day and dust from the six hundred yard strip of land completely covered them. Two bulldozers toiled up and down the rocky terrain until the landing strip was level. Hundreds of men worked at a frantic pace clearing debris, hammering stakes into the ground and raking the land. Several East Germans supervised various sections of the project, and scores of African women were busy preparing meals for the work crew. Since the project would be used jointly by ZINAP and Chief Katumbi's group, a large number of the Chief's men formed part of the labor force.

The airfield was located on a flat piece of land between two mountain ridges. It was three miles from the refugee camp and the site had been chosen because of its strategic location. There was only one way in and out of those ridges, except by air and the field could be well protected against an invasion. Time was of the essence because the first cargo of arms, ammunition, heavy vehicles and tanks was expected to arrive in two days. This meant that work crews would work day and night to get the job completed. One of the main hold-ups was getting gravel from Lukabi to the camp. The lorries were two days late and Frank was worried.

"Sam, what's taking them so long? Are you sure you gave them the correct date and place?"

"Sure. I'm sure, Frank. They've been here before, so they should have no problem. Maybe there was a breakdown or they could be held up by bad weather. Don't worry, these boys are reliable."

"They had better be. The East Germans are getting jittery and I am, too. You realize that big transport planes can not land here until we get the gravel down."

Approaching Frank and Sam were two East German engineers. One wore a Safari hat with a leopard skin band around it and spoke in good English.

"Mr. Myosa, where are the lorries? I need the gravel now. Can you do something about it?"

"The lorries will be here today. I promise you."

"I hope so. If they are delayed much longer, we will not be finished in time."

"They will be here. Is everything else all right including the workers?"

"Yes, yes, Mr. Myosa. The workers are very efficient. It is the material such as gravel and tar that we need now."

"Okay, those things will be here."

The two Germans walked away speaking German. Frank figured they were scorning him. Driving up the narrow road between the ridges was Janice Blanche. She carried two passengers in her Land Rover. One was Chief Katumbi and the other was an East German known only as the Colonel. He was in charge of military strategy and all essential logistics planning, including airlifts. He was shrewd and tough. Although his English was impeccable, he hardly ever used it for small talk. He spoke English only when absolutely necessary and since the others didn't speak German, it was necessary.

In a harsh tone he said, "This road is too narrow here. We will never get a tank through this passage. It must be wider."

"I will speak to Mr. Myosa about it, Colonel," replied the Chief.

"I will speak to him myself!"

Janice drove right up to the field office tent. As soon as she parked the car the Colonel jumped out and stood critically appraising the activities going on around him. Then he went over to a table and sat down.

"Where are the others? Do not they know the time I fixed for this meeting?"

"They're down at the end of the field, Colonel. I'll go down to tell them you're here."

"You do that, young lady."

The Colonel never called Janice by name but addressed her in a condescending and chauvinistic manner. Not only did the Colonel's aggressive autocratic personality rub Janice the wrong way but also he'd had several clashes with Frank Myosa. Frank considered ZINAP, the refugee camp and all its activities to be his own private domain and did not like the East German telling him what to do. Janice returned with Frank and Sam, after having briefed them on the Colonel's mood.

"Good morning, Colonel."

"Good morning, Mr. Myosa. My time says 9:47 a.m. That means we are seventeen minutes late. Do you know that today is November 8th, and we are one week late on this project, Mr. Myosa?"

"Yes, Colonel."

"Well, can we start the meeting now? There are several important points I want to discuss, starting with the cause for the delay of the raw materials we need."

"We shall start the meeting, Colonel."

Personal animosities were soon brushed aside as the group set around the table to discuss a series of issues. They talked about the airfield, road and communication requirements and outlined exactly who was to do what once the new cargo arrived. They also discussed military training and strategy. The Colonel felt that Chief Katumbi's forces could be well trained and ready for military operations in six to eight weeks. He reminded them that the first group of young men to be trained was already well prepared for military maneuvers and this exercise only took four weeks. The Chief expressed reservations about the stringency with which his forces were trained and felt that morale among his men had deteriorated as a result. The Colonel pointed out that the men had received the most efficient and effective training possible given the constraints, one of which was time.

"Our mission is to prepare these young men to fight and win a war as quickly as possible. It is vital that your forces enter Malawi, overthrow the present regime and secure your positions both in the town and the countryside within a couple of months. Already, the enemy is reinforcing troop strength up and around the uranium mining area. Any delay on our part will make the task even more difficult. Those boys will be ready."

Chief Katumbi was anxious to hear the details of the Colonel's proposal for the group.

"Colonel, you are, I understand, in a position to reveal the military strategy you've worked out."

"I am, indeed. I assume, Chief Katumbi and Mr. Myosa, that those of us sitting around this table are trustworthy."

The Chief looked at Frank and then around the table. He then looked at the Colonel.

"You may begin, Colonel."

"Thank you."

The Colonel pulled a folder out of his briefcase and reviewed his own notes.

"According to my calculations, your troop strength should be approximately 1,370 men by the end of this year. These men will have completed our basic training course and twelve percent will have a reasonable knowledge of handling the heavy artillery and sophisticated rocket launches. Each platoon will include one of our military advisors and the heavy armor division will be supervised and in some cases manned by experts not of German origin."

This statement baffled the others sitting around the table.

"Could you explain your last statement, please?" said Frank. "What others do you have in mind?"

"I can be no more specific at this time than to say that they are professional men representing no particular government."

"Then they are mercenaries, Colonel."

"If you choose."

"I did not think that the East Germans operated in that way."

"We operate in the most feasible way we can to get a job done, Mr. Myosa. Are we in conflict over this issue?"

Frank looked at the Chief for a non-verbal response. He signaled no conflict.

The Colonel explained that the coup would be carried out in two stages. The first was preparatory and code-named Operation Stash. This would involve the infiltration of several hundred troops along with the weapons and supplies at strategic locations. The operation would start within the week and each man would be given specific instructions on what to do once he was there. The second stage was execution and codenamed Happy New Year. This would involve the final onslaught and take over of the country. The Chief's forces would be deployed at various strategic locations, and the prime targets included Blantyre Airport, the Presidential Palace, the radio station and certain Army barracks. A substantial force would take over the uranium mining area and a reserve force would be called upon to reinforce the town of Mzuzu.

"This operation should not fail, but if the resistance proves to be formidable initially, our contingency plan is to secure Mzuzu and the mining area and to institute a separate government in that Region. I don't however expect we will need to use that contingency. Within twenty-four hours of executing Operation Happy New Year, you will announce the formation of a new government Chief Katumbi. We expect there will be some pockets of resistance from troops loyal to the present regime, but all resistance should be squelched within seventy-two hours after take over."

The Colonel discussed other details of the plan and entertained a number of questions. After he finished talking about the military strategy be began to talk about other back-up support.

"Our intelligence network, while adequate, has a few gaps in it. For instance, we must have more up to date information regarding troop strength in various parts of the country. The data we have on the Northwest region is much more substantial than that on the Southeast. Can your contacts be of more assistance?"

"Perhaps Janice Blanche is in a better position to answer that, Colonel, don't you think so Mr. Myosa?"

"Yes, Janice, would you take up this issue?"

Janice explained that during the past several months, information had been much more coordinated among her contacts and she felt confident that most of the data requirements could be met. She also mentioned the useful connections she had made with several American Peace Corps volunteers who had access to strategic information. She pointed out, however, that her intelligence network in the Southeast was not as good as she had hoped it would be, but several people were aiding ZINAP forces and could be counted on for additional information.

"Maybe you should tighten up on that operation down South. I would suggest that you do so soon. I have prepared a brief specifically outlining the type of information we require about each phase of these operations and I will go over it with you. How soon can you leave?"

Janice turned to Frank Myosa for the response. He thought for a few moments and replied.

"Miss Blanche can leave tomorrow."

"Excellent," exclaimed the Colonel. "We do not have much time."

Then Frank spoke to the Colonel.

"Pardon me for going over old ground, but one thing you haven't considered in your plans to mobilize the heavy equipment is how we will get such a force through the border guards without being noticed."

"Ah hah! You're right Mr. Myosa. I've not mentioned that. Did I not understand you earlier when you said that the two immigration officials are working for us?"

"I said one is working for us. The other man is an old loyal supporter of President Makube and can not be trusted."

"Remove him then."

"Remove him?"

"Yes, remove him."

"If we did that a lot of suspicion could be aroused. What do you have in mind specifically?"

The Colonel proposed that the immigration official that supported Chief Katumbi be given the job of dropping a drug into his colleague's tea. This drug had the effect of hardening the arteries in the heart after about twelve hours. The old man would die of heart attack symptoms, and since autopsies are not normally performed on low ranking officials no one would suspect anything. If the drug were administered at ten o'clock in the morning, the man would die peacefully in his sleep the following night. The plan was to increase the remaining official's pay-off ten-fold and to bribe the new replacement.

"I don't like the idea of murder, Colonel. This is an innocent man with a family to support."

"Chief Katumbi, let us get our priorities straight. This is no time for cheap sentimentalizing. Once Operation Happy New Year commences, a lot of people will be killed. Such is the essence of war and so too is the price of power. My job is to guarantee your success. Do you want that, sir?"

The Chief was boiling mad inside and refused lo respond. Frank Myosa interrupted.

"If it has to be done, then let's not waste time over it. Sam, I think you should be the one to contact our immigration friend and brief him on the plan. You have had more direct contact with him than any of us. Make sure it's done neatly and quietly, but not just yet. Would you agree with me Colonel that the plan should go into effect a few days before the operation commences?"

"I agree. This means that only one man will guard the border. Our man. There is another aspect of this plan to cross the border. Our vehicles will be painted the same color as the Malawi Army's vehicles and the men who will be visible will wear their uniforms. So if others spot us, they will not be alarmed."

The Colonel then asked Janice if she had up to date information on the location of schools, clinics and hospitals in the country. These would be used as retrieval bases if necessary and also to care for the wounded.

"The clinic and hospital data is up to date. My contact in Mzuzu assured me of that. Unfortunately the school location data is not yet complete. Another contact in Mzuzu is pregnant and has not been feeling so well. However, I will see her in a couple of days and I should have the information when I return. I should not be gone more than a week, assuming the roads down in the South East are not bad. Chikwawa is a long way down."

"You seem to be very efficient young lady," said the Colonel in a rather superior tone of voice.

"It is my job to be, sir, and I would rather you refer to me as Miss Blanche," she replied in an equally superior manner.

The others looked at each other with triumphant smiles on their faces as Janice scored her personal point.

"Ump!" bellowed the Colonel. "Let us get on."

It was after the noon hour when the meeting ended and by then the first of the lorries carrying gravel was grinding its way up the narrow passage through the mountain ridges. Frank was secretly relieved when he saw the lorry. Others were, too. The men who worked on the airstrip gave out a few cheers and then sat back down to finish their lunch. By evening, the entire consignment of gravel and tar had arrived and was unloaded. It had been a tiring day for the men and everyone else. The Chief was beginning to feel his age as he lay down early that evening. His back muscles felt tight and painful and he suffered from a hernia. Keeping pace with younger men like Frank Myosa, Sam Hernandez and the Colonel was proving to be an ordeal and he wondered how he would cope as President. The prospect frightened him. Others were beginning to question whether the Chief was capable of handling the tasks that lay ahead, especially the East Germans.

Later that week Bill Humphries returned from a trip to Washington. He had been summoned by the Director of the Peace Corps about matters relating to his future as Country Director. The American Ambassador to Malawi, The Honorable Hewitt T. Smith had sent a series of letters to the President of the United States and Bill's boss. Based on the Ambassadors 'evidence' they had decided to remove Bill from his present post and give him an assignment in a less politically sensitive country. When he got to Washington, he was told that his transfer was effective immediately. Bill Humphries was a bit of a Maverick and was not prepared to accept the decision so easily. He contacted his wife's uncle, a U.S. Senator from Missouri and a personal friend of the President. After explaining his situation and what the Ambassador had done, the Senator contacted the President and got the decision reversed. Bill Humphries was now in a stronger position than prior to his Washington trip. He sat on his living room sofa with his arms around Sally.

"You should have seen Jack's face when he told me that he'd changed his mind and decided not to transfer me. He must have known that I knew it wasn't his decision. I went straight to the top and he didn't like it one bit. Now as for our Ambassador, I'm glad his wings were clipped. He's absolutely useless!"

"Bill, you should still be wary of him. He's got a lot of influence and he'll probably continue to try and get you transferred."

"I don't think so, dear. Your uncle saw to that. I understand the President's office sent strict instructions to him to say clear of Peace Corps operations in Malawi. He's more vulnerable than I am."

Sally curled up tighter in Bill's arm.

"You know, while you were gone, I thought that maybe it would not be a bad idea if you were transferred. For some reason I feel jittery about this place. Maybe I'm being silly honey, but I've got this nervousness about things here."

"Sally, dear, what do you mean?"

She sat up and took a cigarette out of the packet. Bill lit her cigarette and noticed that she trembled slightly.

"Sally, come on. What are you talking about?"

"I don't know, it's a combination of events I suppose. More things seemed to have happened since the new group arrived in January. I hear rumors about terrorists and people getting killed. Just this

341

week two chiefs have gone missing. Those poor people up in Zambia were massacred."

"Now, that's not true and you know it, Sally. You read the official government version."

"How true was that report, Bill? You don't expect the government to admit to a massacre. I was in the coffee shop yesterday and overheard some volunteers talking about a revolution in this country. From what I could make of their conversation, one of their house boys heard that Chief Katumbi was preparing for a major invasion soon."

"What? Who were the volunteers?"

"I don't know their names. I just recognized them by their accents. They're probably posted somewhere other than Blantyre. Anyway, it sounded like a rumor and I couldn't hear every word, but do you see what I mean? People are getting suspicious."

"Just relax. I don't think there's anything to worry about. Perhaps you're still upset about the Ambassador's attempts to get me transferred. Don't worry dear."

"You're right, honey, I'll try to forget it."

The next morning Bill Humphries arrived at his office bright and early. He was there before anyone else and fixed himself a cup of coffee. Christine Dawson, his secretary, was the second to arrive and she gleefully greeted him.

"Bill, you're back. I'm glad to see you. How did it go?"

"I'm still your boss."

"Oh, terrific, terrific. I was so worried. This is the best news I've heard all week. Let me fix some more coffee for you and I put all your mall in the folder over there."

"Thanks!"

342

Christine skipped out of the office in a happy mood. She too had been worried about her boss's future and her own. If Bill Humphries got transferred, she would have to return to Washington and wasn't guaranteed a job. She also liked Malawi and had established several good friendships she wanted to continue.

Jerry Weeks, the Assistant Country Director, was ill at ease when he came to work. He felt guilty because he wanted Bill Humphries transferred, and during Bill's absence he corroborated with the Ambassador by providing information to support the Ambassador's claim that Bill was inefficient. Jerry had hoped to get Bill's job and thought it was a foregone conclusion that Bill would be transferred. He poked his head through Christine's office door.

"Is he back yet?"

"Yes, he is."

"Well?"

"Well what, Jerry?"

"You know, did he get transferred?"

Christine was aware of Jerry's underhanded activities and she detested him for it. She took delight in replying to Jerry's question.

"Well, Jerry. I'm sure you'll be pleased to know that Bill is still your boss. You are pleased, aren't you, Jerry?"

His facial expression turned sheepish and he shifted his eyes away from Christine.

"What's wrong, Jerry?"

"Oh, nothing. Is he busy now?"

"I'm sure he can find time to meet with his loyal assistant."

"What do you mean by that remark?"

"Oh, nothing."

Bill Humphries was half way through a pile of letters when Jerry came in.

"Hello, Jerry. Come in and take a seat."

"Thanks, Bill. How was your trip?"
"Tiring, Jerry, tiring. Anyway I'm still with you."

"I'm glad for you," Jerry said half-heartedly.

Bill was shrewd enough to know that Jerry's interests would have best been served by his removal. They chatted about several things and then Jerry told him that Phil Harrington called and wanted to see him.

"What did he want, Jerry?"

"He wouldn't tell me. He just said it was urgent and that he would try to ring you again."

"Okay, thanks. Have you seen the Ambassador at all?"

"Ah, yes, I have as a matter of fact."

"What about?"

"Ah, nothing in particular. I think he just wanted someone to talk to."

"Oh, he's changed a lot in a week then. I've never known him to be one for small talk."

"How was Washington, Bill?"

Bill heard Jerry's uncomfortable tone of voice and knew he was uneasy about the questions regarding his meetings with the Ambassador.

"Washington is busy as usual, but I don't expect I'll be going there too often over the next year. I'll be too busy here."

Jerry read between the lines very clearly and cringed in his seat. After several minutes of small talk, Jerry left the room. Bill sipped his coffee, which was cool by them and uttered "yuck." Then he picked up the next letter from the pile. It was postmarked Mzuzu and the return address was Mzuzu Agricultural and Technical Training Centre.

"Umm, I wonder who sent this."

He then opened the letter that read as follows:

Dear Mr. Humphries,

Pardon my poor handwriting and please excuse the brevity of this letter. There is something I think you should know about which I believe concerns all true spirited Americans in this country. First, let me say that this information is second hand but I believe the source is reliable. My source overheard a conversation between Phil Harrington and his girlfriend. Phil was arguing with her because she was spending too much time on a special report for James Johnson. My source thought she heard Phil's girl say that James was the contact agent in the region for Chief Katumbi. My source also said that another friend of hers saw a woman leaving his house one afternoon. This woman is reported to teach terrorists across the border in Zambia.

I can't say for sure whether there's anything to it, but I thought you'd like to know. After all, if this colored boy is assisting those rebels up there, he could jeopardize the program for all of us. I can only speak from my personal experience in training with him, but to me, he never could be trusted. I hope you find this information useful and if I hear anything else, I'll let you know.

Best regards,

Bob Newgate

"Damn!" shouted Bill.

Christine in the next room heard his voice. She ran into his office looking half frightened and asked what was wrong.

"Close the door quickly," he whispered. "Here, sit down and read this. Tell me what you make of it."

Christine read Bob's letter carefully and when she finished she put her hand to her mouth and said: "Oh no, not James! I don't believe this. Anyway, didn't Bob and James have a series of arguments?"

"The story I heard was that they actually exchanged blows. They obviously dislike each other, but I don't think Bob would make a charge as serious as this without a substantial basis. Look, get me Barney Flynn, the Attaché Officer at the Embassy. Make sure you get him direct. I don't want the Ambassador in on this conversation, not yet at least. Also, don't say anything to Jerry about this letter. I want to do a little checking around first."

"Right away, Bill!"

Within minutes Christine got the call through to Barney Flynn. Bill impatiently picked the receiver up on the first ring.

"Hello."

"Hello, Barney? Bill Humphries here. How are you?"

"Okay Bill. How was your trip?"

"Fine, Barney. Don't tell your boss, though. I'd like to do the honors. Look Barney, I'm breaking protocol here but I'd like to ask you to do me a favor."

"Sure as long as it's by the book, Bill. Go ahead, shoot."

"Well, you know as well as anyone about the problems we had with some of our volunteers getting involved in politics. I want to know

346

whether your sources suspect any of my present group of any involvement whatsoever."

"Whew! Bill, you know that's not my territory. Even if I know, I could have my head chopped off for passing on that kind of information."

"Come on, Barney, remember you owe me a couple. I don't expect you to have answers for me right now. Think about it. This is important."

"Yes, you sound anxious. Maybe you're onto something we should know about, eh buddy?"

"Barney, seriously, think about it. Look, I was thinking of taking Sally out to that new restaurant tomorrow night. Why don't you and Jill join us?"

"You picking up the tab?"

"I wouldn't want to break with tradition now."

"We will pick you up."

"Good, about eight then."

"Right."

Click.

The Land Rover seemed to be sinking deeper and deeper into the mud while the rain lashed down hard onto the windshield. No one seamed to be within miles of the vehicle and the road looked as if it stretched for miles across the flat bush country. There were no large trees, no hills, just vast open spaces. Janice was waiting for someone to come along and help push her vehicle out of the mud. She'd been there three hours already and attempted to drive out of the mud several times. By now the axles were covered in the red mucky clay. She dozed off to sleep for a second time and dreamed of happy childhood days when she had not a single worry. Janice often had pleasant dreams during the middle of the day and her nightmares were invariably reserved for nighttime. Suddenly she was awakened by laughter in the distance. Peering across the flat bush country, she saw three men approaching. Janice was patient. Calmly she waited and calmly she drew attention to her predicament. The men were clad in old ragged shirts and shorts. When they got to the vehicle, they stopped and studied the situation. Janice only had to say hello to them—not that she could say much else because they didn't understand English.

After studying the angle of the vehicle and which way they should lift and push, they motioned to Janice to get in and start the engine. The men pushed and grunted and pushed and cursed until finally the Land Rover was out of the hole.

Janice jumped out and said, "Thank you very much. Can I give you a lift? I'm going to Chikwawa."

"Chikwawa! Chikwawa! Zikomo!"

They jumped in the back of the vehicle and off they went. Janice had another three hours drive to Chikwawa and those three men proved to be a blessing in disguise. The vehicle got stuck four times before she got to town and four times the men pushed it out. As they approached the outskirts of the town one of the men knocked on the window. She stopped the vehicle and out they jumped.

"Thank you very much for helping me."

"Zikomo! Zikomo!"

"Goodbye!"

They headed in a direction adjacent to the main street and soon were out of sight. Janice drove through town slowly. She was a stranger and everyone knew it because Chikwawa was so small. Before long she had reached the other end of town and realized she had missed her destination.

"Excuse me please. Could you tell me where the mission school is?"

"Yes, madam. Are you a new teacher?"

"No, just visiting."

"You visit American friends?"

"Friends, thank you for your help. I must go now."

Janice thought the man was a nosey one and drove off. It was late afternoon when she knocked on Cathy Horowitz's door. Cathy's roommate answered.

"Hello."

"Hello. My name is Janice and I am looking for Cathy Horowitz."

"Oh, Cathy's still in class but she should be home soon. Would you like to come in and wait for her?"

"I'm Brenda and I live with Cathy. Is she expecting you?"

"Oh, no. I was travelling through and looking for a place to stay tonight. One of her friends up North suggested I contact her."

"Oh, well. It's no problem putting you up. I'm sure I can speak for Cathy. You're most welcome to stay if you like. You can get your things out of the Land Rover and bring them in. There's hot water here for a bath. I'll put the tea on."

Janice was in the bath when Cathy walked into the house. Brenda told her that Janice asked to see her and explained that she wanted to spend the night there. Soon Janice finished her bath and got dressed. Tea was on the table when she walked into the dining room. Cathy came out of the kitchen.

"Hi, I'm Cathy Horowitz."

"I'm Janice. Pleased to meet you, Cathy. I'm sorry to barge in on you like this but one of your friends suggested I look you up if I was ever down this way."

"Which friend?"

"Stuart Steiner."

"Oh, Stuart. Gee! It seems like ages since I've seen Stuart. How is he?"

"I don't really know now. Stuart left for Israel during the Seven Day War and I've not heard from him since."

"Stuart in Israel? I didn't know that. Wow! Things do change."

"Yes, they do," replied Janice.

"Did you know him well, Janice?"

"Yes and no. We were fond of each other but Stuart was difficult to understand."

"Yeah, I know what you mean. Come and sit down. We can have tea now."

Then Cathy shouted, "Brenda, we're waiting for you!"

The three girls sat around and talked for several hours. It was mostly small chatter about what they did and how they liked Africa. Cathy and Brenda were happy to have a visitor because they were both bored with Chikwawa and with each other. Janice was pleasant and interesting to them. She talked about Zambia and her teaching activities at the mission school, but she gave no hints of her involvement with ZINAP or the revolution.

Later that evening when Brenda was having a bath, Janice said to Cathy, "There are some private matters I want to discuss with you. Is there somewhere we can talk?"

"Sure, if you don't mind local African bars."

"What about Brenda? Will she want to come?"

"No chance. She wouldn't be caught dead in an African bar. She tries to be a goody two-shoes, if you know what I mean."

"I do."

When Cathy and Janice got to the bar there were only three people in the place, including the proprietor and the waitress. He rushed over to the table.

"Good evening, miss. The same as usual?"

"Yes, please."

"And your friend?"

"I'll have a beer, please."

He rushed back to the bar to fix the drinks. Cathy turned to Janice and said.

"You don't look like a beer drinker."

"How does a beer drinker look?"

"Oh, fat and slouchy!"

They both laughed.

The proprietor returned with the drinks and said, "Is your friend from America, too?"

"Yes."

"Welcome to Chikwawa, miss. We like Americans here."

"I'm pleased to be here."

When he left Cathy whispered, "He's a nosey S.O.B., but he's okay."

"Yes. I suppose living in a small town like this most people become curious about strangers."

Cathy was about halfway through her gin and tonic when she asked, "What is it you want to talk about, Janice?"

"Several things, Cathy. First let me say that I am a friend, not a foe. Don't get nervous with what I'm about to say. Believe me it's in your interest."

The expression on Cathy's face changed to sheer confusion.

"What are you getting at, Janice? Who are you anyway?"

"Look, Cathy. I work with a group of people who are fighting for independence in Rhodesia. You probably heard of the Zimbabwe Nationalist African Party—ZINAP."

"No, no I don't know anything about that organization."

"Keep your voice down. You have heard of them because you've been helping their wounded men. Now what I'm here for is to try and protect you and those men. What has happened is that information about your activities has somehow reached the authorities. You are being watched closely and your activities are being monitored. What you must do is to lay low for a few weeks. In the meantime we will instruct our men to stay away from here until the situation quiets down."

"My God! How do you know that? I've only told one person!"

"We know quite a lot about what goes on here. Now, listen and listen carefully. You are not to speak a word of this to anyone. You can trust no one here in Chikwawa. That we know for sure."

Cathy became more confused and frightened as Janice explained more about what was required. She explained to Cathy that although ZINAP was genuinely grateful for her help, it would be better if she did not work in isolation. Cathy was told how vulnerable she was by acting alone and how she could be jeopardizing the lives of many men. During the past several months, several of ZINAP's men were captured after leaving her place, which had become a trap.

"Oh, no. That means I'm responsible for their capture. No!"

"It doesn't mean that at all. You helped out of the kindness of your heart and no one is blaming you for that."

Cathy held her head down and began to shed tears.

"I suppose I have been selfish. I wanted to help those men because it gave me a feeling of personal triumph. They depended on me. No one has ever depended on me before. It's always been the reverse. I don't even know whether I believe in their cause, but I don't agree with their suffering. I couldn't turn them away, Janice."

Janice placed her hand over Cathy's hand and murmured, "I know, Cathy. I know. Here, take this tissue and dry your tears. Those men still need your help, but in a different way."

"What do you mean?"

"There is something you can do to help save a lot of lives, Cathy, but I can't go into details about it. What would be required of you would be very simple and in no way dangerous. If you agree to help, I can tell you now what we need doing."

Cathy raised her head again and perked up.

"Sure, I'll help, Janice. At least I will feel useful."

"First, let me ask you something. To your knowledge, is the only telephone in Chikwawa located at the police station?"

"Yes, why?"

"Are you sure?"

"Yes, I'm sure because one of the teachers at our school got very ill last week and the Headmistress used their phone to call Blantyre Hospital to reserve bed space. There is another phone about seven miles north of Chikwawa though. It's in the power station."

"Really? Tell me more about the station. How many people work there?"

"I don't know. I heard through a girlfriend of mine who is the typist there. I don't think there are more than three or four people, though. The place is guarded. She told me that a small group of soldiers have a camp just next to the station. She says the soldiers are always making passes at her. They also try to date her but she already has a boyfriend. Why is all this important?"

"It's very useful information, Cathy, but I can't tell you why. Just remember, you're still helping those poor wounded boys by doing what I suggest."

By this time the nosey proprietor came over to the table.

"Same again, miss?"

"Yes, please."

"And your friend?"

"I think I'll have something different. Do you have white wine?"

"No, but we have Portuguese red wine, madam. It is a very good wine."

"Okay. I'll have a glass of red wine please."

"Are you visiting for long, madam?"

"No."

"Where have you travelled from?

"Blantyre."

"Are you a teacher, too?"

"Yes."

"How do you like our town?"

"I like it."

The proprietor finally got the message and hurried off to get the drinks. After the drinks were served Janice began to explain to Cathy what she wanted.

"Cathy, first you must do nothing or say nothing about this to anyone. Have I got your word on that?"

"Sure, I'm not looking for trouble."

"Okay. Sometime during the Christmas week, an African will come to your house during the night. He will approach discretely probably by tapping on your bedroom window. He will greet you by saying 'Happy New Year' and then he will leave. When this happens, you are to go immediately to the police station and inform them that terrorists are roaming around the school grounds. Remember, 'Happy New Year' is your signal."

"That's it?"

"Yes, that's it."

"That doesn't seem so important to me."

"Believe me, Cathy, it is very important. You must get down to the Station as soon as you can after receiving the signal."

"Sure. It will be easy. Can you explain why this is important?"

"No, but trust me; it is."

The next morning Janice got up before the others and was dressed and ready to go when they emerged from their rooms.

"You're an early bird," Brenda remarked.

"I've got a long way to go so I must be off. Anyway, thank you very much for your kind hospitality Brenda. Too bad you couldn't come out with us last night for a drink."

Brenda was actually annoyed with Cathy for taking their visitor out to the bar.

"Well, it's not exactly a place for nice young ladies."

"Perhaps you are right, Brenda. Anyway, thanks again and bye."

She shook Brenda's hand and turned to Cathy.

"Thanks to you too, Cathy. Take care of yourself."

"Okay, Janice, but don't you want breakfast before you leave?"

"No, thanks. I couldn't eat a thing this morning. Bye now."

Janice picked up her bag and walked briskly out of the door.

Twenty minutes later she was driving up the muddy road toward the power station. The road followed the contours of the escarpment and on her right was a gushing stream. Soon she entered a small compound with a small wood frame building standing in the center. Next to the building there was an Army jeep and an old motorcycle. Before she parked the Land Rover, two men came out of the building and stood watching. One was in civilian clothes and the other wore a Malawi Army uniform on. She got out slowly and greeted them. The civilian returned the greeting.

"I seem to be lost. I wonder if you could tell me which road to take to Rhodesia."

"There's only one road to Rhodesia, madam. You must have missed it back down at the turn off. I'll give you directions."

Janice tried to think of a good excuse to extend her visit. She wanted to have a quick look around the power station.

"Sorry to bother you again, sir, but I've had some trouble with the carburetor on my vehicle. Do you think you could take a look at it for me?"

"Sure. I'll be glad to have someone look at it for you."

The civilian told the soldier to get the mechanic and then invited Janice in for coffee.

"Oh, this is a very nice place you have here, sir. Is it a forest station?"

"Oh no, this is a power station. We supply power for two-thirds of the region."

"I've never seen a power station before. It must be exciting working here. I imagine you have a huge generator. I've often wondered how power stations operate."

"It's not so complicated. Would you like to have a tour of the station? That's if you have the time."

"Yes, sir. I would like that very much."

Janice didn't know it but she was as good as a guest of honor that morning. The station attendant had not had a visitor in over a year. The only people who came there were government administrators, engineers and Army personnel. Janice walked over to the station that was situated at the edge of a dam. The dam had been financed by South Africa, the white-controlled apartheid regime in the southern part of Africa. A large engineering company in Newcastle, England built the generator. Janice found out that the station generated electric power for the southeastern part of Malawi. A small contingency of soldiers numbering no more than thirty men at a time was positioned near the station to protect it from sabotage. She also learned that one master switch in the station could turn off power for most of the region. Lights, telephone and telegraph lines and other utilities could be effectively halted. Janice acted like a little lost girl who was naive about the station and everything affected by it. But her questions were cunning, and before her tour was over, she knew everything she wanted to know about the entire operation. The station attendant had been most forthcoming in his explanations.

"Sir, thank you very much for the tour and I am grateful to the gentleman who looked at my vehicle. This has been an exhilarating morning."

"Bye, madam. It's been a pleasure."

He looked pleased as he waved to Janice. She looked pleased as she drove away.

Up in Mzuzu, James sat in his office gazing out of the window. He looked as though he were in a trance. The two men who shared the office with him shook their heads in sympathy. They knew he had gone through a rough ordeal recently and had not been the same since. He didn't appear to have much enthusiasm about anything. The grey walls in the room matched the grey desks. On the side of the desks were small metal plates that read 'Manufactured in England'. A series of maps with colored pins sticking in them added a bit of color to the room. Different colored pins represented the location of various types of buildings. For instance the red pins represented clinics, while the blue pins represented schools and so on. This was one of James's contributions to the department and it was used to impress visitors. There were numerous trees and bushes surrounding the Ministry of Health Building and the office was so situated as to provide a good view of the town.

Muwalo Phiri poked his head through the door.

"Mr. Johnson, can I see you a moment in my office?"

"Yes, Mr. Phiri."

They were always formal on the job. James went in and closed the door. Muwalo showed him a new position paper prepared by the government that proposed expenditure on health services over the next three years.

"The Minister has asked our department to take a close look at this report and analyze its implications. He feels that we should be getting more than what's being proposed and he wants us to justify it with facts. Would you read it and let me know your thoughts and recommendations. We can discuss it on Monday morning."

"Sure, Muwalo. I'll study it over the weekend. I'm not doing anything anyway."

Muwalo felt sorry for James and also felt responsible in some ways.

"James, don't let this thing get you down. It's been two months now and you should be getting over it by now. Why don't you take my advice and start dating other girls? Come out with us on Saturday night. I know a nice girl whom you'll like very much."

"Thanks, Muwalo, but I think I'll read the report. I'm just not with it right now, brother."

James went back to his desk. His two colleagues talked to him about a football match, just to try and cheer him up. Then he started to do some work but his mind drifted off again.

"I've got to get Rose out of my mind. Why didn't she level with me in the beginning? Why didn't she tell me she had two children? I wouldn't have been so upset about that. I know these things happen in life. What really hurt me, though, was when she left for Rhodesia without even letting me know. She's been gone for two months and will never come back. That hurt! Oh, dammit! I hate to think about the rest of it. Rose. My flower from Rhodesia. She was still seeing the father of her two children while we were dating. How could she do that to me? Everyone knew it, too, including Muwalo. He's supposed to be my friend. I guess I can't blame him, though. He warned me to stay away from her when I first met her. She acted so innocent and sweet. Even when we made love, she acted as though I was her first lover."

James's anger and frustration reached such a pitch that he banged his fist on the desk.

"Is something wrong, Mr. Johnson?" asked one of his colleagues.

"Hell, yes!" shouted James. Then he grinned and said, "But it won't be for long."

They knew what he meant and both were happy that he was determined to shake off his sorrow. James was quiet for the rest of the afternoon.

When he arrived home that afternoon he was in one of the best moods he had been in in weeks. He hopped off his motorcycle and skipped into the house.

"What's happening, Geoffrey?"

"Good afternoon, James. You are happy today."

"You better believe it. I am free!"

"I am happy that you are free."

"You trying to be funny, Geoffrey?"

"Oh, no sir, James."

"Okay, what's cooking?"

"Southern fried chicken."

"Umm, good. Who taught you how to cook southern fried chicken?"

"I have a recipe book."

"Hey, when you finish come into the living room and have some tea."

"Thank you, Mr. James. Thank you!"

Geoffrey sat down with James and they drank tea. Geoffrey was aware that James was heartbroken and was now attempting to forget it all. Geoffrey talked encouragingly of how James would get over this one and be stronger for it. They chatted for almost an hour before Phil Harrington drove up on his motorcycle. He came right into the house without knocking. He visited James enough times to dispense with protocol.

"Hi, Phil."

"Hello, James."

"Have a seat. Geoffrey, could you get another cup for Phil?"

Geoffrey went to fetch a cup and then left the room.

"You got something for me?"

"Yes. Look, James. There's something I want to talk to you about."

"Okay Phil, what is it?"

Phil Harrington took a sip of tea and reclined into his seat. He seemed apprehensive. He paused before he spoke. James could tell that he was nervous about something because he continuously tapped his fingers on the arm of the chair. Then he spoke.

"Fiona is pregnant."

"Fiona pregnant?"

Phil waited for further reaction from James and predictably James obliged.

"Well, I'll be damned. I mean, how far is she, what are you going to do?"

"She's three months pregnant and we are planning to get married."

James sat up in his chair.

"Well, I suppose congratulations are in order. Let me shake your hand, man!"

James was told that they wanted to get married as soon as possible, and they planned to go to Blantyre to discuss their future with Bill Humphries. Phil wanted Bill to contact the Ministry of Education to ensure that Fiona could keep her teaching post for a while anyway. Phil also wanted Peace Corps office to help him get married quarters for them. After he talked with Bill, they would get married in Mzuzu.

"Gee, Phil, for a guy who's so quiet you really move fast. But it's cool man. I mean you and Fiona getting married. It's funny I couldn't have imagined you with a wife and child before now, but I guess you're beginning to look the part."

"Go to hell, James!" Phil replied jokingly.

Phil got up and walked over to the window. His hands were in his pocket and he seemed as if he had something else on his mind.

"What's up, Phil?"

"Oh, there's something else I want to ask you, James."

"What's that?"
"Would you be best man?"

"Wow! You are full of surprises today. Sure! I'd be honored, Phil. Thanks for asking me."

"Thank you, James. Both Fiona and I hoped that you would say yes."

Before Phil left he explained that Fiona was not feeling too well recently and she didn't think she would be able to help during the rest of her pregnancy. James understood. When Phil left, James opened the large envelope and reviewed the report Fiona prepared. It listed every primary and secondary school in the country and gave the location and number of staff for each.

He thought, "Janice will be pleased with this. Too bad we're losing Fiona."

The following morning a letter arrived from Jesse Jefferson. It was a friendly letter full of chitchat about boring events in Chikwawa. Nonetheless, it carried a coded message just like the previous letters Jesse had written. The coded phrase read, "I hear your momma will have an operation soon. When you find out the date, let me know so that I can send her some flowers."

James was always amused at the coded messages Jesse sent and he enjoyed responding to them even when he didn't have the information. He thought about the message.

"Jesse seems to hear more than I do. I wonder where he gets his information. He's always one step ahead of me."

After reading the letter twice, he tucked it away in a safe place and called Geoffrey.

"You ready?"

"Yes, sir, James."

"Oh, no you're not going to take that shopping basket again are you?"

"Many bargains at the market today."

"I bet."

It was late afternoon when Janice Blanche reached James's house. She was in a hurry and was also in her ironclad official mood. James didn't like her when she was that way. She knocked on the door and was invited in.

"Are you alone?"

"Yes, Geoffrey is gone to the village to shop."

"Good. Have you got the reports?"

"Right here, Janice."

He handed her a portfolio of information and she browsed through them for ten minutes. James was always nervous when Janice Blanche was around and this occasion was no exception.

"Very good, James."

"Thanks. By the way, Fiona will not be able to assist you any longer."

"I know, I saw her today."

"Oh, Janice, I wanted to talk to you about my own involvement as well."

"Yes, what is it?"

"Well, it's like this. I don't think I'll be able to help either."

"Why not, James?"

"Well, this thing is getting too big for me and I'm not too happy about the communist involvement. I understand that these guys don't let loose so easily once they've made an investment in something. Now, it's one thing helping the Africans who are genuinely in favor of positive change, but to put in a communist government to me is no better than what they got now."

Janice appeared to be annoyed but she remained calm, cool and collected.

"Listen, James, just because Chief Katumbi receives aid from the communists doesn't mean he's a communist nor does it mean he will institute a communist form of government. In fact, the Chief is interested in African Socialism."

"Even so, I want out and this is my last assignment."

"James, we need you for a few more weeks at least. There are a couple of things I want you to do and after that, you can quit. I promise."

"Look, Janice, if I want to quit now, I'll quit now! I'm under no obligation to you or ZINAP or Chief Katumbi."

"It's not that easy, James. You volunteered to help us and by doing so you placed yourself under certain obligations."

"I'll be damned if I did! Anyway, you sound as though this thing will be over in a few weeks."

Janice did not reply to that statement. Instead, she gave James a verbal blasting that left him shaking.

"Listen to me and listen good! You're not involved in fun and games here. This is serious business with serious consequences. It will affect the future of people living not only in this country but also in this entire continent of Africa. Now take my advice and do as I say for the next few weeks. Another thing, keep your mouth shut about all of this."

"Are you threatening me?"

"No, I am warning you for your own good. The people we're dealing with will stop short of nothing to achieve their aims, and that includes wasting anyone who gets in their way."

James sat and listened to Janice's instructions intently. She explained that within a week two men in a pick-up truck would deliver some wood crates to his house. These would be hidden under bushes in the woods behind his house. His only involvement would be to make sure no one else was around on the appointed night, including Geoffrey. He was also told to give Geoffrey two weeks off starting December 20th, and to make sure he did not return during that period. There were other minor instructions but Janice did not specify exactly what would happen nor when. James assumed that something big would take place during those two weeks. He didn't know what. He didn't even know what would be in the crates. Janice left quickly and James didn't say a word. He was scared stiff.

That evening he had an unexpected visitor. It was Jennifer Nolan. They had not seen each other in several months and neither was quite sure of how the other would react. Jennifer had let her hair grow long and she appeared to have put on weight. It suited her since she was thin to begin with. As she entered the house she carried a small shopping basket containing a chicken casserole and a bottle of wine. James asked her to have a seat and he sat opposite her.

"Well, this is a surprise. I never expected to see you around here again."

Jennifer sat in silence for a while. She finally spoke.

"James, I'm sorry it all went wrong for you and I've felt bad about what I said about Rose that night at the party."

"No need to apologize now, Jennifer. Anyway, as it turned out, maybe you did me a favor. How have you been?"

"Very busy at school. I've just finished grading my students' quarterly examination papers. I hope I haven't interrupted your plans for the evening."

"Oh, no. No, you haven't."

"I brought a little something for you."

James looked into the basket and was delighted to see its contents. He asked Jennifer to stay and have dinner with him and they busily prepared the dining room table. When they sat down to eat, James lit the candle that was used as a centerpiece. Jennifer noticed that the top of the candle was dusty and she surmised that James hadn't used it for a long while.

"Did Phil tell you the news?"

"Yes, and boy was I surprised."

"I think it's great. Those two are really happy together and I'm sure they'll be happy with a child, too."

"Imagine Phil changing diapers."

"I hear you're Best Man."

"Yes. It was nice of them to ask."

"Fiona thinks highly of you and so does Phil."

"Well, they're okay people, too."

She told James that she was going to be Maid of Honor. They talked about a lot of things before finally getting up from the table. After they cleared the dishes they relaxed in the living room.

"Too bad Fiona won't be able to help you anymore."

"What do you know about that?"

"I helped her with several reports."

"Really? What else do you know?"

"Nothing else, except it's for a good cause. I'm prepared to assist more, James."

"Oh no, not you, Jennifer. Anyway, I won't need any more assistance. I hope Fiona's activities are not general knowledge. Does anybody else know?"

"Oh no, only us two, and Phil of course. I must admit, though, Marg has been nosing about a lot recently."

"That bitch! Oh, excuse my language."

"I know what you mean."

Later that evening James brought out a brand new bottle of Malawi gin and prepared gin and tonics.

"Wow, this is well mixed, James. Cheers, as the British would say."

"Cheers to you, Jennifer. Would you like music?"

"If you want."

"You're the guest."

"It's your party."

"Music it is, then."

Three dances later, they both were able to laugh about what happened at the party that night in Blantyre. She swore she didn't remember performing a striptease and James talked about how professional it looked.

"I mean, you had everybody mesmerized. Even turned me on for a moment or two. Tell me, where did you learn your technique? And the finesse with which you dropped that black dress from your shoulders. . . Wow!"

"Ah, come on, James, I wasn't like that, was I?"

"Has an elephant got a trunk? Here, let me see if I can imitate you."

James got up in the middle of the floor and performed a mimicking version of a striptease. They both laughed so much that their bellies ached.

"Whew, that was something. I sure wouldn't want to do that seven nights a week. I wonder where those girls get their energy?" exclaimed James.

"Practice my dear, practice."

"Hell, there must be easier ways of making a living."

"I agree."

Several minutes went by and they sat opposite each other just listening to the music. The laughter had died down and the small chitchat seemed to have come to an end. Jennifer looked at her watch and noticed that it was late.

"I guess I should be heading back now. It is getting late."

"Do you have to go just yet? I feel like there's something left unsaid."

"Well you have to ride me back, so whatever is convenient for you. I don't want to over stay my welcome."

"You won't do that. I've enjoyed this evening. In fact, it's been one of the best evenings I've had in months."

Jennifer looked down as if embarrassed for James. She could almost feel the pangs in his heart. Then she heard his voice.

"Jennifer, it's all right to talk about it now. Rose was a chapter in my life. I've read it now and I'm forgetting it. You know, I never stopped thinking about you. In fact, that night when you put on that show at the party, I was mad as hell. It was as if you were my woman parading around exposing yourself. Boy, was I jealous that night."

"I don't believe that, James."

"It's true, it's really true. I raise my right hand!"

Jennifer began to blush slightly and then lower her head again, this time because of her own embarrassment. Then James got up and walked over to her.

"May I have this dance, miss?" he whispered.

She didn't answer but simply got up to dance. They swayed slowly back and forth for a long time, holding each other tightly.

Then James asked, "What are we all about, Jennifer? You and me, I mean?"

"I don't know, James. You've always been nice to me and I've always been fond of you. Somehow, my feelings grew deeper and maybe yours didn't."

"Jennifer, do you know that I have liked you since we first met? I never wanted to hurt you though or see you hurt. I knew how I was then with girls and I felt that you wanted a more serious relationship than I was ready for then. Now looking back, it seems as if I caused you a few aches and pains without even trying. I didn't want to do that to you. What I'm saying is that my feelings for you are probably as strong as yours are for me, if not stronger. I've always enjoyed being with you and I want that to continue."

Jennifer began to cry and whispered, "I need you, James, and I want you, too."

"I need you too, Jennifer. I need you very much."

The next morning James woke up and turned to Jennifer.

"Jennifer, sweetheart, it's eight o'clock. I'd better get you back home soon or the girls will be worried about you."

He kissed her on the cheek and she sat up and held him.

"James, did you really mean everything you said last night?"

"Did I mean it? You'd better believe it. In fact I mean it even more this morning."

They both smiled and got up. Upon his return from taking Jennifer home, James sat down to write a letter:

"Dear Jesse,

I appreciate your concern about Momma's operation. I was in touch with the doctor recently, but was not given any specific details. However, the doctor hinted that the operation will be a big one and would probably take place within the two weeks beginning 20th December. There's also a lot of preparation for this operation, which I gather, is underway. I told the doctor that I was very concerned about Momma's operation and I didn't know whether I could face up to it. The doctor specifically instructed me to hold on for a few more weeks because Momma needs all the support she can get for her operation. The doctor was quite forthright, even to the point of threatening me. I am very dubious about Momma's operation and, frankly, I'm scared as hell.
I hope to hear from you soon, brother.

Just One More Goodbye

During the weeks leading up to Operation Happy New Year, a lot of things happened. The Colonel took complete charge of all activities in the refugee camp near Lukabi and antagonism grew between him and Frank Myosa of ZINAP. Chief Katumbi was taken to a hospital in Lusaka, Zambia because he suffered a mild nervous breakdown. He also had his hernia treated. The Colonel was reported to have said he had little confidence in Chief Katumbi's ability to be President and that the Chief was physically and mentally incapable of handling the task. Although no one else admitted it, this view was shared by a few of the Chief's own followers. They thought he was getting soft and had cold feet. The Colonel was instructed by his government to be on the look out for a replacement should one be needed. Two of the Chief's top aides were earmarked. They were younger men who shared political ideologies with the East Germans and they were ambitious.

Sam Hernandez flew to several major European and American cities to recruit mercenaries. He also went to Havana, Cuba to visit relatives and old friends but also recruited a highly-trained force of thirty-five men. Before Christmas day, Sam had recruited over two hundred men from France, Britain, Northern Ireland and America. Some mercenaries were trained pilots and were also responsible for borrowing a highly sophisticated reconnaissance plane from an ally to conduct photographic surveys of strategic locations in Malawi. The information revealed the exact location of bases, artillery depots, troop movements, dams, bridges and numerous other details. Malawi had no air force so the reconnaissance activity went on unimpeded.

Significantly, nationals of Communist Bloc countries would not be engaged in the actual fighting. Only the Colonel and a hand full of his advisors would be involved in directing the operations. The East Germans and their allies wanted to protect themselves against world opinion should Operation Happy New Year prove unsuccessful. That is why they used western mercenaries and western-made weapons. Although the Malawi Army outnumbered Chief Katumbi's forces, the heavy armory that would be used by the Chief's forces was far more modern and sophisticated. This factor along with a well-planned battle strategy that incorporated the age-old element of surprise gave the Colonel great confidence.

During this same period, Bill Humphries learned that several volunteers along with a number of expatriates were under surveillance because of suspected corroboration with Chief Katumbi's supporters. Barney Flynn, the American Embassy's Attaché Officer did not know the names of those under suspicion. He also advised Bill Humphries to take no further action on the situation because higher authorities were handling it. Bill had ambivalent feelings about the situation. He was concerned that his volunteers were involved and upset because he no longer had responsibility for monitoring their activities. Bill and his wife, Sally, also made a special trip to Mzuzu. He gave Fiona away at her wedding, an action that caused all kinds of uproars throughout the diplomatic community. Fiona and Phil first approached the British Embassy and asked a top-ranking official to give her away. At first he agreed, but upon hearing that she was pregnant he politely declined. It became very embarrassing for the British Embassy once word got out that they had refused because the girl was pregnant.

The American ambassador, The Honorable Hewitt T. Smith, put his foot in it again by apologizing to the British ambassador for what he described as "a breach of protocol by a flippant American official." The Ambassador's remarks got back to Washington and subsequently he was reprimanded for making "statements detrimental to the office of a fellow American who acted quite legitimately under said circumstances." Bill Humphries also received an official letter from US Peace Corps headquarters in Washington, D.C. informing him of the death of a former Peace Corps volunteer. Stuart Steiner was killed in action while on patrol in the Golan Heights six weeks after he arrived in Israel. The Washington office received a letter from his mother informing them of the circumstances surrounding his death. He had been killed by a sniper's bullet. Bill Humphries informed those volunteers who trained with Stuart and subsequently Janice Blanche got the news and became very upset. Her nervous tension seemed to increase, and she resorted to biting her fingernails again, this time resulting in painfully blistered fingers. For a couple of weeks she could not use her left hand because her fingers had been so badly damaged.

About a week before Christmas she paid a visit to James's house. A ZINAP soldier drove her. James found out no more than he already knew about the operation but surmised that it would be soon owing to Janice's urgent disposition. She also inadvertently dropped a clue about the date of the operation when she showed a certain amount of anxiety over James's plans to attend the annual New Year's Eve party sponsored by the local regiment of the Malawi Army. Muwalo Phiri was instrumental in getting tickets for two couples to attend this very popular event. Soon after Janice's visit, James wrote to Jesse Jefferson and filled him in on Janice's visit.

On the evening of December 31st, 1967 two civilian air traffic controllers sat in the airport tower at Blantyre Airport. The time was 8:00 p.m. and they were due to be relieved from duty. It had been a dull day for them because no flights had come in, nor were any scheduled. One of the controllers finished a cup of coffee.

"Ah, that tasted awful. Why don't they buy Kenyan coffee? It is much better."

"Kenyan coffee is more expensive, they tell me. What we drink is a Brazilian blend."

"I prefer Kenyan. What are you doing tonight?"

"I'm going to a party."

"Don't tell me that you have accepted the customs of the Nsungu's. They make a lot of fuss about New Years Eve."

"No I have not, but I enjoy the drinks. EEEEI did you see that?"

"What?"

"The two blips on the radar screen."

"No, let me see."

"There are no scheduled flights tonight. Here check the flight schedule again. The blips are getting larger. They are heading this way!"

The two controllers frantically checked all flight schedules for the previous day and the next day just to make sure there had not been a mix-up somewhere.

"I don't understand. There are no flights scheduled this evening. Maybe we should call Mr. Pratt at his home. It could be that a flight was scheduled and not recorded because so many staff took time off."

"No, we'd better not. He may get annoyed and tell us to handle it ourselves. Also, he's going to a big party tonight at the Gymkhana Club. You know how these Nsungus are about their club parties, especially on New Year's Eve. Look, they're about five miles out now. We should be receiving a radio message in a minute. My guess is that they are two flights to Rhodesia but with an unscheduled stopover here. This has happened several times before. They should be asking for clearance about now."

"Umm, it seems too much of a coincidence that two flights are unscheduled. I can understand one."

"Hurry! We haven't got time to figure out the reasons. Contact ground crew and inform them of what is happening."

Sure enough, a few moments later a radio message was received requesting landing permission. The voice with a British accent explained that both planes were destined for Zambia but carried cargo that was to be dropped off at Blantyre Airport. They were granted permission to land. Within five minutes both planes landed and taxied up to the main entrance. The freshly painted signs on the two DC-10s read 'Rhodesia Airways'. The skeletal work crews ran towards the planes to perform their various tasks. They all noticed how strange it was that neither plane had lights on inside and the engines continued to run. Suddenly the doors on both planes were flung open and uniformed men carrying submachine guns jumped out. One shouted at the work crew and told them to line up and not to say a word or they would be shot dead. Within minutes more than a hundred men had seized Blantyre Airport. All airport employees were ushered to the main reception lounge and instructed to sit down on the floor. The two air controllers remained in the tower with guns pointed at their heads. They were told to do nothing unless otherwise instructed. Twenty minutes later, the two airplanes took off again, and according to the radar screen they travelled in a northerly direction.

About the same time a large movement of vehicles carrying troops and heavy artillery crossed over into Malawi from Zambia. There was only one immigration officer on border patrol that night and he knew in advance what to expect. However, five armed men waited with him in his office. By 11:30 p.m. most of Chief Katumbi's men were in position to take over their respective targets. The Chief remained in Lukabi with the Colonel and was to be flown to Blantyre the next day once the coup d'état was successful. Large contingencies of men reached the outskirts of Blantyre City just in time to see the "Happy New Year" fireworks. As the flares lit up the sky, celebration shots could be heard echoing throughout the town. About three platoons along with heavy artillery were on their way to take over the regional headquarters of the Malawi Army when suddenly they were fired upon. One of the mercenaries shouted that they were being fired on. Several minutes later, flares shot into the air, lighting up the sky over the three platoons. Then all hell broke loose. Mortar rockets exploded all around the Chief's men, trucks blew up and rapid gunfire came from both sides of the road.

"We're being ambushed!" someone shouted.

"Oh God, I've been hit!" shouted another.

The men panicked and there was total disarray all around. Unable to see who was shooting at them, they fled in all directions, only to be picked off like flies. Within twenty minutes, more than sixty men lay strewn over the ground. Many were dead. Those who were not wounded huddled behind Jeeps, lorries, bushes and even the bodies of their fallen comrades. Almost as suddenly as the gunfire started, it stopped. The only sounds to break the silence were the anguished screams and groans of wounded men. A voice shouted through a loud speaker.

"Lay down your weapons and come out with your arms raised high."

The men looked at each other in silence and waited. Moments later the voice shouted again.

"You have three minutes to give yourselves up! You are surrounded and outnumbered and there's no hope of escape. Three minutes, starting now."

Three minutes later Chief Katumbi's men slowly walked out one by one. This battle had been lost.

In the northwest region about a mile from the uranium site a fierce battle was raging. Initially the Chief's men had pushed the larger Malawi force into a retreating position. Both sides suffered heavy losses. The battle had been going on for three hours and neither side seemed to be making headway. Suddenly lights were seen hovering over the Chief's forces. The lights came from three helicopters, which began to drop bombs. One of the men operating a bazooka fired at the helicopters and managed to hit one of them. It toppled from the sky like a ball of fire and landed yards from them. When they ran over to inspect the wreckage there were two charred bodies strapped in the chopper seats. One of the mercenaries noticed a dog tag around the neck of one of the dead bodies. The information on the tag revealed that the man was a member of the Rhodesian Security Force.

"Hey," he shouted to the others, "they've brought in outside help. These guys are from Rhodesia!"

The remaining two helicopters had a devastating effect on the Chief's men. Within the hour, most of their heavy weaponry was damaged and many of their men were dead. The survivors retreated over the mountains on foot.

Throughout the night and into the early morning, Chief Katumbi's forces met with unyielding resistance in the northwest and southeast regions. His men had been out-flanked at just about every key strategic point. It was as if the Malawi Army knew in advance of their plans and was simply waiting for them. What they did not know was that the Malawi Army had put into execution a plan called "Operation Sandwich." They deployed most of their troops at each end of the country, leaving the middle that including Blantyre City, virtually unprotected. Having defeated the rebels on the perimeter, they would close in to trap the insurgents. The Chief's forces had met little resistance in Blantyre. They now controlled the airport and had secured the main roads leading in and out of the city. By noon that day they had taken over the radio, power and telecommunications stations. What they found, however, were almost empty offices with little or no equipment. The major transmitters had been removed and the equipment that was left had key components missing. This meant they were inoperative. The men even entered the main Army headquarters and found nothing but empty barracks and offices. Not a piece of military equipment had been left.

The only point of resistance was at the Presidential Palace. A sizeable contingency of men and heavy armory was deployed to protect this multi-million dollar building. The Army was dug in in such a way that they could hold the fortress for several days without losing many men. It would be the rebels who would pay a heavy price in terms of human casualties. Unknown to the rebels President Aleke Makube was not in the Palace but in a secret hide away. Conflicting news of the invasion reached ZINAP's headquarters in Lukabi. Blantyre was proclaimed a success but retreating soldiers confirmed news of heavy losses and defeats in other parts of the country. The Colonel was mad as hell and called another meeting.

"Something is wrong here. I don't like it one bit. Most of the reports we are getting suggest that we're being led into a trap. Someone has passed information to the enemy, dammit!"

They discussed sending a back-up force to Mzuzu and the mining area versus strengthening already secured positions. They decided on the latter but the Colonel still wasn't happy about Blantyre.

"The city by itself is useless to us. We must secure the road to Mzuzu and the uranium mine. However, we have no time to waste. We must fly to Blantyre immediately and Chief Katumbi will announce the formation of a new government under his leadership."

Chief Rodney Katumbi and the East German Colonel arrived at Blantyre Airport about 3:30 p.m. on New Year's Day. Aides and another one hundred-eighty troops accompanied them. They used one of the DC-10 airplanes. After disembarking they left the airport quickly in a convoy containing three jeeps and four troop carriers. The Chief's men were sparsely spaced out over the five-mile road leading to Blantyre. When the convoy reached the center of town they found it deserted except for troops posted at most major intersections. They headed for the radio station unaware that the transmitting equipment had been removed. The station was located in the top floor of a modern building complex owned by a British Building Society. Opposite the building was a block of offices. Since it was a holiday, most of the blinds were closed.

The jeep carrying Chief Katumbi, the Colonel and two of the Chief's top aides pulled up in front of the building and came to a quick halt. The Chief was nervous and turned to one of his aides.

"The moment has come. Have you got my speech handy?"

"Yes, sir, here it is."

The Chief took the white folder containing the speech and tucked it under his arm. He then got out of the jeep and walked slowly up the steps leading to the entrance. When he reached the top he paused and took a deep breath and murmured to himself.

"May my God favor me," he said.

But before he could deliver the speech, the Chief jerked forward and his arms were flung up into the air. His knees dropped to the floor and seconds later he fell flat on his face. His light Safari Jacket showed a red stain. He had been shot in the back and was dead.

"The Chief is dead!" shouted one of his aides.

There was panic as the troops rushed up the stairs shouting.

"The Chief has been shot!"

"This can't be!"

"Chief Katumbi is dead!"

The clamor lasted for nearly three minutes before the Colonel pulled out his pistol and fired into the air.

Everyone became quiet and the Colonel said, "Listen to me. The Chief is dead but his assassin is getting away. I want you to check the front and back entrances to all those buildings across the street and be quick about it. The culprit couldn't have got far."

Then the Colonel turned to the man who wrote the Chief's speech. His name was Benjamin Ngadama and he had been earmarked as a possible successor to the Chief.

"Mr. Ngadama, could you arrange to have some men take the Chief's body back to the airport and afterwards come with me?"

"Yes, Colonel!"

Five minutes later the two men stepped off the elevator. Several men, including a British mercenary, greeted them. He explained that key components of the equipment had been removed and there was no way they could transmit.

"Dammit! Dammit! Dammit! We have been tricked. No resistance in Blantyre, no troops at the barracks, no radio transmitter, and now the Chief has been assassinated. This is a trap!"

The Colonel immediately set in motion plans to evacuate his troops from the city. By then more than six hundred men were scattered at strategic locations and it would take several hours before they could be transported to the airport. The Colonel faced another problem. There were only two DC-10 airplanes available to airlift the men and one was sitting on the airstrip outside Lukabi. Several trips had to be made and the question was whether the men could be airlifted before the advancing Malawi Army reached Blantyre. When he returned to the airport he ordered the pilot to leave right away taking Benjamin Ngadama and three hundred troops. They were crammed into the plane like Sardines in a can. The ensuing hours of waiting for the two planes to return seemed like days and the soldiers were getting nervous. Soon one of the air traffic controllers announced a flight from Dar es Salaam was scheduled to arrive in ten minutes. Instructions were given to let the plane land and get the passengers off as quickly as possible. When the twin-engine prop jet with a forty-eight passenger seating capacity landed the seventeen passengers were hustled into the lounge. Soldiers were rude and abusive and hit several men with their rifle butts. More than one hundred men made a frantic dash to the aircraft. They fought each other and several were shot as they tried to climb aboard.

380

"Enough," the pilot shouted. "There are too many already. I can only take fifty people!"

Someone punched him in the mouth. The Colonel watching the ruckus developing on the runway ordered a group of soldiers to shoot the tires.

"I'll stop this anarchy right now."

After the tires were deflated there was no option but to wait and things quieted down. At about half past ten o'clock two DC-10s landed at Blantyre Airport. As the men began to dash across the runway toward the waiting plane, flares lit up the sky. Rapid gunfire came from the opposite side of the runway. It was effective gunfire as men dropped to the ground. Some managed to reach the plane while others lay on the runway screaming. At the far end of the runway two tanks could be seen approaching. One pilot radioed the other.

"Take off now. We've got tanks on our tails!"

Both planes began to move off quickly with their doors opened. Soldiers jumped into the planes as they moved while others held on to the landing gears. Bodies were run over and smashed to smithereens as the two DC-10s made their way down the runway and up into the night sky. The advancing Malawi Army executed most of their comrades who were left on the ground that night. The Colonel was left on the ground, but he managed to pose as a visitor who happened to get caught up in the fighting. Two days later he was back in Lukabi.

Chapter 8: The Lion Gets the Last Word

The Lion Roars Again

On a January morning in 1968 a special broadcast was heard over Malawi Radio.

"This is President Aleke Makube speaking. I am the Lion that roars and I am your leader and protector. My loyal troops have successfully defeated the jackals that invaded from Zambia. Their leader is now dead. You can now return to your jobs and your normal everyday life without fear of being harmed by those evil men. Remember, you can trust me. I am the Lion that roars and I am the strongest!"

The speech was characteristic of the manner in which President Makube spoke to his people. In some respects he treated them like children. However, the underlying message was that none of his subjects should underestimate his power and strength. Later that day he revealed his anger over what had occurred in a private meeting with the U.S. Ambassador.

"By all accounts, Mr. Ambassador, certain Americans were colluding with the enemy. These Americans are here under the auspices of the Peace Corps. The evidence against them is sound. Based on this evidence, I am terminating the Peace Corps in my country effective immediately. I want all volunteers and staff out within one week."

"But sir—"

"The decision is irreversible, Mr. Ambassador. Now if you would excuse me, I have a busy schedule today."

The United States Ambassador, The Honorable Hewitt T. Smith, left the Presidents office stunned. He walked slowly through the corridors of the Palace and was escorted to his waiting limousine by uniformed Palace Guards. Once inside the automobile he instructed the chauffeur to drive away quickly. The Ambassador took a bottle of scotch out of a compartment, opened it and tilted it to his mouth. The chauffeur watched him drink about a quarter of the bottle's contents before he put it down again. The Ambassador was in a bad mood and the chauffeur knew it.

"Is everything all right, sir?"

"Hell, no! Shut up and keep driving."

"Yes, sir."

On the way down the hill they saw the damage caused by bullets and rockets. Part of the walls were cracked and chipped and both gates leading to the Palace grounds were damaged.

As they got to the bottom of the hill the Ambassador said, "Take me to Mr. Humphries office right away."

Bill Humphries was sitting in his office discussing future teaching requirements with an officer from the Department of Education. This was in preparation for the next group of volunteers planned for September that year. They had talked of enlarging the teaching program by thirty per cent and Bill assured the official that he thought Washington would agree to the increase. The official was pleased with the outcome of the meeting and hurriedly left the office to report back to his superiors.

"Christine, could you get me another cup of coffee, please? Who's next?"

"A Mr. Chad Kanji. He's the man who runs a series of small nightclubs and restaurants and he wants to talk to you about drumming up more business. He wants us to tell all our volunteers about his restaurants and he also caters for big functions."

"Is there no end?"

"I'm afraid not, Bill. It takes all kinds in this world."

"Could you have him wait five minutes, please? I need at least that much time to catch a breather."

"Okay."

Christine left Bill's office and closed the door behind her. When she turned around she got a shock.

"Oh, Mr. Ambassador!"

"Where's Mr. Humphries?" he demanded. "Tell him I want to see him right now!"

"Yes, sir."

Christine hurried back into Bill's office and slammed the door. He noticed how startled she looked.

"What's wrong with you?"

"It's the Ambassador. He's just outside and I think he's in one of those moods again."

Bill said calmly, "Well, show him in."

The Ambassador walked in briskly and slammed the door. Bill greeted him.

"Good afternoon, sir. This is a surprise. Would you like to have a seat?"

"Cut the crap, Bill! You've done it this time. Now you got seven days to pack your bags and be out of here, volunteers and all."

Bill was astonished at both his behavior and his news.

"Sir, what are you talking about? I don't understand you."

"Understand this, then! I've just met with President Makube and he's terminating the Peace Corps program, effective today. He's given you seven days to leave the country and do you know why, Bill? Do you know why?"

"No, I don't, sir."

"Because you've allowed these stupid, flippant radicals parading as volunteers to get involved in supporting an attempted coup in this country. That's why, Bill!"

"Now, hold on a second, sir. They're mighty wild allegations you're making. I've had no evidence to suggest that any of my people were involved."

"You should have. The President sure has!"

"I can hardly believe this—the entire program?"

"The whole shebang! This time he means it, Bill. I shall be wiring Washington straight away and I suggest you get moving on arrangements to get these kids out of here as soon as possible. In the state he's in, he might decide to retain the suspected corroborators for trial."

"Sir, do you know who they are?"

"Hell, if I knew that, those kids would have been sent packing long before this."

During the rest of the day Bill's office sent telegrams to all the volunteers in the country informing them that the program was terminated. He instructed them to pack their belongings and meet at his office in five days time. He scheduled a special charter flight back to the United States. They were to pack their extra paraphernalia into wooden crates and these would be sent later to their homes. News about the program swiftly spread through the country and many of the volunteers and their Malawian colleagues were astonished. Some felt their recall was unfair because only a small number of volunteers were suspected. Bob Newgate was one. Upon hearing the news he went over to Judy Nolan's place and accused her, Fiona, Phil and James of being involved and placed the blame squarely on them.

"Don't be silly, Bob. How can you say such a thing? Anyway, you don't have any proof."

Bob lost his temper with Jennifer and responded without thinking.

"I do have proof. Marg told me she overheard Fiona say that she was preparing information for James."

"That's no proof! Anyway, I wouldn't put too much faith in what Marg says. I'm surprised you haven't learned by now."

Jennifer's remark caught Bob by surprise and left him speechless. She was referring to the fact that Marg had lied to Bob on several occasions about her dating activities. Bob would believe he was Marg's only lover and the following week she was reportedly sleeping with someone else. It had been a volatile relationship.

"That's a pretty low blow, Jennifer."

"What do you expect, after accusing me of something so serious. I think you should leave now, Bob."

"Well, I didn't really mean you. I meant James."

"You hate him, don't you, Bob?"

"Now, did I say that?"

"You don't deny it either."

"Goodbye, Jennifer."

On the morning of January 9th, 1968 three buses pulled up in front of the Peace Corps office in Blantyre City. Young Americans

386

seemed to be everywhere and the walkway was cluttered with luggage, African craft, boxes, musical instruments and numerous other paraphernalia. Some of the volunteers arrived in Blantyre that morning while others stayed the night before at the Blantyre Valley Hotel. There was an odd mixture of excitement and sadness. Many volunteers had not seen each other in months and they happily greeted each other as if the occasion were a high school class reunion. Jennifer and James had come down with Muwalo Phiri the previous evening. Muwalo happened to have a few days holiday and decided to see them off. That morning he dropped them off at the Peace Corps office and said he would see them at the airport. Jennifer spotted Cathy Horowitz sitting on her luggage alone. She appeared to be sad as she twiddled her fingers. Jennifer approached her.

"Cathy, how are you?"

Cathy raised her head slowly and looked at Jennifer as if she were a stranger.

"Hello."

"Cathy, I'm Jennifer Nolan, what's wrong with you?" she responded in a soft voice.

"Nothing."

She then twiddled her fingers. Jennifer became worried because this person was not at all like the vivacious, out-going, stimulating Cathy Horowitz she remembered. Although they had not seen each other in just over a year, Jennifer didn't think anyone could change so dramatically in such a short time.

"Cathy! Are you trying to be funny or something? Where's the Cathy who organized our Saturday night out in San Diego? Where's the Cathy with all the humor?"

Cathy's response was completely nonsensical.

"I'm going home to see my mommy and daddy. I will be a good girl. He said Happy New Year and I went to the police station. They laughed at me and waited. Troops were in the back room and when the three men came to the station, the troops shot them and cut off their heads with panga knives."

Cathy shivered and Jennifer exclaimed, "What are you talking about? Are you sure you're all right?"

Jennifer got up and rushed over to James who was talking with several other people. She pulled him away and explained how Cathy was behaving and then she said, "Do you think we ought to tell Bill Humphries? She doesn't sound quite right James. It's as if she is in a state of shock. Do you remember Maria De Angelo during training?"

"Yes, I'll never forget her."

"We'll, that's who Cathy reminds me of."

"Maybe we shouldn't tell Bill just yet. I'll go and talk to her and see what I make of it. She must have been involved somehow and she could end up in a lot of trouble if she keeps talking like that."

James walked over to Cathy and said, "What's happening, Cathy? Remember me?"

She looked up and smiled.

"Too bad about us all getting sent home, isn't it?" James continued.

Cathy continued to smile. James tried to get her to talk but she only smiled. He understood more than Jennifer that Cathy had been aiding the freedom fighters, but he could not understand why her mind was so blown. He saw Jesse Jefferson standing alone so he went over to talk.

"James, what's happening?"

"You, man, as usual."

"Looks like you're into all the action. Hey, it's too bad about the brothers being defeated."

"Yeah, it is isn't it and what do we get for our efforts? We get thrown out of the country."

"Yeah, man!"

"Jesse, what's happened to Cathy? I mean that chick doesn't seem right in the mind. What did you guys do to her down there in Chikwawa?"

"I didn't do a damn thing to her. Between you and me, I understand she was involved in a plot to lure the policemen away from their station so that the Chief's men could take control of the telecommunications system. It backfired and she saw some gory stuff, man."

"Hey, brother, how do you know all this?"

Jesse was surprised at James's question.

"Hey, I got antennas, too. Hell, you knew a lot of things but I didn't ask you how you found out."

"You don't have to get so uptight, Jesse."

"Who's uptight?"

"Okay, forget it, Jesse. Did you get my last two letters?"

"Yeah. Good stuff."

"You know, I still can't figure out how the Chief's men lost. They seemed so well organized and what little I know of it, they had a good strategy, too."

"I guess these things happen sometimes James. Maybe they underestimated the strength of the Malawi Army."

"No, I don't think it's that. From the rumors I hear, the Army was sitting waiting for them in most places. Do you reckon they knew in advance?"

"Hey, it's hard to tell isn't it? I mean, who would they find out from? I don't know, James. I would just put it down to an ineptly executed heist."

"Wow, what a description. You know, Jesse, you amaze me sometimes."

"How's that, man?"

"You often come out with phrases or words which don't seem to fit your character."

"Well, I ain't totally thick, brother!"

"Yes, I know. You're a long ways from it, in fact."

Just then Bill Humphries came out of the building and asked the guys to help the drivers put the luggage on the buses. He explained that the drivers had to make two trips to the airport and they didn't have much time. A half hour later the first group of volunteers were on their way to the airport. There were a number of sad faces among them as they sat still not totally cognizant of why they were being deported.

There were whispers such as, "What's the attempted coup got to do with us?" and "I wonder who they suspect among us? It's damn unfair to those of us who had nothing to do with it."

One fellow who sat next to Reggie Blackwell said, "I heard from Bob Newgate that James is responsible. Do you think there's any truth in that?"

"If you heard it from Bob, no, I don't believe it for one second," Reggie replied.

Then Fat Ramsey Hall, who was sitting in the back of the bus shouted in a hilarious voice, "Fall in, all you potential soldiers! Uncle Sam is waiting for you right now!"

This bit of irony caused everyone to laugh and then the jokes began.

"He might not have room for you Ramsey." or "He's got a place for jerks like you and it's called Vietnam!"

One of the girls who had come with a previous group sat sobbing.

"I don't want to go home yet. The students haven't finished their science projects. They must finish them. Oh this is terrible!" someone responded.

"Those kids are probably celebrating by now. They don't want to work on those boring science projects anyway, ha."

"What an awful thing to say," exclaimed the girl while continuing to sob.

Soon the group arrived at the airport and took their luggage to the baggage counter. The scars of battle could still be seen around the airport building. Huge windows were smashed and doors were bullet-riddled. Patches of dried blood lay in corridors leading up to the airport tower. So much had to be repaired that the janitors had not gotten around to cleaning the floors. Even the check-in counter was bent out of shape resulting from a hand grenade explosion.

"Gee, whiz," someone reacted. "This place looks like was hit by a tornado!"

When the first group finished checking their luggage and getting their seat numbers, most of them congregated in the coffee shop. There were Malawi officials and colleagues who had worked very closely with the volunteers and had come to see them off. The airport staff was busy catering to the whims and fancies of a group of anxiety prone customers. Many of the volunteers didn't know what they were going to do when they got back to the United

States. Others worried about the reaction of their friends and relatives once they showed up unexpectedly. There wasn't much time for staff to inform their parents.

"Oh my gosh! What's mom going to think when I land on her doorstep unexpected? She's not expecting me back before next year this time. Knowing her as I do, she'll probably suspect that it's my fault. She always blamed me when things went wrong." James overheard these comments as he sat at the next table with Jennifer Nolan, Joe Veto, Phil Harrington and Cathy Horowitz.

"I guess my folks will be surprised, too. I wonder if they heard the news about the fighting yet."

"I'm sure they know by now," replied Joe. Then James turned to Phil.

"I hear you're not going home straight away."

"That's right. I'm meeting Fiona in Nairobi in two days and we're going to her parents house in England."

"Are you nervous, Phil?" asked Jennifer.

"You bet. They know that we're married but they don't know that Fiona is pregnant."

James then added, "Hey, they will probably be pleased about that. After all it will be their first grandchild, right?"

"Yes, you're right."

Steve Manski walked over and joined the group. Everyone joked him about having to leave his bible class teacher behind.

"Who told you about her? Did you, Cathy?"

Everyone pointed to Jesse who was talking to the one of the bus drivers who had become a good friend of Jesse's. This was the same driver who admonished James when he first arrived and stayed at the Blantyre Valley Hotel.

"Jesse!" shouted Steve.

Then Jesse looked across the room at Steve and knew that Steve was annoyed at him. He smiled coyly and Steve gave him a "V" sign. Everyone laughed. Then they sat around telling jokes until the rest of the volunteers arrived. Soon an announcement came over the airport intercom.

"Would passengers travelling on Charter Flight 372 to New York please assemble in the main exit lounge to prepare for boarding."

Everyone began to walk to the lounge. Some volunteers hugged and kissed their Malawian friends and others shook hands.

James turned to Muwalo saying, "Well, I guess this is it brother. I'm sure going to miss you and it's too bad we couldn't stay longer. You've been a good friend. Thanks for everything and we'll keep in touch."

"It was nice knowing you too, James. We had some great times together. I wish you a safe journey back and may be one day I will come to America."

"Hey, that would be great! I can show you around some nice spots."

They shook hands and then Jennifer spoke.

"Thanks for everything, Muwalo. I'll miss you, too."

She kissed him on the cheek and said goodbye.

It wasn't long before the group left the lounge and began to walk across the runway to the waiting aircraft. It was extremely hot that day and most of them wore light summer clothes. There was a certain amount of gaiety among the volunteers as they walked to the plane. James jokingly said it was the shortest two years he'd ever remembered. As they queued to walk up the steps into the plane, James turned to Jennifer and nodded.

"Ladies first."

"Oh, aren't you the gentleman today?"

"Yes, I have always had style, baby."

She nudged him in his side and walked up the steps. When they got to the top, James turned around and waved to the crowds.

"Come on, Mr. Show-Off," whispered Jennifer.

"Okay, okay, just one more goodbye. It's my last, you know."

James turned and raised both arms. His hands waved wildly. Almost in a split second his arms dropped down and he clutched his abdomen.

His body fell over and Jennifer screamed, "James! James!"

As he fell forward, he grabbed the handrail with his right hand and lifted his head. Then screams came from the crowd.

"Oh, Jesus! What's wrong with him?"

"He's bleeding!"

"Oh my God! Someone shot him!"

James's body toppled backwards down the steps and as he landed on the tarmac, arms splayed out. Blood covered his entire chest and leaked thickly from his mouth. By then everyone was hysterical. Jennifer stood at the entrance of the plane screaming. Then she ran down the steps and fell by his side.

She lifted his head and shouted, "Help him! Somebody help him!"

By this time it was too late. The silent bullet was fatal.

On a dirt track running adjacent to the runway about two hundred yards away Janice Blanche calmly closed a black leather attaché case and put it under the front seat of her Land Rover. She drove off slowly towards the main exit of the airport. While driving, she reflected on moments past.

"It serves him right. He was the traitor. He must have been because no one else knew as much as he did except Stuart and Stuart was dead. I warned him of the consequences of talking. First he was keen to help the cause and then he tried to back out of it. The Colonel was right. The leak in information had to come from my end of the intelligence network and I am responsible for what happened. Christ! My own life was in jeopardy. Both the Colonel and Frank Myosa told me to find out who passed on information and deal with him effectively or else it was my neck. James Johnson! You were a stupid, naive little boy. You came out here with the greatest of intentions and now look at you. You are a fool and a dead one at that. If it weren't for you, part of the revolution would have been won. Now we have to wait five, ten, who knows, maybe twenty years to achieve our goals. Yes! It was you. Fiona didn't know much. Cathy was totally out of touch with Chief Katumbi's movement and my African agents didn't know the details. You deserved to die!"

By this time Janice was about two miles away from the airport on the main road. She noticed a green estate car coming up fast from the rear. There was only the driver in the car. From a distance she could not see the face clearly nor could she discern whether it was a male or female. She maintained her calmness since she figured the commotion back at the airport would give her a chance to escape without problems. Her mind drifted again.

"He knew too much anyway. He knew about the East Germans' interest in the uranium mine up North and he knew of our operation in Lukabi. It wouldn't take long for a professional interrogator to squeeze every ounce of information out of him."

Suddenly the honk of a car horn interrupted her thoughts. Her first reaction was to look in the rear view mirror. She saw nothing. Then she looked out of her side window and saw that the green estate car was parallel to her. The man waved to her. She thought it was odd but waved back to him and kept looking ahead. The vehicle continued to run side by side, and this time she looked around with an annoyed expression. What she saw caused her to let go of the steering wheel and cover her face with her hands. There was a loud bang and Janice's vehicle veered off the highway and crashed into the bushes. She had been shot right between the eyes. The green estate car came to a quick halt, reversed and then headed back in the direction of the airport.

Epilogue

It was a cool, brisk wind that blew up Pennsylvania Avenue on the first day of spring. The dogwood trees had survived a severe winter with an unusual amount of frost and snow. Residents of Washington, D.C. rushed about with overcoats and rain jackets hoping for warmer weather. A dark man wearing a light trench coat over his well-tailored brown Brooks Brothers suit hailed a taxi. He quickly jumped in and told the driver where he wanted to go. They rode past the White House and several government buildings before they came to a modest and unexciting block of offices tucked back off the main street.

The man got out and tipped the driver. Then he went into the building, showing a pass to the armed guard who was on duty. Upstairs on the seventh floor were several offices, none of which contained a sign or nameplate. The man was escorted through these offices to a small reception room. A secretary came up to him and asked him to follow her.

They walked down a labyrinth of corridors before they reached a door that displayed a small sign. It read 'Director, Special Overseas Operations, African Division, Central Intelligence Agency'.

"Wait here, please," she said.

Then she went into the room. Inside, a distinguished looking man was sitting behind a desk looking through a series of files. He glanced up just enough to acknowledge the secretary's entrance.

"Sir, Mr. Jarvis is here."

"Send him in, please."

She stepped out of the office and gestured for the man outside to make his way in.

"Jarvis," the gentleman at the desk said, "have a seat."

"Thank you, sir."

"Jarvis, you are to be highly commended for your excellent work under such challenging conditions."

"Thank you, sir."

"The Department looks very favorably upon you and your efforts. It should take you a long way. I've read all the reports associated with this assignment and it appears that you were successful in eliminating Chief Katumbi and one of ZINAP's top intelligence people."

"Yes, sir."

"Tell me one thing, though. Weren't you taking an awful chance of missing that flight when you went after Miss Blanche?"

"No, sir, I figured that the shooting incident at the airport would delay the flight for at least an hour. As it turned out, the flight was delayed for three hours."

"One other thing: Why did she kill that young man named Johnson?"

"Well, sir, I think she suspected him of passing on information. He simply knew too much about their operations."

"Did he suspect you?"

"I believe he was beginning to put the pieces together."

"What would you have done if Miss Blanche hadn't got to him in time?"

"I would have done my job, sir."

The man looked Mr. Jarvis directly in the eye for the first time before speaking again.

"We also appreciate the extra effort you made travelling back and forth to Blantyre at night to meet with your bus driver contact. He passed along information from your reports to top Malawi military officials about the planned coup. I understand the man studied in the United States for a few years and he was a top Malawi government official before being demoted by President Aleke Makube."

"Yes, sir. That is correct."

"Well, tell me this, then, Jarvis. Why would he become an informant for the Malawi government after being so disgraced by President Makube?"

Jarvis paused a beat before responding.

"Sir, it seems to me that this was a chance for him to prove his loyalty to the President in hopes of redeeming himself and regaining his position in the government," he said. "I have to think that was his motivation."

"Interesting, Jarvis. You did a fine job with this assignment. You have several weeks' leave. Why don't you spend part of that time taking a trip to somewhere relaxing? Maybe someplace tropical. Relax and recharge. When you get back, your next assignment will be waiting for you."

"Thank you, sir."

Jarvis walked to the door and was about to open it when he heard the man at the desk call his name.

"Oh, Jarvis. I hope you left all that Black Power rhetoric and radicalism back in Africa."

Then Melvin Jarvis, alias Jesse Jefferson, smiled and said, "It's all part of the job, sir. You dig?"

"I do."

Printed in Great Britain
by Amazon.co.uk, Ltd.,
Marston Gate.